About the author

Gordon d'Venables was born and grew up in Australia and has been, *inter alia*, a farmhand, soldier, teacher, lawyer, and businessman. For some years he even dabbled in politics and was a member of parliament and minister of the crown.

As a lawyer with predominantly international clients, he is widely travelled. The combination of his employment history, life experiences — including dealings and interaction with law enforcement agencies, the military, and global businesses — and extensive travel, has enriched his work.

THE MEDUSA IMAGE

Gordon d'Venables

THE MEDUSA IMAGE

Vanguard Press

VANGUARD PAPERBACK

© Copyright 2020
Gordon d'Venables

The right of Gordon d'Venables to be identified as author of
this work has been asserted by him in accordance with the
Copyright, Designs and Patents Act 1988.

All Rights Reserved

No reproduction, copy or transmission of this publication
may be made without written permission.
No paragraph of this publication may be reproduced,
copied or transmitted save with the written permission of the publisher, or in
accordance with the provisions
of the Copyright Act 1956 (as amended).

Any person who commits any unauthorised act in relation to
this publication may be liable to criminal
prosecution and civil claims for damages.

This is a work of fiction. Names, characters, businesses, places, events and
incidents are either the products of the author's imagination or used in a
fictitious manner. Any resemblance to actual persons, living or dead, or actual
events is purely coincidental.

A CIP catalogue record for this title is
available from the British Library.

ISBN 978 1 784658 93 9

*Vanguard Press is an imprint of
Pegasus Elliot MacKenzie Publishers Ltd.*
www.pegasuspublishers.com

First Published in 2020

**Vanguard Press
Sheraton House Castle Park
Cambridge England**

Printed & Bound in Great Britain

Dedication

To my beautiful wife Diane who has achieved a great deal and could have achieved even more in her life but for her sacrifices to family. To the women of the world, past and present, that possibly don't even realise they are an inspiration to many in our society. By your leadership, by your commitment to justice, by your gentle and honest persuasion, and by your respect for human rights, human values and freedoms, you are a source of courage to the next generation.

Acknowledgements

My wife Diane who has been a constant source of support and encouragement in everything — we are a team. Diane was an honest critic and I really valued her editorial input.

My daughter Lecia constantly pestered me to write my life story. The memoir, *Truth is a Complete Defence*, is not intended for publication, staying within the family circle but I enjoyed the process of writing in more depth and continued writing longer tomes with this story.

Talented and creative Helen Punch made positive comments as I was nearing the end of *The Medusa Image*. I took encouragement from Helen's honest, constructive comments and advice. Helen is an active member of Zonta and, true to the meaning of that word, is honest and trustworthy.

Helen introduced me to Kate Heaslip who does a great deal of work with various groups in the community, encouraging people to express their story through written, visual and oral means. Kate was the founder and creative director of Book Incubator. Thanks, Kate, for your ideas.

My old friend, the late Dr Ian Bell, was an inspiration in so many areas. A voice for refugees, the oppressed and disadvantaged, not just in our society, also globally. A quiet and enormously intelligent man. Until his passing, Ian campaigned unrelentingly for justice and support for victims of domestic violence. IB in this novel is not a coincidence.

Chapter 1

Bangkok Post, Thursday 31 July.

In recent months, local government security and police personnel have reportedly been targeted in an organised recruitment campaign by militants in southern Thailand.

Bangkok Post, Tuesday 5 August.

Colonel Vun-Ung, Commander of the Army Southern Division, reported today that six soldiers are unaccounted for after a recent patrol by a company on the Malaysian border. It was reported that the soldiers, most of whom were highly trained infantrymen, were granted leave after the patrol but did not report back to their company.

Bangkok Post, Thursday 14 August.

A combined force of hundreds of police, soldiers and civilian officials has been deployed to hunt down a small band of armed militants who remain at large after stealthily attacking eight soldiers with machetes in Pattani's Mayo district on Saturday morning.

The attack occurred as the soldiers patrolled on foot near the military base and munitions dump on the outskirts of Pattani. In recent weeks, there have been reports of break-ins at the military facility and firearms stolen.

***

Curtis sat at the front bar of the stately Grand Centara Resort Hotel in Hua Hin, Thailand, perusing the latest edition of the Bangkok Post. Several articles from recent days had caught his attention and, even though on holiday, his curiosity got the better of him. Curtis had an excellent memory. His recollection of several media reports over the past two weeks raised concerns. A pattern was emerging.

In particular, the article dated 31 July jumped from the pages. Appeared the most significant.

An organised recruitment campaign. Other reports refer to highly trained soldiers failing to report back from leave. A pattern. Something big appears to be happening in the south. None of my business. Relax. I am on leave.

At the conclusion of his last assignment Curtis was instructed to take leave. Specifically, he was told to pack his swimming costume, shorts and summer shirts, his workout gear and collect a ticket at Melbourne Airport for his well-earned break. He was unaware of his destination but that was not unusual. Why should his furlough be any different from his usual assignments?

Bell or 'IB', whom he had never met, issued blunt instructions mainly through one of his superior officers. Never direct. Curtis is a professional soldier. He follows orders. That's his job. Never questioning the source.

Rhys Curtis grew up in Myrtleford in country Victoria, Australia. At the age of fifteen, standing six feet four in the old language, he was an imposing figure at school.

He attended Geelong Grammar as a boarder having been recognised by the prestigious independent Anglican co-educational school for his extraordinary athleticism and sporting talent. Awarded a sport scholarship, which supplemented the fees paid by his single mother, the school was rewarded with success in several competitions due mainly to his prowess.

Rhys Curtis hated his given name — why would any parent give their son a name that required him to spell it every time he introduced himself — preferring to be called by his family name.

"My family name has a significant meaning," Curtis told his year eleven Geelong Grammar teacher. "Curtis is derived from the name given to one of my ancestors, Robert Curthose, by his father William the Conqueror.

"Robert was the oldest son of King William but he was deceived by his younger brother Edward, who took the throne as King of England following William's death in Normandy."

"At that time Normans only had first names," his teacher interrupted. "Where does 'Curthose' come from?"

"The French word for short socks," Curtis quickly replied. "Whilst William the Conqueror was a big man, his oldest son was quite short and he only wore short socks. Hence the nickname his father gave him."

Curtis continued with the history lesson amidst a few sniggers in the classroom. "William was nevertheless proud of his son and chose him to ultimately take the crown of England. Robert was on a crusade when his father met with an unfortunate accident whilst riding his horse in the Normandy countryside he loved so much.

"Edward made haste to England and arranged for the Archbishop of Canterbury to formally acknowledge his succession to the throne. The archbishop was unaware of King William's promise, although he may have chosen not to endorse Robert for other reasons."

"Robert Curthose was imprisoned by his brother so how was it possible that he had offspring?" challenged the teacher.

"Yes, but he had an illegitimate son before his imprisonment. Was the Archbishop of Canterbury aware of that? Who knows? What I do know is Robert's illegitimate son is my ancestral link to William the Conqueror, King of England and Duke of Normandy," Curtis proudly announced amidst more classroom sniggers.

One boy, Ferris, also a school athlete much admired by his peers, in an audible whisper clearly intended for those several rows around him, "Curtis is the son of a bastard!" Curtis heard the remark but chose to ignore it — for the moment.

After the final school siren, as Ferris and two of his friends strolled towards the school bicycle rack, Curtis idled out from behind a nearby brick wall at right angles to their direction.

"Bastard, did you say?" Ferris turned towards the voice but a size thirteen boot was the last thing he saw for several hours. For good measure, guilt by association, both of Ferris's friends went to ground. One with a bloody nose and the other with bells ringing in his ears.

Geelong Grammar could not tolerate 'unprovoked violence'. The basketball scholarship and his standing as one of the most outstanding athletes the school had, including being a rising star in football, meant nothing in the circumstances. Curtis was expelled.

Curtis spent the summer toiling on the family farm now managed by his uncle. A tobacco farm at the base of Mount Buffalo. He had disappointed his mother. He felt he had to repay her, a single parent who had sacrificed a great deal to send him and his two sisters to boarding school.

After ten hours' hard work in the baking sun he would alternately jog and sprint fifteen kilometres to the Myrtleford Recreation Ground for pre-season Australian Rules Football training. Over the summer he grew another one and a half inches and muscled up by another fifteen pounds.

Myrtleford had produced some outstanding footballers over the years, notably the great Gary Ablett Snr. And Matt Taberner. Curtis was talked about in the same breath by the locals. At the age of sixteen he was the same size as Taberner and demonstrated elite athletic qualities as Ablett.

In his seventeenth year, Curtis and his mother were frequently approached by Victorian Football League scouts but he remained focused on his studies at Wangaratta Senior High School. He aimed to follow in his grandfather's footsteps and enter the Australian Army, not directly through officer training like his grandfather but through the ranks. The hard way. No 'soft' option for Rhys Curtis.

Upon completing tertiary entrance exams, Curtis attended an army recruitment seminar and immediately made a formal application to join. Aptitude, physical and psychological tests followed. Entrance to the army was a mere formality. He had impressed the recruitment 'top brass' even at the young age of seventeen.

Exceeding expectations at the Blamey Barracks, Kapooka basic training camp, he spent several months at the special forces and infantry training camp at Lone Pine in Singleton. Next came a stint in Iraq and one step up the ladder.

Curtis applied for and was accepted to try out for the Special Air Services Regiment. Gruelling endurance, combative, leadership and other tests followed over many months. He breezed through those and went back to Iraq as an SAS non-com.

Twelve months later Lance Corporal Curtis was on a joint Australian and US mission in a secret Afghanistan location when forced to retreat from a Taliban assault. Eight Americans were trapped. Curtis drew Taliban fire, rescued two badly wounded American soldiers — one a significant American officer — and returned to take out the entire enemy patrol. The location and purpose of the mission was not compromised.

Six months later he attended the White House at the request of POTUS where he was privately presented with a Medal of Honor. The first non-US soldier to achieve such a status. Indeed, the United States' highest military honour can officially only be awarded to US military personnel for acts of valour in combat with an enemy of the United States.

The military command generally nominates the recipients and the president makes the presentation on behalf of Congress. There was no publicity surrounding the presentation to Curtis. The honour had to remain a secret but the acts of bravery for which the medal was presented were of such magnitude and importance to the US presence in the Middle East they had to be acknowledged at the highest level.

Soldiers with heightened athleticism, uncanny senses, no fear and other 'skills' appropriate for black operations inevitably found their way into Operational Intelligence. Curtis gravitated in that direction.

His skills were far too significant to be confined to military purposes. The Australian Security and Intelligence Organisation came knocking on the door. Investigative work for ASIO gained him Interpol recognition. The combination of his investigative and black ops work made him a very important person in intelligence circles.

Curtis was a driven young man. What drove him to excellence and to achieve success on all of his missions was unknown by those with whom he worked. Nobody questioned his commitment. Some regarded him as almost fanatical. His emotional drive was second to none.

Now, after over a dozen successful operations in the Middle East, Korea, the Philippines and north west Africa, Curtis was intent on enjoying a well-deserved break.

Well-drilled habits die hard. Even on furlough.

**

Bell had been working long hours and after the latest national security briefing simply gazed into space standing at the window of the huge office, head spinning.

Is there a link?

Recent attacks on military and police facilities and the disappearance of personnel in Thailand, England, France and now Australia. Reported cyberspace chatter with reference to those attacks was linked to radical and possible terrorist groups elsewhere in Europe.

Security chiefs in the relevant countries surprisingly didn't see a link.

"I don't believe in coincidences," Bell opined.

Chapter 2

The presentation to the high net worth individuals, potential investors, went exceptionally well. For the presentation the brokers had arranged an outstanding venue. One of South Australia's finest restaurants high on a hill overlooking the McLaren Vale, forty-five minutes from Adelaide.

A choice of seafood including West Australian crayfish tails, banana prawns from the Gulf of Carpentaria, Morton Bay bugs, Kimberley scampi, Shark Bay scallops and Coffin Bay oysters. That was starters. The main meal included three choices. Braised squid stuffed with chorizo and garlic with red peppers and cherry tomatoes, veal and tarragon sauce with baked potatoes and beans, or cevapcici, potato, fresh herb and red onion salad with crème fraîche. All washed down with the best Barossa Valley and McLaren Vale red wines and Clare Valley whites.

It doesn't get much better than this, thought Wallace, *the best food, wines and wealthy businessmen all of whom appear anxious to part with some of their money.*

Jim Wallace's company, Green Solutions Limited, was the parent to several other companies registered through a Singapore-based law firm in the Cayman Islands. The corporate structure was designed to ensure Wallace had total control over all of the entities whilst his name did not appear on any business register in the Cayman Islands, Singapore or anywhere else.

Unlike most jurisdictions, Cayman Islands law permits a company to serve as the director of another company thereby casting a veil of secrecy over the structure. The director of the Cayman Islands based Green Solutions Limited was Privatecorps Limited, registered in Samoa. Wallace had a separate agreement with the directors of Privatecorps, which provided him with total policy and administrative control.

Green Solutions Limited had a royalty agreement with NewTechno Forum Pte Ltd, another obscurely registered company that in turn held international patents to a fuel saving technology. It was this unique and ecologically significant technology that had attracted potential investors to Green Solutions.

The technology involved purging diesel engines of material such as iron shavings and non-metallic waste material produced from burning fuel. Following the purge process, a liquid substance is added to the new fuel. This substance was the key to reducing fuel consumption and emissions, most successfully in diesel-powered engines.

Wallace had promised his broker friends responsible for arranging investor meetings they would be appropriately rewarded for their services by way of 'free' shares in Green Solutions. That commitment caught their attention. Their clients were subsequently lined up.

Following lunch and copious quantities of South Australia's finest reds, Wallace's impressive PowerPoint presentation largely focused on Green Solutions' successes in Indonesia. The graphic results of trials with a paper mill in Surabaya and a Jakarta bus company were followed by a video presentation of the engine cleansing process on Indonesian Army trucks.

The presentation ended with a photograph of Wallace shaking hands with a smiling Indonesian General, his Indonesian staff and consultants in the background.

"In Southeast Asia we have contracts with ExonMobil in Jakarta, the largest trucking company in Thailand and a chain of palm oil plants in Malaysia," Wallace informed the gathering. "We expect to be signing a contract with the Indonesian military in the near future. There is much more happening in Asia. We are currently interviewing for an operational person with hands-on experience to manage trials throughout this growing market.

"In Europe, we have contracts with Power Italia, some of the best-known trucking companies including Schmidt Trucking Corporation, Dusseldorf Diesel, Lactoplus Dairy, to name just a few. The quality of diesel fuel in Europe is poor and we see this as a huge opportunity.

"Subject to you all signing a non-disclosure agreement I am happy to provide you with a complete list of companies with which we have contracts," Wallace said.

"We are moving at a very fast pace. Next month we are opening our Moscow office. We already have a general manager working with targeted buyers. Russia is fertile ground for our technology. Russian diesel is amongst the dirtiest in the world and yet they rely heavily on diesel fuel. Their massive rail network, city bus systems, power stations and the military are all heavy diesel users."

Wallace was startled by a comment from one of the wealthy businessmen whom he had noticed wore a sceptical look throughout the entire presentation. "Surely you can't succeed in penetrating into such massive markets. The major fuel companies will simply not allow it."

"You have hit on a very sensitive matter," Wallace replied. "There is no doubt we will be a real threat to the major fuel supply companies but we have cultivated the right connections and those companies will not impede our progress."

"It is all very well to have the right connections," the sceptic interrupted, "but money talks. I don't need to tell you the fuel companies will have huge dollars to spread around. They might even make you an offer to buy the company and shelve the technology. That is a common tactic for the big boys."

Wallace smiled knowingly. "You are quite right. They have the money but we fly under the radar and work quietly with key people at all levels of government so that we are well established before the big boys see the threat.

"We have a general manager in Russia. He is a former Spetsnaz colonel who comes from the same region as Putin and several other key government personnel. Sergei is well known as a hero of the Russian Army and is highly respected. He has opened doors for us and we now have trials being undertaken with Russian Railways, the Department of Defence, and the Ministry of Agriculture.

"We have the backing of the Australian Government through Austrade. You're probably aware Austrade has specific responsibility for promoting trade and assisting private enterprise into new markets. We have been assisted financially and support has also been enthusiastically forthcoming through their various officers in a variety of ways. Introductions to possible customers for example.

"The regional director of Austrade has identified our company as one of the top ten to be heavily promoted. We have Austrade officers on the ground in Russia, Germany, Italy, France and other parts of Europe.

"Again, I can provide more detailed information if you are prepared to sign a non-disclosure agreement," Wallace concluded.

Seemingly satisfied, the sceptic nodded.

Wine continued to flow. Belief grew stronger. Discussion turned to the process of making an investment. The brokers provided their clients with the necessary forms to complete, detailing the number of shares applied for, details of Green Solutions' Singapore bank account for the transfer of the commensurate funds, and the address of the company secretariat and lawyers.

"I don't intend selling a large number of shares in this capital raising," Wallace said. "I do not want to dilute the existing shareholdings too much."

My interests anyway, Wallace reflected.

This comment seemed to please the investors as several turned and nodded approvingly at their financial advisers.

Encouraged by the reaction, the most senior of the advisers, Craig Nelson, reassured everyone. "There is one thing for certain, funds raised now will be used exclusively to inject working capital into the company."

Wallace didn't want the focus of discussion on the company's past expenditure or indeed its budget and quickly redirected discussion to the future opportunities any investment presents.

"Look, I can say with certainty that when we list Green Solutions on the London Stock Exchange the shareholders can expect a substantial return. I cannot say precisely what the return will be but it will be substantial." Wallace exuded confidence. "I am confident the share price will rise dramatically once we list the company. Our plan is to announce a series of contracts soon after we list on the stock exchange."

The sceptic raised his eyebrows and mumbled an interruption, "From a legal standpoint you must reveal every deal that has been completed or is in the pipeline as part of your prospectus."

"Of course. We will take advice on these matters. We have commenced discussions with accountants and lawyers in London. In the next month we have scheduled presentations to nominated advisers, more commonly known as nomads. These are the important people who will make all of the necessary arrangements for listing our company on the stock exchange." Wallace cunningly emphasised 'our' to give the potential investors a sense of ownership, even though he was yet to see the colour of their money.

The luncheon meeting concluded with an air of high expectation and bon ami. Business cards were exchanged. Backs were patted. Hands firmly shaken. Even the sceptic joined in, perhaps no longer a sceptic.

As the last Mercedes Benz sports drove off, Nelson turned to Wallace, grinning from ear to ear. "That went well, Jim. The boys and I will follow up in a couple of days."

Wallace characteristically pouted his lips, raised his eyes sideways and appeared deep in thought. After thirty seconds of contemplation, "Leave the capital raising to the others. I want you to come to Moscow with me. Now that you have seen a few of the presentations you can help me with them.

"We will receive a full briefing on developments in Russia. I have meetings in London after Russia. I want you to finalise contracts elsewhere. I'll give you more details later."

Chapter 3

Bangkok Post, Saturday 16 August.

District Commander Colonel Vun-Ung said he is confident the two suspects captured on security cameras in various locations were indeed connected with the Pattani military facility break-ins. Some weapons and ammunition were stolen at that time.

"We believe these two were also involved with others in the attack on four soldiers last week," the District Commander said in an exclusive interview with the Bangkok Post. "Unfortunately, we did not have a chance to interrogate them as they took their own lives during an exchange of gunfire."

***

As Curtis returned the newspaper to the stand at the entrance to the bar his secure phone vibrated in his hip pocket. A message. As usual, no caller ID.

"Call Frenchy re IB."

"How silly of me to think I was on holiday," Curtis mumbled to himself, but under no circumstances would he ever contemplate challenging the instruction.

'Frenchy' was the sobriquet for one of his superior officers. The instruction was serious — IB was involved.

Returning to his room, he slid past the ubiquitous cleaning trolley parked across the entrance. "Please come back later to clean my room," he instructed Jai Dui, the cleaner. "I must attend to some private business immediately."

"Yes, Mr Curtis," Jai responded as she obligingly vacated his room and moved the trolley along the corridor.

Curtis closed the door behind Jai and habitually angled his gaze at the highly polished floor in front of the entrance to see if the trolley's shadow had moved. It had. Only then did he lower his head to peer through the magnifying peephole to confirm nobody was outside to listen to the ensuing conversation.

The small safe was inside the wardrobe as it is in most hotels. Curtis punched in his four-number code. Inside the safe was another, smaller safe in which Curtis had awkwardly secured his satellite phone — jammed in the rear of the safe at an angle to ensure nobody could readily remove it — together with a spare Glock, his preferred weapon.

"Are we scrambled at your end?" came Frenchy's rhetorical question in a deep hollow monotone metallic voice, much like a computerised sound one would expect in the 'house of ghosts' at a royal show or a county fair.

"As always," replied Curtis with a sigh.

"You will be contacted by an operative in Hua Hin — a Thai national. Don't underestimate him."

"What do you mean by that?"

Ignoring the question Frenchy continued, "IB is concerned about a series of occurrences in Thailand, and England. The reports are strikingly similar. We don't believe in coincidences. A more detailed report will follow. Find the problem and fix it."

Without another word, no clarification, not a single clue about where this might lead to or what Curtis should do next, Frenchy abruptly terminated the call.

Eff you too, Curtis thought.

He hated waiting.

Another waiting game. I wait for a local, who I apparently should not underestimate, to contact me. Who, when and why?

This is becoming an all too familiar theme. Frenchy or some other dickhead sends a message — I wait. Eventually I am tasked with an investigation because nobody has bothered to do the homework. Then usually I have to clean up somebody else's problem.

Curtis went to the resort gymnasium and pumped iron for the next hour. This was always a solution for clearing his head, for removing any sense of frustration.

Following his gym session, during which Curtis estimated he lost three kilos in weight from perspiration, he showered and meandered out of the hotel entrance, planning to find a restaurant that served only Thai food. Hua Hin is renowned for the availability of fine dining but as far as Curtis was concerned there are far too many restaurants catering for European tastes. That might suit unadventurous Europeans but not people like Curtis who preferred the local cuisine.

Why would anybody come to Thailand to eat European food? Stay at home if that is your plan.

As usual, a diminutive man dressed in a hotel security uniform stood near the front hotel steps. Four beautifully tiled white marble steps rose to a wide, open welcoming reception area adorned by large white orchids. The uniform worn by the small man appeared to Curtis to be a hangover from the European — and, more particularly, British — occupation of parts of Asia.

Whilst the British Raj didn't extend to Thailand, its governance was present in nearby Burma, Malaysia and of course throughout India and Pakistan. France occupied nearby Vietnam. Typically, British military officers wore white trousers, gold braided safari jackets and donned a safari or pith helmet, the latter becoming standard head cover for Europeans in the tropics in the nineteenth century.

In similar grand style, the Centara Hua Hin Resort security staff, stationed at every entrance, wore baggy burgundy trousers gathered above the ankles, long tight-fitting white socks, black shoes, an elaborate safari jacket and a white pith helmet. This attire was more ceremonial than battle-ready. Not suitable for exercising security measures if called upon for that purpose.

Curtis observed the diminutive security officer wore clothes that appeared to be several sizes too large for him.

Clearly not tailor-made; one size fits all. Even the shoes appear oversized.

Whilst the uniform was generally unsuitable for dealing with a security issue it was even more so for the little man patrolling the front of the building's entrance.

"*Sawardee karp,*" greeted the diminutive man who wore a fixed, permanent smile. He clicked his heels together and gave the respectful Thai greeting with two hands clasped together in front of his chest as if in prayer, head bowed. The locals call it the '*wai*', pronounced 'why'. It's actually an inverted Y.

Curtis had been deep in thought and did not initially respond.

"*Sawardee karp*," repeated the small man. "Grand Night Market. Very good food. Tonight, I meet you there." He spoke quietly with a rasp.

"*Sawardee karp*," returned Curtis as he took a closer look at the friendly Thai.

No, it couldn't be. He dismissed the possibility of this small man being the Thai operative. *I don't think Frenchy has a sense of humour. No, it's not him.*

Hua Hin has two main night markets selling locally made T-shirts, shorts, beautifully patterned dresses, leather goods, locally crafted jewellery, paintings, copy watches, and genuine 'antiques'. There is also a wide range of street vendor food including roti, deep-fried fish, shrimp, omelettes, and tropical fresh fruits.

The Night Market situated in the centre of the city is contiguous to the large morning market that predominantly sells fresh supplies of seafood and vegetables to the restaurants, but also to the public at large. By day the Night Market is merely one of the roads in central Hua Hin. In the evening, with the addition of the stalls, it becomes a bustling hub of the city.

Although somewhat puzzled by the small man's suggestion, more out of curiosity Curtis first went to the Night Market before realising his mistake and catching a tuk tuk three kilometres down the major road on the outskirts of the central business district to the Grand Night Market.

In terms of the selection of clothing, jewellery, and food produce there is very little difference between the two markets, although the second seemed to Curtis to be less crowded. Perhaps the reason was its location, situated on the main highway entering Hua Hin from the south. Four extremely busy lanes of traffic. Two in each direction and a third used almost exclusively for parking.

He was inspecting the variety of street vendor food, the deep-fried crickets, roaches, grasshoppers, bamboo worms, mole crickets and the like at a stall next to the busy highway when he spotted the small man.

Although no longer in uniform and now dressed in a collarless T-shirt, shorts and sandals, it was unmistakably him. His T-shirt had the words 'Bugs Bunny' emblazoned across the front, overlaying a picture of the cartoon character. The shorts were tattered and stained. The sandals, like his work shoes, appeared several sizes too large.

Small man stood in the shadow of a conglomeration of electricity wires hanging between concrete power poles above the footpath. Some wires connected the main grid directly to market stalls. Free illegal use of the main utility.

A dim light situated towards the top of one pole directly above the small man, combined with the glow of embers from a barbeque near where he stood, made him appear even smaller than he was.

A teenage boy admired the barbequed chicken and other street food delights — hanging out for a decent feed.

Small man's gaze was fixed on Curtis and it was probably the sense of being watched that caused Curtis to look beyond the unappetising meal.

Suddenly a squeal of brakes and sickening cries broke out nearby. A motorcycle carrying three passengers had crossed the two lanes of oncoming traffic to cut into the narrow road that serves both the emergency facility of the hospital next to the market and the rear of the restaurants in the market itself.

Two of the passengers, a man and a woman, were thrown clear but a third person was trapped under the motorcycle upon which the front of the car was seated. The same car was lucky to have escaped being rammed from behind, such was the speed and volume of traffic on the road.

More than thirty people in the immediate vicinity of the accident watched in shock. Frozen. Without hesitation, small man sprang into action and took control of the situation.

"Stand back!" he yelled (in Thai) and pointing to the hospital, "Call a doctor."

In one swift movement and with amazing speed and agility, small man leapt the spinning front wheel of the bike, spread his hands under the car's bumper bar lifting it to free the entanglement.

"Somebody, get the bike out," he barked.

A row of tables and produce combined to form a street stall barrier preventing Curtis from assisting. There was little he could do but watch the proceedings.

Frozen people suddenly thawed and followed small man's instruction. Three bystanders had snapped out of their state of shock and sprang into action, assisting by removing the motorcycle and the badly injured victim. A fourth person ran forty metres to the San Paulo Hospital adjacent to the market.

With a loud grunt, small man dropped the car onto the road. Quickly assessing the extent of injuries to the victim, he immediately commenced cardio pulmonary resuscitation.

His next move was to lift the victim from the road and carry him as fast as possible towards the hospital. Within two minutes a doctor and several nurses rushed forward and relieved small man of the task.

The manner in which small man reacted, his unhesitating action, his agility, his speed and leadership impressed Curtis. Above all, Curtis was surprised at small man's strength.

I have found the Thai operative, thought Curtis. *Or rather, I think he has found me. What a way to announce his arrival.*

Curtis recalled his earlier telephone link with Frenchy in which he was instructed not to underestimate his Thai colleague.

Frenchy was correct. Looks can be deceiving.

Chapter 4

Small man manoeuvred himself through the large crowd that had gathered. He stood directly in front of Curtis, looking up at him, straining his neck.

In a matter-of-fact tone he said, "That was a close call. I think he'll be okay, but I'm not sure about his friends. The police may have a view about that."

"Lucky you were nearby to administer CPR. Shall we eat? I'm hungry. Where shall we go?"

Small man pointed towards a line of restaurants on the northern side of the market and set off in that direction. Curtis followed.

They looked like an odd couple; Curtis, 201 centimetres, trailing behind a local who stood at 147, almost two feet shorter in the imperial system.

If small man wanted to meet surreptitiously, that wasn't a remote possibility here. Crowds of people. We stand out a little.

Following the small man Curtis hesitated as he meandered past an obviously popular restaurant crowded with locals. He stopped and scanned the menu on display at the entrance to Dar Restaurant. Photographs of the food looked delicious. *Always a good sign, a restaurant crowded with locals,* he observed. *Heads bowed over their plates, the patrons seem to be enjoying their choice of menu.*

He looked along the pathway to see the small man enter the Lucky Star Restaurant situated towards the rear of the market further from the highway. Happily for Curtis, a welcoming sign above the entrance read "Thai Food. Aroi."

Trying to look as inconspicuous as possible Curtis slumped his shoulders and followed small man into the Lucky Star where he quickly took a seat directly across the table.

Too many ears. Too many potential eavesdroppers to our conversation.

Small man chose a restaurant with no patrons. Old wooden tables without a tablecloth or mats, a bottle of soy sauce on each, a small box of tissues doubling as serviettes and twenty empty seats. But no diners!

As if reading Curtis's mind, small man grinned. "Sometimes it is best not to try and blend in. Being obvious doesn't matter."

Curtis thrust his hand forward in a customary shake of hands. He was surprised at the firm grip he received.

"I'm Curtis. Do you have a handle?"

"Rat is my nom de guerre," replied small man in a perfect French accent. "Some people call me, "The Rat."

Raised eyebrows were met with an explanation.

"My full name is Jaruth Ratnamphod. When I was young my name was abbreviated to 'Nam' but I stopped growing and that's why people starting calling me 'Rat'. A different abbreviation."

The trademark grin returned and Rat continued, "Actually, there may be other reasons why some people chose that name but I now wear it as a badge of honour."

Curtis continued to look quizzical but said nothing, instead guessing that he might learn more eventually.

Rat was born the youngest of six children; five girls and one boy. Even though he was younger than his siblings, as the only boy he felt obliged to protect them if trouble broke out at school. Trouble seemed to follow him.

When he entered senior school, the Rat was smaller than most of his peers. Size didn't matter though. He continued to stand up to much bigger children if he felt the need arose. It often did, others thinking he would be a pushover. But looks can be deceiving. Sometimes the combination of adrenalin and emotion overcomes the lack of physical strength.

After his first year of high school his parents made the decision that he should finish his education in England. It wasn't just a question of maximising his educational opportunities, there was also the matter of his health. The 'small man syndrome' might mean his early demise.

Surviving school was unlikely unless he changed his attitude. Living with his aunt in the south of London would help both with discipline and schooling.

Rat received a good education at Haling Manor High School, a comprehensive school in the south London borough of Croydon. His aunt was a music teacher at the school, which received special recognition as one of only fifteen specialist music schools in England.

Under his aunt's guidance Rat worked hard and behaved himself at school. Living with a music teacher gave him a sense of obligation to join a music class. Not having any background with western musical instruments, he gravitated towards the school choir.

His aunt figured he also needed to use some pent-up energy and encouraged him to participate in a karate class at the local Police Boys Club. Not that he needed much encouragement. Rat — and it was at the Police Boys where he was given the name 'The Rat' — excelled in the modern version of karate involving vital-point strikes and restraining.

His focus shifted from the choir to karate. Rat preferred the vigorous sport. That was part of the reason for the switch, but his voice had changed. No longer suitable for the choir. He was growing up. A rasp replaced his juvenile, almost girlish voice.

It wasn't the rasp of a flat bastard file running across the edge of a piece of steel. Not the smooth high-pitched type. More like a wooden rasp dragged across the blunt, rough side of pine board.

It was in the Haling Manor High School choir that Rat struck up a friendship with Edward Creighton Junior. Edward was the son of a senior public servant who worked for the British domestic intelligence organisation responsible for monitoring the activities of agencies that may pose a threat to national security, MI5. He convinced his good friend Rat to join him at karate.

Rat had no knowledge of Edward's father's occupation. In fact, neither did his friend. Such is the secrecy that is attached to such a position.

Upon leaving school, Rat returned to Bangkok. Keen to serve his country, he applied to join the Royal Thai Army. His curriculum vitae was sufficiently impressive to earn an interview. His family was excited about having a son and a sibling in the army. They knew the lad well and simply assumed his selection was a fait accompli. He applied, he had an interview, done.

The interview didn't last long. Grasping the application in both hands the captain in charge of the interview process raised his eyes and squinted across his large desk. A blank look coursed across his face.

"Too small." Turning to his second lieutenant, he said, "How did this boy get an interview? Next!" With that insult ringing in his head he was summarily marched from the room.

A second option was more successful. Work in the tourism industry.

The Tourism Training Council of Thailand operated a full-time hospitality course. Within two years, and now in his mid-twenties, Rat had received his diploma in hospitality and tourism management.

During Rat's training in hospitality he learnt that his English friend had secured a job in the secret intelligence service MI6. The intelligence organisation that operated internationally. They maintained a close association with regular FaceTime and Skype calls during this period.

Rat had even spent his semester break with the Creighton family, at Haling Park Estate in London's southern-most borough of Croydon. He had come to love the cooler climate and the Creighton family. Just as importantly, he was able to spend time with his aunt to whom he felt an obligation.

Sir Edward Creighton noted Rat's self-discipline. Early each morning he observed him running laps of the park at the rear of his estate followed by a session in the ancient Chinese art of Tai Chi.

Intelligent, honest, multi-lingual, proficient at martial arts, politically aware and an advocate for democracy, Rat had impressed his friend's father, a senior MI5 public servant. An obvious choice to be recruited as a field operative.

Chapter 5

Heavy rain slowed traffic into the Moscow central business district where Nelson and Wallace were scheduled to meet with the general manager of the company's Russian operation. The weather was uncharacteristically bad for this time of the year.

Nelson gazed through the torrential rain at tall, architecturally uninspiring buildings. Wallace read email messages on his tablet. Grumbling quietly.

The chauffer driven limousine moved slowly, heightening Wallace's irritability. He was unhappy with the apparent lack of progress by his latest employee towards finalising contracts in Malaysia. Geoffrey Coolidge had been dispatched to Southeast Asia to meet with leaders of industry.

A promotional tour starting in Kuala Lumpur and ending in Thailand was, in Wallace's opinion, unsuccessful if the captains of industry did not fall over each other to at least sign a heads of agreement.

Muttering a racist remark and in the same sentence questioning the marital status of Coolidge's parents, Wallace concluded, "I obviously cannot rely on Coolidge to get the job done."

"Shall we follow up on our return flight?' asked Nelson.

"I'll think about it. I have an important meeting in London after Moscow."

To Wallace every meeting was important whether it was or not. At least, that is what Nelson had concluded. Nelson perceived the chairman of Green Solutions as having a rather large ego but he had long ago decided he could live with that.

Nelson was a cold, unemotional individual. He would never ask questions of Wallace. Never challenge him or pursue a line of argument that may not be consistent with Wallace's thinking. He had too much respect for his business acumen. He welcomed the opportunity to be part of the grand plan. The company's business was crucial to the success of that plan. A frigid demeanour was necessary to get it done.

Green Solutions' new office was on the twelfth floor of one of Moscow's monochromatic pieces of masonry. A drab grey building made to look worse by the inclement weather. The official opening was planned for the next few weeks and once inside the building Wallace expected to see a more welcoming office, than the one he had entered. He was unhappy with the paucity of furniture. It was partially furnished, sufficient to accommodate two staff and a boardroom but with no adornments.

"The office needs to be better furnished, Sergei." Wallace spoke in an admonishing tone. "We need to have our literature on display. Posters on the walls. Some greenery. Even artificial plants."

Sergei said nothing but simply turned his palm up and rubbed his thumb over the tips of his fingers in the age-old signal, 'it costs money'.

"If you need funds you only have to ask. We are in the process of raising additional working capital. Craig and his colleagues have clients who are investors of substance."

Retired Colonel Sergei Vasiliev, the company's Russian general manager, ushered Wallace and Nelson into the boardroom. Over his shoulder he muttered to his attractive secretary who had been totally ignored by the Australians, "Serve coffee please."

Vasiliev spent the next two hours briefing Wallace and Nelson on his plans for growing the business. To hold Wallace's attention for two hours was extraordinary. He needed some positive news on trials for the capital raising and listened intently.

"I need break," said Vasiliev abruptly. "I make coffee and have cigarette. You wait."

During the coffee break, principally to allow Vasiliev to exit the building together with his secretary for lung pollution, Wallace turned to Nelson.

"This is painful to listen to. So damn slow at getting the message across but we must be patient. The opportunity for Green Solutions is enormous."

"We have successfully undertaken trials with the Southern Kuzbass mining company," Sergei reported upon resumption. "The operations manager of the Krasnogorsk coal mine is a friend. We joined the military together but took different paths to serve the fatherland. My friend did not join the elite combat group and served in the Supply Division at the Sevastopol Base. Sevastopol is on the Black Sea."

"Yes, yes," interrupted Wallace, now starting to show his impatience. "Tell me about the trials at the coal mine."

"Krasnogorsk is an open-pit mine. It is a huge resource and should be in operation for many years."

Wallace shuffled his notes impatiently. "Forget the preamble, Sergei. Just tell me the results of the trials."

Vasiliev gave a thorough account of how the trials had been conducted, reassuring Wallace the testing protocol had been religiously adhered to. Handing over a single sheet of paper with a description of the end result, Vasiliev beamed with satisfaction. The trials had revealed a massive percentage improvement both in the power of the trucks and the fuel consumption levels. There was also a strong likelihood of a substantial improvement in engine life.

"This is what I am excited about, Sergei. Positive results. Well done. When can we sign this company to a contract?"

Without waiting for a response Nelson added, "This is just what we need to expand our capital raising."

Vasiliev again beamed extravagantly. "We can sign a contract within a week. My friend can meet with you if you want."

"Never mind, just get it done. What else do you have for us?"

"Tomorrow we meet with Lumovski."

"Lumovski?"

Sergei appeared surprised that neither Wallace nor Nelson appeared to know of Lumovski.

"You do not know Lumovski?"

"Never heard of him. Why should we meet with him? Is he a potential customer? Is he the chief executive of Russian Railways or the city mayor?" Wallace asked with more than a hint of sarcasm in his voice.

"Lumovski is a very powerful and wealthy businessman. You must meet with him. He is one of the most powerful men in Russia. Perhaps more powerful than the city mayor," Vasiliev countered with his own dose of sarcasm.

"Simon at Austrade and I have arranged a meeting with him to assist with contracts for the city of Moscow. Lumovski may not be the mayor but he sits on the mayor's shoulder."

Wallace trusted Simon Hunter, one of the Moscow-based Austrade trade commissioners and knew he wouldn't waste his time with a lightweight.

The pair returned to the National Hotel in the Tverskoy District. A grand hotel that still held its old-world charm and within easy walking distance of Red Square. Wallace excused himself and went to his room.

Nelson decided to walk to the Kremlin to view the changing of the guard.

It was customary for Wallace to take an afternoon nap. A 'Jimmy Brennan' he called it, naming his siesta after a long-time friend who refused to attend any meetings between two and four p.m.

He was jerked from his slumber by a sharp noise. He fumbled for the room telephone.

"Jim Wallace."

"Simon Hunter. Are you free? I can drop by in half an hour."

"Sure, Simon. Let's make it four thirty for a drink. There's a piano bar on the first floor but it's sometimes a little crowded. Take the lift to the top floor and we'll meet in the Alexandrovsky Bar."

The top floor bar was spectacular. A glass roof gave Wallace a view of the now bright blue sky over Moscow. He gazed up, a glass of red wine in hand, and admired the jet stream trails at various angles across the sky. The trails are formed by the interaction of burnt jet fuel and humid air at up to twelve thousand metres. A condensation core from jet aircraft commonly known as contrails. Wallace had completed training to fly a smaller prop-powered aircraft. He dreamt of flying a larger jet.

He looked down in time to see Hunter purposefully strolling across the lounge in his direction. Hunter was forced to negotiate a number of turns past empty tables and chairs before reaching the bar.

In contrast to Wallace, who was casually dressed in cream slacks and a tailor-made pale blue short-sleeved shirt, Hunter was still dressed in his work attire. A crimson tie with an angular gold stripe, white long-sleeved shirt, black trousers and three-quarter length black jacket.

"How was your day?" Hunter asked by way of greeting. Without waiting for an answer, he added, "Better than mine, I hope. I had a shit of a day."

"We all have those sometime," replied Wallace with disinterest. "What would you like to drink?"

Hunter ordered a gin and tonic. They sat at the bar for a few minutes, chatting casually about the weather and other matters of no consequence to Wallace. He didn't wish to have a social relationship with Hunter, preferring only business discussions. The gin and tonic was delivered. Wallace was mindful of the bartender's presence and ushered Hunter to a table across the room.

Hunter spoke in a very quiet voice, almost a whisper. Wallace had to lean forward to hear him.

"Thanks for meeting at short notice. I wanted to provide you a background briefing for our meeting with Lumovski tomorrow. Sergei told you about that of course. The meeting is arranged for eleven thirty a.m. at his residence and we will then have lunch together.

"It's not easy to arrange a meeting of this nature. Lumovski is one of the wealthiest businessmen in Russia. He made his money from acquiring controlling interests in oil companies and later diversifying into telecommunications and the media. To build an empire like he has requires friends in powerful positions."

Hunter paused and sipped his gin and tonic. The pause was long enough to allow the message to sink in.

"To make myself clear, Lumovski is a close personal friend to the most powerful politicians in Russia. One in particular." Hunter lowered his voice even further and added, "Putin."

"Impressive," Wallace enthusiastically intervened, nodding with approval.

"Lumovski is actually an oligarch. Many people in Russia like to think they fit that description but the reality is not many do."

The word 'oligarch' is derived from the Greek word *oligarkhēs*. Added to the word *oligoi*, meaning 'few', it became the description of a small group of rich and powerful political figures. An oligarch in Russia is indeed rich and powerful.

"I strongly suggest you do not advertise the fact you have a meeting with Lumovski," Hunter continued in an even lower voice.

"That's easy. I like to fly under the radar."

"In particular, you shouldn't mention his name in your discussions with government officials or financiers in the UK. He is not a popular man in England."

For the first time during the conversation Wallace heard something he didn't like. He grimaced slightly and raised his hand, palm open, to stop the conversation.

After a few moments' thought, a mouthful of his Cabernet Sauvignon, he ventured, "Why should I meet with him? I plan to list Green Solutions on the London Stock Exchange."

"Believe me when I say this man is influential. If I am wasting my time and you don't want to meet Lumovski just tell me but I had the impression the Russian market was important to the expansion of your business. Important too for the initial public offering in London. If you want significant contracts in Russia you will need the help of people of influence. Trust me on this."

Hunter did not wait for any further comment. "According to government officials in various parts of the world there is a dark side to Lumovski. You need to be aware of this and make your own judgement."

Relying on hand-written notes in a 7x4 cm notepad, Hunter explained how Lumovski was mistakenly accused of drug trafficking in Europe. The tabloid newspapers latched onto a story that he was buying property in England. A money-laundering exercise, they reported.

None of the accusations were proven or indeed found to be in any way credible, but the rumours continued to circulate. Where there's smoke there's fire, some would say. But Hunter didn't believe the rumours.

There remained question marks over the accumulation of his wealth and the real purpose of his past regular trips to London. The British authorities had always taken a particular interest in Lumovski's travel schedule.

Lumovski was never able to explain the purpose of his frequent visits to London to the satisfaction of the authorities. But nor was there any reason to prevent his entry to the country. He just stopped travelling to the United Kingdom and sent his trustworthy senior staff if there were business transactions afoot.

Lumovski knew he could continue to travel to London if he wished. It appeared this may not necessarily be the case for the United States. Scrutiny of Lumovski's travel arrangements and business interests was unrelenting in the USA, particularly under the Obama regime. The Magnitsky Act changed things. Lumovski's right of entry was under review due to the passage of the Act through Congress.

Sergei Magnitsky was a Russian tax accountant, auditor and close associate of an American who established a successful investment fund in Russia. The fund had taken advantage of the significant number of privatisations following the demise of the Soviet Union.

Some of the American's close associates were the victims of crime after it became common knowledge the actions of his company prevented corrupt cash flows involving bureaucrats and Russian business heavyweights. Magnitsky was investigating tax avoidance and fraud when he was taken into custody and charged with the very matters he was investigating.

Magnitsky was beaten to death in prison. His American friend immediately campaigned to prevent those who were in some way involved in Magnitsky's illegal incarceration — corrupt judges, lawyers, accountants, bureaucrats and businessmen who benefited from the matters Magnitsky sought to expose — from travelling to the United States.

President Obama signed the Magnitsky Act in December 2012.

Lumovski had a close association with at least two of the officials who were banned from entering the United States and banned from using the American banking system. Olga Stepanenko, director of the Moscow Tax Office, and Oleg Silchenkov, head of the investigation team for the Ministry of Internal Affairs.

Hunter called the bartender and ordered his second gin and tonic. Wallace ordered another bottle of the same Cabernet Sauvignon, not expecting to drink it all but with a plan to take it to his room for supper.

Looking down again at his notes, Hunter continued. "Whilst Lumovski is not on the banned list, his travel status is currently under review. The Americans apparently don't like the company he keeps."

Hunter gave a reassuring smile and waited for a response. Gazing across the room at the row of bottles behind the bar, Wallace appeared deep in thought.

After some moments of uncomfortable silence, Wallace replied firmly, "You haven't described any reason for me not to meet with him."

"I was hoping you'd say that because Lumovski has serious money and is always looking at new investment opportunities. Without telling you how to suck eggs may I respectfully suggest you offer Lumovski a reasonable slice of Green Solutions?"

"Yes, but I'm not giving shares away cheaply. If he has serious money, he can pay serious money. Even if there are question marks about the man, I don't care. His money is the same colour as anyone else's."

Hunter nodded and added, "It would be a good idea if he had some skin in the game so to speak. Give him an incentive to secure contracts."

The bartender arrived with Wallace's second bottle of Cabernet Sauvignon and a gin and tonic for Hunter. He poured the red into a clean glass before Wallace impatiently waved him away. Turning to Hunter he reiterated his earlier comment. "As I said, if Lumovski is willing to make a substantial investment in Green Solutions I'm prepared to listen but the share price has risen sharply in recent times."

Hunter nodded his understanding. Whilst sipping their drinks the pair sat in silence for a time in apparent contemplation of what might be possible before Hunter signalled his intention to leave. "Given our meeting with Lumovski is scheduled for eleven thirty I will arrange for his driver to meet you in the lobby at eleven. If you don't have any other questions Jim, I must be off. I've work to do and arrangements to make."

***

Two large black Mercedes Benz with heavily tinted windows rolled over the Mokhovaya Street kerb at the entrance to the National Hotel. Four bodyguards exited the first and Hunter the second. He held the bulletproof door open for Wallace who carried the demeanour of a man on a mission.

"Leave your briefcase behind," Hunter instructed.

"I need my computer for the demonstration," argued Wallace.

"By all means take your computer but Lumovski is very security conscious and his muscle won't allow your briefcase near the house."

After a rapid drive along the banks of the Moskva River, crossing over at the Bolshoy Kamenny Bridge and circling the Lomonosov University hill, the limo entered a compound. Uniformed security at the gate signalled the vehicle to stop. Two guards opened both rear passenger doors and peered inside before waving to the driver to move on.

Their limousine pulled sharply to a stop in front of a four-storey cream-coloured house. Numerous windows symmetrically placed either side of a large double and ornate wooden door faced the long driveway. Four large grotesque dragon gargoyles were evenly spaced along the roofline of the building.

A tall man dressed in black, the same attire as the bodyguards, opened the rear passenger door. He greeted Hunter with a large smile, exposing a gap between two front teeth.

"Hello, Mr Hunter, Mr Lumovski is pleased to welcome you again."

The pair were ushered into a reading room. There were four large leather chesterfield sofas, a glass coffee table with gold trimmings, a mahogany side table and a wall of shelves laden with books at both ends of the room. Wallace noticed most of the books were leather bound hardback copies. First editions for collectors.

Lumovski stood at the far end of the room facing the bookshelves, thumbing through the pages of a book, his back to the door. In his own good time, after a few moments, with an air of arrogance he slowly turned to face his guests.

Wallace expected a tall, distinguished-looking Russian. Lumovski was neither. A squat balding man with a swarthy complexion, several days of salt and pepper stubble on his chin, a loose-fitting open neck shirt revealing white chest hair. Dark hollow sunken eyes below heavy eyebrows.

Lumovski firmly shook hands and without speaking simply pointed to the chesterfields. As he sat, he reached for a phone on the table next to his obviously well-worn shiny leather chair and spoke sharply in Russian. Without waiting for a reply, he repositioned the handset.

Hunter started to speak but Lumovski raised his hand and stopped him.

"Wait. Coffee," he said.

Within a few moments a servant delivered a tray bearing a pot, a small milk jug, a container full of sugar cubes, a plate of sugar-coated biscuits and three mugs. Coffee was poured. Lumovski pointed to the tray, looked alternately at his guests and said, "Please."

He placed a cube of sugar between his cigarette-stained teeth and sipped his coffee through the cube. Wallace recalled seeing this practice at the McLaren Vale lunch. One of Nelson's Jewish clients took coffee similarly.

Hunter and Lumovski then entered into idle chatter about the performance of their respective football teams the previous weekend. From football they moved to the nature of the weather and debated whether the extreme conditions were the result of global warming.

I don't give a toss about soccer or the weather, thought Wallace. *I'm here to talk business. Money. How much of it are you prepared to part with,* alter trombenik, *'old blowhard'?*

Wallace had learnt the insult from Nelson's Jewish client over a bottle of First Eleven 2010 Cabernet Sauvignon. If only he could vocalise it.

Wallace was excluded from the idle chatter between two friends. From a distance he admired the collection of books. He gazed at the ornate ceiling and the ceiling rose supporting a dimly lit Czechoslovakian crystal chandelier. He was unaware that Lumovski studied him and his every movement. Eyes peering below heavy eyebrows.

After what Wallace considered an interminable wait, Lumovski cleared his throat and said, "Mr Wallace, what do you have to offer me?"

Startled, Wallace immediately opened his computer. The PowerPoint presentation filled the screen. He shifted in his seat and turned the screen for Lumovski to see. He was determined to lead the Russian through the same PowerPoint presentation he used for his recent meeting of potential investors in Australia.

Lumovski appeared disinterested. Wallace had even added the additional information provided by Vasiliev believing this would capture Lumovski's attention. The latest trial results with the Southern Kuzbass mining company at the Krasnogorsk coal mine.

"Simon has briefed me already," Lumovski yawned. "Cut to the chase, Mr Wallace. How much money do you need?"

Chapter 6

Wallace glanced at Hunter who raised his eyebrows and gave a reassuring nod. He had thought this to be an initial meeting to stimulate discussion. To whet Lumovski's appetite. He wasn't ready for the question.

"Er, about five million."

"Dollars?"

"Pounds. We intend to use those funds as working capital until we make an initial public offering to raise more serious money, perhaps up to fifty million pounds."

Lumovski sighed and glared at Hunter before giving his disapproving response. "Don't come to me and ask for a piffling amount of money," he snarled. "I like the project and I know you have other reasons for raising money. I share your philosophy.

"Firstly, you need to establish a company in Russia to run your operation here. Forget five. I will contribute thirty million if you agree not to list the company on the stock exchange."

Wallace couldn't conceal his surprise. Normally catatonic in his approach to business discussions, the glint in his eyes and half-concealed smile was revealing.

Lumovski pushed on, presenting his offer to Wallace as if it was a done deal. There was no alternative to running this business in Eastern Europe.

In return for contributing thirty million pounds to the company, he insisted on fifty-one per cent of the Cayman Islands parent. He would also demand that his key people oversee the management of the Russian subsidiary.

The attraction of the offer for Wallace was Lumovski's desire to keep the company private. Wallace saw the opportunity to provide sufficient funds to meet his main objective. Sufficient for the bigger picture.

This deal would satisfy his associates in England. It would keep them all below the radar. Unnoticed and untouchable. He wouldn't need to go cap in hand to Nelson's Australian investors, although their contribution would be useful as unbudgeted contingency funds.

His mind was wandering in circles, thinking of how he could spend the money and the time he could put into the real project. No longer wasting his time and effort in raising finance.

Hunter knew Lumovski was becoming impatient with Wallace's perceived recalcitrance. He caught the latter's eye, dropped his right hand below the top of the dining table and drew rapid circles, the commonplace signal to 'get a hurry on'.

Wallace was not impressed with the Austrade official's impertinence.

After a longer than necessary pause, Wallace responded. "I'm certainly open to the idea of keeping the company in private hands. We need to discuss the question of board and management control and direction."

Lumovski's dark eyes seemed to darken further. "I trust you to get the job done, Mr Wallace. I need my accountants to look after my investment, that's all. We have undertaken an initial company valuation and we think that offer is more than fair."

A beaming Wallace reassured Lumovski that any investment would reap him a substantial return.

"If we, that is, if I secure new contracts with the city of Moscow and Russian Railways, we will all be rewarded," Lumovski added.

"I expect this business will grow and reward us with strong dividends and the satisfaction of knowing we are doing something positive for the future of mankind.

"Now, on another matter, Simon told me earlier you have concerns about some vested interests trying to discredit the technology. Is there anyone in particular creating a problem?"

How far do I go with this? thought Wallace.

"Simon is right. It appears vested interests have engaged a British consultant with the specific purpose of gathering as much information as possible about our technology. If they get their hands on the results of our trials, I am certain they will lie and manipulate the data to their corporate advantage."

"Who is this consultant? Is he qualified? Where is he based? Is he in Russia?" Lumovski seemed to suddenly come to life.

The cadaver speaks, thought Wallace. The rapid-fire questioning was the first sign that his new Russian friend was really excited by Green Solutions.

"I don't know a great deal about this person other than his name, Creighton, and he is a chemical engineer. My people tell me he is currently attempting to gather information about trials we have undertaken with a trucking company in Thailand.

"I believe the intention of the big boys with a vested interest, oil companies, is to use their consultant's knowledge and expertise in chemical engineering. He has connections in government and the media. Their aim is to use him to kill the project."

"I may be able to help," offered Lumovski.

Chapter 7

"I don't mean to be disrespectful," Curtis addressed Rat, "But how did you land a job in security at such a prestigious resort hotel?"

Curtis was genuinely curious. He held back a smile.

"It's actually my second job. Sometimes one can be lucky. I am fortunate enough to have been provided work by the English authorities. Wink, wink," smiled Rat. "Now I am to work with you and also the resort. As I say, lucky."

Things are starting to become clear, thought Curtis. *I was never going on leave.*

"Are you telling me you were provided with the security job waiting for my arrival?"

"Perhaps." Pensively, "But perhaps not. There has been some trouble in the south of Thailand and I was sent here to wait for my orders."

"So, the hotel management knows about your real job?"

"No!" Rat was emphatic. "But Sir Edward is apparently a friend of a senior executive in the Centara Group and he called in a favour."

Rat elaborated on how he became the most public 'face' of the resort security contingent. There were security personnel at each entrance to the resort complex. The main entrance off Soi 65, a side entrance off Soi 61, and an entrance directly from Hua Hin beach. Security was also placed at the front and rear entrances to the adjoining staff quarters.

Arriving at the Centara Resort office on his first day, Rat was immediately assigned to the least significant entrance at the rear of the staff quarters.

"Chief of security was reluctant to even give me a job. He asked management to assign me to the gardening division. The GM told him I had to be in security.

"So, I was to be sent to the rear of the staff quarters where nobody would see me. I refused. It was my lucky day. I changed his mind."

Curtis could visualise the steel cold glare that accompanied the refusal.

"When I first arrived in Hua Hin, I was issued with the ceremonial security uniform." Rat noticed Curtis raised his head and looked skywards. Unimpressed.

"I know what you are thinking. Yes, the uniform is only ceremonial and next to useless in circumstances of a security breach. So, I immediately modified the pith helmet to meet my requirements. There is no point in being in security if one isn't issued with a weapon, don't you think? I made my own.

"The chief doubted my capacity to respond to a security issue. I said to him, 'see those flowers over there', pointing to artificial flowers attached to the waterproof canopy of a pulling rickshaw on display in the front garden. He nodded. I said, 'Now you see them, now you don't'.

"I had sewn a circular blade into the rim of my helmet. In a single action, I whipped the rim away from the top of the helmet and flicked it frisbee-style at the flower stems twenty metres away.

"It was a lucky hit."

Curtis concluded that Rat was modest about his offensive skills. He guessed the chief recognised talent when he saw it. Without any further argument he had offered Rat the main security position at the front of the hotel.

Chapter 8

Curtis thumbed his way through the menu, flicking over the European cuisine on the first six pages. Next there were various types of Tom Yum soups, five pages of fish and other seafood cooked in various Thai styles; deep fried with garlic and pepper, crispy deep-fried sea bass, soft-shell crabs, and others.

There followed several pages of menu from the Esan district of northern Thailand. Flawless glossy photographs of plates brimming with the most alluring and delectable Thai cuisine accompanied all of the descriptions.

Mouth-watering, thought Curtis.

"Allow me to choose." Rat broke the silence.

He summoned the waiter who clearly doubled as a cook and placed an order of satay shrimp, crab fried rice (the menu said 'crap fried rice'), *ayam* green curry, Massaman beef curry, and mixed vegetables in black bean sauce.

"*Ayam?*" asked Curtis.

"Indonesian for 'chicken' but we use that word here too sometimes."

"Drink?" asked the waiter. "Back page of menu."

Rat ordered *Cha Yen*, Thai iced tea. Curtis pointed at the photograph of black iced coffee, labelled '*oliang*' and instructed, "No added sugar."

The drinks came. Curtis withdrew the straw from the glass mug, placed it to the side and took a sip, sat back in his chair and relaxed. The coffee was good, raising expectations for the food.

Rat used his straw slurping audibly on his *Cha Yen*.

The crab fried rice and vegetables arrived. Curtis helped himself to a sizeable serving of rice and returned to his drink. Rat added some chilli to his plate of vegetables and waited for his guest to start eating.

They ate slowly, in silence, before the balance of the order arrived. The cook-cum-waiter appeared with more steaming hot plates that gave off an assuredly appetising aroma.

Positioning and then re-positioning the plates within easy reach of his customers he asked, "Is everything to your liking?"

Rat merely nodded. With a mouth full of rice and *ayam*, Curtis did not reply but his answer was in the eagerness with which he attacked the curry. Satisfied, the waiter left.

Having tucked away a substantial quantity Rat turned to Curtis and said, "I have something to show you." He fumbled in his pocket and retrieved a cutting from a newspaper bearing yesterday's date.

'British tourist killed in car accident' headlined the article. Curtis read that a tourist driving a hire car had been hit by a truck whilst overtaking on a winding road near the Khao Nam Khang National Park in southern Thailand. There were no witnesses to the accident but 'following police investigations the truck driver has been completely exonerated of any fault,' stated the article.

Curtis silently read on, 'The deceased, one Edward Townsend Creighton Jr had been driving at speed on a narrow and winding road in the Pattani district when he carelessly crossed to the wrong side of the road. It appears Creighton swerved back to the correct side of the road but in so doing lost control of his vehicle. The Creighton family in England has been notified.'

The journalist had made his own assumptions or relied solely upon police comments.

He raised his eyes and peered over the paper. Not unexpectedly Rat carried a forlorn look.

"I'm sorry, Rat."

"That was not an accident. Ed was a skilful and careful driver. I spoke to him before he departed Bangkok for Pattani. He was investigating the recent military camp break-ins and thefts."

"Why would a British agent conduct those investigations? Surely that is a matter for the Thai military police?"

Rat paused the conversation to fill his mouth with Massaman curry. With an audible gulp, he washed it down with ice tea. He used his fork to mix more Massaman with rice as he contemplated how best to inform Curtis of the latest intelligence.

"MI6 believes there is a link between the theft of military equipment, the disappearance of skilled and highly trained soldiers from the Pattani base and paramilitary training establishments in southern Thailand."

Curtis had a flashback to sitting at the bar and reading the newspaper. "I recall reading what appeared to be an inconsequential event recently. The newspaper did not seem to be all that interested in following up on the story."

"It was rumoured that a British citizen was somehow involved," mumbled Rat in between mouthfuls. "An investigative journalist in the UK had been exploring the source of the Brit's unexplained wealth when he came across a familial connection to an Australian businessman. His brother. He migrated to Australia six years ago.

"We have only recently commenced investigations into this matter. Why would we bother?" he asked rhetorically. "Because our people have picked up on coded chatter across several countries that gives us cause for concern.

"The Australian apparently has business interests based in Singapore. How his business is structured we cannot tell, but it does appear he protects his anonymity by operating through company trustees."

"I still don't see the connection between the Aussie and a threat to the UK," whispered Curtis.

"We are not sure if there is a specific threat to the UK. MI6 has concerns that his company revenue, the source of which is so far unknown, is possibly transferred out of Singapore bank accounts to fund terrorist groups. You will be aware of the recent reports allegedly involving HSBC. The Financial Conduct Authority in the UK has been investigating the bank to determine if it has met UK money-laundering regulations."

Curtis nodded his understanding of the issue but was not convinced. He challenged the logic. "Just because this un-named Australian businessman has an HSBC Singapore bank account doesn't mean he is somehow connected to a potential terrorist threat to the UK, or anywhere else for that matter."

"You are quite correct," replied Rat. "But there appears to be smoke and mirrors in the way the brothers operate their business."

"What has triggered the concern?" asked a sceptical Curtis.

"According to the journalist, the UK businessman has acquired an interest in at least one major league team. Large sums of money are involved. Sponsorship money."

"Because of the FCA investigation," Rat added, "the apparent transfer of large sums of money and the secrecy surrounding the movement of funds, our financial forensic experts became involved. But they are meeting obstacles in their investigation."

Curtis understood. "I'm informed there is a great deal of secrecy involving financial transactions out of Singapore. My friends in the federal police have suggested, rightly or wrongly, that it has become a new Switzerland. Hidden wealth. Secret bank accounts."

"Edward Creighton and I talk often." Rat hesitated and appeared to choke on his emotions as he rephrased his last comment. "I should say we talked often," emphasising the penultimate word.

The waiter reappeared and asked if everything was to their liking. Curtis was annoyed with the interruption but acknowledged the courtesy and the quality of the food.

After another pause, Rat wiped his mouth with the wafer-thin tissue that doubled as a serviette before continuing.

"When there was an important matter to discuss I would receive a coded message delivered by way of a crossword in a British community newspaper, 'The Withington Weekly'. The crossword was not regularly published but when it was, Edward was the author.

"I showed you yesterday's Bangkok Post, Curtis. You can imagine how shocked I was to receive a message from Edward on my mini tablet yesterday afternoon. A voice from the dead. No joke. I checked and learnt the car he was driving was only recovered yesterday."

Rat called the waiter and ordered another iced tea. Curtis waited patiently for him to continue.

"Edward's phone was in his car. He'd been out of range when he typed and attempted to send the message. When the car was trucked back into Pattani it was automatically sent. I received the message within minutes."

The iced tea arrived. Shaking his head at the waiter's insistence he order another iced coffee, Curtis was now becoming annoyed at the interruptions. He gave the waiter an impatient wave of dismissal.

"If this message was important, just tell me what it said," he barked.

"Yes, of course," Rat replied reaching for his mini tablet. He unlocked the screen and scrolled down under 'saved emails' at the same time manoeuvring the tablet into position for Curtis to more clearly see the screen and read the message.

It read '28 back, 15 down, 4, 16 across, 27 down. Help me find them.' Nothing more. No greeting or sign-off.

"What in the hell does that mean?" asked Curtis.

"I haven't yet checked but I thought we might work through this together."

Rat punched some letters on the tablet. The signal was weak. The internet moved slowly. After several minutes, the search engine, Rat's slowly written instructions to the web page and the Withington Weekly synchronised and found the latest edition. Rat scanned the top of the page intensely, skimming across the sub-headings of News, Sport, Business, Comment, Property, Classifieds and Contact Us before settling the cursor over Entertainment.

'Entertainment' also had several links. Rat quickly skimmed over Movies, Television, Theatre, Arts, Music, Sudoku, and found Crosswords. There were two. An easy crossword and a cryptic crossword.

Rat double-clicked on Cryptic and, the wonders of the web-wide world, it lifted a crossword to the top right corner of the screen. He held the cursor over the crossword and double-clicked again. It filled the screen.

"The crossword only has across and down and there is only one twenty-eight under the latter. No twenty-eight back as instructed by Ed," Rat stated the obvious.

Most people who regularly work on cryptic crossword puzzles become accustomed to the style of the author. Well-practised exponents of such crosswords more readily solve the puzzle once the author's style becomes familiar. Some use anagrams, others jumble or mismatch words in a sentence. Alphabet soup. Confusing, unless one becomes accustomed to the author's thinking.

The logic of Creighton's message system was clear to Rat but not to Curtis. He was more confused than a stirred alphabet soup.

The characteristic grin slowly reappeared as Rat gazed at twenty-eight down. It read 'Icelandic kitchen'.

"Twenty-eight back," he emphasised, "must mean either kitchen Icelandic or whatever an Icelandic kitchen is spelt backwards."

Curtis shook his head in bewilderment. "Search a translation site," he instructed.

Reducing the crossword to the top corner of the tablet, Rat ran the cursor down his bookmarks on the left of the tablet until he found 'Translations Online'. In the principle box for languages he scrolled down to 'Icelandic' and then typed the word 'kitchen'. He triggered 'Translate'. In the translation box the word 'kitchen' reappeared. The same word he had sought to translate. No difference.

"That didn't work." Rat was talking to himself. He quickly found a generic search engine and typed the two words, 'Icelandic kitchen'. Numerous links appeared, ranging from images of kitchens to the best recipes. Nothing on the first page of any consequence. Nothing on the second page. On the third page under 'Types of kitchens' the word '*nemow*' jumped out at him.

"*Nemow*. Backwards? Women? Let's put that to one side and complete the other clues." Rat was clearly enjoying the challenge his friend Edward had given him.

Curtis nodded agreement.

"The clue for fifteen down reads, 'Digin but it could be suitably or unsuitably French'."

Rat looked up, angling his head to one side and fixing his gaze on a rusted piece of iron bar holding a billboard for the purpose of advertising the restaurant. He was trying to decipher the meaning of the clue but was having difficulty.

Fluent in French, Curtis quickly surmised 'digin' to be the French word '*indigne*' meaning 'unsuitable or unworthy'.

"I get the cryptic nature of this message now." Curtis beamed as he relayed his discovery to Rat.

Rat smiled in agreement. He too was fluent in French, having excelled in the language at school and again at the Tourism Training College, but he accepted the definition Curtis offered. It made sense.

"Neither four across nor four down exist in this crossword," exclaimed Rat. "I know Edward's thinking. He means 'for' not the numeral four. So far, we have 'unsuitable or unworthy for' and possibly the sentence starts with 'Women'. Women unworthy for…"

For a few moments they looked intently at each other before Rat broke the silence. "Sixteen across. It reads 'CHONS in various degrees of chemistry will provide it'. What in hell does that mean?"

Curtis was pleased with himself. He now understood the cryptic system, but frowned heavily as he mentally weighed up the options. Both men again sat in silence for several minutes. Curtis called the waiter and ordered more *oliang*, black iced coffee. "Same, same. No added ice please."

"Everything to your liking?" asked the waiter-cum-cook. "More food perhaps?"

"*Mae au karp.*" No thank you.

"*Mai pen lai.*" No problem.

Rat was surprised at how quickly Curtis had learnt key Thai phrases and told him so. He turned to the waiter and asked for more *Cha Yen* and then spoke rapidly in the local language.

"I told him to bring the drinks and leave us alone. Don't bother us again, however grateful we are for the quality of the meal."

They again stared at the crossword on the tablet and alternately at the clues Rat had scribbled on a page torn from the menu folder. He progressively wrote Edward's message on it.

Eventually this time Curtis broke the silence. Sudden enlightenment. He eagerly told Rat, "I believe CHONS to be an acronym. Since it is capitalised, I reckon it's a combination of chemical elements. Carbon, hydrogen, oxygen, nitrogen and sulphur. The main elements, as the clue suggests, in various degrees or amounts making up important rocks or minerals."

"Important rocks?"

"Yes, important minerals. That includes coal. If that is correct, Rat, and CHONS is 'coal', what does that mean?"

"Energy." Rat almost jumped from his seat.

"Yes, energy or power."

"That's it!" exclaimed Rat. "Women unworthy or unsuitable for power!"

"Hang on, don't get too excited, Rat." Curtis pointed to the torn menu page. "What does twenty-seven down mean and what did Edward mean by his last sentence?"

"Twenty-seven down. It reads 'Sounds like a mirror and a 1970s French-Italian film'." Knowing Curtis had an interest in all things French Rat looked pleadingly at him for guidance.

"Do your thing, Rat, and search 1970s French films."

Rat again went to his favoured search engine. Discovering the list of French films to be lengthy he started scrolling through them with Curtis eagerly translating the titles. Nothing jumped off the screen until half way through the 1972 list. Curtis saw the joint production originally had an Italian title but the words were inescapable.

"There it is, that's it." He pointed at the screen. "The movie *Una Ragione Per Vivere E Una Per Morire*, 'A reason to live, a reason to die'."

Thinking out loud Curtis said, "Edward wrote 'sounds like a mirror'. Of course, it was silly of me not to figure that out straight away. '*Mourir*' is the French word for 'die' and '*morire*' is the Italian word for die. Sounds like a mirror!"

What had commenced as an intense conversation about Rat's friend Edward and his unexplained death suddenly took a new turn. An air of achievement and excitement at the discovery, not the meaning of that discovery.

Rat had written the key words under the clues as they discovered them and quietly read the combination to Curtis.

"Women unworthy for power die."

Chapter 9

"His last message to me said, 'Help me find them'." Rat gazed at Curtis anxiously awaiting his take on the plea.

"Was Edward searching for a terrorist organisation or a group of people whose objective was to prevent a particular woman from holding a position of authority or power? Or was he looking for an individual? But he specifically said 'them'. More than one person?"

Rat thought Curtis was talking to himself — weighing up the likelihood of one scenario over another.

"Good observation," Rat said. "This may well be a group or organisation that takes sexism to a new level where—"

"No, it's not sexism," Curtis snapped, abruptly interrupting Rat's train of thought. "It's misogyny. It's more than discrimination based on gender. It's violence, based on gender."

With that Curtis appeared to drift away in thought.

Rat took a sip of tea and peered at Curtis over the rim of his glass. He thought Curtis looked distant. He was. Deep in thought, contemplating examples of where misogyny was real and dangerous. Remembering his childhood.

"Curtis, snap out of it."

"I was thinking of occasions I have witnessed or been made aware of where misogyny may take several forms. It might be actual physical violence or it might even be emotional aggression.

"Family violence," Curtis continued. "The number of men who emotionally terrorise their wives or partners and eventually physically act upon that torment is staggering. As a community we do nothing. Domestic violence is somehow less important than someone being bashed outside the home. Sadly, our culture regards a familial relationship, even if a violent one, as someone else's problem."

"Not in Thailand," argued Rat. "Our culture demands that we respect everyone in our family, especially women and older people."

The time wasn't right to tell Rat about his family history. He didn't know Rat well enough just yet to tell him that his father was jealous and possessive. That his father would come home from the local bar late at night and beat his mother. That most bruising was not visible. Beneath clothing.

His mother always had excuses for visible contusions. She had stumbled and fallen on the path down the road. She was accidentally hit by a racquet whilst playing squash. She had fallen from her bicycle. Terribly accident prone. Knowing the truth, he felt ashamed that he didn't do anything about it.

He wanted to tell Rat that his father taunted his mother about what he intended to do to his sisters when they were older. But he couldn't. What sort of family did he come from? What man would beat a woman like that? A coward, that's what.

Rat might not believe him. He was afraid for his sisters. So was his mother and she acted upon it. Bruised and battered from her latest encounter with this man of hate, she had left the family home with her children.

It wasn't hard for the father to find them in a small country town. When the children were at school, he broke into her rented accommodation, beat her and sexually assaulted her.

At some point during the violence Curtis's mother found her husband's shotgun that she had stolen for the protection of her children if necessary. Only to be used as a threat. Nothing more. She was certainly not a violent woman notwithstanding she had the best possible tuition from her husband over a long period of time. At the peak of his violence, yelling threats of murder, the pump action twelve-gauge shotgun was used to good effect.

The defence gathered witnesses, prepared witness statements from neighbours near and far, medical evidence and psychological reports. Medical reports included references to broken ribs, collarbones and shattered eye sockets occurring over several years. Potential character witnesses were briefed. Detailed reports from independent experts were requested. Detailed photographs of the crime scene depicting blood splatter were discovered from the crown prosecutor.

The defence barrister ably supported by her local briefing solicitor, the second chair, was ready to mount a solid defence. A compelling defence irresistible to a jury selected after a long and arduous process.

The Crown relied on the gruesome photographic evidence, evidence of gunshot residue on the 'perpetrator's hands and clothes' — an attempt to make his mother an impersonal and cold-blooded killer — and selected statements from her husband's family and close friends. He was, so it was argued, 'a loving family man who never had a violent bone in his body'.

The trial lasted three weeks. In the final analysis of the case in detail, the crown prosecutor had no answer for the plethora of evidence depicting Curtis's father as a violent man. Barrister Joan Symonds SC meticulously stripped the Crown's evidence to the bone. Tore it apart and tore it down.

The photographic evidence of the crime scene and his mother's badly beaten body supported the defence's argument. Members of the jury, so the local press reported, were nodding agreement with Ms Symonds as she demonstrated the husband to be a particularly nasty and violent man.

His mother was eventually found not guilty, her conduct having been found to be consistent with non-insane automatism. She was not criminally responsible for her husband's death. She had absolutely no recollection of the events immediately following the sexual assault. The act of shooting and killing her husband was independent of the exercise of her will.

"Governments have an obligation to protect their citizens," said Curtis. "Unfortunately, sometimes the leaders, by their own ineptitude, send the wrong messages. Or perhaps they are unwilling to address the situation because of their personal bias.

"Let's face it. The reality is the Australian head of government, the prime minister, has the power to influence so much. But since federation in 1901, Australia has had just one female prime minister. Whilst there have been numerous female cabinet ministers, the ratio of men to women has been very lop-sided."

Curtis continued, demonstrating his knowledge of Australian, not just French and English history. "Women have traditionally found it harder to be elected to the parliaments of Australia. Women were given the right to vote and stand for the parliament in 1902 but it wasn't until 1943 that the first female was elected to the House of Representatives.

"Most people will say 'fortunately, attitudes are changing'. But are they really? Shouldn't our political leaders be providing leadership on this issue? But here again we have a problem of attitude. A recent Australian prime minister demonstrated a reluctance to promote women to cabinet and indeed expressed negative views about women.

"Any male government leader — president or prime minister — who excludes women from his cabinet might be described as a 'sexist'. But what is the underlying reason for excluding women from positions of leadership and power? Is it a strategic plan to reinforce male domination in leadership positions? Perhaps. Or is it maybe that some men find it difficult to take orders from women, absurd as that might be?"

Curtis realised he was lecturing Rat. That wasn't his intention. He just wanted to share a taste of his values.

"I would say that government leader is certainly sexist and holds views that are inappropriate. As I was about to say," intervened Rat, "the sexism becomes violent and that is what Edward was chasing."

"It's worse than sexism, Rat. By his actions, that same leader has given expression to a set of values that in turn gives succour to people who are prepared to go further than what they would see as a soft form of discrimination. Demagoguery at its worst. Encouraging the expression of values and extreme views by abhorrent behaviour, even violent behaviour."

Curtis paused. An image of his mother lying prone on the kitchen floor flashed before him. Through the eyes of a boy. At first a solid image, gradually becoming clouded. A clouded vision that slowly dissolved into emptiness returning the boy to the present.

He sighed. "I obviously did not know your friend but it appears to me he was pursuing someone or some people who might fit into that category. He may have lost his life for that reason."

By now it was apparent to Rat that Curtis held very strong views, indeed passionate views on the question of violence against women.

Brilliant, he thought, *he will undoubtedly be a huge asset on this mission.*

Chapter 10

"I think you are exactly right about Edward. He was getting close to exposing the person or people whose objective it is to prevent a woman from becoming a significant leader."

"But why Thailand?" Curtis asked.

"Allow me to explain," Rat said politely. "You would be aware of our former Prime Minister Yingluck Shinawatra. You may also be aware there was a campaign to defeat her centring around legal challenges alleging misuse of public funds. Before her premiership her older brother, Thaksin Shinawatra, was ousted as prime minister in a military coup.

"The Shinawatra family still has a strong following in Thailand. Yingluck has a cousin who is apparently very politically astute and charismatic.

"The information I have recently received is there is concern amongst some politicians that Yingluck's cousin might attempt to continue the family dynasty in politics. Perhaps even avenge her family name.

"Much has been said about the activity of insurgents in southern Thailand. Insurgents are difficult to defeat. The region in which they operate in southern Thailand was originally part of Malaysia but in a bitter and bloody battle in the late 1700s the area was taken over by our country."

"What has this got to do with Yingluck's cousin and, by the way, does he or she have a name?" Curtis realised Rat liked to paint the big picture but he wanted him to focus on the matter at hand.

"She," Rat emphasised. "Dao. Her name is Dao. By the way 'Dao' coincidentally means 'star'. Not only her parents but her supporters also regard her as a star. I have seen her on television and I fully understand the choice of name. It fits perfectly. If you were to meet her, I'm sure you would agree.

"Bear with me, Curtis, while I explain the connection. The insurgency group has demanded the area captured from Malaysia be declared a free and independent Muslim state. The insurgent leaders have a great deal of community support by promising hope and raising expectations.

"Over the years there has been a growing expectation of success. An expectation the Pattani district and several other districts in the south will eventually secure independent administrative control. They are clearly misguided in their view. They aim to stop what they believe is a drain of funds from the area directed in favour of corrupt officials in the nation's capital.

"There are several insurgent groups, the most radical of which is the *Runda Kumpulan Kecil*, known as the RKK. It is a militant Islamic group. They've been responsible for many vicious attacks and bombings, operating in small groups, hitting and running across the border into Malaysia.

"The information I have received is the RKK are being used by another unknown organisation as a diversion. If this group has the objective of targeting women in leadership positions this would suit the RKK for two reasons." With careful deliberation Rat raised his thumb followed by his index finger and ticked them off as he spoke.

"Firstly, they believe in male domination. Secondly, they have a score to settle with the Shinawatra family.

"Dao's uncle and former Prime Minister, Thaksin Shinawatra, took a hard-line approach against the separatist insurgency. He was very much in favour of military intervention in an attempt to wipe them out. No pussyfooting with him.

"So, you see, Curtis, this recent activity in the south was being pieced together by Edward when he was killed. I'm sure he was killed."

From the intelligence fed to Rat he briefed Curtis about the targeted recruitment of military personnel in the south of Thailand. He was able to give a detailed account of the recruiting campaign or 'operation' as he preferred to call it.

Highly trained personnel from the Special Operations Unit had served in the Pattani district for several years. After Thaksin Shinawatra, their role changed from aggressor to peacemaker. It was the intention of the current government to have the SOU win the hearts and minds of the locals and in this way avoid conflict. Were they succeeding? Perhaps not as well as the government had hoped.

MI6 intelligence suggested some SOU soldiers had become quite close to insurgents in the RKK as a result of the policy. There was a real concern that some soldiers had been persuaded to support or at the very least sympathise with some philosophical views of their RKK friends.

"Recruited by the RKK?" asked Curtis.

"Possibly. Possibly recruited to the paramilitary separatist insurgency, or alternatively being used to train them."

"Back to Dao. Is she contesting the next election?"

"At this stage it appears she is merely dipping her toe and testing the water," Rat said. "Given the family history in politics and the strong support she is receiving from around the country, including encouragement from some of the media, there is a strong likelihood she will run."

Chapter 11

Wallace was buoyant after his meeting with Lumovski. Arrangements for Lumovski's Green Solutions' capital injection were to be finalised within days. In the meantime, meetings would be arranged with the mayor of the city of Moscow and the minister for railways. Other ministers would follow.

As far as Wallace was concerned, the really positive thing was he didn't need to attend those meetings but could leave it to Lumovski, Vasiliev and Hunter. He would be free to attend his meeting in the UK.

Real progress is being made in Russia with my company. Generating serious money and providing so much hope for mankind, thought Wallace, wearing a satisfying grin.

Although he had not been invited to participate in the detailed financial discussions, Nelson had also impressed Lumovski with the few comments he directed towards him.

"Your reference to your army background was timely," commented Wallace as he and Nelson were being driven back to their hotel. "He was suitably impressed with the fact you are not only a licensed financial planner but you have got your hands dirty in other areas."

Months earlier Wallace couldn't believe his luck when he learnt Nelson had been headhunted as an instructor at the police tactical response training facility in Sydney. To the elite tactical response group, he was a valuable acquisition; able to utilise the knowledge he had accumulated over the years in the Australian Army.

His expertise in the army extended to the use of explosives in combat, sniper training generally, and precision marksmanship in particular. These were essential skills of enormous value to the tactical response group, especially at a time of heightened police and government concern about terrorism. A concern that was elevated after the infamous Lindt Café shooting and subsequent criticism of the manner in which the New South Wales Police handled the matter.

More important for Wallace was Nelson's loyalty, his commitment and stance on issues central to the Wallace brothers' objectives. Nelson's attitude and philosophy on the natural order of human relations met with approval.

As for his other key Green Solutions personnel, he had less confidence that Coolidge shared the same philosophy, but that didn't matter. Coolidge served a purpose. He would focus on company operational matters. Especially the new Green Solution trials planned for Malaysia and Indonesia.

He was also capable of making presentations to potential customers. That freed Wallace to focus on the more likely successes in Europe and the other issues he wanted to address. Needed to address!

Coolidge annoyed him with his insistence the company should engage a financial controller. He had expressed concern about the burn rate and had asked questions about where the funds were being used.

It's none of his damn business where and when we spend company funds. Unless carefully chosen, a financial controller could create huge problems. I won't allow that to happen. Edgar would be furious if we engage the wrong people, make the wrong moves at this crucial stage of our operation.

On the return drive to their hotel, Wallace was deep in thought.

Sensing Nelson's gaze, he turned to face him. "Is there something bothering you, Craig?"

"When can I expect to meet your brother and the other group leaders? I don't intend to be pushy but I thought I was part of the team."

"You are an important part of the team, Craig, and I think you know that. I have trusted you and taken you into my confidence. Edgar will want to meet you but first it is important to get the job done in Thailand.

"I have booked a flight for you to Bangkok the day after tomorrow. I want you to oversee the operation. This is our first operation of this type. It cannot fail. You will ensure everything goes according to plan. The plans we devised when we became aware of certain political movements. People problems.

"After Thailand we can meet in England. I'll make the necessary arrangements."

Wallace was circumspect in his conversation with Nelson. He was confident Lumovski's driver only understood basic English but even that knowledge was too much.

As the limousine pulled up to the hotel entrance he said, "We shall continue this conversation over a drink."

Wallace ordered a bottle of Dom Perignon P2 Second Plenitude 2000.

"Expensive drop, Jim." Nelson knew the champagne to be amongst the best of the Dom Perignons.

"We have reason to celebrate, Craig, so let's do it properly, in style. We deserve it."

I deserve it and I intend to enjoy the fruits of my labour.

The top floor bar and restaurant where Wallace had met with Simon Hunter late the previous afternoon was empty except for the bartender and the waiter who hovered in the vicinity of the bar. Wallace directed Nelson to a table as far away from the bar as possible.

Although not necessary, more out of habit than fear of being heard in this particular bar, he nevertheless lowered his voice.

"I am flying to London at around the same time as you leave on Thai Airways. We can travel to the airport together. I'll ask Simon's secretary to make the transfer arrangements."

"What's happening in London?"

"You should know better than ask me what I'm doing," scowled Wallace, raising his voice only slightly but by his tone showing his displeasure at Nelson's question. "But I'll make an exception on this occasion and explain."

"I have follow-up meetings with nominated advisers, you might have heard them called nomads, and a meeting with a key person at the London Stock Exchange. Coolidge has made the arrangements."

"What about Lumovski's funds? Wasn't his investment conditional upon us not listing the company? Don't you think he will deliver?" Nelson gazed at Wallace quizzically.

"He will deliver, as you say conditional upon keeping the company in private hands. But existing shareholders need an assurance we are following our original exit strategy," Wallace replied woodenly.

"Simon will finalise matters with Lumovski and the funds will flow to Green Solutions within a week. It will happen, of that I am certain.

"At the right time, and with Lumovski's help, we shall buy out the existing shareholders and give them a small profit. They will accept that arrangement because the return on their investment will be quicker than listing the company, and having their shares locked in escrow for twelve months or more.

"In the meantime, I need to keep up the appearance of moving towards a float."

"Can't you just tell them you had the meetings without actually going to the trouble of doing so?"

Wallace smiled at Nelson's suggestion. "Perhaps, but that would be dishonest and I couldn't do that," he lied.

I don't intend to meet the nomads and the stock exchange but I need to keep up appearances. It's best Nelson doesn't know. The fewer people the better. I wouldn't like to be caught out.

"I have a planning meeting with Edgar and the others in the Somerset city of Bath in the next couple of weeks," Wallace continued.

"Why Bath? Why not London or another major European city where we have plans for offices? Paris?" Nelson couldn't contain his curiosity.

"Edgar's choice. It's all to do with his namesake. Bath is where the coronation of the first King of All England was held."

Nelson again looked puzzled.

Wallace had the capacity to produce his finest English accent, 'the Queen's English' he called it, whenever he chose. And this was such an occasion.

"My brother is a student of history. When he was of an age and able to do so he changed his given name by deed poll to Edgar. My mother was not happy with the name change but Edgar simply ignored her protestations. Our father had already passed, but we know he would have been impressed with Edgar's thinking.

"King Edgar became king at the age of sixteen. Edgar the Peaceful, as he was known, chose Bath Abbey for his coronation in 973, fourteen years after he became king.

"The great King Edgar has inspired my brother and me and we have followed his example over the years. It is his inspiration that has given us purpose. Designed a path for both of us. We have conformed to his leadership.

"The direction King Edgar followed as the first monarch of all of England has offered us hope. Hope the natural order in society can be achieved with strength and planning. You know what I mean by that, Craig?"

"Of course, I do." Nelson grinned broadly.

Chapter 12

Curtis returned to the gymnasium to pump iron for an hour and a half, stopping only once to check his phone for messages. He had flicked the 'silent' switch, not wanting to disturb others in the gymnasium. But he did disturb them by his mere presence. His size turned heads. The weights he lifted had the others in the gymnasium in awe.

Rat resumed his security position at the main entrance to the Grand Centara Resort Hotel. As guests arrived, he greeted them all with the customary '*Sawardee karp*', the Y and a huge grin. Nothing changed.

Both were waiting for new information from Australia. No messages. Curtis hated waiting for instructions or intelligence from Frenchy. If there was a job to do, he wanted to get it done.

Leaving the gymnasium, Curtis walked past the beachside pool and dozens of pool beds occupied mostly by Europeans soaking up the tropical sun. Their newly baked colour was evidence that some guests had clearly been at the resort for some time.

He made his way past the rear entrance to the resort and onto the beach. An ocean swim was in order but first a thirty-minute jog in the heavy sand.

Jai, the housekeeper, had left the air-conditioning temperature control at a ridiculously low level when she had finished cleaning his room. The perspiration streaming from his temples and running down his neck gave Curtis a chill as he entered the room. He quickly flicked the air-con switch to 'off' and opened the door onto his first-floor private balcony. The outside warmth soaked into the room.

Returning to his room had been timely. His mobile phone pinged the arrival of a new message. Unlike many of his friends, Curtis didn't feel the need to constantly check his phone for social media messages or conventional phone messages. Not that he had many friends. He simply didn't have time and wasn't in the one place for any length of time to form new relationships. First a shower and a change of clothes.

Curtis took his time. He had earlier filled his bar fridge with soda water purchased from the 7-Eleven near the resort. After pouring a drink he gathered up his phone and sat on the balcony chair.

A second message had arrived, both from Frenchy. 'Hua Hin weather is forecasted to be unchanged for the next week or so. Relax and enjoy,' read the first message. Curtis knew that meant nothing was about to happen and he should await further instructions.

Scrolling down Curtis found the second abrupt message, which had been sent forty minutes after the first. It read, 'New weather forecast. Getting hotter next week. Call.'

He closed his private balcony door and opened the room's main door, peering in both directions. No potential eavesdroppers. Curtis retrieved his secure phone from the room safe.

"Curtis," was all he said when the phone was answered.

"Are we secure?" came the metallic, hollow sound from 7,500 kilometres away.

"Of course." This was the predictable initial exchange between Curtis and Frenchy. No unnecessary small talk.

"Bell has given me instructions. You are active now, no longer on leave. Bell has specifically chosen you to handle the matter I am about to describe.

"We have shared intelligence with MI5 and MI6. Solid intelligence. Brief our Thai operative but you are in command there."

"Not necessary," Curtis replied. "Rest assured we will work together on whatever is necessary. I will rely heavily on his local knowledge if the matter has to be dealt with in Thailand. Now, what's the go?"

"Dao Shinawatra. You are aware of her interest in politics. It appears her political interest is becoming more serious. There is every possibility she will contest the next election, whenever that might be, to lead Thailand.

"Opinion polls reflect her strong personal following. Her ratings have gone to another level after recent public appearances at rallies in Bangkok."

Curtis listened in silence. It wasn't prudent to interrupt Frenchy. *Although we don't operate on a formal basis, he is my senior officer after all. My job is to follow orders.*

"Dao's campaign is gathering momentum. The military-controlled government is watching developments with interest. The campaign objective is to rally enough public support to force the junta to a general election.

"That is not to say the military is opposed to her. So far, the government has remained silent but there are others who are certain to resist Dao's candidacy. They will go to any lengths to thwart her aspirations.

"We don't know much about those opposed to Dao, but there have recently been coded communications between a group in Thailand and Europe. Possibly France or England. They are quite sophisticated in their communications and it has taken our people several days to break the code.

"We suspect the RKK or people connected to the small patrol units are involved. We know there will be an attempt on Dao's life. Bell wants her protected.

"As I said, you have specifically been chosen to handle this. Bell is concerned that you stay focused. Don't let your family situation cloud your judgement."

So, Bell knows about my father's inconceivable aggression towards my mother. Long ago. It doesn't define me. He should know that by now.

"Dao intends raising her profile in regional Thailand and, to that end, will be meeting and greeting the great unwashed south of Bangkok. We are reliably informed she will travel by train southbound within a week and hold meetings with small interest groups to prepare her campaign team.

"The chatter suggests there will be a hit where you are. In Hua Hin or somewhere in the vicinity of Hua Hin."

At this suggestion Curtis couldn't resist an interruption. "Why Hua Hin?"

"The support for both Thaksin and Yingluck Shinawatra mainly came from the rural northern areas and the urban poor. Opposition to both former premiers came from the Bangkok elite and middle class as well as the royalists in the south. Hua Hin and the surrounding district is very staunchly royalist and also has a strong military presence.

"I am only guessing but I suspect the RKK and their associates believe it will be easier to make their hit and escape capture when it happens. In a community they perceive to be sympathetic.

"Secondly, as you know Hua Hin is a major tourist town and the insurgents now seem interested in raising the stakes. Taking their local protests to a new level. Spreading their separatist message internationally. What better way than creating a problem — perhaps an explosive device — in a tourist area?

"Find the problem, Curtis. Protect Dao. Eliminate the problem."

"You can be sure of that. This is becoming almost personal."

"I know, but most importantly don't let it cloud your judgement. One mistake and lives could be lost. Not to mention the impact that could have on relationships between Thailand and Australia. Also, the impact on both our careers, not that we should be concerned about such matters."

There was a long pause in the conversation. Frenchy often terminated his calls abruptly so Curtis asked, "Are you still there?"

"Yes."

"So, what are my instructions? Do you have any more intelligence that would help us protect her?" A vision of his father beating his mother made an unwelcome return. "Do you have any thoughts about where we should start?" Curtis fired a string of questions at Frenchy.

"Whoa! Hang on, one question at a time." Frenchy raised his voice in protest. "You are to stop the assassination. You and the Rat are our people on the ground there. We don't have any other resources to throw your way. No other intelligence either. If we hear anything you will be the first to know. Good luck." With that Frenchy terminated the call.

Thanks for nothing, thought Curtis. *Where to start!*

Curtis secured his phone in the room safe and made his way to the front of the hotel. He needed to talk to the other half of the Dao protection team. Rat wasn't in his usual position. He found him conveniently standing away from the main entrance in the shade of a tree sipping from a hotel-supplied water bottle.

"I'm glad I found you here. We need to talk."

"*Sawardee karp.*" Rat respectfully bowed his head. "You have new information?"

"I have new — I should say, we have new instructions," Curtis emphasised the plural.

Moving into the shade of the frangipani trees and traveller's palms adorning the long driveway entrance, Curtis relayed to Rat the conversation he had with Frenchy.

"That's not a lot to work with," said Rat, noticeably dropping the broad grin for a worried frown.

Curtis nodded agreement and added, "I need you to get as much information as you can about Dao's proposed schedule. When is the train departing Bangkok? When is it likely to arrive here? How many stops will it make? What is the seating arrangement for Dao and her key people? What carriage will she be in? How many other passengers will be on that train? Are there railway security people aboard and, if so, where will they be located? That sort of thing. Be as thorough and detailed as possible. We need a complete picture."

"I have suddenly taken ill and will have to leave my post," Rat whispered to Curtis, the trademark grin returning with a wink. "I have other work to attend to."

"See if you can find out whether Dao has a supporter base in Hua Hin. We need the names, places of work and home addresses of all the leading Shinawatra supporters in this district. The people with whom Dao is likely to meet. We need to know where she plans to meet these people. What her movements will be. If you can somehow obtain a copy of her itinerary that would make life easier for us. You might have to phone her office and pose as a journalist.

"Rat, I was told there was a bomb incident in Hua Hin a few years ago. What can you tell me about that? Give me some background if possible. Was the RKK involved?"

Rat didn't respond immediately, instead waiting for a group of people who were casually strolling past to walk out of earshot. He slowly drank from his water bottle. Understanding what was happening, Curtis didn't push him.

"Several bombs were found in Hua Hin and other tourist towns in Thailand. A bomb was placed in a pot plant at the front of a bar on the corner of Soi Salekam and Soi Poonsuk. That was the first to explode, about ten thirty at night. Exploded by mobile telephone unfortunately killing a woman. A local street vendor."

Curtis raised his eyebrows then shook his head in disgust at the last piece of information.

"There were two explosions about fifty metres and thirty minutes apart in the same area. The second only caused very localised damage. No other fatality or injuries.

"The following morning another explosion occurred near the main bus terminal. This explosion was bigger than the first. Damage to a nearby Starbucks was testament to that. Another local woman was killed and several other people were injured."

"Did anyone or any organisation take responsibility for the terrorism?" Curtis was anxious to get to the main point of his earlier question.

"Nobody is certain. We never found out who or what organisation, if any, was behind the bombings. There have been arrests of some RKK fellow travellers but they are not significant. We don't believe they were the main players. Nobody has admitted anything.

"The blame game started overnight. The media immediately pointed the finger at the RKK and other insurgent groups in the south. Others blamed the military. Claims they were attempting to strengthen their political power using the terrorist activity as an excuse began circulating."

Curtis interrupted the briefing by reminding Rat the military already had considerable power. "The prime minister is head of the army. The army's power and influence in all government decisions is without question. That suggestion doesn't make sense."

"Of course it doesn't," replied Rat.

"The timing was interesting though," Rat continued. "A new constitution was approved by popular vote in a referendum the week before the bombings. During the course of the referendum campaign some opponents of the proposed constitution claimed it would further cement military power. Provide for long-term military control. Perhaps that was the trigger. We may never know."

"You said both bombs were placed in pot plants and detonated by mobile telephone. How certain are you of the detonation *modus operandi*?"

Now it was Rat's turn to raise his eyebrow. Whilst he had an excellent grasp of the English language the same couldn't be said of Latin.

"Mo-dus op-er-an-di?" he repeated slowly, separating the syllables. I assume that means 'method operation'?"

"Precisely. Method of operation."

"Quite certain. A team of army forensic personnel were called in to survey the entire area over the following few hours. The debris and bomb parts that survived the explosion revealed the use of a mobile telephone for detonation purposes."

Curtis was pensive. If there was sufficient evidence to confirm the detonation technique in such a short period of time the explosive could not have been powerful enough to destroy everything in the bomb itself.

"What else can you tell me about the bombs? Explosive material? Any chemicals involved? Range of the explosion. Anything."

"No chemicals. The army never revealed the type of explosive but leave that with me. I shall explore that further if it is important to you and our mission?" Rat's offer was a question, not just a passing comment.

"Yes, it might be important. How would you stop a train in its tracks, Rat? What force would be required to derail a train?"

Rat thought Curtis was again thinking out loud and didn't respond. Indeed, he was. Curtis had not expected a reply.

"Anything else?"

"The bombs contained some metal pieces and ball bearings but if I remember correctly the police and army investigators did not think they were heavily laden with that material. They suggested the bombs were not intended to cause major damage and the resulting deaths were just bad luck. Collateral damage as you army people would say."

Perhaps. It all sounds amateurish.

"Righto, Rat. You sign off from work and gather the information we need. I will meet you later tonight at the Lucky Star Restaurant. Say, eight o'clock."

Chapter 13

Curtis decided to find the streets, Soi Salekam and Soi Poonsuk and inspect the site of the bombings three years earlier. He was certain the passage of time would prevent anything of substance being found but he wanted to talk to the owners and operators of nearby bars and shops.

Foremost in his inquiry was the need to obtain more information on the explosive material used and the extent of damage.

There was no dramatic repair to the road or nearby buildings. It was clear to Curtis the bomb was not particularly powerful. A planter box had been replaced in front of the bar. Amateurish cement work patched areas of two buildings, the damage presumably caused by small projectiles. Ball bearings. Different, newish paint revealed the precise location of damage.

After talking to the bar owner where the bomb had been planted, the restaurant staff on Soi Salekam and the staff of the massage centre across the road on Soi Poonsuk, Curtis was about to leave the vicinity of the blast when he was approached by a very angry man.

"Are you still investigating the bombing?" he asked in a heavy European accent. Before Curtis could respond he continued, "I heard you are asking questions about the explosion. Stop asking questions and find the fucking people responsible. Those fuckers have to pay."

Word travels quickly around these parts. He feels the need to vent his spleen against the police or anyone who might be investigating the matter.

"Don't get angry with me, my friend. There is no need for that language either," Curtis said in a moderate tone.

He only wanted to calm the man, not reveal the reason for his enquiries.

"I'm sorry. I'm still angry because the bomb has badly affected my business. Tourist numbers have fallen. That's my hotel," he exclaimed pointing at The Mermaid forty metres along Soi Salekam. "Easy to get a room there now — and cheap!"

"Rest assured the authorities are doing everything possible to hunt down the bombers," Curtis said with confidence as he walked away.

"Yeah, sure."

To confirm his suspicions about the impact of the explosives, Curtis ventured to the second site near the major tourist bus terminal. Without asking the staff at Starbucks or any of the tour operators he cast a look around the concrete wall of the terminal and the nearby planter box. He immediately saw where the bomb had been placed.

Repairs to the structure supporting the signage and the flowerbed were rough. Easy to see where the device was exploded. There were even burn marks that hadn't been cleaned or painted over.

His thoughts drifted back to the last conversation. *The hotelier is right. These people do need to pay for the senseless act that has cost lives.*

Several hours after arriving at the first bombsite, Curtis was satisfied that other than the tragic loss of life the explosions had minimal impact. Interviewing the locals, who had either been at work and within the vicinity of the explosions or were aware of the extent of the damage, convinced him both bombs contained small amounts of explosive material.

The entire operation was amateurish. Several other bombs failed to detonate. *If this was the work of the RKK our work might be easier than I initially thought. Careful, Curtis*, he thought reproachfully, *don't become complacent.*

Strolling along the main road that entered the central business district from the direction of Bangkok, Soi Phetch Kasem, Curtis noticed the street vendors starting to erect their gazebos in readiness for the night market. This signalled to him that it must be approaching happy hour at the resort and it was time to return there.

With still time to kill before happy hour and his later meeting with Rat, Curtis took a circuitous route and found his way to Soi Naresdamri. Here there are several bars, restaurants, clothing and a variety of other shops. Naresdamri is a long road. It passes the Hilton Hotel, several smaller hotels offering cheap accommodation and the main entrance to the Grand Centara.

Walking past a leather goods shop, he glanced through the wide-open door and saw a familiar face. He had an uncanny ability to remember people he had seen many years previously.

Nelson — Nelson. Now, what is his first name? Hmmm, Craig. That's him. Craig Nelson. What is he doing in Hua Hin? On holiday?

Curtis remembered Nelson from his Special Air Service Regiment training. He had left the SAS and the army only weeks after Curtis had been enlisted into the elite group. But he remembered him.

If he recalled correctly, Nelson had become tired of the army after many years of service as a non-commissioned officer. He didn't mind sharing his discontent with the troops.

In any work environment with a large number of employees there is a good chance one would find an associate with whom one disagrees on occasions. With whom one cannot have shared values. For whom one has disregard.

A person remembered mainly for their ideas, intellect and intolerance towards others, or a person lacking respect for others. Nelson was such a person.

Twenty metres past the leather goods shop was a small saloon bar. One that offered a free beer for every two purchased. Curtis went in and took a seat at the far end of the beer garden. From there he had a view through the foliage of the direction in which he had been heading and, with a sideways glance, he could see the opposite direction in a large bar mirror.

He ordered a lime soda. The bartender asked, "Are you sure? A lime and soda?"

"Yes, I'm sure."

I don't need to justify my choice of drink to you. This could be my private happy hour, he thought sarcastically.

A glass of ice containing a small quantity of soda water and a large slice of lime was delivered with a smile.

Best I don't make any comment. Remember to order without ice in future.

Within a few minutes Nelson walked past. Turning on his bar stool to avoid being seen, Curtis watched Nelson in the bar mirror. He turned down a narrow side street.

Curtis left two hundred baht on the bar with his unfinished drink. Payment for the drink and a healthy tip. Long strides took him quickly on to Soi Naresdamri, the main thoroughfare.

Nelson paused occasionally to look at his mobile phone, reading incoming messages and responding. At a discreet distance Curtis followed along the narrow side street, occasionally stepping into a tailor shop or a souvenir shop to avoid being seen when Nelson stopped.

A slight turn of the head. Barely perceptible but Curtis noticed it. Nelson was scanning the central police station as he casually strolled past. He turned in the opposite direction, retraced his steps past the City Beach Hotel, turning into the side street and strolling behind the police station where the officers' accommodation was situated.

Is he assessing the police numbers or entrance and exit points to both the station and accommodation? He has walked right around the block. Odd for a man on holiday.

After the central Hua Hin peregrination, Nelson arrived at his destination, looked in both directions along the road and entered the Golf Holiday and Resort Hotel. A tired hotel. Two — or at best three — star.

Golf Resort Hotel. Not exactly a holiday resort. Nelson must be alone.

Curtis returned to his room at the Grand Centara and made a telephone call. The information he requested could be sent by email to his mobile phone. Time to relax and assess the situation.

He made his way to the beach bar. Ordering his usual lime soda without ice, Curtis lounged under a frangipani tree in full bloom and listened to the music of the seventies played by the resident band. Sounds of the Bee Gees, the Beatles, Billy Joel and Barbara Streisand were just what the doctor ordered.

The sun was speeding its descent. Creeping lower in the sky. Curtis nibbled almost feverishly at the basket of chips, cheese and biscuits provided with his second drink of happy hour. He now realised he had forgotten lunch and his stomach rumbled as it welcomed the tasty morsels. Dinner at the Lucky Star Restaurant couldn't come soon enough.

Chapter 14

The Grand Night Market was busy, mainly with locals buying fresh produce presumably for the preparation of their evening meal. Thais love their food and tend to buy fresh produce on a daily basis.

Tourists congregated around the copy watch and jewellery stalls. Some stood at length in front of the leather goods shop offering inexpensive wallets. Examining items, replacing them on the racks, examining them again.

Some were circling the racks of cheap clothes. Others were sitting on benches listening to the busker strumming his guitar and singing what Curtis assumed were popular Thai songs. Everyone seemed happy.

A large bus stopped on a side street and middle-aged Asian tourists cascaded onto the footpath. Some stretched. Others wandered off in the direction of the street vendor food. Dried grasshoppers, deep-fried crispy crickets, bamboo worms of various shapes and sizes, were on offer.

Curtis was very early for his dinner meeting with Rat. He too meandered around the market stalls. For the first time feeling conscious of his size, standing considerably taller than the much shorter tourists surrounding him, Curtis joined the music lovers on the bench. Sitting. Shorter and less noticeable.

Approaching the scheduled meeting time, he drifted off in the direction of the Lucky Star Restaurant. Passing the Dar Restaurant, he hesitated and considered stopping, as it was again full of diners obviously enjoying the local cuisine. The aromas that brushed his nose sent his saliva glands into overdrive.

Walking slowly Curtis reluctantly left the Dar Restaurant and meandered towards the Lucky Star. The same waiter doubling as the cook greeted him as if they were long lost brothers. He was ushered to the same table he shared with Rat two nights earlier. "*Oliang?*" cook asked. "No added sugar?"

"Good memory. Lime soda please. No ice."

Cook darted to the commercial refrigerator at the rear of the small restaurant. One of his newest and best customers who tips extraordinarily well, extremely generously, had returned. He must be doing something right.

The lime soda was delivered with some haste and a smile. Cook wanted to please and rushed off to find the menus. Curtis drank slowly, scanning the passers-by lest Nelson should decide to eat at the Grand Night Market. From his understanding of Nelson, he considered that highly unlikely but one should always be on one's mettle.

"*Sawardee karp.*" The Rat stood before him.

"Where did you come from?"

Curtis was thorough and attentive but was surprised at the arrival of Rat. He hadn't seen the small man walk into the area around the restaurant.

The trademark grin returned. "An advantage of being small, I suppose. I watched your movements and the rhythm with which you looked beyond Lucky Star." Rat beamed. "You looked in the wrong direction, you looked high into the crowd and your scrutiny was slow and measured giving me ample time to move unnoticed."

The little man is quick. A good lesson. I must be more careful.

The Rat sat and both turned their attention to the menu as the waiter returned with another lime soda, no ice, and stood waiting. Rat again offered to order and before Curtis responded he gave instructions in Thai, concluding with an order for iced coffee.

"I have all the lowdown on the explosives as you requested," Rat eagerly informed Curtis in a quiet voice.

"I have been doing some investigations of my own," Curtis replied. "I doubt the type of explosive material is important now but tell me anyway, just in case."

Rat explained both the police and the army had been involved in every aspect of the investigation, and whilst there was the usual inter-agency difficulty, all information had eventually been shared at the insistence of the government. He had verified the information from several sources. As usual, Rat relayed the information he had gathered about the bombings in detail.

"Thank you for being so thorough. Did you know FBI crime data for the United States revealed that just two years ago there were over sixteen hundred women murdered by a man with a gun? A single victim and single offender, not mass murders. Okay, I know the vast majority of those murders involved people in a relationship or at least an intimate acquaintance, but not always."

Rat frowned, attempting to understand where this conversation was heading.

"I believe the attempt on Dao's life will be with a firearm. I'll explain why I believe that in a moment but first — aah, good work on the bombings by the way — but what about the other information we need. Details on Dao's train trip?"

"Aah yes, you want to know what time the train is departing Bangkok? What time it is likely to arrive here? How many stops the train will make? Where Dao is likely to be seated on the train, including her carriage number."

Rat was progressively ticking them off on his fingers. "Seating arrangements for Dao's organisers and advisers, her key people. How many other passengers, if any will be on that train? Will there be railway security aboard and where will they be located?"

He stopped and gazed at Curtis. "Is that all?" he asked.

Although impressed with Rat's impeccable memory Curtis shifted in his seat, leaning forward to make his point. "Just give me the information, Rat."

"Dao apparently wants to get a feel for her level of support, and to commence organising her team in the south as soon as possible. She has scheduled the journey south for the next two weeks, commencing the day after tomorrow. The train is the normal scheduled train operating between Bangkok and Hua Hin. It departs Bangkok at 9:20 a.m. and arrives here in Hua Hin at about 1.35p.m.

"Dao's schedule is designed to include meeting as many of her family's supporters as possible. Her group will stay overnight in Hua Hin for such a meeting. She has a reservation at the Hilton Hotel. The following morning, she will proceed by train to Hat Yai further south.

"I am guessing the assassination attempt will not occur at the hotel or its surrounds because of the high level of security proposed for her visit," Rat mused, "but I cannot be certain of that. We need to secure the hotel."

Rat proceeded to outline answers to the other issues previously raised by Curtis, concluding with an expression of disappointment about the lack of security on the train. One security officer for every two carriages.

"That won't be a problem, Rat. You can handle it. I want you to board the train at the stop before Hua Hin. That would be Cha-Am wouldn't it?"

"Yes, Cha-Am, but do you really think it wise that I board a train that may blow up while I'm on board?" Rat looked genuinely concerned and even a little bit hurt that Curtis should regard him as dispensable.

Curtis grimaced ruefully adding, "I know what you are saying," he sighed, "but somebody has to do it, Rat, and one thing's for sure, it aint gonna be me!"

Rat noticed the hint of a smile slowly gaining traction on Curtis's lips.

"Okay. I get it. You have a weird sense of humour, Rice."

"Call me that again or anything like it and you will be strapped to the cowcatcher on the train. And it isn't 'Rice'. My first name is pronounced Reece but I don't answer to that."

The mispronunciation and Curtis's correction of the same broke the tension. They both laughed audibly, such that the diners at the nearby Dar Restaurant swivelled to determine the source of the raucous noise.

Both sat back in their seats and sipped at their drinks as the food started arriving. First, as always, came the rice. They looked at the rice, at each other, at the rice, and again burst into laughter.

"While you were gathering the information, I was doing my own investigation. I saw a man in town that I know to be an expert marksman. He was the sniper instructor when I was in the SAS. I made some enquiries. He left the army to take a position as the principle marksman instructor with the Tactical Response Group in the New South Wales Police Force."

"Did he see you?" Rat asked with genuine concern.

Before Curtis had time to answer he was interrupted by the cook placing two more generously laden plates on the table. Red curry chicken and lamb curry, Indian style.

Curtis waited for the cook to leave and said, "No, I am certain of that.

"Nelson is the worst kind of misogynist. When he became aware of women being elevated to senior roles in the army, he was vocal in his disgust. It was all he talked about. His views were met with widespread opprobrium amongst the senior ranks, so he spat the chewy and left the army.

"The top command was probably relieved to see him go. There had been reports he had flaunted his contempt for Australian Army rules by torturing Al-Qaeda suspects in Iraq. In fact, he openly bragged to junior soldiers about embracing horrendous torture techniques. At the time we thought he was joking.

"Nelson had a profound effect on some junior soldiers he trained. It was reported that at the time of Australia's strong military presence in Afghanistan one of his men flew a Nazi flag above an armoured truck whilst on patrol. The commander became aware of this when he saw photographs that were circulated of a flag, bearing a swastika, flying above an army vehicle. The soldier was disciplined but not his mentor, Nelson.

"The man has no moral compass. No moral inhibitions when it comes to hatred. Hatred of women in leadership positions in particular.

"Some of my colleagues once saw him at the beach when off duty, wearing a T-shirt depicting Australia's first female prime minister with cross hairs on her head, and a bullet in flight directed at her. He sang the praises of a talkback radio jockey who repeatedly said Prime Minister Gillard should be 'put in a chaff bag' and dropped at sea.

"Gillard led a minority government but still negotiated the passage of legislation though a hostile environment. She is intelligent and competent. Sadly, there was a great deal of hatred towards the PM. Not because of her policies, which incidentally I don't know much about, but merely because she is a woman. Nelson openly expressed his hatred for her, just as he did those women who were promoted above him in the army.

"Now you know the type of person this man is. It wouldn't be hard for him to pull the trigger on Dao, or to train someone to do the job."

Rat looked concerned at the last suggestion. "Is he still in the police force? Do you think he could be involved with the English businessman or his Australian brother?" he asked.

"Possibly. I am told he is now a financial planner. He mixes in the right circles. Although his licence doesn't allow it, he uses his position to raise venture capital. As I say, he doesn't necessarily follow the rules. In fact, he has contempt for rules he doesn't like and makes a point of showing it."

"Okay, but how does that translate to stopping the train and assassinating Dao?" Rat urged Curtis in the direction of the matter at hand.

"A hunch. I watched Nelson for some time and he didn't act like your average tourist on holiday."

The expression on Rat's face had been one of doubt turning to concern, back to doubt.

"I know what you are thinking. You want evidence and not just a hunch. Trust me on this, Rat. My instincts are rarely misplaced."

"Your dislike for this Nelson fellow doesn't cloud your judgement, does it, Curtis? You obviously have an intense dislike for him."

You're beginning to sound like Frenchy — and Bell apparently — but for a different reason.

Ignoring the question, Curtis proceeded to outline a plan for his colleague. Not merely suggestions but clear and firm instructions. He told Rat that when he boarded the train in Cha-Am he should show his credentials to Dao and advise her to follow his directions. He was to ensure she changed carriages, and most importantly did not sit near a window. That was critical. She mustn't create an easy target for a skilled marksman.

"She is a politician. I am sure she will insist on sitting near a window. She wants to be seen," Rat objected.

"I don't care what she wants, Rat. We alone have the job of protecting her. Tell her of the threats if you must, but get her away from the window."

"It is not a good idea to tell her of the threat to her life. We might be alarming her unnecessarily. If nothing happens, we would look stupid," Rat argued.

As before, Curtis ignored him. "Better still, as this is a normal passenger train suggest that she might care to walk along the aisles and talk to the passengers. No, don't suggest, insist. Keep her moving. We want her to be invisible to everyone outside the train.

"Rat, I have had mud on my face in the past but never thrown by Frenchy. This is real, not just a threat. There will be an attempt on Dao's life and it involves a sniper. I know it."

Chapter 15

Curtis sought and obtained a meeting with the Hua Hin District police commander. He was forced to show his military crime investigator and Interpol credentials. Both covered a wide discretion, even liberty not revealed by the documentation.

Even the most senior of law enforcement personnel are usually impressed by my creds. If only they knew my usual line of duty.

The meeting was fruitless. Curtis had sought additional resources from the police but without proof of a crime there was no interest from the commander.

"I cannot act on a hunch or a possible future crime. I don't have the resources," Curtis was emphatically told. "I'm unable to take preventative action, as you call it, on the basis of a hunch!"

Curtis stood and firmly pushed back his chair. It toppled to the floor with a loud metallic clang. He grimly said, "If anything happens to Dao Shinawatra, be it on your head."

With that challenge the commander responded. "I'll tell you what. I'll increase the security between the railway station and the Hilton Hotel. Even at the Hilton. That should keep you happy and deter any assassin." The last comment came with a sarcastic tone and a wry grin.

Curtis ignored the sarcasm and, deciding nothing was going to change, left the office.

In the late morning heat Curtis walked the train track. The heat radiated off the blue metal and the iron tracks as he purposefully walked the line from the railway crossing at one end of town to the crossing at Soi 8 (Eighth Street) near many of the popular restaurants. His eyes darted left to right, scanning both sides of the line for the most likely locations for a possible hit. He was experienced in such matters and knew exactly what a sniper would look for to make a shot.

There were no tall buildings from which a sniper would have a clear view of the train. The Hilton Hotel was a possibility from about seven hundred metres in a direct line of sight but the security was tight and the exit routes were limited.

A sniper needs a certain, unimpeded escape strategy. An exit route. He would not want to leave his gear behind.

There were no obvious alternatives to the Hilton. Ground level shots were certainly out of the question. No vantage points where a gunman could set up and make a hit without being seen in the entire process. He mentally wrestled with the options and concluded it simply wasn't possible in the areas he had seen.

Beyond the Hua Hin central business district perhaps? Frenchy said in the vicinity of Hua Hin. I'd better hire a motorcycle and look beyond the central business district.

Two hundred metres along Kamnoadvitee Road near Sa-Song Road is a motorcycle rental shop. Small bikes could be hired for a mere three hundred baht per day. Curtis paid the three hundred and with the fuel gauge in the red he drove to the nearest fuel station before the last drop was used. Typically, rental shops siphon any 'excess' fuel from the tank and recommend to the hirer they fill the tank as soon as possible.

Curtis filled the tank, circled the central business district and returned to the railway station. From there he headed south along the rough dirt track contiguous to the railway line. He dodged holes in the track and the wheel ruts left when wet clay soil baked under the sun. He rode at just above jogging pace. Unlikely to cause any damage to passers-by or him should he lose control on the wheel ruts.

Again, there were no appropriate vantage points for a sniper. Even the best of snipers couldn't be sure of hitting a moving target unless he or she was exceptional and had the right equipment.

Unless there is a reason for the train to stop.

He found the reason ten kilometres from central Hua Hin. Nong Kae Railway Station.

Curtis stopped suddenly and parked in the small parking lot at the front of the station. He walked around the area, eyes darting in all directions particularly looking for a possible sniper location. The vector origin. Standing on the station platform, he quickly concluded this mission would be extremely difficult but not impossible.

Any sniper would have to use sophisticated equipment and be highly competent in order to pull this off. From what I've seen and heard the RKK don't have the expertise to do it. Nelson could. Or perhaps someone Nelson has trained using a firearm and telescopic equipment provided by him.

Behind the railway station a new hotel was under construction. To the south was a hill with a Buddhist temple standing proudly at the top. Further to the southwest of the new construction there was a larger hill and another temple.

Unlikely they would use a temple for the shot.

Gazing into the distance Curtis concluded there was only one building within two thousand metres that would possibly meet the requirements. From where he stood using his powerful binoculars, he had a clear vision of the rooftop, which appeared to carry unusual structures. There was only a small gap between the new construction and the hill.

Difficult. Very difficult but not impossible.

A competent sniper with a cosine indicator attached to the telescope, a small device that assists in computing the horizontal range allowing for gravity, and possibly a bullet drop compensator, could perform the task.

Curtis stretched to ease tight muscles after riding a motorcycle more suitable for a person of 1.6 m, and then stood rigidly, deep in thought.

The sniper would need to dial in the range and target allowing for the train's movement. A moving target could be hit if the sniper correctly calculated the vector cosine. He would need to use the Kentucky windage technique of aiming to the side, in this case in front of the target.

Calculating the vector cosine would be less of a problem than calculating the windage and lead. If the sniper studied the angle of other passenger trains from his proposed vector origin, he could easily ascertain the vector cosine. But a shooter would have to be sure the train was moving at a constant speed and allow for wind, or any other movement to determine the lead.

Shooter would have to be certain of Dao's position on the train too. Assuming only her head would be visible she would present a small target. The other problem is the wind. Normally not a problem but I have noticed occasional unexpected gusts. He would have a fraction of a second to get it absolutely right. Extremely difficult and possibly too hard, I think. Not impossible but why take the risk of missing. He would only have one chance.

I doubt that will happen. There has to be a way the shooter or his assistant, perhaps his spotter, would stop the train. Yes, the train will have to stop in a precise location.

Curtis decided to take a closer look at the building which could be a sniper's nest. His mind was working overtime.

Having not parked his ride in the shade, the vinyl seat of the motorcycle had absorbed the afternoon sun. Curtis gingerly sat down. The motorcycle was battery started with an automatic transmission. He turned the key and pressed the ignition button.

Moving carefully to avoid bare skin touching the vinyl seat, Curtis manoeuvred his ride in the direction he had come. He left the Nong Kae Railway Station and again dodged dips in the hardened clay track as he made his way back towards the main road through the district.

At times the motorcycle seemed to struggle in the heat. *Perhaps the fuel isn't clean or the engine needs a service*, he surmised.

With road repairs underway near the flyover joining two roads with the main southbound highway, the traffic was funnelled into fewer lanes. Moving at a crawl. Traffic was heavy. He patiently waited at the railway station exit road for a gap in the traffic. Having estimated the distance between the railway line and the tall building, he figured the latter would be near the main highway. The easiest route to follow would be to first head north and then circle back to get onto the flyover.

After waiting some time for the passing traffic to thin, Curtis gave up on the rules of the road and followed other motorcyclists in cutting into the traffic, slowing the cars even further. Turning across the traffic, he slowly headed in the direction of the flyover that would place him back into the southbound traffic.

The road widened and a relatively new surface was certainly easier to deal with than the railway track. It was quite a relief to the stress on his back. The roads department had even marked an extra lane, a narrow lane, especially for motorcyclists.

Not being familiar with the highway, Curtis rode with care. Heavy trucks with canvas billowing from the sides as they travelled at faster than necessary speeds almost grazed him. He constantly scanned both sides of the road looking for the building with the rooftop structures.

As he rounded a bend, he could see the building was inside a compound, quite close now. A high razor-wired fence running parallel with the road seemed to bustle up to a side road and a sentry box. A large sign embraced the fence where it met the box. It read 'Non-Commissioned Officers School'.

Army. Curtis immediately decided he was on the right track. His instincts told him Nelson was involved. Nelson was a marksman of some note in the Australian Army. His gut told him there was a connection with the missing elite soldiers from Pattani and the plan to assassinate Dao. His gut rarely got it wrong.

Returning to the resort hotel, Curtis again sought the assistance of his newest friend. This time he asked Rat to make discreet enquiries about any recent transfers from the Pattani military barracks. Any movements from the elite corps in particular and if there were transfers, where did they go?

"We need a quick answer. You're looking pale, Rat. Go home sick. Get on to it."

"As a matter of fact, I have been feeling a little off colour," Rat replied with a wry grin. "Is this part of your hunch?"

Curtis didn't reply. Rat didn't press the point.

Chapter 16

"You could be onto something," Rat hastily informed Curtis after the customary greeting. "Four months ago, two soldiers applied for a transfer from Pattani to undertake a training course as NCOs and were immediately transferred to the Hua Hin school."

"Were they from the elite unit?"

"Yes, I meant to add that. Where are you going with this?"

"I suspect they may be involved with Nelson and whomever he works for. Nelson couldn't do this alone. Rat, there is much more to this than just taking down a political aspirant in Thailand."

"Unless of course he is under contract to a group here in Thailand. An organisation with that political objective. I haven't told you everything. There is more."

Curtis waited expectantly while Rat wiped the perspiration from his brow before continuing.

"My sources tell me about four or five months ago the NCO school's commanding officer met with a former soldier who excelled as a marksman. He was on a long-term holiday in the area and told the CO he could assist with training on a voluntary basis. The CO was convinced when he became aware of the man's professional background. He saw an opportunity to improve skills and save money at the same time. I think he may have had promotion in mind. Oh, and by the way, the volunteer was an Australian."

Rat grinned widely. He thought he was revealing the most startling piece of information.

"I'm not surprised. Is there anything else, Rat?"

"Not of major significance."

"Tell me everything you know, Rat. Is there anything else?" Curtis asked more firmly.

"Only that the Australian started work at the school about three months ago and spent a solid month training several soldiers. It seems most of his attention was given to two soldiers whom he described as being particularly suitable for leadership positions."

"It all fits together. Tomorrow Dao leaves Bangkok. As discussed, you will meet the train in Cha-Am. Get an early night, Rat. You know what your role is, what you have to do on the train. I trust you to ensure Dao is mobile and importantly does not occupy a window seat when she isn't moving." Curtis reinforced his earlier instructions.

"This attempt on Dao will not be with a bomb. It will be by an accomplished sniper. I trust my instincts."

After returning the rented motorcycle, complete with a full tank of fuel for goodwill, Curtis again followed the road adjacent to the railway line on foot. He avoided the area around the Golf Hotel and Resort where Nelson was staying before turning down the road that would take him back to the Grand Night Market. He strolled casually in the direction of the Lucky Star Restaurant. Eyes darting in all directions as usual.

It was 2100. He had expected to see Rat dining there but hadn't expected to see him eating with the cook.

"*Sawardee karp*, Rat."

Rat tried to mask his surprise. He had been deep in conversation with the waiter-cum-cook whilst looking at tourists passing by.

"*Sawardee karp*, Curtis. Where did you come from?"

"Reversed roles. Sometimes being tall has its advantages. One can see past shorter obstacles." Curtis laughed. "I watched your movements. The rhythm of your movement is predictable. When you looked in the wrong direction and then became engrossed in your food, I was able to enter the restaurant area. Bingo!"

Rat knew he had said something similar to Curtis twenty-four hours earlier. He saw the humour in this exchange and laughed, joined by his companion.

So, cook understands English perfectly.

"Allow me to introduce you more formally to my friend, our favourite cook. This is Noi. Noi is a very useful man to know. The Lucky Star is his ticket to escape the regimen of the army. He is the breakfast and lunch cook at the officers' mess of the NCO school but wants to permanently operate his own restaurant.

"This is Curtis, Noi. He is a trusted friend of mine from Australia."

"I had a hunch — sorry, Rat, there's that word again." He continued, "I had a hunch our favourite cook could be one of your sources. That's why I came back here. Guess what, Rat? My hunch was right."

Curtis winked at Noi as he made that comment. He realised Noi had probably heard much of what had been exchanged with Rat on their several visits to the restaurant over the last few days. He was nevertheless confident Rat would choose his friends carefully. He was well trained by MI6.

"You really should have told me about Noi."

"Sorry, Curtis. The expectation of my employer in the UK is that I keep my contacts to myself. Don't forget, I'm only on detachment from my usual position for this assignment."

Turning to the cook, Curtis gave a brief, incomplete explanation of his role in the covert operation. A matter of great importance to Thailand and the region. He informed Noi that he needed his assistance and assured him of the legitimacy of his activities. He was convincing. Noi nodded agreement and appeared to relish the responsibility he carried with this new clandestine knowledge.

Curtis asked for Noi's assistance in gaining access to the NCO school. His task would be made much easier if he had early, unimpeded access and inside information on the layout of the buildings.

Noi gave an assurance he would be able to help.

Chapter 17

Most of the local restaurateurs were early risers to buy the freshest and best produce at the Hua Hin fruit and vegetable market. Noi was no exception. The NCO school officers would expect nothing less. He had to be there when the market opened in order to allow sufficient time to buy seafood caught during that night in the nearby bay, and produce delivered from local farms, before returning to the mess to prepare breakfast.

When does the cook sleep? Curtis thought as he waited near Starbucks for Noi to collect him at 0445. He had briefed Noi selectively and insisted on the need for secrecy but had not provided any information on the mission itself. He had made Noi feel special and privileged to be privy to the Australian's campaign against terrorism.

Curtis had slept soundly knowing exactly how the day would proceed. He had mentally played it out on numerous occasions. He was confident Rat would perform his task in providing good backup defence. Additional security for Dao. His plan was to eliminate the threat before it got that far but, without question, Rat was a good backup.

The previous day, the day after his reconnoitre on the railway line, Dao had arrived in town and spent the afternoon and night at the Hilton without incident. Rat reported to Curtis that he did not need to show his credentials. He told her he was an enthusiastic supporter and she had accepted his advice to meet and greet passengers on the train. Dao had invited him to her meeting with supporters after he had informed her he was travelling on to Hat Yai the following day.

Curtis had risen at 0345, spread out on his bedroom floor and stretched his limbs into unimaginable positions. He retained his athleticism and nimbleness from his football days. After his stretch he had jogged to one of the hotel pools and swum laps. The pool was officially closed at that hour of the day but Curtis was not inclined to follow the rules when it came to his fitness regime.

Back in his room, he had showered whilst boiling the kettle for coffee and then dressed in his choice of combat clothing. Sufficiently close fitting but allowing flexibility of movement in any direction and with ease. Strong but flexible lace-up canvas boots with plenty of cushion on the sole. Curtis never liked the boots issued by the Australian Army. Even the boots issued for black ops personnel left much to be desired in his view. He had his black canvas boots specially made.

Fully kitted, he sat on the sun lounger on his balcony and sipped coffee from a mug borrowed from the Railway Restaurant at the resort.

He counted off on his fingers the matters needing to be dealt with during the day and again ran through the day's plan, especially the timetable.

The train leaves Hua Hin at 0945. It would normally reduce speed to pass the Nong Kae Railway Station at precisely 0957 but today, allowing for slowing into the station, it will stop at 0959. What causes the train to stop doesn't matter. It will stop. 0959 precisely.

He thought about his equipment and was satisfied he had all he needed. Everything would run smoothly. He was supremely confident. He sipped his coffee and again visualised how the encounter with the shooter and the spotter would play out.

As the picture took shape in his mind with cinematographic clarity, Curtis smiled. He wasn't complacent and overconfident but the picture forming gave him a sense of satisfaction. He was going to stop the assassination of a woman who was apparently a potential leader.

Curtis had holstered his Glock 43, a single stack sub-compact semi-automatic 9 mm pistol. Although not a fan of all equipment used by the US military, he was certainly a fan of the Glocks they used. He packed two Glock 78 field knives — one strapped behind his shoulder blades within comfortable reach and one in a narrow leather holster strapped to his lace-up canvas boots. The perfectly balanced Glock 78 was always his first choice when he decided a throwing knife might be necessary.

At 0445, driving a Thai Army jeep, Noi pulled to a halt in front of Starbucks. At that hour there was no need to be concerned about the 'No Parking' sign. In any event, a soldier's privilege to park wherever he or she wants is unquestionable.

Within a few moments Curtis appeared from behind a billboard, quickly climbed into the vehicle and buckled up. Noi was impressed with his speed and agility. The gears crunched as the jeep lurched forward and somehow found synchronisation despite Noi's failure to properly engage the clutch. Perhaps he had. Perhaps this was the best the army could do for their breakfast chef.

There was very little traffic on the main highway out of Hua Hin to the south at that time of the day. Most traffic was heading into the city although it was still relatively quiet compared to the usual rush hour.

Twenty minutes later, as the jeep slowed to turn into the NCO school, Curtis lowered himself in his seat. He didn't have right of entry to the camp and, unaware of Noi's standing with the sentry, he thought it best to be as discreet as possible.

Noi noticed his passenger's attempt at being less noticeable, smiled broadly and said, "You can't hide, Mr Curtis. You are way too big. Don't worry, I know the sentry really well. We won't be stopped."

True to his word, Noi simply waved as the jeep approached the sentry box and the boom gate was lifted. A few minutes later the vehicle was parked in front of the officers' mess. Curtis helped Noi unload the produce he had purchased from the market. Assisting Noi in transferring it to the galley also helped him survey the mess.

At 0520 there was now some movement around the NCO facility as a few soldiers started their early morning jog. It wasn't organised exercise as part of the army regimen. Just their own regular fitness programme. Several officers emerged from their quarters situated near the mess and jogged ahead of the NCOs.

Of course, ahead of the NCOs.

The early morning haze started to lift as the sun began to glow behind coconut trees across the main road in front of the garrison entrance. Already the fresh morning sea breeze was making way for the humidity, which would linger until well after sunset.

"Thanks for the ride, Noi," Curtis said.

"You're welcome, Mr Curtis."

"Forget the formality, Noi. Just call me Curtis."

"Okay, Mr Curtis."

What's the point?

"I think I'll take a walk around the grounds."

Curtis glanced at his robust watch that had multiple purposes, not the least of which was to tell the time. It was still three hours and fifty-five minutes until the train was due to pass Nong Kae Railway Station. This particular train was not scheduled to stop at Nong Kae. The afternoon train always did, but the morning passenger train to Hat Yai only stopped at the major towns. Nong Kae was not one of them.

However, it happens today will be an exception. It will stop. A moving target creates and adds to the already numerous imponderables. I just need to be standing next to the shooter when the train comes to a halt.

He chuckled to himself. *What a silly thought. Standing next to him. I will be there but not next to him. Take him down from anywhere but take him down before he pulls the trigger!*

He needed all the time he could spare to properly survey the NCO school facilities, including the administration block and the taller building, the garrison barracks and short-term accommodation. He believed the shooter and his spotter could only use the latter building to have an unimpeded view of the area around the Nong Kae Railway Station. That was the shooter's nest. No question.

Like so many of his colleagues in the elite army corps, Curtis was a trained sniper. He knew precisely what it took to get the job done. He surmised this shooter would have a trained spotter who could double as the shooter if something unforeseen occurred. A spotter would most likely be used in circumstances where the shooter was not totally familiar with the environment, and where meteorological circumstances are subject to change.

Pure conjecture but this guy will have his spotter. Two soldiers from Pattani are enrolled at the school. Thwo soldiers have had additional training. It only takes one to pull the trigger. One soldier will have learnt the special skills required to be a spotter. The additional training was by an Australian marksman. I have no doubt that person was Nelson. Learning from the best. Probably with the best sniper rifle.

Walking the garrison grounds was surprisingly not a problem for Curtis. He had expected to be stopped at some point by security. Questioned about his credentials and reason for being at the school. Not so. Having thought through that possibility he had an answer in mind but he concluded Thai soldiers were trusting people.

He had no concerns about being seen by Nelson. He was sure Nelson would not be the shooter and would therefore not be on site. Curtis guessed that Nelson was currently in Hua Hin to ensure the mission actually occurred, that the shooter, for any reason, wouldn't abort it. He expected Nelson to be in his hotel room awaiting news from the RKK recruits.

He will certainly receive feedback. Ultimately not the feedback he is looking for.

When Curtis earlier made enquiries about Nelson's recent past, he asked one of his contacts, an investigator with the Australian Securities and Investments Commission, to ascertain more information about Nelson's business activities. He had a raft of questions for his friend that might require him to research beyond his jurisdiction. Most importantly, he wanted to know if Nelson had any partners in his financial planning business, who his main clients were, the names behind any companies with which he was in any way involved as a consultant, a director, or securing venture capital.

The ASIC investigator was to inform Frenchy of the information gathered and convey to him a request from Curtis that he research the background of any names he has been given. Going directly to Frenchy would speed up the process. Curtis had other matters on his plate.

After he had informed Rat about Nelson's character, the conversation had jolted him into the reality that Nelson might not be working alone.

He may be part of a larger group with the same sick values. The same ultimate objective, whatever that might be. When this immediate task is completed, I must contact Frenchy. By then he should have the answers.

Curtis never contemplated failure. He had carefully thought through the possibilities with respect to an attempt on Dao's life and was now certain he had the measure of his opponents. He could have asked Noi to see if the two from Pattani were in the NCO class today but decided against that idea. There was always a risk they might learn of someone asking about them.

He had to take the risk to learn about their accommodation in the NCO barracks however. It was easy for Noi to obtain that information without showing obvious interest in the pair. Noi had told him they shared a room on the western side of the building, third floor. The western side had an outlook to the mountain range. The railway line was on the eastern side.

Perfect. The shot cannot be taken from their room. There are no balconies they can access on the eastern side. They won't use someone else's room because that would potentially expose them.

The train will stop about 1,300 metres away as the crow flies at 0959. They have to use the rooftop to get the right bullet drop and vector cosine. Living in the same building gives them an easy escape plan. No doubt the rifle will be fitted with a sound suppressor. Almost the perfect hit by an anonymous person.

They need to be caught in the process of committing a crime. That's what I will do. This remains a one-man job.

Normally a sniper and a spotter would be in position well in advance of the shot time. They need time to thoroughly assess and evaluate all possible eventualities. Since both sniper and spotter have been living in the building from which the shot will be made, I don't expect they will need as much time. All they need is sufficient time to dial in the numbers to compensate for crosswinds and the downward trajectory, the angle of the shot. Certainly made easier, if the rifle is fitted with a bullet drop compensator.

They need to be in position to dial in the rifle and then relax. A sniper must slow his heartbeat and his breathing. Relaxing is crucial. A minimum of thirty minutes. Longer would be better. Forty-five should do it.

Timing is important. I need to be on the roof, in position, at 0944.

0637. Time to visit the officers' mess galley for a quick coffee then take a closer look at the shooter's building, especially the rooftop.

Chapter 18

0916.

At last all the hard work, the months of training, practice at the range, practice in various impossibly difficult positions, the planning comes down to this.

We will be well paid and Nelson promised us more jobs. Perhaps even in another country. No, Keng, this is not just about the money. We serve a greater purpose. A noble purpose. Nelson said the natural order must prevail. Subhumans should not hold positions of power.

0922

Dial in the numbers. No laser rangefinder. The scope's mil dot reticle is good enough, better for me actually. Nelson has provided the height of the target based on his research so I can calculate the range. Nelson is the man. Only the best equipment, especially the 8.6 TKIV 2000 rifle. Manually operated bolt-action holding five cartridges but I'll only need one. A beautiful instrument of death. I wish Nelson could somehow get her out of the train onto the platform — an easier shot — but Nelson's calculation of her height sitting on the train will do the job. She's as good as gone.

0931

Don't even whisper, Spotter. Silence. Relax, Keng, relax. Now to load the cartridges. Wow, these boys are powerful. .338 Lapua Magnum. Designed for long range military sniping use. Unbelievably accurate over distance. Outperforms everything. Supersonic range a minimum of 1,500 metres but I don't need that. No need to worry about armoured glass on the train either but it could still penetrate that if they were smart enough to build such a carriage. They aren't. They suspect nothing.

0937

Ready to go. Relax. Deep breaths. Have I got everything right? Of course, you have, Keng. Relax. They'll never know what happened.

Where the bullet came from. We are doing this for mankind. Dao is just the beginning. There will be more, whoever they are. Wherever they are.

0944

Nelson paid the train driver to make the unusual stop. Collecting a significant passenger. I don't need long once the train stops. It won't stop for long. Just one passenger to step on board. If he hasn't paid the driver enough, we have the backup of a detonator on the rail. The driver will have to stop when alerted by the small detonator to a problem on the line ahead. He won't want to be responsible for a derailment by ignoring the warning detonator. Stop thinking, Keng. Relax.

0946

There he is. That's Nelson on the platform waiting for his ride. The train must have left Hua Hin. He won't board of course. Breathe deeply, Keng. Slowly, slowly.

0951

Spotter is checking the range again. Good. He knows what he is doing. Double-checking for windage even though we have the BDC and Finndot reticles on the scope. Professional. What is he writing in his notebook? Oh, again calculating the gravity pull and dividing it into the vector range. Ignore him, Keng. He's doing his job. Relax. Breathe deeply, breathe deeply.

0956

Here it comes. Slowing. The train driver is doing the right thing. Stop thinking, Keng. Slow breathing. Get ready to meet your maker, Dao Shinawatra. Fifth window in the first carriage. Slight pressure on the trigger.

Chapter 19

0753

Curtis completed his reconnoitre of the grounds and the building and returned to the galley of the officers' mess, entering from a rear door near where Noi had parked his jeep. It was best to avoid being seen.

Not all officers took their breakfast in the mess. At this hour it was almost empty but Noi, being the only person responsible for the preparation of breakfast, worked feverishly making toast, scrambled eggs, fried sausages and crispy American bacon. He kept small pots of baked beans warm, and cooked easy over eggs for the late-rising international officers. As expected, there was plenty of Thai food for the early risers. Tasty rice porridge, pork dim sum, marinated minced pork, and fried garlic.

The combination of aromas made Curtis salivate as he furtively entered the galley from the rear door. He had left his resort hotel well before the availability of breakfast and hadn't even thought about eating until this moment. Like all good chefs Noi sensed this. He nodded in the direction of the trays of food.

The main preparation area in the galley was not clearly visible from the mess hall. Curtis helped himself to a pot of coffee, munched on a slice of toast topped with crispy bacon and relaxed in a corner by the pantry.

For Curtis sleep was an irregular occurrence when on a mission. Never sure when he might be able to sleep comfortably in a bed, he had learnt to take ten- or fifteen-minute naps in some of the most uncomfortable and unusual places. He moved his chair inside the walk-in pantry and found a bag of white rice to rest his head against. He set the timer on his watch to vibrate after fifteen minutes. No need. His internal alarm would awaken him at fourteen minutes. He quickly drifted off.

0817

Fourteen minutes exactly. Curtis woke and reached for another coffee.

Time to freshen up and move into position on the fourth floor. Train stops at 0959, he reminded himself. *0944 I'll be on the roof.*

Noi had earlier told him the NCOs were required to be in the gymnasium by 0600 for weights training after their morning run, followed by a session of yoga. Ablutions at the gymnasium were usual for some, although the communal facilities were often crowded. Others went to their barracks for that purpose. Wherever the ablutions were performed they were expected to be on the parade ground by 0730 before commencing classes at 0800.

The barracks were empty and after cleaning the administration block cleaners commenced work at 1030 on the ground floor, working up and concluding on the seventh by 1500. Even the cleaning staff kept to a strict timetable in the army.

0831

By now the mess was empty of staff. He thanked Noi for the breakfast, left the galley and went to the bathroom at the rear of the mess. Curtis performed his regular morning ablutions and splashed water on his face. He checked that his essential equipment was in place and quietly left the building.

0847

He moved into position in the cleaner's storeroom on the fourth floor. *My guess is shooter and his accomplice will take the fire escape to the seventh between 0900 and 0915. Need to make each move with plenty of time to allow for unforeseen circumstances. I'll start my move to the rooftop at 0935. Twenty-four minutes before the train stops. Not too early. In position behind the air-conditioner, while they are preoccupied with their preparation, at 0944.*

0935

Curtis quietly commenced climbing the internal fire escape stairs. He was familiar with every turn and irregular marking on the walls on each landing.

Floor numbers in the Thai language.

He moved with care. No noise. Cushioned feet on concrete steps.

Apart from my essential equipment, these strong but soft-soled boots are my best acquisition. Stealth is the name of the game.

0940

Long steps took him to the seventh floor. From there he had to scale to the rooftop on a grated steel ladder with aluminium railings. He could see the rooftop door above as he climbed stealthily.

0942

He reached the door and gripped the painted brass handle. It wouldn't turn. It turned with ease when he went to the roof earlier in the morning.

Ssshit! They've locked the door from the roof. Why didn't I think of that? I don't have my lock pick tools.

With no time to waste, Curtis ran down the fire escape stairs and darted behind the accommodation building. He ran as fast as he could, bustling along so as not to dislodge any of his essential equipment, as he liked to call it.

Curtis threw open the rear door to the galley and rushed inside.

0946

"Noi, I urgently need your two sharpest carving forks."

"Carving forks?"

"Yes, meat carving forks," he urged as Noi rushed to the drawer containing the cooking utensils.

0947

Without waiting for any further response from Noi, he started emptying the utensils onto the bench.

0949

"This is what I want." He waved a meat fork and addressed Noi with urgency. "Quick! Quick! Do you have another one?"

Noi realised the urgency and rushed to the sink to find another, quickly handing it over. Curtis wiped it under his armpit and using the side of the bench to lever against, bent one of the prongs on each of the forks at right angles.

0951

"Thanks, Noi," he yelled over his shoulder as he rushed out the mess, makeshift lock picks in hand.

0953

Curtis scaled the internal barracks steps two at a time. When he reached the seventh floor, he ran the length of the corridor and pushed the fire escape door. It was reluctant to open.

0956

He took half a step back and rammed his right boot into the door near the handle. *I doubt they will hear that on the rooftop. Too bad if they do.*

0957

The door no longer resisted. Curtis stepped over the debris. With long steps he reached the steel ladder and bounded up it.

0958

Using the sharp prongs of the meat forks he manoeuvred the locking mechanism and turned the handle.

Glock drawn, Curtis stepped out onto the roof in bright sunlight. Now just seventeen direct metres from the sniper's nest he first had to take four long steps around the corner of the air-conditioning unit, placing him side on to the shooter, fifteen metres away.

At 0959, Curtis yelled as loud as he could.

"Stop! Hands in the air!"

Simultaneously, shooter's finger closed on the trigger. The discharge did not cause any rifle movement. It remained precisely in position. Curtis fired. Shooter fell to his right over the top of his rifle. He wore a new bright red spot like a Hindu woman's bindi dot but this one wasn't on the forehead. A centimetre above his temporal bone. Instantaneously dead.

Shocked, the spotter swivelled when Curtis yelled, and as he fell sideways, he reached for his pistol, not quite making it.

Curtis wanted him alive and capable of talking. A painful injury would be best. Although a brilliant shot he still didn't want to take the risk of permanency. Two shots would bring the cavalry. A split-second decision. He whipped the Glock 78 knife over his shoulder and in one action placed it with a surgeon's precision directly into the spotter's calf muscle, just missing the fibular artery. Not bad, a surgeon operating fifteen metres from the 'patient'.

Spotter was still trying to unholster his pistol at the same time as he screamed in pain. Adrenalin pumping, the initial pain seemed to subside.

He managed to lift his weapon. Before he moved to take aim at Curtis the pistol was wrenched from his grasp.

As he grabbed the pistol Curtis planted a clenched fist from short range directly onto the point of Spotter's chin. A short but powerful left jab. *Goodnight, Spotter.*

Chapter 20

As suggested by her new friend Jaruth Ratnamphod, Dao Shinawatra had vacated her seat in the first passenger coach and moved along the aisle of the train to meet and greet. Grinning with satisfaction, Rat followed her.

Rat had been experiencing excruciating stomach cramps from a bout of gastric enteritis. He gripped his stomach and waited for Dao to move beyond her carriage. She was now in the second car. Safe to do so, he rushed to the water closet.

A few minutes passed. Dao sensed the train was slowing and probably stopping at a railway station. She decided to resume her seat and moved quickly back to the first carriage.

In a passenger train water closet, there is no sound insulation. Everything external to the train — steel wheels rolling on iron rails, couplings squealing, and brakes applying — is clearly audible. Even seemingly amplified.

Rat's senses were acutely tuned at all times. He heard the train brakes being gradually applied, probably before the engine driver even moved the brake lever. Possibly even before he thought about it. Knowing there was no scheduled stop so soon after departing Hua Hin, Rat thought it was probably normal procedure when passing another railway depot.

Thirty seconds later. *We're still slowing. Something is wrong. Surely, we're not stopping?*

Feeling better and the stomach cramp having subsided, Rat left the bathroom at the rear of the second passenger coach. He looked along the carriage. No Dao. He quickly pushed on the end door and, standing in between the carriages above the coupling mechanism, he cupped his hands at the side of his eyes, placed them against the glass and peered through the window into carriage three. No Dao.

He had no time to waste. She had returned to her seat. Rat ran the length of the second carriage excusing himself as he roughly brushed past standing passengers. He threw back the exit door of carriage two and pushed through the second door in front of him. He was alarmed by what he saw. Dao sat by the window peering out, row five.

The train pulled to a stop. Dao looked to her right and could see there was only one person standing on the platform. Directly in front of carriage two and the sign, *'Nong Kae'*. Curiously, he was gazing in her direction but not boarding the now stationary train. She waved, smiling.

Rat lunged forward and grabbed Dao as the window shattered. He felt sharp stinging on his arm and neck as he was hit by small shards of glass.

Squeals erupted. Passengers squealed hysterically. Others were fixed in their seats, horror-struck. People clambered away from the destruction and blood.

Blood everywhere. Loud banging.

What Rat thought was loud banging were footsteps beating along the aisle of carriage one. The impact and his forward and sideways thrust had thrown him into the aisle. Head hard against the floor. Semi-conscious but drifting away.

The train started to gradually move. An alert and quick-thinking passenger ran to a small box at the front of the carriage labelled 'Emergency Stop' and smashed the glass panel with her high heeled shoe. She pulled the lever and the train jolted to a stop.

Dao! Where is she? Blood! Whose blood?

Still drifting into an abyss.

Rat wasn't seeing things clearly. Everything was a blur. He could only just make out the base of a seat against which he had hit his head.

***

Satisfied, Nelson walked away. His planned exit route took him behind the railway station building where he dropped to the blue metal and stepped over the iron lines on the other side of the platform. Without hesitation he pushed through shrub onto a narrow dirt track that opened onto a bitumen road. He moved briskly down the narrow street.

Three blocks from the station he reached his parked hire car. Nelson retrieved his mobile phone from under the driver's seat and placed his thumb on the 'Home' button to activate the screen. He tapped the green 'Message' app followed by the new message symbol in the top right corner. He commenced typing 'Wallace' and after inserting the first three letters, one name appeared. He tapped on the name, adding it to the recipient space and then typed his message: 'Mission accomplished.' With a smile of satisfaction, he pressed 'Send'.

***

There had only been one shot. The NCO school security couldn't get a bearing on its source. One of the soldiers at ease on garrison security duty in front of the administration block told his colleagues of the general direction. It was narrowed down to the accommodation barracks by an agonising scream. A brief scream that ended as abruptly as it started, but it was enough.

It was further narrowed down when soldiers carrying German-made Heckler and Koch MP5 sub-machine guns charged into the barracks to be met by a soldier who had been confined to barracks for disciplinary reasons. He was in his seventh-floor room with his window open when he heard the commotion directly above him.

At the risk of facing more disciplinary action he left his room and ran down the fire escape until he came face to face with a group of his colleagues. He was quick to alert them to a more accurate location of the shot.

Had a soldier lost control of his senses? Was there an intruder in the garrison? Whatever the problem, the soldiers who continued to the top floor had to use their initiative. Several soldiers immediately went to the ground floor to close off a possible escape route. Others stood at the ready by the lifts and still others by the fire escape door waiting for the offender to appear.

They didn't have long to wait. A huge man carrying a body slowly opened the door and peered into the corridor. Curtis moved cautiously, facing several soldiers he observed to be pointing MP5s at him. Within a short time, before he could explain, they were joined by military police.

Curtis noticed this group carried Israeli made Uzi sub-machine guns. He was impressed by all the ordnance.

One soldier stepped forward and silently pointed his Uzi at Curtis and then the tiled floor. Message received, Curtis lowered the spotter onto the tiles and kneeled beside him.

"Lie flat on your stomach and spread-eagle your arms and legs," the lead soldier barked.

Curtis followed the order. Another soldier slid his hand into Curtis's shirt behind his neck where a slight bulge was revealed. He retrieved a Glock 78 knife.

That's the one with traces of blood. Shall I tell them I have another knife and a handgun? Nah, I'll let them make the discovery if they're switched on.

The NCO school commanding officer emerged from a lift at the end of the corridor. Heavy steel-capped boots echoed on the tiled floor. Lying flat on the floor looking sideways Curtis could see the CO walking steadily towards him. Not in a hurry. He halted close to Spotter's shoulder and nudged him with his toe. There was no movement, just heavy breathing. Lying next to the comatose body Curtis smiled. The CO saw it and he too couldn't resist half a smile.

Instructions were given and Curtis was ordered to lift the unconscious soldier onto his shoulder. He was ushered into an elevator.

A little crowded in here. In a more hostile situation, I could cause some mayhem. They really should have checked sleeping beauty for weapons that I could access. I still have mine too.

Exiting the elevator, Curtis was nudged forward by the barrel of a sub-machine gun. He walked ahead of the group at gunpoint to the military police office.

At the rear of the office there were two rooms, each with a small barred window and a peephole in the door. Curtis knew these to be temporary lock-ups. He was instructed to place Spotter, who was starting to stir, in one and he retreated to the other with several Uzis still pointing at him. As he lowered Spotter onto a bunk bed, he briefly considered rendering him completely unconscious again but thought discretion was the better part of valour. Apart from that, he needed to talk to him soon.

Inside his three-metre square cell Curtis was frisked at gunpoint, having to relinquish his Glock pistol, the throwing knife attached to his boot and his wallet carrying his Interpol and Australian Army Military Police credentials. Those were the creds he had decided to carry for this job. The other choices were locked in his room safe.

Curtis sat on the hard bunk and waited for the commanding officer. He knew the CO would want to question him once he became aware of the creds. He certainly had some explaining to do. Not the least of which was an explanation for not informing the Thai Army of his mission, and not seeking permission to enter upon the garrison grounds. He would definitely not involve Noi.

As he waited, his anger returned. Curtis was furious with himself. He hadn't considered the possibility of the rooftop door being locked. It wasn't locked when he reconnoitred the rooftop early in the morning.

He recalled every aspect of the rooftop action. An internal debrief. An assessment of how he would improve on the performance. It was bad enough not being in position early as he had planned, but it was unforgiveable knowing the shooter had made the shot.

Hearing his neighbour groan from the pain of his leg wound, Curtis realised the walls between the two cells were not thick. He decided to play a mind game.

"Get some rest, Spotter, you dog. I'm coming for you shortly. I'm your worst nightmare. Do you have a sore leg? You haven't got the worst of it yet! Shooting a civilian just because she's a woman. Trust me, you dog, you are about to experience serious pain."

Spotter did not respond but Curtis knew he had heard the tirade. There was no more groaning. He pictured the spotter breaking into a sweat.

Curtis closed his eyes and the unwanted vision returned. He again saw his father beating his mother. The vision was powerful. He was part of the scene, a little boy cowering in the corner of the kitchen by the pantry, watching clenched fists rain on his mother as she tried hard to protect herself. A young Rhys Curtis covered his eyes, then eyes shut he covered his ears. "If I had a gun, he would be dead," young Rhys told himself.

The door opened and Curtis snapped out of his daydream.

"So, Agent Curtis, I am sorry to take so long," the commanding officer said as he pulled back the door and entered the room, "Should I call you 'Agent' or 'Sergeant'? No, I think 'Agent' will cause us less problems right now, don't you think?"

Curtis took that to be a rhetorical question and didn't respond. He stood upright and towered over the CO, noticing for the first time the officer's insignia on his shoulder strap. Three stars with a Thai emblem attached. Colonel.

Curtis stood to attention and although not in uniform he acknowledged the colonel with a salute. The Australian requirement to salute only applied when a soldier is dressed in uniform but he knew this was not so in Thailand. One always saluted whether in uniform or civilian clothes.

"At ease, Agent Curtis," the colonel said as he handed Curtis his essential equipment and credentials. "My name is Juntarsa, Colonel Juntarsa. I prefer not to acknowledge your Australian Army credentials. That would create too many problems for us, no? I choose to acknowledge your position as a senior agent of the Australian Security Intelligence Organisation. Oh, and Interpol of course. Yes, I have been made aware of your ASIO connection.

"With the permission of my lieutenant general I spoke at length to your superior officers and another very powerful person in Australia. Although it was left unstated, I have a feeling your credentials do not offer up everything about your role. Your people did tell me you also work for ASIO. I chose not to ask about any other, covert work you may undertake. For whatever reason, the people to whom I spoke did not go into detail about what your plans were or are in Thailand."

Probably Frenchy. No detail because he didn't know.

"I was reassured," Colonel Juntarsa continued, "of your propriety. That you are a trusted agent," emphasising the last word.

Curtis nodded appreciation of that recognition.

"They said your — what you Australians call — *modus operandi* is entirely at your discretion, but within the boundaries of local and international law of course. The man with whom I spoke in Australia asked me to have you call him as soon as you have a clear picture of the events that have transpired. You see I was not in a position to tell him anything other than you were in our custody. Perhaps you may care to tell me more, Agent?

"I reported everything I know to my lieutenant general. My orders are to cooperate fully with you."

"Thank you, sir," Curtis spoke for the first time.

The colonel appeared surprised, either at the courtesy shown him or the deep, throaty voice.

"Having made further enquiries, I am starting to have a clearer, although incomplete picture. I should also inform you, your associate is in hospital. Nothing serious. Nothing life threatening but serious enough to stay there for a few days. Perhaps a week or so."

"Was there anyone else hurt on the train, Colonel?" Curtis asked anxiously.

"There was a female passenger shot, but I have no further information. Your associate is in the Bangkok International Hospital, the private hospital on the highway near the new Blueport shopping centre.

"Now, Agent Curtis, what should we do with the soldier next door? It appears he was involved with the shooting. He may even have been the shooter. Only you and he would know that.

"My military police officers will question him and get to the bottom of it. I expect he will eventually be dealt with by the Royal Thai Police, but he is a soldier first and foremost."

Curtis understood the dilemma the colonel faced. A soldier had committed a criminal offence on public property from an army base, but a criminal offence nevertheless. He could see the Thai Police, the railway police and the army all being involved.

"I would like the opportunity to interrogate him first," Curtis asked.

"I expected you to make that request, Agent Curtis."

"Without interference," Curtis firmly insisted.

Colonel Juntarsa nodded and continued, "As you know, the Royal Thai Army is like every other. We have rules we must follow. I don't have any jurisdiction over an Interpol agent, but I trust you will respect our rules of interrogation."

"Of course, sir."

Chapter 21

Two chairs were placed facing each other in the soldier's cell together with a small table that was situated to the side. At Curtis's request, the prisoner was seated on the chair closest to the table. Curtis entered the three-metre square room and placed his Glock 43 on the table.

He noticed the spotter's almost imperceptible glance sideways at the weapon within easy reach.

Eyes flicked left ever so slightly. *Do me a favour, scum. Go for the Glock. Give me an excuse. Self-defence. Do it!*

Silence. No movement from either man. They merely eyeballed each other. After a few minutes the prisoner lowered his eyes and clasped his hands into his lap.

He's decided against it. Pity. I'll have to give him some encouragement.

Curtis broke the silence. "I'll cut to the chase. Who recruited you?"

Silence. Spotter did not reply. Curtis noticed the grip of his clasped hands tightened slightly.

A few minutes passed in silence before Curtis asked, "Who gave you the order?"

No response.

Spotter's leg was heavily bandaged. The garrison's medical officer had first applied stitches to the wound. A tinge of red edged the bandages. The wound had continued to bleed enough to escape the gauze laid over it before the bandages were applied.

Whilst still sitting directly opposite Spotter, Curtis suddenly stretched his legs and as he did so his size thirteen boot hit the centre of the bandaged area. Bullseye! Spotter didn't see it coming and didn't have time to avoid the kick. He screamed in agony.

"Oops, sorry." Curtis unconvincingly attempted a look of concern.

The cell door flew open and a sergeant of the military police stood in the entrance gripping a Type 86 semi-automatic pistol.

"Would you mind stepping outside, Agent Curtis?"

Curtis obliged after collecting his Glock.

"We do not condone torture, Agent," the MP said emphatically. "It is against Royal Thai Army rules and international law."

"Torture? Don't be ridiculous. The prisoner has an injury that is likely to cause ongoing and sudden pain. Everything is under control in there, Sergeant," Curtis nodded towards the cell and spoke with reassuring confidence. "No need for you to come back in unless I call you. Please do not interrupt my interview."

With that, smile upon his face, Curtis re-entered the cell, closing the door firmly behind him.

"Now, where were we?" he said placing his Glock back on the table. "Did you have something to say to me?"

Spotter noticed Curtis deliberately staring at his bandaged leg.

"What do you want to know?" Spotter asked through clenched teeth, still holding his leg and in obvious pain.

"Names. I want names. Who and why."

The prisoner lost his resolve and started talking. He told Curtis everything he had already deduced. The separatist insurgents, the RKK initially recruited him and his associate, the now deceased shooter, to help restore the natural order of things. He explained how a *farang* had paid them well with a promise of more when they got the job done.

"*Farang*?" Curtis enquired.

"Foreigner."

Curtis listened. Said nothing more but stared hard at the prisoner. He lived by the old adage, 'we are born with two ears and one mouth, and we should listen twice as much as we talk'. He also knew when a person under interrogation starts to talk, silence by the interrogator encourages the other side to fill the space. Even light meaningless chatter sometimes carries more meaning than one might expect.

The spotter rambled. Curtis listened without a hint of interest or emotion.

When the spotter had exhausted his pot of mostly, but not all, useless information, Curtis asked, "Does the *farang* have a name?"

"Neelson."

I'm surprised he used his real name. Shows the arrogance of the man.

Curtis decided he couldn't allow Spotter's ill-conceived notions to go unchallenged.

"Let me explain some things, shithead. Over sixty countries have had female prime ministers or presidents. Some of those have been so satisfied, indeed ecstatic and optimistic, about their leaders they have re-elected them. I applaud the people of those countries. They recognise women can do just as good a job of running their country as men. Better in many cases.

"Nothing you have done or your scumbag mates attempt in the future will change that. Countries will continue to have democratically elected female leaders.

"You should know the army is a better teacher of moral responsibility than the RKK or radical groups like them. You work in an environment where there is an expectation of moral responsibility. Responsibility to your fellow Thais, young and old, male and female.

"I know you have been influenced by the RKK, you weakling. The RKK have an extremist agenda. They espouse a radical Islamic agenda that is not in keeping with the teachings of the Koran. Their views are at odds with the philosophy and religious beliefs of the vast majority of Muslims. Did you know that a significant number of those sixty plus countries are predominantly Muslim?

"It is not a cultural attitude in Thailand. You had a female prime minister in this country not that long ago. From my observation, most people in Thailand respect women.

"Why are you different? Why do you have this sense of superiority? What are the circumstances that give you a sense of superiority? As a soldier on a steady income, you are not facing economic hardship. You cannot describe yourself as a victim, nor the people you work and live with as victims, after having a female prime minister. Not that either of those things are a reason to commit violence or kill anyone.

"As you sit there and squirm, I can tell you are certainly not superior to anyone. Just brainwashed. Weak!

"You will have a long time to think about what I have just told you, as you sit behind bars inside a square concrete box. You're going away for a long time."

Curtis stood and holstered his Glock. He moved towards the door and hesitated. He turned slowly and gazed at Spotter's bandaged leg again. Sensing what was coming, Spotter braced for the impact and raised his hands in what would have been a futile attempt to shield himself from the ensuing pain.

Shall I? No, why should I lower myself to his level. To the level of a coward. He cannot defend himself. If only he had the courage to reach for my essential equipment.

Chapter 22

Geoffrey Coolidge did not entirely tell the truth to Jim Wallace in his interview for the position of Green Solutions operations manager. He mostly told the truth. He just omitted certain parts of his employment history and problems he had with the authorities.

He omitted to tell Wallace about the Australian Securities and Investment Commission investigation into his handling of a share transaction on behalf of a client when he was employed by one of the big four accountancy firms.

After months of investigation Coolidge was exonerated, but the company remained dissatisfied. It believed Coolidge's *modus operandi* in dealing with the disgruntled client left much to be desired. There were no grounds for dismissal, but the managing partner of the accountancy firm was more than happy to provide a reference and encourage his employment elsewhere.

Wallace was given a glowing account of Coolidge's performance. Indeed, the managing partner was so effusive, so gushingly praising, that Wallace suspected the praise might be misplaced.

He had connections in the chamber of commerce and asked questions about Coolidge. He was told Coolidge had made some silly mistakes that caused enormous difficulties for a client. Mistakes involving the Corporations Law, including continuous disclosure, fundraising and related party transactions.

Wallace immediately decided he would be perfect for the job. He had information about Coolidge that could be used against him if necessary. Apart from that, his background, varied and international as it was, would provide the flexibility that Green Solutions would need in an operations manager.

In his youth, Coolidge had attended Leeds Grammar School in Yorkshire, England where he excelled at athletics. His sports involvement developed into an interest in statistics and performance analysis. After receiving outstanding high school grades, he moved to London and attended the London School of Economics, studying managerial accounting and financial control.

Coolidge was a one hundred and two hundred metres junior sprinting champion in the North of England track and field junior championships. He had the athletic ability to represent his country internationally. But his parents convinced him he would never reach a level capable of making substantial money from the sport.

"Focus on your schooling, boy, not playing," his father told him. "You are good at mathematics and you have a level head. Good for business. Focus on accounting and you will go places."

Obediently following his father's urgings Coolidge was accepted at the LSE, but it was his athletics prowess that caught the eye of the registrar at the Mendoza Business College, Notre Dame University in Indiana, USA.

Coolidge was attracted to the college because it had a reputation of developing leaders with excellent analytical skills. Skills that were required by the big accounting firms. It also provided a tough athletic environment, being situated near the Notre Dame athletic stadium. He was offered a scholarship and jumped at the chance to work with the best in both fields of interest.

The accolades poured into the business college when he consistently won inter-college sprint meets. When representatives of the Bank of America, Ernst Young, KPMG, JP Morgan, and Deloitte, attended Mendoza College, as they frequently did, they sought to interview the young man. His athletic ability was widely discussed. The big companies wanted a well-rounded young graduate. One who could easily deal with difficult clients and who had the determination and stamina to succeed.

As a sophomore he was offered a position with Boston Consulting Group on the basis he completed his studies. As tempting as it was to work with such a reputable organisation, he decided it would be best to wait and see if he received a better offer from one of the big accounting companies. The offer came.

Whilst working in New York for five years, Coolidge had become friends with a senior manager of the Boston Consulting Group. At a BCG Christmas party he introduced Coolidge to some of his staff, one of whom, a pretty Australian woman, immediately took more than a passing interest in the young, good looking, easy-going athletic Englishman. The chemistry was evident.

When Coolidge returned to England two years later, he did so with Mrs Veronica Coolidge. Both Geoffrey and Veronica worked for BCG in London. This gave Coolidge the opportunity to work with developing businesses throughout Europe and thus broadened his experience.

The couple decided they would prefer to raise their now expanding family in Veronica's home state of New South Wales, Australia. Veronica's family lived in the Sydney suburb of Vaucluse. The Coolidges settled nearby. Geoffrey Coolidge spent several years working with his father-in-law in the family civil engineering business before he accepted an offer from KPMG.

By the time he started work with KPMG, Coolidge was anything but the athlete he once was. He had not exercised in years and had spent most of his time sitting at a computer, waiting in airports or flying across Europe and occasionally to the USA. None of this was conducive to a healthy lifestyle.

Veronica was concerned for her husband's health. He had allowed himself to become overweight. Dark shadows were formed on the puffy bags under his eyes. He constantly looked stressed.

"I can see the work you are doing for ungrateful clients, and the exceedingly long hours are taking its toll, Geoffrey." Veronica looked concerned as they sat on their rear balcony overlooking Sydney harbour for their daily routine of after-work drinks. But she didn't know Coolidge was also under pressure from ASIC. He had wanted to shield his wife from the stress of the investigation and chose not to tell her.

"You should look for another job. We don't need the money. We own our house. We have accumulated enough property, savings and shares to enable you to take a more relaxing job. You could even return to work for my father on a part-time basis. I'll talk to him if you like."

The last thing Coolidge wanted to do was to return to work with a man he regarded as a control freak.

"I have been thinking about an offer I have received from a company known as Green Solutions, Vee," he replied. Coolidge always referred to Veronica by the initial of her given name. She liked that.

"I had planned to discuss it with you when the kids have gone to bed tonight. It sounds like a great job but involves a fair amount of overseas travel. Perhaps you can travel with me some times if I take the job?"

"Sounds interesting, Geoffrey." Veronica envisaged an occasional visit to her friends in the UK and the USA. "Is it a good offer financially?"

Coolidge reached across the small tiled table and poured another glass of Pol Roger champagne for Veronica. He helped himself to a local Hunter Valley red wine.

"An income exceeding what I currently earn by fifteen thousand dollars but the real attraction is the parcel of shares our consultancy company will receive. That is the real attraction."

"As long as you don't have the stress levels, it sounds like an offer you can't refuse," concluded Veronica.

Coolidge smiled and nodded.

Chapter 23

His mobile pinged an incoming message. Wallace stared at the text message with huge relief. The mission in Thailand was the first of that nature. He had funded campaigns against women in leadership positions, some successfully, such as the Australian experience, but this operation was quicker and less expensive.

He smiled broadly. *More permanent too. No return. Edgar was right. This is the way to get it done.*

If I talk to Nelson in riddles, he will understand but nobody else will. Nobody suspects anything. I need to know for certain that we succeeded and I want to hear the detail.

Not able to contain his excitement, he dialled the number.

Nelson answered quickly, unambiguously. "You received my message."

"Yes. How certain are you we completed the deal? The major shareholder has been taken out?"

Nelson chuckled at Wallace's use of corporate language in the circumstances. Acknowledging the reason, he responded accordingly. "I was there when the transaction was completed. It was smoothly done and the new operator responsible for arranging the takeover has walked away with cash in hand."

He had a mental picture of Wallace's beaming face. Could almost feel his excitement.

"It's been a great week, Craig. Our new friend in Moscow has made an initial deposit into the company's Singapore account. He will make a further more substantial contribution in the next ten days. Simon tells me he is sold on the technology but we must keep him informed of progress towards completing contracts."

"What do you want me to do now, Jim? Shall I meet you in London?"

"No, Dubai. The office will make the arrangements. Talk to Melissa about flights. I will give you the details of a similar problem to the project you just completed. Our new Russian shareholder said there could be an issue in St Petersburg. He will have someone meet you there. But first come to Dubai. We have some serious planning to do."

Wallace terminated the call and pondered a celebration. He had told his brother he would send a message once he had confirmation the mission was successful. He immediately sent Edgar the same message he had received from Nelson.

Nelson. What a find. The perfect recruit for what we aim to achieve. That Thai woman was the first of many. A trial run really. Minimal security for her, no bodyguards, but others will be more challenging.

Now for my meeting with Coolidge. He should be at the hotel by now. Perhaps we can even have a drink to celebrate the addition of Lumovski to our shareholder's list. He'll never know about the other reason for a celebration.

The Jumeirah Mina A'Salam resort hotel in Dubai was one of Wallace's favourite hotels in the world. It has outstanding accommodation, swimming pools, spa facilities and is connected by gondolas to some of the finest restaurants he had dined at.

Wallace frequently stayed at the Mina A'Salam or the nearby Jumeirah al Qasr when travelling to Europe. From Dubai he could easily fly to most European cities. He appreciated the warmth of Dubai after spending time in London during the cold months.

With Lumovski's funds in Green Solutions' Singapore bank account, and with the promise of many millions more, Wallace planned to reward his trusted senior staff with luxury stopovers when they travelled in this part of the world. Coolidge was to be the first beneficiary of Wallace's generosity.

A message was left at the resort hotel reception for Coolidge to meet him by the Mina A'Salam pool bar, arguably the best pool bar in Dubai. Wallace lounged on the Arabian Gulf side of the pool with views towards the famous seven-star Burj Al Arab. The azure sea glistened in the late morning sun. Luxury motor launches drifted past, their ultra-wealthy passengers soaking up the sun and the best French champagne.

That could be me soon, he thought.

Wallace browsed the menu whilst waiting for Coolidge. The à la carte menu offered some of the finest cuisine available in the city.

When Coolidge arrived, and having exchanged pleasantries, Wallace caught the eye of the nearest waiter and with a beckoning wave summoned him. They placed their order, a beer with a slice of lime. Wallace ordered an Arabic tasting plate including hummus, shish taouk, mutabbaq, and olives.

Wallace likes the good life, thought Coolidge, ever mindful of spending shareholders' money. *I can't make any comment or I'll be looking for a new job.*

"I need you to go to Russia. We have a new investor who is extremely well connected and has arranged a contract with the government of St Petersburg. You will need to meet the chief minister and sign the contract on behalf of Green Solutions."

"But I don't have authority to do that," Coolidge meekly protested. "It should be a director."

"That's not a problem, Geoffrey. Don't worry, just sign the thing. Write your name in as 'director' if you want. Just get it signed."

"Have you seen the contract? Can I have a copy before the meeting in Russia? What does it propose?" Coolidge wanted more detail. Having worked for one of the big five accounting firms, he was always conscious of good corporate governance procedures. Shareholder interests were paramount. He was also well aware of sovereign risk in dealing with Eastern Europe.

"I told you not to worry, Geoffrey," Wallace replied curtly. "You've got a job to do, just do it! Oh, and so there are no surprises you might see Craig Nelson in St Petersburg. He will be meeting with some of the new investor's friends and making a presentation to them. You need not be concerned about that. In all probability, you may not even see him."

"Tell me about the new investor. Did you give him an information memorandum on Green Solutions?"

"Look, Geoffrey. I run this company and I know what I'm doing. I know how to deal with potential investors, as does Nelson. I don't need you to tell me how to run the business. Your job is to follow my instructions and not concern yourself about peripheral matters."

"Sorry, Jim, I'm only trying to protect you as the principle shareholder in the company. If Craig is in Russia, why can't he sign the contract? Or Sergei Vasiliev for that matter. After all, he is our Russian general manager."

"There are other things for you all to do. When you have signed the agreement, I want you to start looking for a factory in which we can store the product. Get prices on a large enough space in the light industrial area to accommodate expected demand for the St Petersburg region. The chief minister will tell you what that will be.

"I know you are trying to do the right thing by me, Geoffrey. Sometimes you ask too many questions. I am tired of receiving your emails about our expenditure. Our burn rate. Don't bother yourself. Get on with finalising the contracts and we will never have to think about such matters.

"Do the logistical stuff, moving product as required. Meeting our orders. Ensuring the manufacturing process is secure and the formulae protected. Liaise with the manufacturers about future demand and make sure they can meet it."

Following this brusque, almost uncivil reproach from Wallace, Coolidge realised he might be pushing him too hard. It wasn't so much the words he used but the manner in which he delivered them. His tone was almost hostile. Coolidge needed this job and the pay was generous. Time to retreat.

He nodded acceptance of Wallace's comments and chewed on a piece of mutabbaq.

No point in arguing with him, I suppose. He thinks he knows best. He sometimes shows disrespect for my background, qualifications and the contribution I make to the company.

Wallace sat back on the pool chair, sipped his beer and then closed his eyes. A signal to Coolidge the conversation was finished.

Chapter 24

Curtis took a circuitous route to his room, intending to avoid attracting attention to his unusual attire. Unusual for a hot tropical afternoon. Perspiration ran heavily down his face and across his neck. He walked along the beach and cut through the side entrance adjoining the staff quarters. He knew the guard on duty there during the day considered him to be strange anyway so it didn't really matter.

"Mr Curtis," the Grand Centara general manager rushed up to him as he walked across the lawn and started up the stairs past the gymnasium.

The GM looked at Curtis from head to toe and frowned. "Good afternoon, Mr Curtis," the GM said in a heavy French accent. He continued to gaze at his guest's attire.

"Unusual clothes?" Curtis acknowledged the stare. "I feel I need protection when I ride a motorcycle just in case I fall. One can never be too cautious, can one?" A quick response seemed to satisfy the GM.

"Of course, Mr Curtis. Your friend, our security officer, reported unwell yesterday. I call him 'your friend' because I know you talk to him a great deal. He also seems to be very fond of you. He talks about dining with you some times. We don't encourage staff to mix socially with hotel patrons but if that is your choice, who are we to argue." The GM smiled as he made the last comment.

"He seems to take a great deal of time off work lately. Do you know how he is?"

"I understand he has a gastric problem." Curtis attempted to look concerned. "Sometimes these illnesses can take some considerable time to correct themselves. I am sure he is on a heavy dose of antibiotics whilst he is recuperating at home."

"No doubt we will hear from him about a date for his return to work?"

"I'm sure you will." With that, Curtis walked briskly to his room.

The cleaning had been completed in that area of the hotel and as usual his cleaning lady had turned the room air-conditioning down to an intolerably low temperature. Uncomfortably so at ten degrees. A shock to the body.

Cold air hit Curtis as he entered his room. He rushed to the air-conditioner controls and flicked the temperature up. Turning to the wardrobe he opened his safe and secured his essential equipment. Curtis reached for his secure satellite phone but stopped.

I can't give Frenchy a thorough report until I have spoken to Rat. Frenchy can wait. I need to make certain my little mate is okay first.

He showered and dressed in shorts and a Hard Rock Café collarless T-shirt. He loved the XXXL Hard Rock material even though the shirt was still a little tight around the biceps and chest. He placed the clothes he had worn all day into a hotel laundry bag, together with his gym clothes from the previous day. After calling housekeeping to facilitate collection, Curtis placed the laundry bag in the corridor outside his room. Before doing so he looked in both directions along the corridor for any unwanted visitors. A habit. Not really expecting to see anyone.

Curtis walked out the front entrance of the hotel and was greeted in the traditional Thai manner by a new face. The security officer from the side entrance had been relocated to the front.

Probably a temporary move. I hope so anyway. The little man is tough and I don't expect a bullet would stop him too easily. If in fact that was the cause of his injury. No, that can't be right there was only one shot. The CO said a woman passenger had been shot. One shot could take out two people though. I've done it.

He walked to the main entrance and turned into Naresdama Road, where the tuk tuk drivers usually congregate. As usual with all tourists, a driver casually enquired if he needed a ride, seemingly resigned to the fact this big man walked everywhere. He thought about it for a millisecond then waved to the driver and walked past, in the direction of the Grand Night Market.

Two kilometres along the major highway heading south he negotiated the heavy traffic crossing Phetch Kasem Road during the late afternoon rush hour. Thai rush hours are not usually rushed but this highway is busy at any time of the day, with three lanes in each direction interrupted by the convenience of a wide island. Curtis waited on the island for a break in the northbound traffic, eventually crossing the highway between slow moving buses directly in front of the grounds of Bangkok International Hospital.

The doors to the hospital slid open as he approached and a uniformed man wearing a pleasant smile and a quiet "*sawardee karp*" greeted him. Curtis was impressed at the hospital entrance, ultra clean and modern. Two nurses at the reception similarly greeted him. He enquired about the room number for a man who was admitted in the morning.

"His name is Rat," Curtis said before realising how silly that was. "Ah, actually that is his nickname."

The more senior of the two nurses smiled and asked, "Under what name would he have been admitted?"

"Probably not Rat. I know this might sound ridiculous but I cannot remember his actual name. I have always called him 'Rat'. Perhaps if I can look at the recent admissions on your computer, I will be able to identify him."

"I'm sorry, sir, for security reasons we cannot allow that."

"I understand. Can I talk to your registrar please? I can then explain why I want to see Rat."

"Explain to me." The senior nurse was not in the slightest bit intimidated by the very large man standing in front of her. She took a step backwards as she spoke to ease the stress on her neck.

"I work for the Australian Government and it is important for intergovernmental relations that I talk to him."

Curtis thought that might be enough to convince the nurse to give him Rat's room number. Wrong. The recalcitrant nurse simply eyeballed him. Unmoved.

"I don't want to create a nuisance of myself," Curtis said in a conciliatory tone, "But it really is important that I see this man."

The nurse confidently stared at him. No hint of relenting. "Tell me his name and I will consider giving you the room number."

"Ma'am, I must see your registrar. This conversation cannot continue like this. I'll tell you what, if you don't agree to my request, I will walk the corridors of this hospital checking in each room until I find my friend." Curtis felt the nurse was being overly bureaucratic and was tired of her resistance to his simple request.

"I shall call security," she abruptly answered. "You cannot wander around this hospital as if it is your right to do so."

Curtis noticed the nurse's right hand move slowly, almost imperceptibly, towards a red alarm button.

"Go on, push the button. Do you think I would be intimidated by your security? You will be making a grave mistake and your security people will never forgive you for it. I am sure they don't wish to be patients in this hospital."

The nurse dropped her shoulders, again looked at Curtis from head to toe, and decided to make the call to the registrar. She turned away from him, speaking quietly into the mouthpiece. He couldn't hear either end of the brief conversation but knew the registrar would appear shortly.

That worked. I didn't intend adopting an aggressive stance but enough is enough.

Within thirty seconds a well-dressed grey-haired man exited the offices across the lobby. His demeanour was grim as he spoke abruptly to Curtis, "Please come with me to my office, sir."

With that he wheeled around and retreated to the office from whence he came. Curtis followed.

"What is your name?" the registrar asked without a greeting or offering to shake hands.

"Curtis," came the equally abrupt response.

"Aah, Mr Curtis. I've been expecting you. My apologies for the introduction to our hospital but I'm sure you will understand our strict rules about patient confidentiality. Our patients always come first.

"Your friend Ratnamphod informed his doctor that an important man from Australia would visit him today. He urged his doctor to offer any information you requested and to provide whatever assistance you required. Because of the nature of Ratnamphod's injuries I was informed of the request and his doctor insisted I call the police."

"What are the injuries? Is his condition serious?"

"When you see him, Ratnamphod will explain everything. He asked me not to contact the police until after I've talked to you. He assured me that you would know best how to handle what he described as 'a delicate situation'. Oh, and no, he is not in a serious condition."

"Let me talk to him before we go any further with this. What room is he in?"

Curtis walked past the reception and smiled at the senior nurse. The smile was not reciprocated. She turned away. Curtis looked at the second nurse, raised his hands to waist height, palms upturned. His expression said 'what's wrong with her?' The junior nurse smiled, turned her head to ensure her senior colleague wasn't watching and then shrugged her shoulders.

He winked at the nurse and walked briskly to the nearby stairs. On the third floor Curtis entered the private room at the end of the corridor. He was greeted with '*sawardee karp*' and a beaming grin, partly restrained by bandages strapped over Rat's face.

"What happened?" Curtis was straight to the point. No niceties.

With a little difficulty as a consequence of inconvenient bandages, Rat relayed the sequence of events. "At your request I convinced Dao to 'meet and greet' as you say. She was busy talking to passengers in the second passenger car. I had been suffering all morning from a terrible stomach cramp and needed to go to the bathroom. When I finished and left the toilet, the train was slowing and Dao had returned to her seat. I ran to carriage one and saw her in her allotted seat by the window. I think she was waving to someone on the platform."

Curtis thought he was listening to one of Rat's long rambling stories but noting his long face chose not to interrupt.

I guess he needs to explain why Dao was shot. He'll be blaming himself for leaving her alone. Best I let him tell the whole story. In any event, I will need to explain to Frenchy how it played out.

When I tell Rat the worst of it was my failure to stop the shot, he might feel better. Frenchy will be pissed!

"I rushed forward and threw myself at Dao as the train jolted to a stop. A single bullet shattered the glass in front of her. That's how I have these cuts over my arms and face. Shards of glass. There was blood everywhere. I am a little concussed from hitting my head on the iron feet of the passenger seat in front. Feel the lump. The doctor said I must stay in hospital under medical observation for a few days. Concussion, he said."

Rat paused his sad soliloquy. A lengthy pause. Appearing to drift deep in thought or to gather himself for the next piece of news.

Bad news.

"I never saw the person she was waving to but she told me he was definitely not a local. A European."

With Rat's pause Curtis had gazed out the hospital window at the buildings below. The last comment caused him to swivel, jerking his head in surprise and looking hard at Rat as if he thought him insane. "She spoke to you?"

"Yes," the smile returned. "The impact knocked me. I saw stars. Dao was there when I awoke in the ambulance. She is in the room next door. The bullet hit her hand as I fell over her. She may not wave to strangers again," he laughed, "But she is a politician I suppose."

Chapter 25

Following this revelation, Curtis recounted the events of the morning from his perspective. He omitted the part about not expecting the rooftop door to be locked and leaving his lock-picking pieces at the hotel.

"Your friend Noi was a huge help in getting me into the compound without being noticed. He cooks a pretty good breakfast too, Rat. You should try it some time.

"The shooter won't ever fire another shot. The spotter is in custody with a very sore leg. My throwing knife found its way into his leg." Curtis wore a look of satisfaction. "The soreness was compounded by an unfortunate accident in the lock-up."

Both laughed at this point. Rat understood what sort of 'accident' the spotter might have inflicted upon himself.

"There is always a silver lining though. I think he now has a better understanding of our attitude towards violence against women. A crash course on human relations, so to speak. He now understands he is assuredly a coward.

"By the way, the NCO school's commanding officer, Colonel Juntarsa, was enormously cooperative. He spoke to my superior officer who apparently gave him an assurance of my bona fides. You have been left out of the conversation so far, but I'm sure it won't be long before the CO knows of your involvement. He will be talking to the local police.

"The hospital registrar believes he should tell the police that firearms have landed two people in his hospital. What do you think, Rat?"

"He probably has an obligation to do so but if you think it advisable to keep the police out of it, I am sure he can be dissuaded from that view," Rat replied. "On the other hand, we may need the police involved to provide around the clock protection for Dao."

"You're reading my mind, Rat. That is precisely what I was thinking. Great minds think alike."

Idle chitchat occupied the next fifteen minutes. Eventually Rat asked Curtis for a more complete description on how he took down two elite Thai Army soldiers. He felt he had been given a summary of events. He wanted it all.

Curtis obliged. He outlined the events from the time Noi met him near the Starbucks café. This time he told Rat about the locked rooftop door and how he improvised with meat carving forks to pick the lock. They laughed in unison at the description.

The spotter's arrest and interrogation brought more laughter. Rat was amused at how Curtis left one piece of his 'essential equipment' within reach of the 'douchebag' as Curtis called him.

"It was surprising how the douchebag eventually wanted to spill the beans."

"What do you mean 'spill the beans'?"

"Talk," Curtis answered. "He just wanted to tell me everything without any further prompting from me. Well, maybe a little prompting.

"There are two things I need to do, Rat, before talking to my superior officer. I need to tell Dao about the background to this awful attack; why she was targeted. She needs to be aware of the attempt on her life and she needs to upgrade her security.

"Secondly, I need to talk to the hospital registrar about police involvement."

Curtis left Rat's bedside and entered the adjoining room. Dao Shinawatra was not in her hospital bed. Dressed in a fleecy white gown she sat on a chair beside the window, peering into the distance in obvious contemplation. Her right hand rested in hospital strapping.

Dao didn't hear or notice Curtis entering the room. He politely said, "*sawardee karp.*" Startled, she turned to see which doctor or other hospital staff member had such a deep but comforting voice. The accent was almost perfect Thai.

Wow, I doubt I have ever seen such a beautiful woman, Curtis thought.

Even though Dao was seated, Curtis could tell she was quite tall. Taller than the average Thai woman. Long black hair tied into a ponytail. Some strands of hair had escaped, forming waves running across the side of her face. Light brown, smooth, unblemished skin. Perfect facial features. Dark but sparkling eyes that reminded Curtis of the women he had seen in Iran. A striking feature, the eyes. Like cat's eyes. Alive and beautiful.

He smiled. The biggest and warmest smile he could muster. A look of puzzlement was returned. She was surprised and puzzled by the presence of such a large but obviously friendly man. He was clearly not part of the medical staff.

Curtis stepped forward and started to reach out to shake hands when he realised that was not a good option. Dao's right hand did not move. Could not move. Heavily bandaged in a sling across her shoulder.

"*Sawardee karp.*" A mellifluous voice. A broad smile despite the discomfort of a bullet wound in her hand.

"I'm sorry to disturb you, ma'am, but there are matters we need to discuss."

After more formally introducing himself by way of his status in Interpol, for the next thirty minutes Curtis outlined the information he had been given. He explained to Dao the attempt on her life was not simply because she was a member of the Shinawatra family, but because she was a woman with leadership aspirations and a likelihood of success.

"I am not a political person, Ms Shinawatra, and I am not aware of your policies or your background, but please don't be deterred from your ambition. At the same time, you must not ignore the threats. I urge you to be careful. It shouldn't be necessary and I believe it's outrageous, but I also firmly believe you need improved security."

A flash of Curtis's unwanted vision returned. His father's violence. Only a flash. Dao's soft and soothing voice quickly returned him to the present.

"Since there have been rumours about my possible candidature, I have been subjected to messages of hate on my Facebook page and Twitter," Dao informed Curtis with sadness in her voice. "Fortunately, the moderators quickly remove the bloggers, most of whom come from overseas.

"In Thailand we generally show respect to women, Mr Curtis, although there have been some notable exceptions of a highly public nature. There is no point in discussing those. Suffice to say, I can assure you I will not be deterred. I don't intend being intimidated. Your former

Australian prime minister refused to back off, and by her comments and actions she was an inspiration to many women around the world."

"I'm pleased about that," Curtis replied. "When Prime Minister Gillard spoke out against misogyny some commentators continued to criticise her, suggesting the malicious attacks on her were part of the cut and thrust of politics. That is nonsense of course. No other Australian prime minister before or since has been the subject of such aggressive verbal abuse. Often ridiculously based on her hairstyle or even the clothes she wore. The attacks mainly came from weak, insecure men."

Dao smiled at the description. She instantly liked this man. Liked his human values. More than that, he and his little friend next door had saved her life.

"Ms Shinawatra, with your agreement I intend talking to the Hua Hin chief of police to ask for around the clock protection whilst you are within his area of responsibility. We don't know whether the group responsible for the attack knows of your survival. We don't know if they would take further action if they were to hear their initial attack failed."

A nod of approval at the plan, together with a tender smile was the acknowledgement Curtis needed.

"Thank you. I shall be in touch." With that, Curtis left the room. He walked briskly to the office of the hospital registrar.

The registrar was given a potted account of the recent events. He was informed of the Royal Thai Army's involvement and agreed to leave the matter in the capable hands of Colonel Juntarsa. He also agreed to place a security officer in the corridor on the third floor, but this would only be a temporary measure. The hospital treated all patients with equal care and attention. He acknowledged he would not want any of his patients to feel insecure and agreed to allow a police officer's presence in the short term.

A visit to the Hua Hin chief of police did not yield the same immediate results, largely because Curtis was reticent in revealing the complete story. A need to know basis and the chief didn't need to know everything. It was a matter for the army to settle even though a civilian was involved. Curtis would leave it to Colonel Juntarsa to involve the police if he considered it necessary. By then he would have left Hua Hin.

Consistent with his covert operations he wanted to avoid questions, avoid more involvement than was necessary.

Curtis told the chief that Colonel Juntarsa would be in touch. He was confident the colonel would be discreet.

The chief looks relieved. No paperwork necessary, I suppose. Coppers everywhere hate paperwork.

After Curtis had relayed as much of the detail as he considered necessary, he requested a police officer be posted on the third floor of the Bangkok International Hospital, "In the interests of good relations with the Royal Thai Army and to ensure there is no further violence against Dao Shinawatra."

"I am under-resourced Mr— err, what is your name again?"

Curtis hadn't revealed his name and chose to ignore the question. "Sir, I remain concerned there may be further violence against a Thai citizen within your jurisdiction and I urge you to place an officer at the hospital. It won't be for long. A matter of a few days, nothing more."

"Two days then. From tomorrow," the chief replied.

"*Copun karp.*" Thank you. With that Curtis stood and walked briskly from the chief's office.

From the police station Curtis retreated in the direction of the Grand Centara to locate a tuk tuk. It was now late afternoon. The evening glow of a setting sun hung in the air with the humidity. Whilst at the hospital the skies opened up and torrential rain had swept across Hua Hin. The usual afternoon tropical cloudburst for this time of the year. Steam rose from the roads.

Somebody needed to stand guard in the hospital for one night before the police took up their position. He wasn't confident the hospital security could perform the job. It would be left to Curtis. He couldn't waste any more time in returning to the hospital.

His stomach rumbled slightly, reminding him he hadn't eaten since a snack in the army officers' mess at dawn. An essential stopover at the Lucky Star Restaurant for food on the go, while the tuk tuk driver waited at the front of the Grand Night Market. In any event, he owed it to Noi to give something of an explanation, a partial explanation, of the day's events. He did so whilst watching Noi ply his trade.

Delivered to the front doorstep of the Bangkok International Hospital, he juggled the generous containers of food and passed a decent tip to the tuk tuk driver. Back to work.

Chapter 26

A lounge chair was positioned for Curtis across the corridor from Dao Shinawatra's room by a hospital orderly. Keeping one eye along the length of the corridor, he munched on takeaway green chicken curry with rice. Although it wasn't ordered, Noi had also prepared a container of mango rice. Dessert. A generous serving of fresh mango accompanied by sticky rice sprinkled with sesame seeds and a small container of coconut milk.

The registrar was satisfied. The police had been informed of the use of firearms in the commission of an offence. There was nothing more he need do. All hospital facilities were made completely available to Curtis. Accommodating this big *farang* for one night would not be a problem.

Upon his return to the hospital, with access to bathroom facilities Curtis had taken a shower and rinsed his shirt, soaked and stained by perspiration. He dried his hair as best he could. Folding the shirt into the length of a clean towel, he stood on one end and twisted the other to wring out any excess water. Without allowing time for it to fully dry, he dressed and made his way to Dao's room. Although a little untidy in appearance at least he felt clean and alert.

Rat's room was first. He decided to share more intelligence with the little man but found him asleep. A deep sleep. Curtis couldn't see Rat below the sheets but he could certainly hear him.

If Rat keeps up this performance tonight, nobody in the hospital will get any sleep.

He quietly and slowly opened the door to Dao's room. A nurse was busy taking her blood pressure. A clip that looked to Curtis like a clothes peg was attached to her middle left finger to record her temperature. Satisfied that everything was in order the nurse recorded the data on a clipboard. In a quiet reassuring tone, she spoke in Thai to Dao and then turned towards the door to leave the room.

Startled, she dropped her clipboard. "Where did you come from? I never heard you."

Curtis bent down and gathered the documents, speaking in a hushed tone, "I'm sorry to have frightened you. I did not wish to disturb you whilst you were doing your duty."

"You have no right to be here after visiting hours," the nurse scolded.

Dao quickly intervened. "It's okay. I invited him. He is my very good friend. My very close friend."

With that, the nurse turned in the direction of the door and left the room. As Dao spoke, Curtis had experienced an inner glow, a feeling of warmth not known to him. Was it the voice, the warmth of her smile, her startling beauty or a combination of all three? It took a few moments for Curtis to gather his thoughts.

Curtis reassured Dao that her security was his prime concern. He told her of his discussion with the chief of police. The chief's commitment to place an officer outside her room for added security from early tomorrow morning.

"I will be outside your room tonight. You need not be concerned about anything or anyone. Have a good night's sleep. Err, *lab sa bai*." Sleep well.

Dao smiled approvingly at his use of her native Thai language.

As Curtis left the room he was thinking, *my very good friend, my very close friend*.

Just after midnight his mobile phone vibrated. He had muted the sound in accordance with hospital policy. Knowledge of the policy was inescapable. The phone-off symbol was posted at the hospital entrance, in the stairwell, and along the corridor. He couldn't miss it as he periodically patrolled the corridor, checking the stairwell and carefully scrutinising medical staff that either entered rooms or were stationed at the ward reception.

Curtis looked at the screen. 'Unknown caller' appeared. Frenchy, he assumed. He pressed 'Accept' and was surprised at the accent.

"Colonel Juntarsa, Agent Curtis. You are a hard man to find. You didn't answer the phone at your hotel. I was forced to contact the person in Australia to whom I spoke yesterday to obtain this number."

"One moment please, sir. I need to find a quiet spot to talk."

Curtis walked along the corridor and stood in a recess where the water fountain was situated. From there he still had a clear view of the length of the corridor.

"Okay, I'm listening," he told the colonel.

"I'm sorry to call you so late, Agent Curtis, but there are three matters in which I think you will be interested. First, you will understand the death of a soldier on our grounds requires an autopsy. We contract to a civilian medical officer for such a purpose. The autopsy was conducted tonight.

"As you well know, the cause of death was a lead projectile penetrating the brain."

Well now, why wouldn't I know that? I put that projectile there, Colonel. Too formal methinks. Almost bureaucratic. Shot dead will do.

"The more interesting aspect of the autopsy was the markings on the soldier's body. He had a tattoo on his back that appears to be the face of a bearded man with flames emanating from his head, or possibly surrounding it. It is rare to see a tattoo on a soldier, especially one of this size. Thai soldiers generally do not wear tattoos, Agent Curtis. That is unusual in itself. The coroner took a photograph of the tattoo and I shall have him send it to this phone number as soon as possible.

"Second, on a closer examination the coroner found a very small rectangular lump in the middle of the tattoo. He cut the lump and extracted a wireless sensor implant about the size of a one-baht piece. Our technical people told me the implant was designed to track the movements of the carrier. As you are apparently heavily involved in covert operations, I thought you should know this.

"Third, your senior officer said he is still waiting for your call. Your report. I have told him as much as I know, which, by the way, is very little, but he said he needed to talk to you."

"Thank you, Colonel. I shall attend to that. One last favour please, sir. It would be interesting to know if the imprisoned soldier, the dead man's accomplice, also has a tattoo. Would you mind checking that as soon as possible, even tonight? You can text this number as soon as you know. That would be appreciated."

"Certainly, Agent Curtis. I am still in the office and shall deal with that immediately. I shall text you shortly."

The commanding officer signed off, but before doing so he made a passing comment that perhaps it would be in everyone's interest if Curtis were to leave Thailand.

Before returning to the lounge chair outside Dao's room, Curtis asked one of the staff on duty to arrange a strong coffee. His concentration was such that he didn't need the caffeine to stay awake and alert, but it would help.

The hours passed slowly and uneventfully. Curtis patrolled the corridor, occasionally stopping at the reception to chat to the nurses. The ward came to life soon after six a.m. when the cleaning staff and the tea trolley arrived. As promised by the chief of police, one of his officers arrived before seven a.m.

Relieved from his post, Curtis visited Rat. He had just been served breakfast. Rat was having difficulty in attempting to spoon porridge between partially opened lips held firm by bandages.

"I'd help you, Rat, but I'm not experienced at spoon feeding. It wouldn't hurt for you to lose some weight anyway," he laughed.

Rat responded by raising his foot from under the bed sheet and flashing it in Curtis's direction. The nurse standing at the foot of the bed entering data onto Rat's chart giggled and left the room.

"What's that all about?" Curtis enquired.

No response. Rat was busy with his breakfast. Progress with the porridge was slow, spilling more than he consumed.

Curtis briefed Rat on his discussions with the Hua Hin chief of police and the late-night discussion with Colonel Juntarsa. He would call Frenchy for further instructions, but his expectation was that he would be told to leave Thailand as soon as possible. He asked Rat to maintain a watchful eye on Dao.

"I believe she may be out of immediate danger. We have slowed her opponents. But if Nelson is involved there will be others," he said. "We need to be vigilant. She needs to be vigilant."

Curtis reached for Rat's hand and gripped it firmly. "I'll be in touch, my friend."

With that he turned towards the door, turned again and smiled at Rat. "*Lin jor aa kae*," he said with a smile. A tongue like a crocodile is a Thai description of a person who eats a plate of food as if it will be his or her last, regardless of the taste, good or bad. He had learnt the phrase from Noi at the officers' mess.

A quick visit to Dao was in order before leaving. He was disappointed. Dao was taking her morning shower. Curtis couldn't wait. He left a note, 'I may have to leave Thailand but I shall be in touch. Take care. Curtis.'

As he walked past the nurse's station on the third floor Curtis spotted the nurse who had been in Rat's room earlier. She was talking to a doctor who had just arrived to do her rounds. Curtis waited patiently until there was an obvious break in the dialogue.

"Excuse me, ma'am, I hope you don't mind me asking but I'm curious to know why you laughed when the patient in room 325 pointed his foot at me."

The nurse looked at the doctor and they giggled in unison before replying, "In Thailand, sir, when a person shows the bottom of their shoe or their foot it is like doing what I think a *farang* would say is 'flipping the bird'. Or showing their middle finger, if you prefer."

"Thank you. I must remember that," he laughed. "Despite his obscenity I want you to take special care of my *nit noi* friend please." My little friend.

Curtis walked briskly to the Grand Centara Resort. First, breakfast at the Railway Restaurant, a more fulsome breakfast than what was on offer at the hospital. Most early diners were dressed ready for golf. Hua Hin is renowned for attracting tourists on golfing holidays. The area boasts some of the best golf courses in Asia.

Each of the restaurant staff greeted Curtis with a *wai* and the warmest of smiles. The typically friendly greeting he had become accustomed to at the resort. The restaurant boasted a large outdoor dining area surrounded by tropical plants. An assortment of cuisine formed a backdrop to an indoor air-conditioned dining room. A mélange of Thai, Chinese, Japanese and European food and juices.

Curtis piled his plate with American-style crispy bacon, four fried eggs, baked beans, several hash browns, garlic spinach and mushrooms.

He ordered American coffee with a dash of milk and retreated to the outdoors dining area. Fresh air.

"Good morning, Mr Curtis," the heavily French accented voice of the general manager caught him by surprise as he filled his mouth. "Is everything to your liking?"

Does this guy have a home to go to? He is always here. At least he shows real interest and concern for his guests.

Curtis politely greeted the GM and informed him the little security man from the front entrance was recovering well from his bout of gastroenteritis.

He is over the gastro, just not quite over the flying glass he caught as a result of the gastro.

Chapter 27

The phone call to Frenchy was revealing. Curtis had asked his contact at the Australian Securities and Investment Commission for information about the financial planning business operated by Craig Nelson. To expedite the investigation the information was passed directly to Frenchy. On the surface the business was purely about offering financial advice and planning, particularly for wealth accumulation and superannuation purposes. Nelson used his judgement on what best suited a client's needs and accordingly made recommendations on which products to acquire. He was not licensed to sell listed securities.

Deeper investigation had revealed Nelson to be heavily involved in the business of raising venture capital. Such activity was potentially in conflict with his advisory role unless merely assisting company lawyers or accountants with business plans. He didn't promote himself as qualified or having expertise in this area but his results spoke volumes.

For several years numerous small to medium enterprises had engaged Nelson for this purpose. More recently he had been involved with offshore registered companies. It was difficult to obtain information about those companies in some jurisdictions.

Curtis's ASIC connection had informed Frenchy of an Australian registered company that had untraceable links to an offshore entity. That company was a wholly owned subsidiary of the offshore company. Frenchy told Curtis the Australian company appeared to exist for two reasons; for the purpose of raising capital locally with the help of people like Nelson, and for securing support from the Australian Government through Austrade. Austrade provided financial support. Its trade commissioners actively pursued overseas markets for its clients.

"What is the name of the company and who runs it?" Curtis asked.

"Green Solutions Australia Pty Ltd," Frenchy replied. "The sole director is one James Langton Wallace. We did a check on him. He emigrated from the UK six years ago. He appears clean. No police record. He owns a house in Vaucluse, Sydney. Obviously has a few bob.

"Wallace became an Australian citizen three years ago but doesn't appear to have renounced his British citizenship. The Australian Constitution would therefore prevent him from becoming a member of parliament," he laughed.

Frenchy's last comment was an aside. A reference to the chaos in Australian federal politics as a result of a high court ruling that excluded a number of elected members and senators with dual citizenship, including the deputy prime minister, from holding their positions in the nation's parliament.

"It is now starting to make sense," Curtis said, ignoring the last remark as irrelevant. "Nelson is connected with Wallace. Together they are using this company and possibly the offshore entity to fund opposition to Dao Shinawatra and possibly other women."

Frenchy gave an uncharacteristic sigh. "Curtis, I know you believe that to be an irresistible inference. I can hear it in your voice. You are confident there is a connection and, although I trust your judgement, I confess to being less certain than you. Let's get the evidence.

"Our people are tracking Nelson's movements. When I have more information, I shall contact you. In the meantime, stay low. Do not leave the hotel. I shall be in touch within twenty-four hours with further instructions."

With that, Frenchy concluded the discussion without any warning. *Typical Frenchy. No niceties. No 'Have a good day, Curtis'. Nothing. 'Stay low,' he says. A little difficult. Time to catch up on sleep.*

***

As a young athlete and aspiring professional footballer, Curtis had thought sleep was a waste of time. He didn't need to spend a third of his life in an unconscious state. His time in the SAS had made him aware of the studies undertaken by the Walter Reed Army Research Institute into sleep patterns, sleep loss, the effectiveness of recovery sleep and the impact on a soldier's cognitive and psychomotor performance. He knew he needed sleep to continue to perform at the level expected of him in the days, perhaps even weeks, ahead.

When one is sleep deprived there comes a point when overtiredness makes it difficult to fall asleep. Such is the case when one has a particularly active mind. The last thirty-six hours had required constant alertness. Curtis lay on his bed, fan turning slowly overhead, eyes shut but brain not so. Turning faster than the fan. His training meant it was usually possible to take a nap as required, but on this occasion, he couldn't shake the thought of further attacks against Dao Shinawatra.

Eventually sleep took over. A fitful sleep. Night visions, as episodical as his initial attempt to sleep, also returned. A vision of his parents arguing leading to more sinister, graphic pictures of violence. A little boy cowering in the corner of the kitchen whilst his father unleashed his temper. This time the dream was interspersed with visions of Dao caught in cross hairs.

The room telephone jangled. An unfamiliar ringtone. Curtis was jolted from his sleep. It took a few moments for him to realise where he was and what the noise was that awoke him. Dripping in perspiration he fumbled for the phone as it slipped from his fingers. It cluttered across the bedside cupboard hitting the lampshade.

"Hello," Curtis mumbled into the mouthpiece when he recovered the handset.

"Good afternoon, Mr Curtis," came the introduction. The mellifluous and assertive voice of a young Thai woman. Still in a haze, he didn't recognise the voice.

"*Sawardee karp*," Curtis replied. "Who is calling?"

"Dao. It's Dao Shinawatra speaking. I have been told the full story of how the attempt on my life unfolded. I realise I never had the opportunity to properly thank you for everything. If there is anything I can ever do for you, please don't hesitate to ask, Mr Curtis. Anything. I owe you my life."

"Curtis. Just call me Curtis, ma'am." He didn't respond to Dao's last comment.

"And I'm Dao. If I decide to pursue a political career, I know I will need a good person to head my security team. I would dearly like that person to be you. Would you be interested?"

"I'm flattered, Dao, but may I respectfully suggest the person you need is in the hospital room next to yours. Don't underestimate him."

"Yes, I know he is a good man and the two of you working together would make a perfect team to have around me. By the way, a few hours ago I had a long discussion with the Rat, as he likes to call himself. He told me you have an uncanny understanding of the mind of an aggressor. He called it a 'hunch', a sixth sense. He said he has never met anyone like you. Anyone with the ability to get into the head of an assailant."

Now fully awake Curtis laughed at the last comment adding, "Experiences, Dao. Life's experiences coupled with experiences in the military have provided me with that ability. You owe me nothing, Dao. I merely follow instructions from my superior officers in Australia."

If she knew what particular experiences have shaped the ability...

"I am leaving the hospital tomorrow, Curtis, and shall continue with my original plan. I shall also take your advice and increase my security contingent. Can we meet for coffee before I leave Hua Hin?"

"I'm afraid we will have to take a rain check on that. I am waiting upon further instructions, but I expect to be leaving tonight or very early in the morning."

The conversation concluded with an exchange of mobile telephone numbers together with positive vibes about plans to meet again.

Time for a quick workout, Curtis dressed appropriately and went straight to the gymnasium. Thirty minutes of pumping iron was enough for today. He returned to his room, showered and dressed. Khaki knee-length shorts, burgundy collared polo shirt bearing a Hua Hin Golf Resort logo and slip-on sandals that Curtis liked to call his 'Jesus shoes'.

Bell had given instructions, via Frenchy, to remain in the resort and lay low for twenty-four hours. Time to relax. Curtis ventured to the Ocean Bar and Restaurant to listen to the music of the seventies and enjoy a quiet drink. He also felt the need to again think through the manner in which the assignment had been conducted. To contemplate the options that were available to him and how he and Rat could have perhaps better handled the mission.

"Lime and soda, no ice, Mr Curtis?" the drinks waiter asked as he took his lounge seat.

"Yes... er, no dammit. I think I'll have a beer for a change. A celebration. A Chang please."

"You have something to celebrate, sir?"

"Yes, always. If you are vertical there is a reason to celebrate."

The waiter looked somewhat puzzled by the comment but didn't ask for clarification. "Of course, Mr Curtis. One Chang beer, sir."

He had chosen a single lounge seat positioned under a white flowering frangipani tree with a clear view of the beach and bay beyond. White beach sand under the lounge.

The music of Simon and Garfunkel, a setting sun, green lights from squid boats glistening across the still water, a slight waft of breeze and an ice-cold Chang. *It doesn't get much better than this.*

Curtis sat back in his chair and thought about the events of the last few days. His hunch had proven correct. A sniper team trained by Nelson. Should he have involved the Thai military when he sensed the NCO school was involved? Was it right to risk Rat's life by placing him on the train? What if it had been a bomb and not a bullet? He made a mistake by not taking his lock pickers. Should he have interrogated the spotter in the manner he did? Question after question. The answer was always, 'Trust your gut, Curtis.'

He thought about the pain he had inflicted on the spotter. Not the initial pain from his Glock 78 field knife but the follow-up 'accident' in Spotter's cell. The interrogation 'accident'. Should he have been more cognizant of the army rules of interrogation? *No, absolutely not. It's in the DNA. My grandfather. Army is in the DNA and his modus operandi is too.*

Curtis doubted the genes that affected his behaviour could come from his father. In the recesses of his mind he nevertheless carried that fear. Sometimes when he looked in the mirror, he saw the dark completed look of his father. His fear that more than just his looks — the square chin and dark eyes — are fundamentally transferred in the DNA.

We all have failings; some we are not prepared to acknowledge. I know his failings. Lack of self-control, a bully, a misogynist. Not me. At least I don't succumb to such impulsive, erratic behaviour. Yes, I did the right thing by inflicting pain on the spotter. Now we know what and with whom we are dealing. At least I do. Frenchy might not, but I'm in the field. I know.

Curtis slowly sipped his beer whilst listening to the band play Simon and Garfunkel's *The Sound of Silence*.

The lyrics poignantly reflected his dreams.

And the vision that was planted in my brain still remains. How do I rid myself of that vision? Will I ever rid myself of that vision?

The vision had presented itself a great deal more than usual of late. Curtis knew this must be the consequence of the mission with which he was charged. A mission to protect a woman whose life was threatened. It became personal.

Chapter 28

After a late breakfast following his vigorous gymnasium workout, Curtis had spent the morning relaxing by the ocean pool. It was early afternoon. He felt the vibration just before he heard the ping on his mobile phone. 'Bell has spoken,' read the message from 'No Number ID'. A clear message to phone Frenchy.

As always, having sworn an oath to his country and justice, his duty to Bell and Frenchy couldn't wait.

He rushed to his room and went through the usual routine to make the call. Check for possible eavesdroppers in the corridor, unlock two safes, and dial a number that automatically rotates to a new number each time it is used.

"Scrambled?" asked Frenchy, his usual introduction in a monotone, metallic voice that could be from another planet.

"As always," was Curtis's usual reply.

"As you know, through passport checks and facial recognition at airport immigration checkpoints we are, to some extent, able to track a person's international movements," Frenchy said. "It may take time to obtain the information, depending upon how sophisticated the local system is and whether the other end responds expeditiously to our request.

"Thai Immigration only has an electronic checking system for locals but Thai officials are excellent with their visual checks and response time. Given the number of travellers between our two countries we have an automatic linking system. When they record the passenger's name and passport details at the checkpoint, it links to our border security system within minutes. We had a flag on Nelson.

"Nelson left Thailand two days ago at 1625," Frenchy told Curtis.

"The same day as the attempt on Dao's life. He may not even be aware they failed. The attempt was at 0959. Allowing about three hours from Hua Hin by car we can probably assume he left within an hour or so. Check-in at the Bangkok Airport requires at least ninety minutes," Curtis said.

"Without going to Thai Airways, we didn't initially know his destination," interrupted Frenchy, "but we searched the flight timetables out of Bangkok and narrowed it down to either Dubai, Frankfurt or Paris. Dubai won. We only know that because our people checked with Emirates and discovered he flew with that airline to Moscow within twelve hours. A very brief stopover in Dubai.

"Our people have followed your suggestion, Curtis, your hunch if you like, that Nelson is involved in something sinister. Personally? As you know I have yet to be convinced.

"Like you, Bell suspected an international connection between various criminal activities from the very beginning. So far, there is no evidence to suggest any criminal connection between Nelson, Wallace and the business in which Wallace is involved. I need more information before I am convinced of any sinister motivation or criminal activity between those parties.

"Let's say, hypothetically, you are right, Curtis…"

"Trust me," interrupted Curtis, "I know I'm right."

"We'll see. If you are, how do Nelson or Wallace select their targets? Are they targeting people with political aspirations? People who hold different political views from them? Or are they acting for others. Political groups or individuals that pay to eliminate their opponents? Is it based on a financial reward or is it political?

"I have decided to go down your path a short distance and test your theory. In truth, Bell instructed me to do so. Bell is my superior and I have no alternative despite my doubts."

Curtis could hear a slight change of tone in Frenchy's voice. He knew the man well enough to know he disagreed with the strategy.

"What is now interesting given that he was only recently there prior to travelling to Thailand, according to our immigration department people, Nelson has returned to Russia. He has landed in Moscow. Travelling within Russia makes him harder to track but our people are doing their best."

Curtis's doorbell chimed and from the corridor his housekeeper yelled, "Housekeeping!"

"Excuse me, sir, I need to answer that."

Curtis carefully placed the cumbersome satellite phone on his bed. He turned and took one step towards the door. The housekeeper, assuming the room was empty as it normally was, impatiently twisted her skeleton key in the pin tumbler lock and opened the door.

"Sorry, sir, may I turn down your bed?" Jai, his regular cleaning lady, asked.

Curtis was anxious to continue the telephone discussion and quickly responded, open palm pointing Jai towards the door with a smile. "Not necessary, thank you."

He closed the door and stared at the highly polished floor to see if the cleaning trolley shadow had moved. It did so as he watched. He then looked through the door peephole and the fish-eye lens gave him a clear view of Jai moving along the corridor.

Curtis had followed this procedure thousands of times. On one occasion in a hotel in Bogotá, the capital of Columbia, when his room was to be cleaned, he asked the young male cleaner to return later but noticed the trolley did not move. He waited a few seconds and then jerked the door open. The cleaner was standing behind the trolley with a pistol, silencer fitted, pointing directly at the pcephole. Had he looked into the lens he would have been dead. The 'cleaner' was smashed between the trolley and a brick wall opposite the door. Never to 'clean' again.

Returning to his secure phone he again apologised to Frenchy for the interruption.

"Was Nelson met at Moscow Airport?" Curtis asked.

"Yes, he was. Two large, muscular men dressed in black. You know the look. The bodyguard type, thugs."

"Where did they take him?"

"Interestingly, he didn't leave the vicinity of the airport. He sat in a black extended limo in a loading zone with the two thugs standing kerbside nearby. After forty-four minutes in the limo he left the vehicle and went straight to the domestic terminal. He took a flight to St Petersburg."

"Do we know who he met with in Moscow? Curtis asked.

"The limo was heavily tinted. It wasn't possible to see precisely who was inside, although our person said it was a man. He only caught a glimpse of him. We checked the car registration, a private plate. It belongs to a company called Meshech which is connected to the Russian oligarch Lumovski."

"What do we know about him?"

"We know he is well connected politically. He had to be to accumulate such wealth in a relatively short period of time since the break-up of the Soviet Union. An oligarch. It is rumoured Lumovski has a dark side. Some of his business activities have attracted accusations of corruption and other serious criminal activity. It has also been suggested he uses his many international investments to cultivate powerful political connections. Nurturing relationships with campaign donations and the payment of consultancy fees. Highly questionable activities.

"Bear in mind, we can't be absolutely certain of this as much of the information we have obtained is from the media in the UK. Whilst the media is not necessarily a reliable source of information at least those reports come from more trustworthy sources than one might expect from the tabloids; The Financial Times and The Guardian.

"That's the best we have been able to do in a short time because, strangely, our Moscow trade commissioners claim to know very little about him. They have heard of him but that is all."

Strange indeed, thought Curtis. *It is an irresistible assumption that he met with Nelson. Why would a comparative financial lightweight like Nelson meet with an oligarch? What business could he be involved with?*

Curtis was jolted out of his contemplation as Frenchy continued, "In the last twenty-four hours we have cobbled together as much information as possible about potential political candidates in Russia, based upon your hunch and your report about the Thailand operation.

"We cannot be involved in political machinations, of course. If we become aware of illegal activities, or even potential criminal activities involving an Australian citizen overseas, it is incumbent upon us to report the matter to the appropriate authorities. We will not take an active role unless requested by other governments or Interpol. We usually only provide information if requested."

"I don't mean to be rude, sir, but if this matter crosses international borders shouldn't we at least endeavour to better understand what is happening? What clandestine activity an Australian might be involved in?"

"My thoughts precisely, Curtis. More about that in a moment. Further examining possible targets based on your hunch, we have discovered there is one potential Russian politician likely to be contesting a gubernatorial election next year. A judge from the General Jurisdiction Court of St Petersburg.

"The city court is supervisory for the local courts and is an appellate court. On occasions it acts as a court of first instance, hearing civil and criminal matters with three judges sitting to hear serious criminal matters. Okay, 'so what' might you ask?

"We understand this particular judge has taken an aggressive stance on matters of corruption, often vocally and publicly at odds with the other judges.

"More significantly, and without other judicial support, this particular judge has also made recommendations on legislation to the Supreme Court of Russia. Taking a public stance on important and popular issues.

"Even issues with international significance that have absolutely nothing to do with the city court. The Yukos matter, for example. In 2007, the state of Russia seized control of one of the country's largest oil producers, claiming the company had fraudulently failed to pay tax.

"Perhaps coincidentally the major shareholder of Yukos was a vocal critic of the Russian president and financially supported his opponents. He spent ten years in jail for his troubles. Tax evasion apparently.

"The European Court of Human Rights ordered Russia to pay the Yukos shareholders about two billion dollars in damages.

"In a letter to the Russian Constitutional Court that somehow found its way to the media, the St Petersburg judge to whom I referred supported the ECHR ruling. You can imagine what the Russian establishment thought of that. Not surprisingly, totally ignoring the judge, the Constitutional Court subsequently claimed the ruling violated the Constitution.

"This judge is increasingly making waves. Comments on issues popular with the public at large, probably with the imminent gubernatorial election in mind. Issues that are mostly, or at least not always, popular with the Russian establishment but have public support. In summary, Curtis, the judge is vocal and takes a public stance on matters that are certainly unpopular with the Russian mafia."

Curtis couldn't restrain his curiosity. "You said the judge is likely to contest an election for governor. I presume that's for the St Petersburg District?"

"Correct."

"Do you know if the judge has even higher political ambitions, higher than governor?"

"Correct again. We understand that to be the case."

"Another hunch, sir, I bet the judge is a female, am I correct?"

"Yes, Curtis, you are correct again, but what makes you think that is so?"

"As I said, just a hunch."

Curtis smiled so widely it altered the tone of his voice. Frenchy sensed that his subordinate was being a smart-arse. He decided to let it slide.

"Actually, more than a hunch this time, sir," Curtis continued. "Remember, I know Nelson. I know how he thinks. As I said earlier, it is a distinct possibility he is either a hit man, training terrorists or planning hits on political figures or potential leaders."

Frenchy was silent for a few moments whilst he contemplated how best to convey Bell's instructions. He was conscious of his obligations but needed to ensure a mistake would not be made that embroiled Bell or the government in an international crisis.

"Other than her name, Judge Angelina Vasilek, we don't have enough detailed information nor the support in place for you to undertake a mission like the one you have just completed." Frenchy chose his words carefully.

"Having said that, we believe it appropriate that you explore the options. There will be a great deal of investigative work to determine if a target actually exists. If Nelson or any other Australian citizen is indeed involved in clandestine and criminal activities in a foreign country. The purpose of your investigation, should you discover the same, is to determine if there is a way of — ummm — putting an end to the situation.

"Make no mistake, Curtis, you are very much on your own with this mission. Or perhaps as you seem to believe, a continuation of the same mission that I suggest you have just completed. As far as we are concerned you are totally off the grid with this.

"The earliest flight we can get you on is at 2010 tomorrow. One way. Air Italia. Unfortunately, it's a twenty-five-hour flight including a stopover in Rome. You will not need a Russian visa. Your Russian passport will be at the international flights check-in number seven at Bangkok Airport for collection by an Alexeev Lomot." Frenchy spelt the name and repeated it slowly in full for Curtis to memorise.

"Alexeev is probably derived from the Greek name Alexey, meaning 'defender'," Curtis said with a smile.

"Hmmm, if you say so. Contact me again when you have left Russia. Good luck."

With that, Frenchy was gone.

Chapter 29

Nelson relaxed in business class on the seven-hour Thai Airways flight to Dubai, enjoying delicious offerings of Thai cuisine. An entrée of satay king prawns, a main course of red curry chicken with steamed rice, followed by tropical fruits, all washed down with more than his share of Veuve Clicquot. He privately raised his glass in a toast to his Thai military recruits and the success of the Dao Shinawatra operation.

The French certainly know how to make the best champagne. Here's to the Thailand success. Here's to political certainty and stability in Thailand. Here's to the natural order.

He reached for a set of headphones in the pocket behind the chair in front, pushed his wide-bodied chair back into a comfortable semi-reclining position, and fitted the latest in padded headphone technology. Business class headphones have a stereo jack connection with noise cancellation circuitry. Perfect for listening to one's favourite music.

How good is this? Wallace rewards his consultants. Normally I wouldn't enjoy such small luxuries in cattle class. But he needs me. My success deserves such rewards. Good food, outstanding wine and easy listening music.

Nelson, the professional, reappraised the Thai mission. He closed his eyes and visualised the scene at the Nong Kae Railway Station.

The hot concrete platform devoid of any activity. Standing in the cooler shadow of the ticketing office. The train was now visible, still travelling at normal speed. He stepped out into the sunlight and sensed the train was slowly braking. He turned in the direction of the military barracks in the distance, above the palm trees. He was confident his men would be in place with his best and most appropriate sniper equipment for this location, geography and meteorological conditions taken into account. He had trained them well. He knew the spotter would have informed the shooter of his presence in case the latter, with a much narrower field of vision, hadn't seen him emerge from the shadows.

The train is stopping, supposedly to collect me. Exactly as required. I paid the driver enough to make it happen. He risked everything if he hadn't agreed to stop. I'm sure he realised that.

There she is. Precisely where she is supposed to be. The stupid woman is waving at me. Goodbye, Shinawatra. Get ready to meet your maker.

Nelson visualised the shattering glass. Through the cobweb, the haze and shards of glass flying into the carriage, he could just make out the waving hand disappear and with it the person to whom it was attached.

Job done. He smiled with satisfaction that everything he had planned — the recruitment of personnel, the training, the weapons, the location, the bribes and the timing — had proceeded just as devised. Working with the *Runda Kumpulan Kecil* group, the RKK small patrol units, had been easy. They wanted to learn. The hardest part was recruiting the soldiers but once on board they were loyal to the cause.

Professionals. They will be used again elsewhere if Wallace and his brother Edgar allow me to take full control. No interference. Just give me the targets and let me choose appropriate targets too.

"You are booked on an Emirates flight to Moscow at ten a.m. tomorrow, arriving Moscow just after two p.m.," Wallace told Nelson when they met at the exclusive Jumeirah Mina A'Salam.

"You will be met by Lumovski or one of his men. He will give you further details of the target.

"In the short time Lumovski has been a shareholder I have been able to understand what motivates him. It isn't about money. It isn't about improving the environment. It's more about the exercise of power and influencing people in powerful positions. Some may call it 'greed' because at the end of the day the influence reaps financial rewards, but Lumovski is already extremely wealthy.

"Lumovski very quickly realised what our objectives are and immediately helped us in Thailand. I told you about the Creighton accident, didn't I? He has invested in the company and has already invested in our plan. King Edgar's plan."

"King Edgar's plan, Jim? Do you call your brother King Edgar?"

"No, of course not." Wallace pouted his mouth in a characteristically contemptuous expression. "The philosophy of the first king of England," he scoffed. "A great man."

Wallace continued to outline his understanding of his newest friend. "Craig, you might not be aware but Lumovski has powerful friends. You have already met some of his people when we went to his compound. For his personal security purposes and for the security of his senior employees, Lumovski employs highly trained personnel previously in the *Spetsnaz*. Their controllers are former leaders of the renowned Alpha Group, previously part of the KGB. People not to be meddled with. I'm glad they're on our side.

"Lumovski's people will assist you in your new mission."

"Assist, Jim, or control?" asked Nelson.

"Assist. You will be in charge, Craig. It will be your plan. I have more confidence in you than a team I do not know. They might be strong, have all the attributes of good soldiers, but are they leaders?" Wallace's question was not directed to anyone in particular. "I don't know the answer to that but I do know you are proactive, can lead and get the job done.

"Lumovski wants to maintain the political status quo in Russia. He supports the current president and other political leaders. My guess is he can influence decisions to his financial gain.

"I understand his political friends are concerned about the growing public support of a Russian judge who may have her sights on the ultimate position. The presidency. She has made outrageous public statements in opposition to everything the Russian government stands for.

"Her liberal philosophy would be worse than a return to the communist era. She has even supported foreign organisations in opposition to the Russian leadership.

"According to Lumovski, Putin believes her to not only be a security threat but also an agent provocateur, or *agente provocatrice* as the French would say, inciting others to protest. Giving the loony left encouragement."

Nelson smiled at what he thought was a typically Australian expression. *Either Wallace has learnt Australian slang quickly or it's a universal expression, the loony left.*

"Russia has a strange legal system. The highest court of the land, the Supreme Court, has the power to present legislation to the Duma, the parliament of Russia. Although a regional judge, this woman has taken it upon herself to make recommendations to the Supreme Court on her pet lefty subjects. Mostly promoting feminism. Dangerous. She chooses her timing and subject matter carefully. A popularist."

"I know the type," Nelson opined. "She fits Groucho Marx's description. He once said, 'Those are my principles and if you don't like them, well, I have others' — that pretty much sums her up by the sound of it."

Wallace hadn't heard that quote before and promised to remember it for future use.

"Where is this woman based?" asked Nelson. "Is she in Moscow? Does she have the protection of the Moscow police or court police?"

"No, the task doesn't present those challenges. She is based in St Petersburg."

Nelson needed more information. "What is her name? Do we have a private address for her or just the courthouse address?" Nelson asked.

"The bitch!" Wallace laughed. "Lumovski calls her '*blyat*', which apparently has a stronger meaning than just 'bitch'. I think you and I would use the more accurate description of 'whore'.

"Seriously though, her name is Angelina Vasilek. You might not know this, Craig, but Angelina means 'God's messenger'. Her parents obviously had a sense of humour. She probably thinks she is a messenger from God. Your job will be to see that she gets to meet her God earlier than expected.

"The president regards her as a threat, Craig. Our friend and also the president's friend, Lumovski, believes she poses a threat to all of his friends and associates. End the threat, Craig. Maintain the natural order in Russia.

"Lumovski will provide all the information you will need. Addresses, future court hearings over which she is presiding, names of her enemies, and also her friends. You only have to ask and Lumovski will provide. He is very resourceful.

"The bitch thinks she is untouchable. A big fat ego. Apparently very popular because she is outspoken and is the people's politician. She walks the streets of St Petersburg without any protection. No security. Frequently dines out at low cost cafés just so she can be seen to be in touch with the ordinary people of Russia. But she is no ordinary person, Craig."

Wallace looked intently at Nelson, believing he could read his mind. "Yes, I know what you are thinking, Craig. An easier target this time."

"From what you have told me, Lumovski is impatient for results?" Nelson asked rhetorically.

"Absolutely! You don't have much time on this job. Lumovski expects quick action. The rewards will be huge," Wallace said as his thoughts drifted to Caribbean cruises and luxury hotels.

"I was thinking I do not have the certainty of my marksmen. I don't know if Lumovski's people are well trained, have the right equipment, and can be trusted to achieve what we just did in Thailand," Nelson added.

"So, what are you thinking?"

"Too early to tell how to approach this. I need to talk to Lumovski before going to St Petersburg. If security is as poor as you say, perhaps I might take an interest in court proceedings. Better still, perhaps I will start to use public transport," Nelson laughed. A heinous laugh.

Wallace understood the meaning of the last comment. For a moment he was unsettled by Nelson's macabre laughter. Only a moment. Wallace would not get his hands dirty. He appreciated Nelson's resolve. His uncompromising determination and animalistic hunger for success.

Yes, best leave the dirty work to others. Keep a distance between the action and me. Untouchable. Edgar and I are policy people.

"Is a public transport hit in busy St Petersburg wise?" Wallace asked.

"Yes, public transport might be best," replied Nelson coldly. "There will be collateral damage but as Ned Kelly said as the hangman's noose was placed around his neck, 'such is life'."

Chapter 30

Lumovski listened intently to Nelson's description of how he 'took down the woman in Thailand, Dao Shinawatra'. He was happy to claim total credit for the planning and the end result.

The two men sat in Lumovski's bulletproof black limousine at Sheremetyevo International Airport, the main airport situated approximately thirty kilometres from the Moscow central business district. The limo was parked in a loading zone at the end of a row of drop-off bays where cabs continuously unloaded outgoing passengers. An airport official urged the cabs to move quickly whilst other cabs were held in a line blocking ordinary traffic. It was a busy airport.

After waving at Lumovski's driver to move the vehicle, a gesture that was ignored, an exasperated security officer strode purposefully past the line of cabs towards the limo. The bodyguard opened his passenger door and climbed out as Security neared. He was a big man, the bodyguard. Security stopped in his tracks and fumbled for his two-way radio.

Not wanting to cause a scene or appear hostile, the bodyguard extended his right arm in a friendly gesture to shake hands. His big hand held a folded green consultancy fee that was surreptitiously passed to Security with a smile.

"I see you are busy unloading," Security quickly acknowledged, speaking in his native Russian. "Take your time, sir. We don't expect any trucks this afternoon."

Bodyguard nodded and retreated to the limo wherein both occupants of the soundproof rear of the vehicle were unloading verbally.

"Jim Wallace has told me a little about our new target, the judge." Nelson had decided enough was said about how good he was and the success of the Thai mission.

"*Blyat*, not a judge. *Blyat*, the bitch!" Lumovski shot back. "This woman encourages public discontent. My objective is to create harmony.

We need to be strong. That is the only way to end the discord in the community, the civil unrest caused by minorities such as the so-called Chechen separatists, for example.

"There are many examples of how this *blyat* has promoted civil unrest." Lumovski's usual dour demeanour had been transformed with excitement.

He continued with all the enthusiasm he could muster. "I'll give you an example. We have ways of dealing with homosexual men in our society. You have to understand we had to change the law and appear more tolerant for the rest of the world to accept us as a reformed society but behind the façade we will not tolerate this abominable crime. And nor should we. You wouldn't, would you, Mr Nelson?"

Nelson merely shook his head in agreement.

"We have places we send such people to in Chechnya for rehabilitation and re-education," Lumovski continued, invective spilling from his mouth.

"The *blyat* has encouraged public unrest on this issue. We have seen intolerable demonstrations in the streets of St Petersburg as a result of her speeches. Some Chechens have protested, alleging the existence of concentration camps. Led by the *blyat*, some *Leningradtsys* have protested.

"She has to be stopped. The *blyat* is gaining in popularity. You must understand how popular this woman is and what a threat she poses to stability in government. Her public comments often refer to, in her belief, our government's wasted expenditure. For that she receives public accolades. It's a nonsense. Our leaders do not waste the state's resources." Seemingly, without taking a breath, Lumovski had jumped from the treatment of gays to management of the government's finances.

Nelson patiently listened to the rant, not wanting to upset the oligarch by interrupting. *Wallace needs his money. I might need his other resources.*

"This woman is popular but dangerous to our society," Lumovski's tirade continued. "Popular and dangerous. She aspires to high office.

"Do you know what that would mean?" Without waiting for Nelson to respond, Lumovski continued, "I'll tell you. It would mean instability in our country. It would mean civil unrest. It would mean a society dominated by women. Yes, she is a radical feminist."

Nelson was keen to learn about the judge's personal and working habits. Her likely movements and asked, "I understand she has scorned the use of security personnel or even a court driver?"

"Of course. What would you expect? Only men are employed in security," came Lumovski's sarcastic reply. "She uses public transport, will not accept free tickets to the ballet or any such little benefit that usually attaches to people in her position. She is so damn righteous."

Lumovski is obsessed with the judge, thought Nelson, *and will do anything to curb her influence. 'Curb' is not the right word. Apply a stricture to her breathing more likely. I can handle that. As Wallace would say, maintain the natural order.*

Lumovski returned to his vituperative attack on the judge, repeating his immediate concern, "She wants the top job. Do you know what that would mean for my friends? We stand to lose everything. You may have heard of the traitor, Magnitsky. That former radical black US president even passed a law named after him. Good law-abiding citizens of Russia can't travel to the United States. The Americans are even thinking of preventing me from going to there to look after my investments.

"We are spending a great deal of time and money to convince the president of the United States to repeal the ridiculous law. The *blyat* would bring all of our good work undone. Treasonous. She is a traitor to Russia."

"Other than her political views, what else can you tell me about this woman?" Nelson asked, keen to have the subject return to the tactics and mechanics of dealing with her. "If she doesn't have security and travels on buses and trains that will make things easier."

Lumovski glared at Nelson and snarled, "You think you can do it all in Russia without help? Wrong! The good thing is the *blyat* believes she is untouchable. No need for security. That certainly makes it easier but you will need my people to help."

For the next fifteen minutes, Lumovski briefed Nelson on the assistance he could expect from his former *Spetsnaz* employees. He outlined a plan that he and his ex-Alpha Group leaders had devised. Nelson liked it.

"I shall embrace that strategy as long as I can choose the time, location and people involved," Nelson said.

"You will have my full support, but you don't have long and don't mess it up. This is too important."

Chapter 31

The night was black. No stars. An occasional glimpse of a waning gibbous moon mostly obliterated by heavy clouds. Light from flames in an open fire cast some dancing shadows. Enough light from within the small house to see the drunken episode. Again. Becoming more frequent.

Two shadows. One male, one female. One aggressor, one victim. The yelling had started immediately the aggressor had thrown open the door on the back verandah. He was shaky in the legs but stood twenty-seven centimetres, or ten inches in the old language, above the woman, fists clenched.

She knew it was coming and so did the boy. Both powerless to stop it. Fists rained as hard as the heavy weather outside.

A darker than usual night. Thunder echoed off the nearby hills. Rain fell heavily on the tin roof. From his corner in the kitchen he could see the shadows. Just the shadows, shimmering and dancing across moist eyes. Two shadows, distorted by the haze.

Flames licked the mallee roots and sent small sparks in search of something to grasp. Flickering light made the shadows dance and fall. The entire affect, twisting, flicking light combined with wet eyes made the body fall faster.

Fists still rained. Kicking started. The man wobbled with each kick and then he overbalanced and fell too. The boy could hear crying interspersed with screams of 'stop!'

The loudest scream woke Curtis in a lather of perspiration. His last vision was that of the cross hairs in a rifle telescope.

Curtis sat on the side of his bed, perspiration beading his upper body. The nightmare haunted him more frequently from the time he was assigned the mission in Thailand. His instructions were to protect Dao Shinawatra and in that regard he and Rat had been successful but it hadn't stopped the visions. It didn't help that he hadn't slept much in the last thirty-six hours. A long economy class flight to Moscow with a stopover in Rome was difficult to handle for a man of his size.

The travelling time and waiting at airports had one benefit. It gave Curtis ample time to use Google and Google Maps for researching information about St Petersburg. Curious, he had also checked the name, Alexeev Lomot. He was correct in his comment to Frenchy in respect of his assigned first Russian name. It was indeed derived from the name of a third century BC Greek poet. Defender and quick thinker were the meanings attached to the name.

I can handle that. Frenchy has given me a compliment but the attached surname reveals his thinking. Lomot. Russian for 'hunch'. Give me a break, Frenchy. I trust my instincts. By now you should too.

He chuckled at Frenchy's tactlessness. His raffish insensitivity.

Rude. Will he apologise or have more respect when I prove my hunch?

Curtis had booked into the four-star Courtyard Marriott Hotel on Vasilyevsky Island near the Malaysia Neva River. More upmarket than he was used to. At the height of the tourist season cheaper accommodation was hard to find.

From the hotel Curtis looked across the water to the busier part of the city. The beautiful city of St Petersburg, home to the magnificent Hermitage Museum of art and culture. The second largest art museum in the world directly across the river houses the world's largest collection of paintings. The Hermitage also includes the Winter Palace, home to many Russian emperors and empresses including Catherine the Great who was responsible for the establishment of the museum.

Ironic. Perhaps there is something in the St Petersburg water? A tough, uncompromising leader who became Catherine the Great. An outspoken and obviously strong female judge who aspires to leadership and with a little help will hopefully make it.

Entrance to the museum is free on the first Thursday of each month. It is also the week of an annual event, the Festival of the Arts. Not surprisingly a large number of tourists visit St Petersburg at that time of the year, making accommodation at a premium.

The city is crowded. That might create a problem. I need to find the judge. More importantly, I need to find Nelson.

Despite the lack of sleep, Curtis made his way to the hotel gymnasium on the eighth floor, unsure if it would be open at 0430. It was. The gymnasium wasn't the best equipped he had ever experienced, certainly not as good as the gymnasium at the Grand Centara in Hua Hin, but it would do. It had the essential equipment, even if a little outdated and inadequate.

He was joined by several older people after some time and was surprised to see them working out so early in the morning. He continued to pump iron — again turning heads — whilst waiting for a treadmill to become free. Several people watched as the larger than average automaton seemingly jogged across Europe.

One of the onlookers was an older man who clearly did not spend a great deal of time on a fitness programme. His ample belly overlapped the elastic on his shorts. He wore a pale green polo shirt bearing a small boxing kangaroo emblem. A receding grey hairline emphasised his furrowed brow. A look of head-scratching discombobulation.

Alighting from the treadmill, Curtis merely smiled in his direction and walked to the water fountain to replace some of the liquids he had discarded in the previous two hours.

"It's important to workout, to defeat jet lag, but your performance takes exercise to another level," the stranger said to Curtis's back, in admiration of the big man's effort.

Curtis gulped down his third plastic cup of water. He recognised an Australian accent, turned and noticed the emblem. He smiled again.

"What makes you think I might have jet lag?" a grumpy Curtis asked with a practised Russian accent.

"Just a guess. I'm sorry. None of my business really. I was in the Lobby Bar having a drink when I saw you arrive last night and head to the reception counter. You looked rather tired and I guessed your appearance was from travelling."

"Was it that noticeable? I see you are an Australian so I suppose you would know," Curtis replied. "You are a long way from home."

"Yes, I'm an Aussie. I travel a great deal and sadly about the only time I get to a gymnasium is when I'm staying at a hotel. Please accept my apology for being so presumptuous."

The Australian thrust his hand forward, eager to accept the big man's forgiveness.

"Geoffrey Coolidge is my name. Perhaps I can buy you a drink later? I haven't met many locals in St Petersburg with whom I can have a conversation. Most people either don't speak English or lack the confidence to use it."

"Alexeev Lomot. Pleased to meet you."

Curtis gripped Coolidge's hand with his usual vice-like firmness. As he pulled his hand away Coolidge absent-mindedly looked at his hand as if expecting to see protruding pieces of bone.

"Are you a local?" Coolidge asked, picking up the Russian accent.

"I was born in Moscow and have lived in Russia most of my life," Curtis lied, "but now I live in Australia."

"What brings you back to Russia?"

"I always visit St Petersburg at this time of the year to attend the Hermitage Arts Festival. What about you? What are you doing in Russia?"

Curtis was uncomfortable with answering questions from this stranger. He wanted to shift the focus of the discussion back to Coolidge.

"My company, Green Solutions, has an agreement with the government of St Petersburg. But why don't we chat over breakfast?" Coolidge added. "I can tell you about the exciting business in which I am involved."

"Are you travelling alone?" asked Curtis, "or are you with others from your company?"

"No, I'm on my own."

"Okay, let's have breakfast then. In, say, forty-five minutes. I'll meet you in the breakfast dining room."

During a long hot shower, he contemplated how he might deal with this fellow, Coolidge, quiz him about the real purpose of his visit. Ascertain if anyone else from his company was planning to be in St Petersburg and if so, who and for what purpose.

Curtis dressed in jeans, a long-sleeved dark blue casual pullover and brown leather RM Williams boots. Appropriate for this time of the year he also wore tight-fitting long thermal underwear. It was probably several sizes too small but thermal underwear was difficult to find in his size. He carried a fur-lined jacket for additional wind protection later. He made his way to the Pierrot breakfast restaurant.

Strong Java coffee was available. Just the way he liked it. He thumbed through the menu whilst waiting for Coolidge to join him. The lunch and dinner menu made reference to the Australian dessert named by Bert Sachse in 1926 after the famous Russian ballerina by the same name, Anna Pavlova, when she visited Australia. He was pleased the hotel acknowledged the history of this iconic Australian dessert.

"It tastes just as good as a homemade Pavlova too," Coolidge said as he walked past Curtis and took his seat.

"You have tried it?" Curtis resumed his Russian accent.

"Indeed, I have. I have been here for only two days but I have eaten it twice already. Nothing like good old Aussie cuisine."

Methinks you could probably do without so much sugar, Curtis reflected on Coolidge's appearance in the gymnasium.

The waiter appeared and Curtis ordered a large American-style breakfast of sausages, a 300gm sirloin steak, mushrooms, hash browns, crispy bacon, three fried eggs easy over, and toast. Not content with the French-style offerings of heavily buttered croissant chosen by Coolidge.

More coffee arrived. Having already told Coolidge about his purpose for visiting St Petersburg, Curtis wanted to avoid further discussion on the subject. He was anxious to hear what Coolidge had to say about his visit and his company.

"So, tell me, Mr Coolidge," the Russian accent kicked in again, "what is this agreement you talked about? Did you say an agreement with the district government?"

"Geoffrey. Call me Geoffrey. Yes, I signed an agreement with the governor. It means the government will purchase Green Solution's technology and use it in all buses, diesel trains and trucks. Having said that, it is only a heads of agreement at this stage and requires my company to establish a warehouse to store our products."

"Is it your private company?" Curtis asked, knowing the answer.

"No, I'm a shareholder but I work for the company. I'm responsible for the procurement of materials that go together to make the end product — the ingredients if you like — and I handle all operational matters."

Curtis asked Coolidge to explain more about the technology, how it works and where the company operated. He received a thorough explanation of the technology, its purpose, where Green Solutions sold its products and details of recent successful trials.

"Are you making good money out of this business?"

"We are selling some product and expanding rapidly into new markets. I probably shouldn't be saying this but, to be honest, my only concern is that our burn rate is high. There is huge upside to the business though."

"Why is your burn rate high?"

"The CEO tells me our working capital is largely spent on marketing. Although I am a qualified accountant and could therefore take on the role of financial controller, the CEO doesn't want me in that role. I guess he thinks I am more valuable in managing the logistics."

"Perhaps he likes to control the finances himself for whatever reason. Is your company — what is the company name again?" Curtis knew the name but he was on a fishing trip and wanted the bait to drift slowly towards the catch.

"Green Solutions."

"Of course, you did say that. You told me your technology reduces fuel consumption. Is your company involved in any business other than producing fuel additives?"

"We're not just producing and marketing fuel additives. That's just part of the process to reduce fuel consumption and emissions. It is important to recognise we sell a procedure. As I said, we have a particle purging technology as well. Use of the whole system maximises the benefits."

Curtis said he understood. "But are you in any other business? I have known chief executive officers, who are the principal shareholders, to use company funds on the development of a secondary business. It occurred to me that might contribute to your burn rate."

"Not as far as I'm aware," Coolidge replied.

"It sounds like an exciting business. My family invests in companies that have an environmental purpose. We are shareholders in an Australian company called Eco-Safe Technologies. for example."

Curtis had recently read of the valuable work the Victorian company was doing in the area of odour control. He sounded genuine.

"Are you looking for investors? If my family or my Russian friends wish to get involved in an eco-friendly business like yours, is that possible?" Curtis asked. His objective was to find out as much as possible about the company and the people behind it. Already Coolidge had provided more information than he expected but none of it was useful to ascertain the objective of those involved. He was looking for a weakness.

"Over the last few months, we have been actively raising working capital but I believe that is no longer necessary," Coolidge replied. "We have recently secured a major Russian investor. In fact, the financial planner behind much of the company's fundraising is apparently here in St Petersburg at the moment. Craig Nelson. I haven't seen him and don't expect to, not that I'm losing any sleep over that. I don't particularly like the man."

Curtis intentionally and quizzically raised his eyebrows to elicit a response from a talkative Coolidge. The latter did not follow Curtis's philosophy.

Born with one mouth and two ears means one should listen twice as much as one talks. You learn by listening, not by imparting one's own thoughts.

Coolidge laughed at the quizzical look. "Yes, perhaps your relatives or friends are already involved," he said.

"Give me a name and I will tell you. Did this Nelson fellow present to the investor?"

"I'm not sure how Nelson was involved. Unfortunately, the principal of Green Solutions doesn't include me in many of the discussions."

"The investor?" Curtis asked again.

"Oh, yes. The investment came from a Russian company called Meshech Alliance."

"That sounds familiar. One of my cousins has a company with a name like that. Do you know who is behind Meshech?"

"Is your cousin's name Lumovski?"

"No. Obviously a different entity."

Coolidge had unwittingly confirmed Lumovski's involvement in Green Solutions.

Nelson is working with him. Lumovski has 'skin in the game'. Investment in Wallace's business. Probably not just corporate involvement. He has the money and the muscle to meet their crazy objective. Perhaps Thailand. Perhaps elsewhere.

Whilst Coolidge was busy outlining the nature of the business in which he was involved, Curtis chewed vigorously on his breakfast. He now emptied his third mug of strong Java with just a dash of milk.

"When are you departing St Petersburg, Geoffrey?" he asked as he stood to leave.

"Tomorrow morning. I'm catching an early flight direct to London."

"Perhaps we will have time for that drink you were talking about earlier. I'll be in the Lobby Bar at about eight p.m. I hope to see you then."

They shook hands again and both went their separate ways after charging breakfast to their respective rooms.

The unexpected encounter at the gymnasium had reaped some rewards, however minor. Curtis was satisfied with the morning's work so far.

Chapter 32

Nelson is a step ahead of me. No, not a step, a mile. He has been in St Petersburg for several days. No doubt he has a plan by now. I need to get to work. Quickly.

Curtis had to find a way to talk to the judge but first had to locate the courthouse. In a large city with several courts that wasn't going to be easy. Understanding a little of the language helped. He had to break his rules of investigation and ask for help from a complete stranger. The hotel concierge was his best bet.

"Can you please tell me where the main courthouse is located?" he politely asked the concierge.

"What is your legal problem, sir? I have a cousin who is a lawyer and will be able to help you. A very good lawyer. Always wins his cases."

"I don't have a legal problem — I would just like to visit the court."

The concierge smiled knowingly.

An embarrassed man. He most definitely has a problem and obviously a big problem. He is too embarrassed to admit it.

"Don't be concerned, sir. I have referred many people to my cousin. His fees are very reasonable too."

"I told you, I don't have a legal problem. I just want to visit the court as a tourist and don't require a lawyer." Curtis firmly reinforced his position with a step closer to the concierge's desk, a raised voice and it seemed to the concierge, an aggressive demeanour.

To the concierge, the last statement, borne as it was with a harsh tone and stern look, confirmed the big man's need to attend the court was almost certainly as a result of a grave crime. Something more serious than a mere misdemeanour. Tourists don't attend court.

Given the size and apparent attitude of the guest, the concierge decided discretion was the better part of valour and chose to cease touting for clients on behalf of his cousin. Without removing his eyes from the big 'criminal' staring down at him, he reached under the counter and produced a map of the city.

"I'm more than happy to help, sir. These are the courts," he said as he used a lime-coloured highlighter pen to mark the approximate location of the Primorsky District Court, the Charter Court, the Kalinin District Court, the City Court of Arbitration, and the Mirovyye Sud'I, naming each court as he marked the map. The concierge then looked up and gazed nervously at Curtis who in turn merely shrugged his shoulders.

"The criminal court is obviously the one you are looking for, sir," concierge unthinkingly commented.

"What makes you think that?" Curtis laughed. "I'm actually looking for a judge who I believe may be a relative and would merely like to see her whilst I'm in St Petersburg."

"My sincere apologies. Err, I just assumed—" the concierge tailed off.

"Judge Angelina Vasilek. Have you heard of her?"

An embarrassed concierge joined the laughter. Still nervous he replied, "Yes, everyone knows of our judge. She is a favourite with the majority of *Leningradtsys*."

Curtis assumed a *Leningradtsy* was a resident of St Petersburg but a furrowed brow caused the concierge to further explain.

"Many of the older folks of St Petersburg, those who lived here during the soviet time, mostly still call our city Leningrad and a resident a *Leningradtsy*. Locals are increasingly referring to a man as a *Peterburget*. Such people would refer respectfully to our Judge Vasilek as a *Peterburgenka*. I'm surprised you don't know that, Mr Lomot?" The last comment delivered as a rhetorical question with raised eyebrows that horizontally creased his forehead and created vertical lines between the brows.

Curtis ignored the question and drew his eyebrows together also causing a deep furrow of the brow. He was not aware his assumed name was known beyond the reception and Coolidge. The concierge noticed the change of facial expression and quickly responded.

"We have a very high standard of hospitality in our hotel, sir. We make it our business to know the names of as many guests as possible. I had to check your name when your friend gave me your description, wanting to confirm that you are staying here. I was pleased to help him, Mr Lomot."

Coolidge is checking on me. Or was it someone else?

"Did my friend give his name?"

"No, sir, he didn't leave his name. He asked for your room number but, of course, I would not divulge such information. He said he would call back this afternoon to see you."

"Describe my friend."

"Not a *Peterburget*, a different Russian accent. Sounded like a *Moskvich*. About 195cms, 120 kilos. Short dark hair, perhaps a number 2 haircut, maybe 5 or 6mm. He looked really physically fit, just like you, Mr Lomot. Not as tall as you but I would guess he works out just like you."

Very observant man. Definitely wasn't Coolidge, but who? Nelson? Maybe, but I can't imagine Nelson attempting a Russian accent let alone sounding like someone from Moscow.

Curtis questioned the concierge about the court where Judge Vasilek would operate. He gathered as much information as possible. The name of the court, a description of the building, it's precise address, directions for getting there, best means of transport, a description of the Honourable Judge and her office telephone number. Satisfied, Curtis gave him a healthy tip in US dollars. Eyes darting around the lobby, he left the hotel.

Although walking distance to the courthouse was not far by his standards, Curtis decided to take a cab. The concierge hailed the cab on his behalf and gave an address.

"Mirovyye Sud'I Court," the driver was instructed.

Curtis didn't recognise the street names but he heard the concierge mention number seventeen. The same address highlighted on the map.

"Are you sure that is the right place?" Curtis asked. He understood enough Russian to know the name given to the cab driver was the Court of the Justices of the Peace.

"Of course, sir," the concierge replied. "The driver told me to tell you he had another job so you should make up your mind if you want him."

At that insistence, Curtis squeezed into the front seat and fastened his seat belt. Before he had completed pulling a recalcitrant belt over his broad chest and buckled up, the cab lurched forward, gears crunched and the car hopped a short distance away from the hotel entrance. It found its rhythm and a grim-faced driver accelerated.

The cab roared past the Children's Hospital and the University of St Petersburg before stopping abruptly on a tree-lined street in front of an uninspiring brown brick building. It was devoid of grandeur, unlike many of the other buildings in the central business district. Not even a hint of resplendence. Curtis was aware many government buildings in Moscow were similarly drab but had not expected the same of a federal government building in this grand city. The government had spent enormous sums to make St Petersburg attractive to tourists.

"Please wait," Curtis instructed as he opened the cab door.

The driver protested in vain, saying something about money. Curtis didn't hear him, or didn't want to hear him as he slammed the door. Without hesitating he rushed across the pathway to the building entrance. Through the glass door he approached the receptionist's desk and asked to speak to Judge Vasilek's secretary. The receptionist looked at Curtis as if he had two heads.

"Whom do you want?" she asked.

"Judge Vasilek's secretary," Curtis repeated.

"You have the wrong court, sir. This is the Court of the Justices of the Peace. If you are looking for Judge Vasilek or her secretary you want the federal court, the General Jurisdiction Court."

Damn incompetent concierge. I thought it might have been the wrong court.

The receptionist wrote the address of the General Jurisdiction Court onto a note pad, tore the page free and with a cavalier wave passed it to Curtis, turning away.

Curtis rushed from the building and crossed the road to where the cab was parked, engine still noisily throbbing and intermittently missing a beat. Time was of the essence. He passed the slip of paper to the now very annoyed cab driver and urged him to proceed with haste.

"I waste my time on short trips with you. I miss out on long fares," exclaimed the driver.

"Where I come from you are obliged to take a fare no matter where the passenger needs to go," Curtis snapped. "I'm paying good money. Now get moving. You are wasting my time!"

The driver threw the vehicle into gear, another loud crunch, and it again leapt forward for twenty metres before finding some rhythm. The driver looked like a frightened gazelle. The cab almost took flight.

Grumpy is doing his best to make this ride as rough and uncomfortable as possible. Care factor? Zero.

Upon arrival at the court, Curtis paid the required fare plus a small gratuity. The cabby looked incredulous at what he obviously saw as a meagre offering.

Curtis noticed the cabby staring at his hand and said "Too bad. That is all the cumshaw you're getting. Take it or give the whole damn amount back and take a hike." He was in no mood to bicker over the tip. He pushed the passenger door, which was clearly in need of oiling, and left the vehicle, not bothering to thank the driver. There was a more important matter on his mind. A woman's life.

Stepping onto the footpath, Curtis hesitated then cautiously made his way to a park directly opposite the entrance. He gazed back at a large eggshell white building with flax coloured trimmings. Large Roman Tuscan styled columns stood either side of the grand entrance. To Curtis they appeared to be free standing. For aesthetic purposes only, adding to the grandeur of the building. This was a far more impressive structure than the courthouse he had just visited.

He casually walked across the freshly cut grass towards a park bench. The park was several acres in size, large enough to accommodate neatly trimmed spruce and birch trees. Some children played with a soccer ball on a grassed expanse. Others climbed wooden structures and still others screamed with delight as they swivelled and swirled on playground equipment presumably supplied by the city government. Mothers watched on, seated on picnic blankets and park benches.

Occupying a bench for some thirty minutes, he watched for any sightseers that might look out of place. Always vigilant and even more so today because he had an uncanny sense he'd been followed. Not as strong as his usual hunches but a hunch nevertheless. There was nothing obvious, just the occasional attorney entering the building with trolleys of files. He stood, stretched, casually gazed around one last time, and then slowly crossed the road and entered the building.

He needed to ascertain the physical layout of the establishment. Where precisely was the judge's office located in relation to the court entrance? How did she enter the building, front entrance or rear door?

Before asking for details of the judge's office, as best he could with limited knowledge of the language, Curtis read the daily hearing list to ascertain if Judge Vasilek was dealing with any matter. The judge's name was not listed.

Not hearing a matter today. Hopefully she is in her office.

Uninhibited by security or court staff, probably because he gave the appearance of being in control, seemingly owning the place, Curtis roamed the corridors searching for Judge Vasilek's chambers. The marble tiled floor gave way to timber planks at the entrance to small courtrooms and meeting rooms. The larger courtrooms were distinguished by solid oak doors surrounded by timber columns. Inlaid gold lettering on the door announced the significance of the room.

Nearer the court and meeting rooms, members of the Bar Chamber, attorneys at law and their assistants were intensely discussing matters important to the next court sitting or a mediation meeting shortly to be conducted. Some didn't even notice Curtis shuffle past. Others only gave him a passing glance, intent on their own deliberations.

He found Judge Vasilek's chambers near one of the small courtrooms in a narrow corridor towards the rear of the building. Wanting to familiarise himself with the building layout and check for any security measures in place, he walked past the office to the end of the corridor. He peered in both directions at the T-junction. An 'Exit' sign was illuminated at the end of the shorter side corridor. There was no activity in this area.

Curtis returned to the entrance of the judge's chambers and knocked. No response. He knocked again. Nothing. Curtis turned the doorknob and edged his way into the office.

He immediately understood why there was no response to the knocking. The judge's secretary was busy typing. A solid woman in her forties. A more than ample buxom blond. The signs of early greying at a parting in the centre of her forehead. Her facial features gave a stern appearance. High cheekbones and what would best be described as a bulky nose. A contrasting striped embroidered cream and white blouse was conservatively buttoned under her chin.

She wore earphones connected to a Dictaphone. The only sound was light tapping on the computer keyboard, surprisingly light for the size of her hands and fingers. There was an occasional muttering, a click of the foot on a sensor pad that stopped the Dictaphone's operation. Another click rewound the tape and the typing continued. She looked and acted with a no-nonsense attitude.

Curtis audibly cleared his throat. No response. Louder, he said, "Excuse me, ma'am."

Nonchalantly the secretary raised her head and slowly removed the headset.

"Yes?" she scowled.

Curtis noticed the secretary's name on a large tag held by a silver chain around her neck. Valeriya. He used her first name in explaining that he had an important matter of a deeply personal nature that he had to discuss with the Honourable Judge. That comment only elicited a grunt and the roll of eyes. He persisted, stressing the importance of the matter. Not important to him but of considerable importance to Her Honour and her future standing in the community.

"Judge Vasilek is a very busy woman," Valeriya said. "She is not here today but, in any event, she does not have time to meet with every person who walks in here off the street claiming to have matters of importance to discuss. Even matters of national importance," she said sarcastically. As she spoke, Valeriya raised both hands in a gesture of dismissal.

Curtis knew the sarcasm was intended to dismiss him from the room.

"How did you get in here anyway?" An afterthought.

It was Curtis's turn to remain silent on that question. Instead he asked if it might be possible to make an appointment to meet with the judge as soon as possible. "I cannot stress enough the importance of this matter," he firmly responded. "I'm sorry but I will not leave until I have an appointment. Where is the judge today?"

Valeriya could see this man was not going to take 'No' for an answer. She emitted a loud sigh. Not wanting to reveal too much about her employer's movements, she told him to return in the afternoon and talk to the judge's associate. She was currently unavailable but would be in the office after two p.m.

Certain the secretary wouldn't be forthcoming with more information he didn't even bother to ask about the judge's residential address. There was no option other than to return to see the associate. He smiled disarmingly at the taciturn, restrained secretary and politely thanked her for her time.

Whenever Curtis entered an official building, even a familiar one in Australia, he would scan the outside perimeter and internal corridors to locate closed-circuit television cameras. He had checked the corridors near Judge Vasilek's chambers. Not unexpectedly, CCTV cameras were placed at regular intervals in the main corridors and strategically located in the main reception area.

They look as if they were installed a long time ago, at least not recently. An old system. Probably point to point. I doubt they would have facial recognition technology in place. But at least they have CCTV.

It was mid-morning. Time to kill. The Hermitage Museum would certainly be a good place to visit. Apart from housing the largest collection of paintings in the world it consisted of magnificent historical buildings, one of which was the Winter Palace, former home of Russian emperors. If Curtis was to meet with Coolidge tonight, he needed to sound convincing about his reason for being in St Petersburg. A visit to the annual arts festival was imperative.

In Palace Square, people were gathering in large numbers and groups for guided tours. Some were moving in the direction of the General Staff Building where the French impressionist paintings are now held and others into the Hermitage itself. Nothing much overawed Curtis but he stood in the square for some time gazing in awe at the majestic dusty green and white state museum.

A guided tour would have him meander slowly along the many kilometres of corridors. He didn't have time for that. He entered the complex through the Great Courtyard and followed a tour group to the magnificent Jordan Staircase. The opulence was overwhelming. He heard the tour leader describe the grand entrance as formerly the Ambassadorial Staircase where foreign envoys were meant to be, and were no doubt, impressed by the wealth and power of the Russian Empire as they made their way to the staterooms for official functions.

Curtis pushed past the group and entered the War Gallery of 1812. He knew his French history and was keen to study the portraits and uniforms of the military commanders who were involved in the defeat of Napoleon's force. The centrepiece of the room featured Tsar Alexander I gloriously astride his white stallion, ironically presented to him as a gift by Napoleon himself. The victorious tsar was riding into Paris.

Tchaikovsky's 1812 overture pounded strongly in his head. The overture was written to commemorate the victory over Napoleon by the mighty Russian forces in defending Moscow.

After twenty or so minutes in the War Gallery it was time to explore the corridors and art in the numerous rooms. Having collected a brochure and map of the Hermitage exhibits from the hotel concierge earlier, Curtis was keen to see some of the exceptional pieces of work. The Rembrandt collection. In particular his *Return of the Prodigal Son*. Leonardo da Vinci's work, *The Madonna Litta*. Picasso's paintings including the *Two Sisters*. All of these are in the top ten most popular, famous and valuable held by the museum.

The hotel brochure had a striking copy of Thomas Gainsborough's *Portrait of a Lady in Blue*. That centrepiece jumped off the pages at Curtis. Caught his eye. The featured lady bore a striking resemblance to a photograph he had seen of his mother when she was young. Before the already troubled marriage worsened and added to her appearance in a negative way. The dark rings around her eyes, stress lines, and scars.

Curtis stood near the *Two Sisters* and stared fixedly at the image on the brochure. A striking likeness to the image he remembered seeing in a family photograph album.

"Do you need assistance?" a female security officer asked in English but with a heavily laden Russian accent. "I can point you in the right direction if you like?"

Startled at the husky, almost masculine voice of security, Curtis responded, "No. I have a very good map, thank you. I should be able to find my mother."

"Your mother? Your mother is on the map?"

"No, not really. Just a very good likeness," Curtis laughed.

Security looked puzzled by the expression, apparently not understanding what this large man was telling her. She didn't join in with the laughter but merely shrugged her shoulders and returned to her seat by the corridor entrance door. From there she could watch tourists hovering around the priceless works of art.

I suspect nobody would dare get too close to the paintings lest Stalin's sister scolds them or worse. Look at those forearms and biceps!

Curtis waved in Security's direction before making his way down the corridors to the Gainsborough exhibition.

There seems to be a reminder of that horrendous domestic violence almost daily of late, Curtis thought. *I, nevertheless, want to see the likeness, a positive reminder of my dear mother.*

Curtis returned to the General Jurisdiction Court at two p.m. on the dot and immediately encountered a problem. A minor problem compared to what was soon to happen.

The judge's secretary was still busy typing. She still wore a headset connected to the Dictaphone, typing Judge Vasilek's latest opinion on a civil matter to be delivered at the end of the week. A lengthy judgement.

Her eyes flashed at Curtis as his shadow loomed over the reception bench in her direction. "Judge Vasilek is in Moscow." The secretary scowled in annoyance and in that short sentence provided more information than she had hitherto given. "Judge's Associate has not returned to the office. She may have decided to take the day off work."

"I must speak to her. Now!" Curtis raised his voice, becoming anxious. He took the plunge. "It could be a matter of life or death. The judge's security is being threatened. I need to talk to her. I need to help her."

The secretary laughed, shook her head and waved her arm dismissively. "Don't be ridiculous. Our judge is very popular. Who would want to harm her?"

It seems she is indeed popular but that could be the problem. Popular and electable.

"I have information which is cause for concern. Why take the risk? Please call the associate and let me talk to her."

"Okay. No harm in that. If I can reach her, I will transfer the call to the telephone on the side table." She pointed towards several chairs. A small oak coffee table buttressing the end chair held a telephone extension. Curtis didn't move. Secretary dialled a number and again pointed towards the chairs. Curtis still didn't move. He was sharp of hearing and listened intently to a ring tone followed by a distant clicking sound and a recorded message.

"Just as I guessed." Secretary exhibited annoyance this time. "The associate has taken the day off and will be in the office tomorrow. She usually starts work early. I suggest you be here at eight a.m."

There was nothing else he could do but return in the morning. Curtis thanked the secretary, turned on his heels and left.

Chapter 33

The corridors near the judge's chambers were poorly lit. Only a glimmer of light emanated from ornate Czechoslovakian crystal wall lights positioned periodically along the narrow corridors. As he approached the building exit, Curtis slowed his pace to allow his eyes time to adjust to the brighter light outside. The average person doesn't think of such matters and is blasted by brighter light after leaving a dark space, taking a minute or so to adjust during which time the individual sees very little, if anything. But Curtis is not your average person and was always prepared for potential surprises.

It was a beautiful day in St Petersburg. Cold, but clear blue skies. In the distant north there was a bank of high clouds drifting slowly towards Russia's second largest city. Not rain or snow clouds. Not nimbostratus. No threat. The weather did not impose any impediment to a brisk walk back to the hotel.

A white Chevrolet Cruz police car was parked directly in front of the courthouse, engine running. A wide blue stripe carrying the word '*Politsiya*' in reverse block ran the length of the vehicle. The police insignia was emblazoned in the centre of the front door. An officer occupied the driver's seat above the insignia waiting for his partner to return from a drop-off.

A tall, lean police officer, neatly dressed in a Marengo coloured uniform bearing two shoulder stripes signifying his status as a junior sergeant, brushed past Curtis as he took the final two steps to the pavement. The officer's weapon holster made contact with the side of Curtis's upper leg. He immediately apologised in his native language, however minimal the contact was.

Realising the officer was apologising, Curtis responded, "No problem. You're a busy man."

Turning to acknowledge the police officer he noticed a large black car turn the corner into the main street and accelerate rapidly. The bright afternoon sun caught the glint of a firearm protruding from the passenger's rear right-hand window. The opposite side from the driver.

As the first spray of bullets from the Kalashnikov semi-automatic machine gun hit the rear trunk of the police car, the echo reverberating off the building's concrete walls, Curtis threw himself at the police officer in front and to his left. A plunge like cornerback Sheldon Brown's hit laying out Reggie Bush when he was playing for the Philadelphia Eagles. A blind-sided tackle. Hit of the year. The officer went to ground heavily. Shielded by the car.

In one continuous action, Curtis pushed away from the stunned police officer, stopping just before he rolled from the kerb. Bullets continued to whistle past, some thudding into and ricocheting off the concrete behind him. Others tore through the car's metal, fibreglass and plastic.

Lying prone on his back, he swivelled to his right and saw the police officer struggling to his knees.

"Get down," Curtis yelled. "Stay down. I'll handle it." He had been trained for this type of action.

He knew the Chevvy had been severely riddled with bullets. The driver couldn't possibly survive the barrage. Curtis blocked out the sounds of people running and screaming. He had to stay focused.

He heard the squeal of tyres as the perpetrators roared into a U-turn about two hundred metres past the courthouse, crossing in front of oncoming traffic.

Here they come again. Who is the target? The police officer? Me?

From a partially prone position Curtis reached for the handle and wrenched the car door open. His fears for the driver were confirmed. He lay slumped to the passenger's side. Blood could be seen in two places on the side of his uniform. A lot of it. Curtis reached for the lifeless body and groped for the officer's handgun.

He won't need his firearm again.

Manoeuvring the pistol from the holster of a leaden body was awkward but he managed. Withdrawing the weapon from below the body he brushed against the belt holding a second magazine and retrieved that too. He snatched up the handcuffs lying on the seat next to the driver's head.

Just in case…

A great weapon. A 9mm Yarygin PYa Grach, semi-automatic with 18 in the clip. A second magazine. Probably one in the chamber. 37. I might need them all.

One's capacity to recognise and think of a myriad of things at a time of stress and crisis is amazing. All in the space of seconds. Curtis was familiar with the 'Grach' although, like most Russian police officers, he hadn't been trained to use it. No matter. He could use any weapon.

He thrust the second magazine into the front inner pocket of his leather jacket and the handcuffs into another pocket. On hands and knees Curtis scuttled towards the front of the car, police revolver gripped firmly in his right hand. The shooter's car was approaching more slowly now. The perpetrators knew they had immobilised at least one police officer and possibly two. This approach was to ensure the job was done. To empty another magazine into the police car and any curious or threatening heads that might emerge.

Curtis stayed low next to the front right wing. He could again see the barrel of a sub-machine gun protruding from the rear passenger window, directly behind the driver. Left-hand drive. On the opposite side of the road.

Slowing. Thank you. Thank you. Now, meet your maker.

Small bursts came from the behind the driver's head, ripping into the radiator guard and the front and side windows of the police car. Stray bullets shattered the strobe light bars on the roof.

Poor shooting. Too high.

Curtis rose on his knees to peer above the bonnet and returned a short burst. Just as he did, he heard shots ring out from behind. The second officer, against whom he had laid a brutal tackle and in so doing saved his life, had recovered enough to lay down some fire. He turned to Curtis, smiled and then winced. Broken ribs.

A single shot from Curtis found its mark. At the same time the police officer fired twice with his old Makarov pistol. The Makarov is being phased out in Russia. The most senior police are the first to receive the replacement now in Curtis's possession. The old Makarov is about as useful as an air rifle. One can probably throw the lead projectile further than the Makarov will send it. But on this occasion the junior sergeant made good use of it, twice penetrating rubber. The perp's car swerved violently to the right, jumped the kerb and charged into the park.

"Let's go!" yelled Curtis, taking control.

Seeing the mayhem up ahead, the traffic had stopped. Curtis raced across the road with the junior sergeant struggling to keep up. After ten paces the officer simply stopped running and grabbed his chest. He gasped but couldn't suck in enough air to satisfy his needs. He was struggling with short breaths. His chest felt like it was on fire. Curtis looked over his shoulder.

"Stay there. Leave this to me," he yelled.

The perp's car came to a sudden stop against the park bench that Curtis had earlier occupied. He sprinted across the concrete walkway into the grassed park, dodging past shrubs damaged by the out of control vehicle.

Obviously, the limo had been travelling at a speed sufficient to deploy the airbags as it smashed into the concrete block at the end of the park bench. Approaching the immobilised limo, he could see the airbags had now deflated. The driver was motionless. The rear passenger door on the opposite side of the driver was open.

Parents pushing prams in the park and others playing with toddlers froze. Stunned by the mayhem. Coolant steamed from the punctured radiator condenser creating a haze that impeded Curtis's clear view of the park ahead.

Tourists cringed in fright as a man wielding a sub-machine gun ran from the direction of the immobilised vehicle. Curtis saw him too, crouched into a shooter's position, and raised his pistol. But he didn't squeeze the trigger. The risk of collateral damage was too great. Too many spectators.

The sight of the big man pointing his firearm towards the crowded park set off a series of screams, adding to the drama. The shooter had escaped. Curtis lowered the revolver, turned back to the wreck and wrenched open the driver's door. He quickly extracted a bloodied body from behind the steering wheel and laid him on the grass unseeing eyes facing the sky. A familiar face.

The spotter from the attempt on Dao Shinawatra's life. That explains why the commanding officer at the NCO school in Thailand never contacted me after promising to check his prisoner for tattoos. He had escaped. Or, perhaps, set free?

Still struggling to breathe and trembling slightly, the second police officer stood nearby, just a few feet away, watching as Curtis rolled the dead man onto his stomach. He gripped the base of the deceased's jacket and pulled it over his head, tearing his shirt away in the process. Curtis then lifted the man's thermal undershirt and found the answer to the question he had asked the commanding officer — did his prisoner have a tattoo the same as the soldier he had shot on the roof of the NCO school? There it was. The same tattoo photographed and sent to Curtis by the CO.

He now knew he had been the target of the drive-by shooting.

Nelson knows he's been made but he won't know by whom. I've possibly been described to him. He certainly knows where I am staying but he won't have any idea if he is being hunted or who the hunter is. Time to move.

Curtis was sure the turmoil, the cacophony of noise, the rapid movements and his blind-sided tackle had meant the policeman didn't get a close look at him. Could only provide a partial description. Without offering any explanation and without looking at the bewildered officer Curtis strode away from the scene.

He had a thought. Stopping and without looking back, he yelled to the police officer over his shoulder, "Take the credit for this *moi drug*" (Russian meaning 'my friend'). "You can be a *geroy* [hero], good for *prodvizheniye* [promotion]."

With that he pocketed the revolver in his jacket, zipped it and buttoned the extra flap over the zip to the neck. A cool breeze had engulfed the area. Curtis walked briskly through the park as stunned onlookers started to gather their composure.

For some, curiosity got the better of them. They surrounded the bullet-riddled car, the body lying face down on the grass and the police officer, looking shaken but unscathed, patting him on the back for a job well done. Others couldn't get away from the scene quickly enough and rushed past Curtis in the direction of the far exit.

Chapter 34

Lumovski's jet sat on the tarmac at Pulkovo international airport, about twenty-three kilometres from the St Petersburg central business district.

The jet, a Gulfstream G550, had undergone serious modifications from the original design to permit long international flights. It accommodated a queen-sized bed and en-suite, a separate lounge partitioned from a galley and a dining area capable of fine dining for six people. It also featured a bar with a suitable range of cocktail mixers, spirits and quality wine, in a lounge with luxury leather seating for twelve people.

Nelson had placed a call to Wallace who was still in Dubai advising him he needed more time to execute his plan to make good on the latter's promise to Lumovski. Without going into detail, he told Wallace his plan required the careful selection of capable people to assist him. To follow his instructions.

He failed to tell Wallace he had been informed by one of his well-trained snipers from Thailand that his team had encountered a problem. The problem had been spotted at the airport. He needed time to deal with him. He couldn't divulge such information. Wallace would be furious and might end his involvement in restoring the natural order. His reaction would be predictable.

"No delays," Wallace had said. "Lumovski's target is our target and must be dealt with as quickly as possible. There is no time to go sightseeing in St Petersburg, Craig. Get the job done and do it quickly, without fuss and without a trace."

As was often the case when talking to Wallace, Nelson had been frustrated by an interruption. *There always seems to be a more important person with whom he must talk,* he pondered.

This time Wallace had an incoming call from the Russian oligarch. "I'll call you back shortly," Wallace told Nelson before disconnecting.

Nelson waited. Thirty minutes passed before Wallace resumed the call. His instructions were short and concise. He was told to meet the Gulfstream at St Petersburg's Pulkovo Airport, Terminal One.

***

When he entered the terminal Nelson immediately recognised one of Lumovski's musclemen, dressed in a black polo shirt, black-rimmed dark shades even though he was indoor, black jeans and black Yeezy military boots. Barrel-chested, massive biceps bulging the polo. Perhaps the head honcho.

A juicer. On steroids, surely.

With a nod of his head Muscle walked casually in the direction of a lounge door. He passed through the lounge and pushed on a door on the far side of the room. A sign above the door read 'Strictly No Exit'. Muscle ignored the sign, exited the lounge, stepping onto a concrete walkway and glanced behind to ensure Nelson was following. He was.

Muscle walked five paces stopped, stretched and gazed skywards. The sun appeared behind a bank of clouds. Muscle stood still, face turned to the sun soaking in the vitamin D whilst he had the opportunity. The sun was visible on few occasions at this time of the year. Nelson waited inside for Muscle's next move, contemplating whether he was extraordinarily tough and didn't feel the cold or just plain stupid. He decided he didn't wish to find out.

After a minute or so Muscle turned to Nelson, and with an arrogant manner spoke for the first time. "Come," he barked as he started towards a jet standing alone on the tarmac about one hundred metres away.

Nelson boarded the Gulfstream. The pilot greeted him and pointed to the lounge, inviting his passengers to make themselves comfortable for the flight to Moscow's Vnukova Airport. Formerly an international airport for public and commercial use Vnukova is the oldest airport in Moscow, now most frequently used by wealthy Russian businessmen with private jets. It is conveniently located near the M3 motorway with a direct and fast route into the city.

Upon arrival at Vnukova the Gulfstream taxied past a terminal shaped like a light bulb and came to a stop in front of a grey hangar.

Yellow snowplough trucks were lined up at the ready nearby. The pilot interrupted the whine of slowing jet engines by announcing their arrival. Muscle turned to Nelson and barked his second word, "Wait".

Nelson gazed out the window at grey clouds and a misty rain enveloping the 'light bulb' nearby. Airport workers moved slowly in their heavy-duty wet weather gear. He was happy to wait. It looked cold outside. It was cold outside.

Across the tarmac a black Mercedes Benz limousine came into view and drove past the line of snowploughs. A mobile staircase had been wheeled across from next to the hangar and pushed up against the Gulfstream. Cold air rushed into the passenger's cabin forcing Nelson to upturn his jacket collar as the aircraft door was opened by remote control.

Still gazing from one of the jet's passenger windows Nelson saw a heavyset man in a dark overcoat, collar upturned wearing a ushanka hat with the flap fastened on top alight from the limo's front passenger seat and open the rear door. The oligarch stepped out.

Lumovski climbed the stairs and entered his private jet, shaking moisture from his coat as he did so. Moving along the corridor without a word he waved dismissively at Muscle and reached for Nelson's hand. Muscle left the jet. After shaking hands, the two men sank into beige coloured soft leather chairs. Very comfortable.

No sooner had he sat, Lumovski was on his feet again. Gaze fixed on Nelson.

"Dringka?" he asked. "Vodka? I have the best."

"Thankyou. A small one." Nelson knew by now there was no point in refusing Russian hospitality. Vodka was always on the agenda for meetings, especially when a toast was likely to be in order.

The short, unshaved man with dark, deep-set eyes meandered to the bar, and opened a cupboard above the sink. He retrieved an unopened bottle of Faberge Art's Applied Craft Imperial Collection, Super Premium Vodka. "This is from Moskovskaya Oblasti (Moscow region)," he said as he poured the first glass. "Soft, smells like pine nuts. Very good and not expensive."

Opening the small bar refrigerator integrated behind a brown leather covered door and retrieving another bottle, Lumovski proceeded to pour a larger glass of cranberry juice.

The oligarch deposited both a nip of vodka and the juice on a table at Nelson's right hand. More sophisticated Russians like to drink a cranberry juice chaser, which apparently lessens the impact of the high alcohol content in the vodka. He turned and walked back to the bar. Whilst standing there he quickly downed a nip and then poured another before returning to take a seat opposite Nelson.

"Dringka!" he said.

Nelson responded by taking a sip and then a larger mouthful of juice. *Hmm, not bad*, he thought.

"Now tell me your plans," Lumovski ordered.

For the next twenty minutes, Nelson briefed the oligarch on his plans. He explained how he had spent three days observing the judge's movements.

"*Blyat!*" Lumovski snarled.

"Of course," Nelson responded with a smile. "A healthy tip for the doorman at her apartment block loosened his tongue. I learnt the judge… er… took her luggage case with her when she left the apartment this morning. A clear indication she was again visiting Moscow as she regularly did over the last few months, according to the doorman. He said the size of her case meant she would not be expected back for possibly a week."

"In Moscow," Lumovski interrupted. "Best chance."

Nelson knew what he meant but didn't intend to seek approval on how to do the job, only to seek his help, reluctantly. He needed men. Men who would carefully and thoroughly follow his instructions to create a diversion in order for the second part of his plan to succeed without the impediment of confronting the *politsiya*.

Outlining the plan drew a smile from Lumovski. Nelson had not hitherto seen the little dark-eyed Russian mafioso show any such emotion.

Lumovski clearly liked what he heard but nevertheless asked a question, "Why don't you simply use nerve agent poison? That has been successfully used on numerous occasions in other countries where our people don't want to create a scene or leave their prints over the alleged crime."

"Several reasons. Creating a scene is part of the purpose. We want the incident to be thoroughly reported. We would like to ensure the Chechen rebels are blamed for this atrocity. They have been quiet for a while. No harm in resurrecting animosity towards them."

"I like your thinking, Mr Nelson. Your planning is very thorough. My best men are at your disposal but don't put them at risk."

Nelson continued to provide the detail of how Judge Vasilek would be taken down. Unwittingly referring to her as 'the judge' again brought an angry reaction.

"*Blyat, blyat*! Bitch!" Lumovski hurled the words at Nelson. "Enough!"

Not entirely satisfied that Nelson had absorbed all he had told him previously, or perhaps it was because he was fanatical, Lumovski launched into a diatribe about feminism. He didn't refer to the natural order, a term adopted by Wallace and his team, but described to Nelson how gender discrimination is a way of life in Russia.

"The weak must never run our country. They must submit to the strength and dominance of Russian man," Lumovski told Nelson. "The *blyat* is a feminist. Her mentality is to be disruptive. She threatens our very way of life. She threatens our leaders by her public babble."

I don't need the rant, thought Nelson. *Doesn't this idiot know he is speaking to the converted?*

"I want you to know I'm not concerned about your attitude to the *blyat*," Nelson interrupted. "What you have to say about her makes no difference. It is my job to ensure she doesn't continue to agitate, that's all."

"Yes, I know you agree but I want to strengthen your resolve. You must know how important this is. What a danger to our society this woman is. She frequently makes public comments about so-called domestic violence and what she describes as 'gender discrimination'. The *blyat* hides her political fundamentalism behind language that may appeal to women, totally ignoring the rights of man.

"Our parliament, a democratically elected institution that reflects the views of the majority of Russians, has been criticised by the *blyat* for decriminalising so-called 'domestic violence'. You and I know there is no such thing as domestic violence. That woman is trouble. Imagine if she was elected to high office in our country. We must ensure that never happens."

"I agree," Nelson sighed realising nothing he said would stop Lumovski's rant.

"It doesn't bear thinking about," Nelson added. "Her attitude seems to be taking hold in some countries. I recently read about the prime minister of Iceland, for example. Katrín Jakobsdóttir, a radical greenie feminist."

"Don't worry about Iceland. A small country. A near neighbour but not near enough to be of concern. That woman will have no effect internationally but we must ensure those very same attitudes never take a hold in Russia. We are a powerful country and we influence the world economy and political decision-making.

"A crazy movement called 'hash MeToo', or something like that has developed in the United States over the last few years. Isn't it strange how some famous actresses have become involved in this campaign? Even some from your country. Unfortunately, it is spreading but it won't succeed here in Russia," Lumovski said with confidence. "It is led by aggressive women. Women opposed to sex or even the suggestion of some play in the workplace.

"Russia will not tolerate such ideological power-seeking behaviour. Fortunately, so far, many female Russian journalists have had the good sense to reject the 'hash MeToo' movement. They've seen it for what it is. It is a reflection of the decadence of American, Australian, English and other societies. Even Iceland. Our journalists understand that Russia is a much better nation with strong men in control.

"Yes, Mr Nelson. You will have all of the help you require to rid us of the *blyat* Vasilek and put an end to her movement. Do not let me down."

The last comment was delivered with a glare. Nelson was rarely intimidated but he felt a little uneasy at the tone of delivery. Almost threatened.

Hmm. Russian mafia don't play games. They probably have access to the nerve agent poison even if it is only available at military facilities. Knowing how disloyal Russian spies have suffered and died from their poison, I don't like the idea of being another victim. But I don't play games either. This task will not be difficult. A service to mankind.

Chapter 35

Despite the chill in the air, Curtis managed to work up a lather of perspiration as he walked at a brisk pace back to the hotel. His thermal underwear combined with the jacket was working a treat.

Entering the welcoming hotel lobby on the first floor and seeing the concierge, he recalled the conversation they had earlier in the day. The concierge said a friend had called to see him. The friend had described Curtis and asked for his room number. Concierge had acknowledged that such a man was indeed staying in the hotel but hotel policy prevented him from divulging the room number for Mr Lomot. The friend said he would return in the late afternoon.

My 'friend' apparently said he would see me this afternoon. I think he's already seen me.

Curtis strode purposefully across the lobby towards the Market Bar and Restaurant, intending to make a reservation for dinner. As he approached the entrance, he had a thought, turned on his heel and returned to the concierge's desk. The same young man was on duty but was in the process of handing over to the next shift.

"Good afternoon, Mr Lomot. Have you had a good day? Did you find the court? Did you see your relative, our judge? Is she a relative like you thought?"

The accent kicked in. "Yes... yes... no... not sure," replied Curtis. The concierge couldn't recall the order of his questions and merely shrugged his shoulders in response.

"If the friend that called this morning returns and asks for me, please do not call my room. Simply ask the housemaid on my floor to attend my room to inform me. I don't want you to mention my room number, just my name. Take your time, pretend to talk to reception and then tell him I have checked out."

The two men at the concierge desk looked puzzled.

"No questions. Just do as I say."

Curtis handed both a sizeable gratuity and walked away as they stared at the largesse in their hands.

That should seal it. Curtis smiled at the thought.

An hour and a half passed. Curtis showered, shaved and used the bath sheet, an oversized bath towel, to dry. As he finished the doorbell chimed and a loud voice yelled, "Housekeeping!" Curtis quickly pulled on a pair of stretch jeans. No time for other clothing. At the door one eye passed over the fish-eye lens and he stood quickly to the side, never allowing himself to become a target. It was indeed the housekeeper.

"Errr... Mr Lomot, concierge has asked... errr... me to errr... tell you there is a friend in the lobby asking about you," Housekeeping was flustered at seeing Curtis half naked. Averting her eyes, she added, "That's all, Mr Lomot."

"Thank you."

"You're welcome." She quickly walked away and as an afterthought said, "Have a good day, sir. It's cold outside."

Curtis smiled realising Housekeeping was making a reference to his lack of clothes. He quickly dressed in a clean thermal undershirt, jacket and his favourite RM Williams boots. He tucked the stolen police Yarygin pistol into the belt behind his back and rushed to the service elevator.

Having pressed the button, Housekeeping was standing by the elevator doors. "This is only the service elevator, Mr Lomot. You walked past the two main elevators just along the corridor."

"I know, but I'm sure you won't mind if I take this one to the basement," Curtis winked at her. "You see, the man in the lobby who wants to see me is a relative. He is always borrowing money from me. I have discovered he has a drug problem so I want to help him shake the habit. The best way to do that is to call him from outside the hotel and get him into a cab and then a rehab centre. I don't want to cause a scene in the lobby." *Quick thinking.*

Housekeeping had not heard of a rehab centre in Russia but who was she to question such a handsome man. A man with such a physique. She smiled and nodded approvingly.

Curtis weaved his way past cleaning trolleys, cleaning apparatus and laundry bags to find the basement 'Exit' door. Outside, he jogged up the ramp leaving the Marriott Hotel precinct on the side street. He turned right and right again, passing between the hotel and a nondescript office building. Had he turned the other direction his 'friend' could see him leaving the hotel. He jogged towards the Makarova embankment on Neva River.

The Marriott is on a corner. The hotel's main entrance is on Malyy Prospekt Vasil'yevskiy Ostrov, a major thoroughfare that runs towards the Neva River. Always prepared and thorough, Curtis had previously walked around the building to familiarise himself with the area.

Knowing the lay of the land is always helpful. If my 'friend' is professional he won't wait long. He'll soon realise he is being stalled and probably leave.

The Neva usually starts to freeze in late autumn but in recent years anomalously warmer winters meant this had not occurred until two or three months later. With an influx of tourists for the arts festival and warmer conditions than usual, river cruises were still popular.

Curtis was in luck. As he rounded the corner of the hotel onto the Makarova embankment, he saw a cruise vessel parked at the jetty. Tourists were disembarking and another larger group were standing to the side, waiting to be called aboard. Mingling with the tourists would give him a perfect view of the hotel entrance. The group waiting to board the vessel stood on the pathway that ran parallel to the main road and the embankment.

If I step down onto the jetty, I will be three feet lower and less conspicuous.

He didn't have to wait long. Two men appeared at the hotel entrance, took several steps towards the road and stopped. The taller man was dressed entirely in black and wore shades. He stood two feet taller than the other man. A giant hulk.

A good-sized target.

After looking in both directions and then scanning the small crowd of people on the pathway at the end of the road near the river, the hulk directed his portlier companion to a sports utility vehicle parked in a 'No Standing' zone across the road.

Curtis had hoped the man purporting to be his friend might be on foot and he could follow him. If not, he had hoped to learn something else about the man. Anything. He thought it likely the hulk was the same man in the drive-by shooting at the courthouse. He was of similar stature and from a distance appeared to be dressed the same.

The shooter, I'm sure of it. Come back for a second go have you, buddy? Finishing what you started? We'll see about that.

Traffic signals on the embankment changed colour and the traffic was momentarily stopped. The hulk and his companion took the opportunity to manoeuvre past the stationary vehicles. They climbed into the SUV, whilst Curtis pushed past the tourists and crossed the road. His objective was to get closer to the hulk's ride.

On a one-way road the hulk's car had to pass where he was standing. Taking care not to be noticed he peered down the road at the silhouettes in the front seat of the SUV. The hulk was gesticulating wildly. Making a strong point to his companion. Curtis waited. Suddenly the SUV's passenger door opened and the shorter of the two men climbed from the vehicle.

He looked to his left. There was a large gap in the traffic. He took several steps towards the hotel, stopped and looked to his right in the direction of the intersection with the embankment. Curtis could clearly see him before he disappeared inside the hotel.

Coolidge.

Curtis stepped out from the corner of the building. Still on the footpath he was in full view of the SUV's driver, the hulk.

Come and get me.

The driver saw him. At the intersection behind the SUV, on Malyy Prospekt, the lights had stopped the traffic. With ease the hulk pulled into the break in traffic, gunning his engine. He accelerated faster than one would expect of a SUV. A vehicle obviously mechanically adjusted to satisfy his requirements. As he approached the corner where Curtis stood apparently waiting to cross the road, he swerved onto the low kerb and mounted the footpath.

Curtis threw himself backwards behind the building out of harm's way. The hulk momentarily lost control of his vehicle as he jerked the steering wheel in the direction of his target. The car clipped grey brickwork. At the speed he was doing the building redirected his car across the traffic now moving along the embankment. Out of control, the car involuntarily swerved, but not enough to avoid the heavy-duty front bar of a lorry. The lorry flipped the SUV towards the river.

Observers would later report that the driver appeared to have collapsed over the steering wheel. Perhaps a heart attack. With the noise and commotion of a roaring engine, car brakes squealing to avoid the mayhem, and the piercing sound of metal on concrete and metal on metal, the observers did not hear gunfire. It was part of the confusion. The cacophony.

The first shot hit the driver in the head. A second shot exploded into the SUV fuel tank igniting the vehicle.

One less threat to Judge Vasilek.

Pistol replaced in the belt behind his back, not visible, Curtis stared at the scene in feigned amazement for a time, just as any bystander would.

After returning from his stroll in the park near the courthouse he had taken the precaution of using a hand-held technical device to remotely disable the closed-circuit television cameras attached to the building across from the Marriott. The hotel had cameras in the entrance but they would not provide a view of the action.

As police and fire-truck sirens wailed in the direction of the burning vehicle, Curtis casually strolled along the embankment and returned to the hotel from whence he came. No cameras in the service area.

Now, for the truth, Mr Coolidge!

Chapter 36

Curtis decided not to have dinner in the Market Bar, instead ordering room service. Warm prawn, peanut and mint salad followed by French lamb cutlets with anchovy, mint and young peas. Sweet potato cornbread was an accompaniment.

While waiting for his dinner to arrive, for the first time he switched on the television. A welcoming message for Alexeev Lomot greeted him. Curtis pressed the remote to change channels and commenced scrolling, looking for Cable Network News.

Breaking news. "Chechen rebels have been blamed for three separate attacks in Russia this afternoon," the newsreader announced. "An assault on the federal court in St Petersburg was foiled by a quick acting and brave police officer. Our Russian correspondent reported that a police officer was killed at the entrance to the court. We cross to St Petersburg and Simone Garcia. Simone?"

Simone Garcia stood at five feet nine inches (177 cm), wore her long black hair tied into a ponytail, dark eyes, full lips. She was dressed in dark blue slacks, a faux fur-lined jacket, and leather gloves. Looking up from her mini-iPad tablet, Garcia addressed the camera with confidence. When she opened her mouth to speak, she revealed large protruding top teeth that gave even greater definition to her lips.

The Hermitage Museum was in the background. Garcia was definitely in St Petersburg. Curtis concluded that she was unable to film the actual scene of the attack. Being a government building precluded the use of photography.

"Dramatic scenes at the federal General Jurisdiction Court in St Petersburg this afternoon as a vehicle, believed to have been stolen and occupied by Chechen rebels, twice drove past the court at high speed. Shots were fired at police standing guard," Garcia reported.

Just a little journalistic twist and exaggeration methinks. But then, why let the facts get in the way of a good story.

"One police officer was killed as bullets sprayed the front of the court," Garcia continued. "A second police officer manoeuvred himself into position behind a bullet-riddled police vehicle and shot the driver of the assault car. It is believed the dead man was a foreign national, possibly a mercenary hired by the rebels. Investigations are ongoing. Simone Garcia reporting from St Petersburg, Russia. Aiden."

"In other news," Aiden, the news anchor read on, "School children around the United States have staged their second national demonstration calling for tighter guns laws. This follows the first national march after a Florida school shooting several months ago."

The newsreader, Aiden O'Byrne continued speaking over live coverage of the rallies in various American cities. "The protest movement appears to be gaining momentum with scenes like this around the United States. Pressure is mounting on state and federal governments to restrict the type of firearms that can be sold over the counter, and to raise the age of licence holders."

Come on, Aiden, tell us about the other attacks in Russia today. You said there were three.

"An earthquake of 7.3 magnitude on the Richter scale has been recorded in southern Chile; a grade four hurricane, or tropical cyclone as it is called in Australia, with winds up to 140 miles per hour has hit the northern coast of Australia near Darwin; and freezing weather just like the so-called 'beast from the east' has been forecast in Britain over the next week, with cold air sweeping across from Siberia dropping temperatures to 10 degrees Fahrenheit or minus 12 degrees Celsius.

"Those stories and more in a moment, but first we return to Simone Garcia in St Petersburg with an update on incidents that have shaken the Russian government. Simone."

"Thank you, Aiden. Police are continuing their investigation into a shooting incident at the front of a federal court in St Petersburg this afternoon. Unofficial reports suggest that a Chechen gunman escaped and is still at large after a brave policeman who was standing guard at the entrance to the court killed the shooter's accomplice. Another policeman was killed."

Garcia swiped her tablet, refreshing the page and reading her notes.

"It appears this attack on a federal institution was part of coordinated action by Chechen rebels. Sketchy reports are coming in about two more serious attacks that have resulted in the deaths of innocent people."

Garcia continued in an even more serious tone as she adopted a reproving look. "There have been two separate attacks against trains on the Moscow to St Petersburg line. The police are not revealing any information to the media at the moment but it appears the two attacks were coordinated and professional. Sources suggest Chechen rebels are behind the attacks. I will hopefully have more information to convey to you in our next news bulletin. Aiden."

The newsreader then gave updates on various matters that had earlier been scantily reported upon.

The chime of the doorbell was followed by a woman yelling, "Room service."

Curtis walked closer to the door and waited for the second call. The doorbell chimed again and a louder but still melodic voice yelled, "Room service!"

Curtis crept closer to the side of the door where it was hinged to the wall. Without hesitating he went through his usual routine, eyes darting across the fish-eye lens. Enough to recognise a trolley bearing food. He threw open the door and stood to the side, taking the waitress by surprise.

Dinner had indeed arrived. Curtis glanced in both directions along the corridor as he ushered the room service inside and pulled the door shut.

Room service extracted the trolley extension arms to provide more room for Mr Lomot to comfortably eat. She then swivelled the trolley to the side of the bed where he could presumably eat and watch television.

"I see you watch CNN news, Mr Lomot. Terrible tragedy, no?"

"CNN have not reported the full story yet," Curtis replied.

"I listen to radio in kitchen," room service continued. "Yes, terrible, terrible news."

"What is the news? Tell me more please."

"One train bombed. Ran off railway track. Other train, the fast train. Many people shot and killed. Men with guns. Chechens. Yes, Chechens. Must be.

"Many problems in our city today. Shooting at a court. A policeman killed. Very bad accident near our hotel and car burnt with a man inside. And now this — the two trains."

"They say things happen in threes," Curtis said. "Perhaps the car was driven by a man connected to the other incidents."

"Yes, Mr Lomot, but that makes four things today, not three. The rebels must be stopped. It is not good for tourists, especially during our festival.

"You have everything you ordered here, Mr Lomot," said room service pointing to the food trolley. "Is there anything else you would like, sir? Is everything to your liking?"

"Perfect," snapped Curtis, anxious to hear the news.

As room service shuffled from his room, Curtis quickly scrolled through the television channels looking for more current news. Local news was reporting on the developing tensions between China and the USA over trade tariffs. Scrolling across the bottom of the screen in Russian was a reference to breaking news and 'chaotic scenes at a train derailment near St Petersburg. More to follow'.

Anxious to hear of the latest news Curtis flicked the remote control, changing channels back to CNN. He recognised the voice of Simone Garcia as the screen was filled with a picture of disaster. A freight train was partially derailed with the diesel locomotive resting on the side of a rail embankment. Smoke was billowing from the side of the engine. The film was taken from a helicopter, or perhaps a drone, overhead.

"Police reports suggest a group of militants discharged an explosive device by using a mobile telephone," Garcia reported. "As the freight train approached Chudovo in the Chudosky District, sixty-two miles south of St Petersburg on the Moscow line, an explosion occurred on the line. The train was unable to stop and was derailed. We have reports from witnesses that four heavily armed men wearing balaclavas fired shots at railway employees who attended the scene, although no-one was killed or injured."

Either very poor shots or they deliberately missed. Professionals don't miss. A smokescreen for something else. Their main target.

Curtis watched the screen intently as he finished a slice of sweet potato cornbread. He did not shift his eyes from the television but, having very good peripheral vision, lifted a French lamb cutlet by the 'handle' and started chewing.

At this point, the television camera overhead honed in on the shattered concrete railway sleepers and twisted lines where the train had left its tracks. The camera retreated to reveal a large number of police scouring the bushes thirty metres away.

The scene of the tragedy receded and Simone Garcia's pretty but sombre face again stared out of the television.

"Almost simultaneously with the attack at Chudovo, another group of militants attacked the historic passenger train that operates between Moscow and St Petersburg. The attack occurred near Lyuban, about fifty miles from St Petersburg. The famous Krasnaya Strela or Red Arrow. Police believe the first attack was a smoke screen. An attempt to divert police attention away from the second attack."

Curtis nibbled on the crusty meat at the edge of the lamb chop. *Well planned, well-orchestrated. Preventing the authorities from sending assistance to the ambushed train.*

"News of the second attack is sketchy," continued Garcia lamenting the lack of news. "It has been reported by witnesses at the Chudovo station that a group of men boarded the train there. The authorities believe those men may have been carrying firearms and were likely involved in the second attack.

"Nobody has claimed responsibility for either of these terrorist attacks. I will bring you more news as soon as it comes to hand. Aiden."

In the studio, Aiden looked up from a slip of paper handed to him by the producer. "Breaking news from our Moscow reporters, the gunmen who hijacked the second train — the famous Red Arrow — have killed innocent civilians on board and left the train.

"In a statement released a short time ago, the Russian minister of internal affairs said the manner in which the gunmen had stormed the two trains had all the hallmarks of terrorist attacks by Chechen rebels. He said the Russian government had acted quickly to secure the area, and when caught the perpetrators would be brought to justice."

A euphemism for 'killed'. If caught. I doubt that will happen. Planned by Nelson, orchestrated by Lumovski. Both dystopian. Judge Vasilek was the real target. This venomous, aggressive campaign of male dominance, of fear about women in leadership must be stopped. I need to cut off the serpent's head. If Frenchy doesn't believe me, I'll just have to finish it on my own.

Chapter 37

Coolidge had ordered a Baltika Draught beer on the recommendation of the bartender. He had been told the beer was "One of Russia's favourites with the right blend of pale barley malt, hops and purified water. A rich flavour using unique Russian technology. No pasteurisation." The bartender sounded convincing.

With slow sips, pursed lips and a mouth swilling process, Coolidge appeared to the bartender to be something of a connoisseur. But not so. Coolidge just liked beer.

As he approached the bar, Curtis observed the interaction with the bartender and the manner in which Coolidge appeared to make love with the contents of his glass.

"Good evening, Geoffrey," Curtis interrupted the exchange with the bartender. Russian accent. "We have much to discuss. Let's find a quiet area."

As an afterthought, Curtis ordered a lime soda without ice and turned briskly on his heel to find a small table in the corner of the bar. He sat with his back to the wall. He peered around the room to see if a closed-circuit camera watched the occupants of the room. It didn't really matter to Curtis in the circumstances but old habits die hard. He observed a camera above the entrance to the Lobby Bar.

He watched Coolidge's every move as the latter meandered between tables across the room.

Study the subject matter. Look for strengths and weaknesses.

Coolidge wore a dark green shirt with sleeves turned back one wrap just above his wrist. It revealed an expensive watch. Without lowering his eyes, he noticed black partially bleached jeans and black casual suede shoes.

"Have you been waiting long, Geoffrey?"

How many beers have you downed?

"No, not long."

"You are a racing car enthusiast, Geoffrey?"

Coolidge looked surprised. "How do you know? I didn't tell you that, did I?"

"Your watch. A Tag Heuer Carrera Formula 1. Usually only bought by rev heads, if you'll excuse the expression. You're not the type of person who would buy an expensive watch like that without having an interest in Formula 1 racing."

Coolidge again looked surprised. He smiled. "You're very observant."

"You obviously enjoyed the beer. That is your second."

"How do you know? Are you psychic?"

"The beer is 5.3% alcohol by volume. I noticed that on a stubby behind where the bartender stands. The average drinker usually consumes the first beer a little quicker than subsequent beers. I noticed you sipping this one fairly slowly as I entered the bar. Had you consumed two already with that alcohol content your movements would be more measured than they were when you walked over here."

"Observant and an analytical mind, Alexeev," Coolidge responded.

Curtis laughed, then added, "You like the colour green too. You wore a pale green T-shirt in the gym this morning, a dark green pullover to breakfast, you are wearing a dark green shirt now. Oh… and you work for a company called 'Green Solutions'."

Both men laughed at the last comment.

"How was your visit to the Hermitage?" Coolidge asked.

"Excellent as always. I particularly enjoyed the 1812 War Gallery and the Rembrandt collection. The Gainsborough exhibition was worth a visit too. Did you have a good day? What did you do?"

Curtis watched intently as Coolidge hesitated and fidgeted slightly. Weighing up his response.

"Nothing special. I only went for a walk along the embankment, took an afternoon 'nana nap' and followed up on some administrative matters for the company."

"Administrative matters?" Curtis had decided to break the façade. "Was that why you had a meeting with the big Russian in his car parked in a 'No Standing' zone across the road?"

A bank of wrinkles formed across Coolidge's forehead. He was clearly disturbed at this comment.

"Err… Alexeev," he stuttered nervously, "Are you somehow connected to that Russian? You… err… don't appear to be an average Russian tourist."

"No, I'm most definitely not connected to him but you are. Before I explain why you could be in deep trouble, I need to know what the meeting was about. I can assure you, Geoffrey, it is in your best interests to be totally honest with me."

Beads of perspiration had now formed across Coolidge's brow.

"Why should I tell you anything? It is none of your business. I don't need this pressure. Thanks for the drink, Alexeev."

Coolidge pushed his chair back and rose to leave. Curtis reached forward and wrapped his huge hand around Coolidge's forearm, pulling him back down onto the chair.

"Sit! As I said, you could be in serious trouble. Only one person can help you and that person happens to be me. Now, either you tell me the purpose of your clandestine meeting, or we can deal with this another way."

Curtis reached into his pocket and extracted a wallet, flipped it open and flashed his Interpol credentials at Coolidge. One side of the wallet carried a gold badge bearing the words 'International Police' on the top and 'Interpol' at the bottom. The other side had a photograph of Curtis and, in smaller lettering, more detailed information that for obvious reasons he chose not to reveal. He didn't give Coolidge time to absorb anything more than the gold badge and photograph, returning the wallet to his pocket.

The result was a huge sigh and a look of defeat. Coolidge lifted his glass, gulped at the beer and slumped back in his chair.

"I knew you could not be a normal tourist, Alexeev," Coolidge said in a tone of resignation. "What do you want to know?"

"Start by telling me the purpose of your meeting with the Russian."

"I received a phone call from the CEO of Green Solutions, Jim Wallace. He told me there is a person staying at this hotel who intends to sabotage our company's plans to develop a closer relationship with the government of St Petersburg. He said this person is working with oil companies that do not want to see Green Solutions succeed. Those companies threatened by our technology and products. He said our Russian investor and major shareholder…"

"Lumovski?"

"Yes, Lumovski."

Curtis nodded an invitation to Coolidge to continue.

"Jim said Lumovski wants to meet with the oil company representative and that I should assist in facilitating that meeting. He said I would be contacted by one of Lumovski's people with instructions.

"To be honest, Alexeev, I was not happy with the approach. Later, reception phoned to say there was a gentleman waiting to meet me in the lobby. When I went there, I was instructed to follow him. We went to his car. That made me nervous and I was even more nervous with the conversation that followed. I almost didn't join you for a drink as promised because the Russian said he didn't know your name but you fitted the description he gave. He told me I was to leave a message that you should meet me tonight at the front of Restaurant CheerDuck but I must not turn up. He said he would meet you instead and deal with the matter."

"Why didn't you follow his instructions?"

"I told him I didn't want to become involved in what sounded like corporate malfeasance. We argued. He threatened me. I said I didn't want anything to do with bullies and immediately left his car."

That explains the wild gesticulations I saw. That took some courage. Perhaps Coolidge has more intestinal fortitude than meets the eye?

"What are your plans now?"

"I am booked on a flight to London tomorrow."

"Good. But you need not be concerned about the Russian. He was involved in a fatal accident soon after your meeting. His car hit a concrete street lamp post at high speed and rolled, bursting into flames. He was trapped inside but I suspect he was already dead from the horrific collision."

"How do you know that?"

"I saw it happen. I'm surprised you are not aware of it. The hotel staff are talking about the terrible accident diagonally across the road near the river. But, of course, you don't speak Russian."

"I need to talk to Jim Wallace," Coolidge continued. "I left a message on his mobile phone for him to call me. He needs to know about the threats against me from Lumovski's assistant. I'm sure he will have an explanation, but if he doesn't it suggests he doesn't really know who he is dealing with."

Now Mr Coolidge, I'm about to find out what you are really made of.

"Trust me, Geoffrey, he knows."

Coolidge was puzzled by this remark. "How can you say that, you don't know Jim?"

"And it appears neither do you."

Without further interruption Curtis spent the next fifteen minutes explaining how he believed Lumovski's investment in Green Solutions would be used to fund a campaign against women in leadership positions.

"My use of the word 'campaign' understates the seriousness of this action. An assault on democracy. An assault on human values led by scumbags of the worst order," Curtis spoke bitterly.

This is personal too.

He continued by explaining how there had recently been an attempted assassination of a potential prime minister in Thailand. Intelligence gathered from and by various international sources revealed an attack on a judge in St Petersburg was also planned and that had brought him to Russia. A party associated with Green Solutions and Jim Wallace had orchestrated both attacks.

"I have reason to believe Lumovski has embraced the philosophy, and Wallace is the prime mover. Another zealot, Craig Nelson, completes his work. My role is to stop this movement and bring the perpetrators to justice."

"This is hard to believe, Alexeev. But I guess Interpol wouldn't be involved if there were not perhaps an element of truth in this. Is that right? As they say, where there's smoke there's fire," Coolidge said as he gazed into space.

"Still, the old adage innocent until proven guilty should hold." As an afterthought he added, "That might explain why Wallace didn't want me to look at the company financials."

Curtis noticed how Coolidge had adopted a new reference to the head of Green Solutions, from 'Jim' to 'Wallace'.

Coolidge sat, dumbfounded and staring into space. "Hard to believe," he said, voice fading, "hard to believe… hard to believe."

"Believe it, Geoffrey, and believe also that you will be caught up in this scheme."

Curtis knew what Coolidge was now thinking. "Even if you were to leave the company as you are suddenly contemplating you will be caught up in it as a Green Solutions executive whilst this criminal action had been undertaken. If you leave and survive the certain attack on your life by Nelson or Lumovski's people, you will be forever looking over your shoulder. Make no mistake, Lumovski's tentacles are long and reach into many corners of the globe."

The realisation suddenly hit Coolidge. Beads of perspiration returned. "Wh… wh…what can I do?"

"There is only one thing you can do. Continue as if nothing has happened. You know nothing. You will be my person inside. Your only chance is to feed information to me and I will ensure you are protected."

"What sort of information? They aren't likely to suddenly trust me with their secrets."

"Of course not. You will purchase a throwaway mobile phone and call me with details of their movements. Where Wallace is at all times. With whom he is meeting. Where Nelson is and what his planned itinerary is. Don't place yourself at risk by asking too many questions. Play it cool. If Wallace returns your call tell him the meeting with the Russian never occurred. He just didn't contact you."

"Alexeev, you mentioned a judge from St Petersburg. Was she the judge referred to in the afternoon news?"

"I only saw the CNN news before meeting with you. I believe she was a passenger on the train, the Red Arrow, that was ambushed between Moscow and St Petersburg. Several people were killed. She would certainly have been one of them. She was the target, I've no doubt. I'm sorry I couldn't save her," Curtis said grimly.

"No, I mean the judge that was taken into custody in Moscow earlier today. A judge was arrested for allegedly causing insurrection. An allegation of treason and income tax fraud has been levelled against her."

"Her? Did they give a name?" Curtis asked.

"Yes. It was a typical Russian female name. I can't remember it."

"It wasn't Angelina Vasilek was it?"

"That's it. That was the name of the judge arrested. Apparently, a popular local figure."

Curtis smiled and gave a sigh of relief. *She is alive and has a chance. A slight chance against concocted charges and a corrupt administration, but a chance nevertheless.*

Chapter 38

Nelson was angry, very angry. He had gone to a great deal of trouble for no purpose.

Wasting time. The authorities had dealt with the judge. Time and energy spent in planning and training. Causing a distraction for the police and the ambush of the second train. All unnecessary because they had other plans for her. Surely Lumovski knew what was planned!

He was seated in the Gulfstream G550 private jet again waiting for Lumovski. Waiting for further instructions.

There had been a light fall of snow at Vnukova International Airport in the last few days. Nelson gazed out of a Gulfstream passenger window, noticing the yellow snowploughs had been repositioned.

Airport workers moved slowly around the snowploughs and other airport ground support equipment. Non-powered equipment, the catering and cargo dollies, stood in line awaiting the arrival of a passenger aircraft. A refuelling truck and a potable water truck stood at the ready. Nelson knew an incoming flight was imminent. Truck snorkel exhausts emitted hints of fumes from overhead, indicating diesel engines sitting quietly in operation.

In total disregard for airport protocol and vehicular movement restrictions, a black stretch limousine rounded the corner of a nearby building and traversed the tarmac. Baggage handlers and airport security personnel didn't move. They watched the vehicle pass as if it was a common occurrence.

So much for security, thought Nelson.

As the limo slowly moved in the direction of the Gulfstream, a mobile staircase emerged into view from somewhere in front of the jet. It nestled up against the aircraft by the port side front door.

Just as before a large man wearing a *ushanka* hat and a heavy overcoat climbed from the front passenger seat and opened a rear door. Out stepped Lumovski, buttoning his black overcoat. Nelson watched as

Lumovski panted condensation into the air. The flow of condensation increased as he climbed the stairs.

Taking his leather gloves off, Lumovski thrust his hands forward and to Nelson's surprise grabbed his right with both, gripping firmly and shaking vigorously.

"We have reason to celebrate, Mr Nelson. Very good work."

This was disarming for Nelson. He had primed himself to confront Lumovski about the complete waste of his time in focusing on the judge.

"We celebrate," Lumovski repeated. "Vodka from Moskovskaya Oblasti. I pour."

"I understand the *blyat* was arrested in Moscow. Was that always planned? Did you know about that? Of course you did. Why did we bother with our operation?" Nelson fired off a string of questions.

Lumovski didn't respond immediately, instead pouring the vodka, handing one over and taking a seat opposite Nelson. He looked tired. Too many celebrations.

After a few pensive minutes his reply took Nelson by surprise. "The decision to engage you to dispatch the *blyat* was mine alone. I had no knowledge of any other plans to deal with her. Other than Wallace, I did not consult with another person. Nobody in Russia consulted with me. Nobody," he emphasised.

"Be assured the *blyat* is finished. The authorities will have a very tight case against her. They have much experience in manufacturing… I mean, dealing, with such matters. She will not pose a threat to anyone.

"Your work was not a waste of time as you suggest, Mr Nelson. There was no media interest in the arrest. All the attention was given to the Chechen attacks on our trains and at a government building in St Petersburg. Thank you. I will ensure the right people learn of your good work. You will be well-rewarded."

"Just doing what is right for society."

"And you did it so well, Mr Nelson. It is a pity I lost one of my best men in the operation though. Your man from Thailand was also killed. Shot by a police officer at the federal courthouse in St Petersburg."

"A pity, but nobody is indispensable," said Nelson shrugging his shoulders. "What happened to your man?"

"He had a car accident. Always liked his vodka too much."

Chapter 39

Another very uncomfortable night. Tossing and turning. He awoke in a lather of perspiration, his mother's face fresh in his memory. There was a difference this time though. His mother was unscathed. In his dream they were both cowered in a corner of his bedroom whilst his drunken father staggered around the house, falling over furniture until at last the noise stopped. His father had knocked himself out when he fell onto the tiled kitchen floor.

If only a fatal fall. Anything fatal.

Curtis rose early as usual. He dressed in sports shorts, a polo shirt and joggers and set off for a run along the embankment. He passed the burn marks left by his assailant's car a day earlier. *One down. How many more to go?*

The streets were quiet and so were the walkways. *Nobody, except me, is stupid enough to be out in this cold weather and this early.* Curtis smiled at the thought. *Softies live here.* He glanced back at the rubber marks, furrowed bitumen and scattered rubble. *Softies and idiots.*

An hour later he was back in his room. Time to kill. He pressed the television remote. CNN news sprang into life. The news anchor Aiden O'Byrne was providing an update on student rallies in the United States over firearm laws following more shootings at educational institutions.

"Protests continue with students turning out in their thousands in cities all over America," Aiden announced. "The voice of young America is demanding to be heard."

Good on ya, kids, thought Curtis. *Somehow the brutal deaths must stop. Keep protesting until governments listen. Remind the politicians you will vote one day.*

Curtis watched the news for twenty minutes or so but there was no report on the judge's incarceration. Simone Garcia featured again with a summary of the major events in Russia over the last twenty-four hours with the 'Chechen attacks' taking priority. The judge's plight, the undoubted wrongful arrest, wasn't apparently worthy of international attention.

He knew there was nothing more he could do in Russia. Not now anyway. He had already checked with the concierge and found the shortest most direct flights to Singapore were via Qatar Airways. He made the call. The first available flight to Singapore was late afternoon and there were several economy-class seats available.

He found Coolidge in the Pierrot breakfast restaurant and gave him the number for one of his mobile phones. After a strong Java coffee and some idle chat, they went their separate ways. Coolidge to the airport for his flight to London, Curtis to the gymnasium.

After a solid workout, Curtis showered, dressed in dark blue jeans, a thermo skivvy, and his favourite RM Williams boots, then returned to the Pierrot breakfast restaurant.

First things first, another strong Java. After a waiter had attended his table several times, impatient for an order, Curtis ordered the same breakfast he had consumed a day earlier. An American-style breakfast and plenty of everything. Washed down with another strong Java.

I had this yesterday. Yesterday! It seems like a week ago.

Curtis ate slowly and contemplated the next forty-eight hours. In their last communication before he boarded the flight to Russia, Frenchy had instructed him to send a coded message when he was departing St Petersburg. They were to meet in Singapore.

No matter what Frenchy thought, he had a task to complete. Frenchy said he was yet to be convinced the two attempted assassinations were linked in a wider campaign against women. "On the basis of two attempts, Curtis, I'm not sure how you can be so certain," Frenchy had said. "I am prepared to be persuaded otherwise, but I need more evidence."

Strongly believing he was on the right track, Curtis had to persuade him otherwise. At least it appeared Bell agreed with the possibility. *Bell is Frenchy's superior officer. Surely that should be enough?* He would have to brief Frenchy on his recruitment of Coolidge and convince Frenchy to allow him to follow any leads that provided. He hoped Bell would agree.

After a leisurely breakfast Curtis checked out of the hotel and placed his meagre luggage in storage with the doorman. With time on his hands he again took a brochure from the stand near the concierge desk, intending to visit the Hermitage in a more relaxed frame of mind than his last visit.

His first stop was the 1812 War Gallery. From there he strolled the corridors, stopping occasionally to admire the works of art in various halls. Exceptional pieces by Rembrandt, Michelangelo, Picasso, Monet and masterpieces by less renowned artists he was not familiar with.

After three hours of wandering the corridors he found himself standing in front of the *Portrait of a Lady in Blue*. The Thomas Gainsborough painting that could very well have been a portrait of his mother in younger, less stressful years. He contemplated the magnificent paintings he had had the pleasure of viewing over the last few hours.

I love the work of these amazing artists but the thing that strikes me as unfair and disappointing is the stereotyping of the era. Why is it the male is mostly depicted in uniform, sitting high on horseback, or in some other commanding position? Women are typically portrayed as sweet, glamorous, lamblike or servile. I suppose we have to understand the attitudes of years past. Wallace, Nelson and their cohorts would have us mired in that time.

"You again," came the husky almost masculine voice of the female security officer Curtis had encountered a day earlier in a different section of the museum. "Do you need assistance today?"

Surprised, Curtis smiled and replied, "No, thank you. I remember seeing you yesterday near Picasso's painting of the *Two Sisters*. This Gainsborough painting could be my mother."

"But she is not," husky voice replied, this time with a smile.

And there are no paintings from the same era of anyone like you, thought Curtis. *No paintings depicting a woman of obvious strength, just the usual stereotypical aristocratic women of those times.*

It was time to find a café and have a quiet lunch before heading to the airport. During the entire time he was at the Hermitage, and the long walk back to the hotel, Curtis constantly checked his surroundings. He concluded that he was no longer being followed. Those who had previously tailed him were either dead or had given up after the 'success' of the attacks on the trains. He could relax a little.

His scheduled flight was at 1725 departing Pulkova Airport, landing in Doha soon after 2300. The stopover at Hamad International Airport would be just over three hours and the seventeen-hour flight in total would have him in Singapore at 1545 the following day. He sent the coded timetable to Frenchy and added, "It's more than a hunch."

Hopefully I shall hear from Coolidge tomorrow and commence the hunt. Yes, Frenchy, we must cut off the serpent tomorrow

Chapter 40

Wallace was born in Southampton, England, and, ironically, as a child lived in the suburb of Shirley, near Southampton Common. After emigrating and choosing Australia as his destination he then chose never to return to the city in which he was born and where many relatives still resided. He visited the UK frequently and spent most of his time in London.

He liked to stay in the luxurious Mayfair House Serviced Apartments on Market Mews, in the historic Mayfair area near Green Park. From there he could readily catch the underground train to Victoria Station where he could link up with trains to most suburbs, Heathrow Airport or other UK destinations. From a public transport perspective, it suited his requirements.

The other advantage of the Mayfair area was the proximity to five-star restaurants, the theatres in and near Soho, and old English pubs. Wallace loves old English pubs. The ambience, Guinness on the tap and bangers and mash. The Market Tavern on Shepherd Street as his favourite.

Shepherd Market boasts many small restaurants in quaint old buildings that could really tell a story. Wallace liked to take his breakfast at the Piccolo Bar where many of the Black Cab drivers dine. That's where he met Nelson five days after he had arrived in London.

For the preceding four days Nelson had been occupied at Her Majesty's pleasure. Four days in a police lock-up.

Upon arrival at Gatwick Airport on Aeroflot, a detective chief inspector and a detective constable had boarded the aircraft. The DCI held a copy of the passenger manifest as he was engrossed in deep discussion with the senior flight attendant. The flight attendant approached Nelson and asked him to remain in his seat when the other passengers left the aircraft.

"I'm DCI Andrew Hodgson, Mr Nelson. This is Detective Constable Peters," Hodgson said pointing at his colleague. "We have received intelligence reports that suggest you are carrying a concealed weapon into the UK. A plastic handgun. One that may not have been detected by the metal detectors or wands at Moscow Airport. Are you aware, Mr Nelson, that it is an offence to carry a handgun in the UK? Is there anything you wish to declare to us now?"

Nelson was stunned. After a few moments he broke the silence with a laugh.

"Where did you get that idea from?" Nelson asked the police officers.

"As I said, sir, we have a reasonable belief. Since the scanners may not detect a 3-D printer weapon, are you prepared to allow a body search?"

"That is crap and you know it!" exclaimed Nelson.

"I'll ask you again, sir. Are you willing to allow a body search or do we have to take you into custody to proceed and verify this information?"

Nelson shrugged, stood and raised his arms to allow DC Peters to pat him down. At the same time Hodgson rummaged through Nelson's hand luggage. Nothing.

"We need you to accompany us to our police headquarters, Mr Nelson," Hodgson instructed. "There are other matters we need to discuss and it is in your best interests to cooperate."

"Do I need to have a lawyer present?" Nelson asked. "What is this all about?"

"You may need a lawyer if you have committed a crime," Hodgson replied, a furtive glance as he returned to the hand luggage. "You are a person of interest in relation to organised crime in Southeast Asia. At the moment only in the sense you may have information that can assist us in our inquiries. At this stage we only need to ask you questions relating to drug trafficking. Our colleagues in Hong Kong and Bangkok will be very interested in what you have to say."

Over the following days Nelson was questioned about his recent travel history. During the course of the so-called investigation he began to realise the police were on a fishing expedition. They knew nothing but if they continued to question him on matters entirely unrelated to his recent travel in Thailand and other parts of Southeast Asia, he might reveal something of his real purpose for travelling.

Nelson was told he had been detained pursuant to the Serious Crime Act 2015 where there are three or more people involved, possibly constituting organised crime, and where the alleged offence was carried out either in England, Wales, or in a country where the law in force would constitute a criminal offence.

He was also told the police had followed the current Code of Practice for detention and questioning where there are reasonable grounds to believe a serious crime had been committed.

He was entitled to make a telephone call. On the fourth day of his detention he made the call. During that call he told Wallace the police were making 'trumped up claims' just in case his call was tapped. Police questioning had revealed nothing. No organised crime in Great Britain or in any other country.

Wallace called Lumovski asking for help with a legal matter. Within hours a team of lawyers attended Gatwick Police Headquarters in the East Sussex hamlet of Lewes.

The chief inspector was warned about the 'illegal detention of an Australian businessman on claims that are clearly not sustainable'. False imprisonment that could result in Nelson taking legal action against the police. They demanded Nelson's immediate release.

In the lower level of the Piccolo Bar in Mayfair, Wallace waited patiently for Nelson to arrive. When Wallace entered the bar, he had told one of the Italian chefs behind the counter that he would be dining at his usual table downstairs and would have the Italian sausages, fried tomatoes, hash browns and ciabatta.

Downstairs the grey granite tables, surrounded by four red metal-framed chairs, straddled brown tiles. As usual, Wallace sat at a corner table with his back to the wall facing the direction of the staircase. A group of five cab drivers — a spill over from the upstairs dining area — sat at the table closest to the stairs. They ate in a relaxed manner and clearly enjoyed each other's company.

He heard the heavy footsteps on the wooden stairs before Nelson came into view. Nelson glanced around, saw Wallace had occupied a table at the far end of the dining area, and walked purposefully to the table.

"Good morning, Jim," he said and without waiting for a response, "What a harrowing few days that has been."

"I'm concerned about the reason for the detention, Craig. What do you think motivated the police?"

"I have no idea, Jim. They simply asked many questions about my business activities and reasons for travel."

Wallace looked anxious. "What did you tell them?"

His raised voice attracted the interest of the cabbies. They all turned and looked intently at Wallace's red face. Nelson glanced back at the only other occupied table, noticing the attention they had received.

He waited a few seconds, peered around the room and then lowered his voice, "All of the things we agreed on when we started this venture. I told them the truth. I have a financial planning business and I regularly meet with my clients, potential clients and potential investors. I meet with company executives to learn about the businesses my clients may consider to be a good investment. Nothing more. They hounded me but I just kept repeating the same lines. I think they were more frustrated than I was," he laughed.

Still looking at the cab drivers Nelson noticed they had lost interest in the mumbler at the end of the dining room.

"Well done. Legal counsel said you have reasonable grounds to receive damages for wrongful arrest and illegal detention. I think it is best to let 'sleeping dogs lie', Craig. If we pursue damages that may open a can of worms."

Jim likes to use metaphors, Nelson thought.

"I agree. I never even contemplated it. The few days in a police slammer was a new experience for me but I have experienced worse in the military. The spare time I had gave me the opportunity to do some serious thinking. More than ever before I am resolved to stay the course, Jim."

Wallace nodded, and then changed the subject. "Geoffrey Coolidge will be joining us shortly. I told him a later time so that we could have a chat first. Craig, you must ensure he doesn't get wind of your activities over the last few days," he said earnestly.

"What has Coolidge been doing?" Nelson asked.

"He has been in Cardiff talking to the company we have contracted to blend the ingredients for the liquid products. We need to increase our production given the success of trials in Malaysia, Indonesia and Thailand. We also need to increase our inventory for the St Petersburg government."

"I don't trust Coolidge," Nelson added.

"Coolidge does a good job in running the operations side of Green Solutions. He will never be in the loop on the more important operational issues we deal with," Wallace winked at Nelson as he made the last comment.

"Edgar and I have been talking about our strategy in restoring the natural order for mankind, Craig. We are limited in personnel. Obviously, it is important that we limit our… aah… direct action campaign I shall call it, to those people we are absolutely certain we can trust. But we are contemplating a more substantial movement."

"A small vigilante group is always best though, Jim. If too many people are involved, we run the risk of mistakes being made and, worse still, leaks to the authorities," Nelson said emphatically.

Wallace looked pensive, pursed his lips in a typical contemplative manner and replied, "Our current *modus operandi* will not be changed. Your role is set in stone. We value your commitment and expertise and, most importantly, you get the job done. But, Craig, there are other imposters who are just too difficult to get at without risk.

"You will recall how I described to you our campaign against that woman prime minister. *Blyat*, our friend Lumovski would have called her. We need to run similar campaigns elsewhere. We have the brainpower to achieve that and now the money too. We intend creating a seismic shift away from the interests of politicians and activists' intent on promoting women to roles they are incapable of performing. Enough is enough!"

The two ate in silence. After a few minutes, Wallace told Nelson he intended meeting with his Malaysian and Indonesian distributors in Singapore at the end of the week. Nelson should accompany him. It would provide an opportunity to hear first-hand how successful the trials had been with palm oil companies in Malaysia and the largest paper mill in Asia, based in Indonesia. This would be useful information he could pass to other financial planners.

"Travelling together will also give us time to discuss our next target. Without swivelling heads trying to hear what we are talking about," glancing in the direction of the cab drivers.

When breakfast was finished and the table cleared, Wallace reached for his mobile phone. Before making the call, he asked Nelson to go upstairs and order coffee. He phoned his secretary in Sydney. It was midnight in Sydney but a demanding Wallace expected his secretary to be available twenty-four-seven.

Coolidge arrived and reported on his visit to Wales. He reassured Wallace that everything was in place to increase the production rate as long as the essential ingredients in the additive were available. The Welsh company was very efficient and he was satisfied they could meet whatever demands were placed upon them.

Wallace's phone chimed. He raised his hand, signalling to Coolidge to hold the conversation whilst he was on the phone. He took the call while moving away from the table. After a few minutes he returned.

"I have some good news and some bad news," he said addressing Nelson. "The good news. Our flight is booked to Singapore. The bad news, well… aaah

… mixed news really," he said with tongue metaphorically placed firmly in his cheek, "We have to stay at the Ritz-Carlton because the less expensive mid-range hotels are largely booked by conference attendees.

"There is a conference in Singapore next weekend promoting women in leadership. Women from Europe are the keynote speakers. I'm not sure why Amanda, my secretary, told me this although she seemed unusually excited about the subject matter. The focus is on women from throughout the Asian region including Australia. Apparently, the conference is entitled 'Conscious and Unconscious Bias — Breaking Down the Barriers'."

"Breaking bones is more like it," Nelson mumbled out the side of his mouth just loud enough for Wallace to hear.

Chapter 41

The same scene. The back door, away from the public view, smashed open. The same small house and a frighteningly large, aggressive man stumbling, yelling, venom spewing from his twisted mouth. The same two shadows. An aggressor almost out of control. In a drunken rage. Fists clenched hunting for the woman who would be powerless to resist the rage.

The open fire flared as a gust of wind shot across the lounge room. As before, flames licked the mallee roots. Small sparks shot out and upwards, some searching for timber to grasp, others making their way into the night sky. Shadows danced.

Fists clenched, he charged across the room. He hesitated, balance a problem in his drunken stupor. Hesitated long enough for the boy to charge at him with his baseball bat. The first blow only struck a turning shoulder. The boy's vision was blurred by rivulets of tears. He swung the bat again.

"Sir, sir, wake up," the flight attendant said quietly.

No response.

"Mr Curtis!" Louder this time and with a gentle shake of his shoulder.

"I'm sorry to waken you, sir, but you have been dreaming and thrashing your arms around, disturbing the other passengers."

Curtis rubbed his eyes and apologised to the passengers next to him in the exit row. "My sincere apologies. I've had very little sleep in the last two days. Heavy negotiations on an important business deal in Doha."

His contiguous neighbour, the pretty dark-haired woman occupying the centre of the three exit row seats, couldn't help her curiosity. "Obviously the negotiations were heavy, very heavy. Is that how you normally negotiate? Arms waving and yelling 'take that'?"

Curtis smiled and said, "Actually, I'm just a gentle lamb. A recurring nightmare. One of the reasons I haven't slept much. I'm almost afraid to go to sleep."

His new friend looked genuinely concerned and reached out, gently touching his forearm. "You need help."

She reached into her handbag nestled on the side of her chair and extracted a small wallet. Holding her business card between thumb and forefinger in both hands she presented it to Curtis with a slight nod and continued, "I'm a counsellor. If you acknowledge you need help here are my details. Even a chat over coffee might help deal with some of your demons."

I doubt it. Perhaps a coffee is not a bad idea, though.

Mindful of the importance of business cards in Asia and the custom of showing respect by immediately reading the card, Curtis closely examined it before saying, "I'm sorry, I don't have a card. I see you're a counsellor with the Singapore Police Force."

"Correct," Jolanta Chan replied. "But I am always willing to help people in need. As I said, don't hesitate to call."

"Thank you. I just might do that."

Idle chat about the weather in Singapore at this time of the year and plans for the weekend took them into Changi Airport, Singapore.

"I have been calling you for the last two days, Alexeev," Coolidge anxiously announced immediately Curtis accepted the call. "I'm sorry, I should have asked how you are first," in a more contrite tone.

"Obviously, I am only able to call when the others are not around, others meaning Jim Wallace and Craig Nelson."

Curtis reverted to his acquired Russian accent, "I've been travelling. What's the news?"

"Wallace and Nelson left overnight for Singapore. They plan to meet with the company's distributors in Malaysia and Indonesia."

"Is that all?" Curtis asked.

"I overheard Wallace tell Nelson there is a conference in Singapore this weekend about women in leadership."

"Is that all?" Curtis repeated.

"Nelson commented on that news with a scowl on his face. I didn't catch what he said but it was obviously negative. Like you said, don't ask too many questions. Just listen. That's all."

"Where are they staying?"

"The Ritz-Carlton."

"Anything else? Where do they plan to go after Singapore?"

"I don't know about Nelson but I understand Wallace plans to return to London. He told me to stand by here and await further instructions."

"Thank you, Geoffrey. Good work. Call me any time if you learn anything else, however insignificant you think it might be. Especially news about their movements. I appreciate it."

Curtis had been checking in to the Park Royal on Pickering when the call came. He had politely excused himself and walked across the lobby and stood behind a partition, away from any prying eyes. After terminating the call, Curtis resumed his check-in. With the process completed he was shown to his room on the twelfth floor, near Frenchy's.

The Park Royal is a prominent building, covered externally with hanging gardens. Several acres of greenery. Its proximity to Clarke Quay and Chinatown made it an attractive place to stay. For Frenchy's purpose it was within his budget, conveniently located close to relatively inexpensive but agreeable restaurants, and where he could meet with whomever he wished in total privacy.

At 1630 on any Thursday, the afternoon traffic on the roads near the hotel is heavy so instead of his customary walk in the sun to minimise the effects of jet lag, Curtis went to the pool deck for a swim. It provided a few moments in the late afternoon sun. He called the waiter, ordered a soda water and lime without ice and eased onto a poolside recliner.

He took a sip, placed the glass on the small side table, retreated into the comfort of the recliner cushion and closed his eyes. The long night flight had taken its toll.

"I thought I might find you here."

Curtis immediately opened his eyes and sat bolt upright. "Frenchy! I just closed my eyes."

"No. You have been fast asleep for about forty minutes. I've been waiting patiently but you were in a deep sleep. I had the impression you might sleep for some time. We have matters to discuss."

With that, Frenchy turned on his heel and made his way to a nearby poolside cabana, gesturing to the waiter as he went. He ordered a Tiger. A beer locally produced by the Dutch brewer Heineken, his favourite beer.

Curtis stood, stretched, and walked slowly to join his boss. He was still dressed in swimming trunks and a towel was wrapped around his neck.

Frenchy watched the big but lithe man take casual strides towards the cabana. He couldn't help noticing the size of Curtis's biceps and forearms. The sheen of perspiration highlighted his abdominal muscles. His six-pack.

Twelve-pack more like it, thought Frenchy.

Frenchy was casually dressed in a loose-fitting tropical short-sleeved shirt buttoned to a cluster of grey chest hairs, beige coloured shorts and brown suede leather boat shoes. He wore Ray-Ban shades. From his comfortable position he gestured to Curtis to sit opposite.

"You look tired, Curtis. You have dark rings around your eyes."

Curtis ignored the comment. He launched into a briefing on the happenings in St Petersburg. How he visited the federal court to be confronted with a murderous attack; that he had been followed by a Russian who met an untimely death when his car burst into flames in the vicinity of Curtis's hotel; and the chance meeting with Coolidge. He told Frenchy about the latter's role in Green Solutions.

Frenchy was aware of the news about the Chechen rebels attacking two trains on the Moscow-St Petersburg line. He didn't know the detail. Nor did he know there might be a connection with the judge he had asked Curtis to protect.

"The first attack on a freight train was merely a distraction," Curtis told his boss. "Local police and the regional National Guard rushed to that ambushed train where a small group of alleged Chechens was shooting at railway station employees and the train staff. Strangely, nobody was hit. Doesn't that strike you as strange?"

"Of course. Chechen rebels are supposed to be well trained and I'm certain they would have selected capable marksmen for such a task."

"It wasn't the Chechens," Curtis added abruptly. "It was a group of hit men organised by a friend of Wallace. Remember you told me about the oligarch Lumovski? Him. His men were responsible for the shooting at the courthouse. One escaped the chaos there and later charged at me in his car," he repeated. "The man died before his car was incinerated. I am certain of this, Frenchy.

"You told me Wallace is the CEO of a company known as Green Solutions. You might recall I insisted there is a link between Wallace and Craig Nelson. They are using Green Solutions to raise capital and fund opposition to women seeking positions of power and influence."

"You have said that before, Curtis, but still haven't produced evidence."

Curtis was becoming annoyed. "They targeted Dao Shinawatra, tried to stop my investigations in St Petersburg, shot women, only women," he emphasised, "on the ambushed passenger train and incarcerated the judge. Isn't that enough?"

"Not convincing evidence. As I previously told you, Curtis, IB supports your activities and wants me to give you a free rein on your hunch, but me? I'm not convinced."

Curtis paused, took a few sips of his lime soda and waited for Frenchy to do likewise. He looked beyond the cabana to see if they were still alone. Of no interest to anyone else.

"I took a small risk and recruited Coolidge. He was on the verge of leaving Green Solutions. I had no choice and I made sure he didn't either. He was left with no alternative than to assist by staying in the company and feeding me appropriate information."

Frenchy looked somewhat alarmed.

"Don't worry, Frenchy. He knows me as a Russian by the name of Alexeev Hunch. I mean Alexeev Lomot."

With that, Frenchy almost smiled. A glimmer of recognition in his eyes. He nodded, acknowledging that Curtis had understood the meaning of the surname he had assigned to him.

He is sharp. I'm impressed with what he has done but I'm not about to tell him that.

"Coolidge phoned me a few hours ago." Curtis continued with more than a hint of sarcasm in his voice. "His first report. Wallace and his 'financial planner' are now here. In Singapore. Is it merely a coincidence that Singapore is hosting a conference on 'Women in Leadership' over the weekend?"

Without waiting for a response, he answered his own question. "Of course it isn't. Mr Hunch… aah… Mr Lomot might have to get to work."

Frenchy gave a deep sigh. Both men sipped their drinks in apparent contemplation for a few minutes, before Frenchy broke the silence.

"I know Nelson is in Singapore. As you know, we need to take action if an Australian is committing a criminal offence in another jurisdiction. We were tracking his movements. So far, we have nothing to support your hunch. No evidence."

"I understand that, but we can't wait for hard evidence. It will be too late," Curtis said firmly, bordering on anger. "Is it just a coincidence that Nelson happens to be in the same country as the attempted assassinations? Twice!"

"We don't have enough information and we can't just act upon circumstantial evidence," Frenchy calmly replied. "If we do, he will just walk away."

Silence. Frenchy contemplated whether to share his latest information with a simmering Curtis. He shared Curtis's views about gender equality. He acknowledged there were some in the world that would stop at nothing to reinforce their misogynistic views. Their belief in the superiority of man, that women are less capable.

A man of principle, Frenchy thought. *But it is also personal with Curtis. His anger mustn't cloud his judgement but I have always been open with him. I expect the same of him. I can trust this man like no other I've worked with.*

"I arranged to have Nelson taken into custody at Gatwick when his flight arrived from Moscow. The English gendarmes couldn't hold him for long of course and the four days he spent in the lock-up was clearly beyond reasonable," Frenchy informed Curtis in a quiet voice, the latter surprised at this new information.

"He was illegally detained. We had hoped that by questioning him at length he might give us something. Anything. Just a slip of the tongue that might give us a lead to something bigger but he didn't. He is very disciplined."

"Wrongful arrest," Curtis said, "Surely an innocent citizen detained for such a time without being charged would take action against the authorities?"

Usually a very serious person, Frenchy smiled for the first time during their meeting. "You are right onto it, Curtis. I figured if Nelson didn't immediately commence legal proceedings against the police, there was a chance he had something to hide. More would possibly be revealed if this matter went further with a court hearing.

"The other really interesting thing is what happened on the fourth day. For the first time Nelson made his permitted phone call. He was obviously pissed off with the quality of the food he was receiving and the standard of Her Majesty's accommodation. The police gave him access to a telephone but they didn't listen to the conversation, of course."

Frenchy actually has a sense of humour.

"Okay. What's interesting about that? What happened?"

"We think he phoned Wallace. Not certain, but the detectives said he may have started to say a name before thinking better of it. Five hours after the call a team of lawyers arrived led by one of the more prominent British barristers. It was amusing really."

"What's funny about that?"

"Picture this. A leading British barrister with two lawyers in tow carrying a pile of books and loose-leaf source material on criminal procedure, torts and other common law reference sources arrive at a relatively small, police lock-up. Thomson Reuters Westlaw reference books on criminal procedure, Clerk and Lindsell on torts and others."

"Yes," smiled Curtis. "Just for an ordinary citizen of Australia with nothing to hide?"

"Precisely. We shook the tree but nothing fell out. Where would a man like Nelson get the money to pay for such legal counsel? Why was it necessary?"

"They made a mistake. Should have hired a no-name local solicitor."

"Yes, Curtis, his choice of law firm raises more questions. Points the finger to his collaborators. Big money doesn't normally think of such things. They want the best."

Curtis realised where Frenchy was heading with this line of thinking.

"Interestingly, the legal firm that attended the police station demanding his release is the same firm that acts for Lumovski in the UK," Frenchy announced.

"Surely this additional information must convince you I'm on the right track, sir?"

Frenchy noticed a change in Curtis's complexion. He was again becoming agitated.

"Perhaps," Frenchy calmly replied. "But I say again, we don't have the conclusive evidence to hold Nelson, Wallace or anyone else. Yet!"

"Bell wants you to push on though. I want you to push on. Just be careful and don't do anything that links you to…" His voiced tapered off.

"You look tired. Have an early night, Curtis. Get some sleep. We'll talk in the morning."

Without further comment Frenchy downed his remaining beer, rose and left the cabana.

Chapter 42

A feature article in the *Straits Times* announced the conference. 'Conscious and Unconscious Bias — Breaking Down the Barriers, is to be held at the Raffles City Convention Centre on Bras Basah Road. Speakers will include political and business leaders from France, England, Australia and Malaysia,' the article said.

Curtis focused on the article before flicking through others in the *Straits Times*. He was enjoying a coffee in the lobby restaurant at the Park Royal.

'The conference aims to inform the public at large of the difficulties experienced by women in breaking through the glass ceiling,' the article said. 'It will provide women with the opportunity to discuss individual experiences and workplace practices.'

The article highlighted excerpts of a paper to be delivered to a plenary session by a leading Australian business figure, referring to the negative use of social media. It quoted a former prime minister who said social media was 'kind of like electronic graffiti'.

'Women are disproportionately victims of abuse in this online age,' the excerpt stated. 'There are of course major structural barriers to women advancing in politics and business. There is also sexism and misogyny expressed by the anonymity of online abuse. That must be addressed. We must challenge and defeat this blight on our culture.'

Across the city at the same time Wallace and Nelson were deriding the article over breakfast in the Summer Pavilion at the Ritz-Carlton Millennia Hotel.

"Feminism is cancer," Wallace smirked. "That's how our friend Milo Yiannopoulos described it."

Not wanting to appear totally uninformed Nelson asked, "Remind me again please, Jim. Who is Milo?"

"Milo is an author and public speaker who stands up for men's rights. I recently attended his public address to a crowd of people in

Sydney. He was invited to Australia by a senator. He talked about the myth Jews perpetrate about the so-called holocaust, the alternative right, and he lambasted feminists. Some feminists and other radicals protested outside the hall. Boy, did he give them a serve! Inspirational stuff," added Wallace with a grin.

"I would have liked to have been present for that speech," Nelson agreed.

After a few minutes' chat about their shared philosophical position on such matters, the two discussed plans for the day. A meeting was scheduled with the Southeast Asian distributors of the Green Solutions products.

"More importantly, are any of your Thailand… er… distributors on the way here as I requested?" Wallace asked, the smirk returning.

"Colonel Juntarsa, the commanding officer at the training school, has sent one of the men I trained to a combat service support course." Nelson deliberately dropped Juntarsa's name and rank into his reply to impress Wallace. "He is arriving mid-morning. I plan to reconnoitre the convention centre following the distributor's meeting, and then meet with him."

"You will of course assign him a serious task as we discussed," Wallace instructed.

"Yes, of course. He is the best man for the job."

"It's important that we also obtain a list of people attending the conference," Wallace said.

"Absolutely. To help with our plans for the future. Oh, and by the way speaking of our future plans, the soldier arriving from Thailand is the one I told you about. The one who speaks fluent French."

"Good work. Was he with the RKK?"

"Yes, he was. My man at the NCO training school handpicked him. The most disciplined, skilful and fundamentalist of the RKK recruits."

"How long does the course last? Can we ensure it lasts some weeks so that we may use him elsewhere?"

"I have already arranged that. He knows he will be undertaking military work of a different nature. Military work, but in a non-military environment." Nelson laughed at his last comment. "We can send him wherever we choose. As far as the Thai Army is concerned, he is engaged in training with the Singapore Army."

Wallace merely stared at Nelson. "This is serious business, Craig."

"Yes, of course. Where do you intend using him after he completes this task, Jim?"

"I will think about that and talk to Edgar later today. You will be the first to know. I'm thinking of either England or France. Brexit should take care of the English problem. A problem appears to be emerging in one of the regional cities in France. Your man would be perfect to solve that."

That explains why you wanted him to learn French. Good thinking, Jim. Forward planning.

"Okay, Jim. Let me know what your brother thinks and we will forge ahead as instructed. In the meantime, we have work to do. This stupid conference shall not proceed."

***

One name in the article caught Curtis's eye. A reference to Jolanta Chan of the Singapore Police. 'Ms Chan will chair a session entitled "Gender Equality in Government — a Singapore Experience". Her emphasis will be on all of the positive initiatives taken by the Singaporean government towards gender equality in recent years.'

Curtis found Jolanta's business card in his wallet and dialled her mobile phone.

"Curtis here, Jolanta," he said when she answered. "We met on the flight from Doha yesterday."

"Yes, of course. How are you?" Without waiting for an answer, "Better after a good night's sleep in one of our comfortable Singaporean hotels, I hope?"

"I'm fine. Do you have time for coffee today?"

"I am free this afternoon, around three p.m. I will be in the Raffles City Convention Centre, which is in the Raffles City Shopping Centre. I recommend the Saint Marc Café. They make great coffee. Does that suit you?"

"Perfect. I'll meet you there at three. One small favour, Jolanta. I know you are working at the 'Conscious and Unconscious Bias' conference tomorrow. Would you mind bringing the speaker's list?"

"Now, why would you want that?"

"A long story. I'll explain my reasons when we meet."

His usual practice was to arrive early. He attended the Saint Marc Café well ahead of schedule. At the counter he ordered a mug of strong coffee with a dash of milk and then found a vacant table away from other diners. Back to the wall, facing the entrance.

Curtis sipped on his coffee whilst working on sudoku in the latest *USA Today*, retrieved from a nearby vacant table. Occasionally he would glance towards the entrance and around the café without raising his head.

A number of heads were raised and turned towards the entrance when Jolanta walked in. She was dressed in a pale rain blue jacket and a royal blue Wenmore fabric skirt. A single button in the centre of her jacket was fastened, highlighting her trim figure. Her black shoulder-length hair shone under the café's entrance lights.

She's carrying some papers. Good. The conference programmes.

Curtis stood and greeted Jolanta with an extended shake of hands.

"How do you take your coffee, Ms Chan?"

"Jolanta. Please call me Jolanta. Cappuccino please."

Curtis quickly moved to the counter, ordered and paid for a long macchiato in a mug and a cappuccino also in a mug.

"I have the programme, Mr Curtis. Actually, I don't know your name. You introduced yourself as 'Curtis' on the telephone. Is that your given name or surname?"

"Surname, but it is the only name I answer to. As a boy I was tired of always having to spell my first name, Rhys. So, Curtis it is. As simple as that," Curtis chuckled quietly.

"You said you would tell me why you wanted the schedule of speakers. Are you with the media?"

Curtis laughed at that suggestion. He told Jolanta he was with a special operations unit in the Australian Defence Force, and also worked closely with Interpol as an accredited agent. For security reasons he didn't elaborate on the Operational Intelligence Unit nor tell her he always worked alone. As far as he was concerned, the unit had a membership of one.

"We are always mindful of potential security risks surrounding events such as the conference this weekend," Curtis added. "I am personally concerned to see this conference is a success and not in any way interrupted."

Jolanta gave a broad smile at this comment. She felt very much at ease with this man. His intentions appeared honourable. The security of attendees and the success of this most important conference. She handed Curtis a bundle of documents. Photocopies of the original documents including a list of conference speakers, chairpersons of each session and registered attendees.

They sat quietly for several minutes whilst Curtis cast his eye over the names under each category. He was searching for one name in particular and there it was.

"I notice one woman, Dao Shinawatra from Thailand, was to be a speaker but her name has a line though it and another name written in," Curtis commented still looking at the lists, "Is she attending?"

"No. I'm a member of the organising committee for the conference. By chance I was in the office the day when she phoned and cancelled. I tried to persuade her to at least attend the conference if she was no longer willing to be a speaker but she said her doctor recommended against the travel. She seemed upset and passed the phone to her security adviser to complete the call."

Curious! Obviously, a new position on her staff. From all of the information I was able to glean she was complacent about security. Not so now. That's good.

"Her adviser, a man who had a rather long name as do many Thais, was adamant that Ms Shinawatra was unable to attend as she was recuperating from an operation."

"Do you remember the man's name, Jolanta?"

"Hardly," she laughed, "But I can tell you it started with an R. That's all I can remember. It was Rabt or Ratt-something."

She has accepted my recommendation.

Chapter 43

The Park Royal has an outstanding gymnasium. Curtis made good use of it in the early morning. He half expected Frenchy to put in an appearance too but it didn't happen. Instead, Frenchy had gone for a long walk along the Singapore River. He walked from Clarke Quay, crossing the river on Esplanade Drive, and passing along the bank of the river to Lower Delta Drive. There he again crossed over and returned to the hotel. A reasonable walking distance.

Frenchy enjoyed walking in the early morning. It gave him time alone to contemplate. This morning he had also taken the opportunity to make a call and brief his boss as he walked.

Bell: "Don't you think there is an irresistible inference, based upon what Curtis has told you that this Nelson fellow was involved in the attacks in Russia?"

Frenchy: "I cannot confidently draw that conclusion."

Bell: "Nelson was in Thailand… more than that… in the vicinity when there was an attempt on Ms Shinawatra's life. Second, Nelson was in Russia when there was an attempt to silence Curtis and when there were attacks on the train apparently, but mistakenly as it now appears, on which the outspoken female judge was a passenger. And now you tell me Nelson is in Singapore and there is a conference on this weekend for women in leadership? Come on, Frenchy. Surely you might think there could be a connection?"

Frenchy: "I can understand why you might think that but I can't just give Curtis free rein on the basis of a hunch or even these events coinciding with Nelson's presence in the area. I need more."

Bell: "Frenchy, you have often told me you don't believe in coincidences. Right?"

Frenchy: "Yes, but…"

Bell: "But nothing! This is not just a coincidence!"

Frenchy: "We will have egg on our collective faces if we make a mistake. I'm just being cautious with how we pursue this matter. If indeed there is a matter to pursue. My strong recommendation is that we wait and see how things transpire. Let's see if we can gather some hard and conclusive evidence."

Bell: "No. My instructions are to allow Curtis to discretely follow his hunch. To deal with the people involved… aah… as he should."

Frenchy: "I understand. I shall convey your instructions to Curtis. Tell him he must exercise restraint. Tell him to act according to his training and scope of work and responsibility in the circumstances. Is that what you want?"

Bell: "Absolutely. I couldn't have put it better. Well, perhaps I could have."

***

The front page of the *Straits Times* carried an article about the forthcoming elections in Singapore and Malaysia. Curtis skim read that and turned the page. Page two carried a follow-up article on the weekend's women's conference. It was more of an advertisement listing the main topics for discussion and inviting early registration.

In the centre of the article, highlighted by a strong square border intended to catch the eye of the reader, was a quote from the French author Simone de Beauvoir. It read: 'Representation of the world, like the world itself, is the work of men; they describe it from their own point of view, which they confuse with the absolute truth.'

Freedom of speech is a good thing, thought Curtis. Having read the quote, he chuckled quietly.

"What amuses you this morning?"

Curtis turned towards the voice as it approached his breakfast table.

"Good morning, Frenchy. I expected to see you in the gym this morning."

"Took a long walk instead. Phoned Bell."

"And?"

"And your instructions are to continue. You have Bell's full support. But make no mistake, Curtis," he added drily, "You are to proceed with restraint and within the scope of your responsibility as a Special Ops soldier."

"Gather more evidence? Deal with any situation that may cause embarrassment to the government? Uphold and enforce international law? Defend and protect?"

"Continue. Despite my reservations. Be careful, Curtis."

"Continue until when, sir?"

"Until we no longer have reason to be concerned about those particular Australian citizens breaking the laws of another jurisdiction. Until the job is completed."

"I understand." Curtis smiled and nodded acceptance of the mission. "With both Wallace and Nelson in Singapore, my next move will be to attend the conference today. I cannot register to attend but I have a contact who has kindly provided me with a security accreditation and tag for the Raffles City Convention Centre."

"This morning I received an intelligence report that revealed both Wallace and Nelson left Singapore last night. Wallace flew to London and Nelson to Sydney. You probably have no need to be concerned about the conference, unless you have other reasons to attend of course," Frenchy said with what appeared to Curtis to be a sly grin.

Curtis almost admonished his boss with a stern reply. "You don't think those scumbags would do the dirty work themselves, do you?"

"I am merely providing you with an update, and have you contemplate all the options."

With that comment Frenchy rose and took a few steps away from the table. He stopped, turned to Curtis and said, "Don't do anything I wouldn't do."

Typical Frenchy cynicism. Always a man of few words.

Curtis also knew the last comment was an indication of Frenchy's intention to depart Singapore that day. As Frenchy made his way towards the hotel lobby, Curtis caught him by the arm. "One other thing, Frenchy. Can you please text me a photograph of Wallace? His passport photo will do."

"Easy. Immigration will send it to me and I shall immediately forward it to you. I'm surprised you haven't asked for it before. I've been waiting for that request. Be thorough, Curtis. Don't let anything else cloud your judgement."

Curtis thanked Frenchy, told him he would be in touch and returned to his coffee to plan his next move.

Frenchy is right. Perhaps I haven't devised a strategy as well as I should have. Time to think.

Chapter 44

For those conference attendees who had not registered online, registration was to commence at 0900. Curtis arrived at 0800 and walked around the relatively empty shopping centre. As night shopping is common in Singapore, most shops open after 0945. He noted the position of closed-circuit television cameras, the position of the centre's security office and the location of exit doors. He would remember the precise location of each camera.

The Raffles City Convention Centre is on the fourth level of the shopping centre. At approximately 0815, Curtis took the escalator to that floor. Already there was a group of women standing at a registration counter, about five metres from the main door.

Curtis approached the counter just as a security officer rushed forward and urged the women to stand on the opposite side of the carpeted lobby.

"We have a security issue. Please stand well back from the doors!" he exclaimed, ushering the women away from the counter.

Security glared at Curtis before noticing the tag on the lanyard around his neck.

"Please help to keep the women away from this area," he muttered nervously.

Curtis obliged, calmly ushering the women backwards before returning to Security and asking, "What's the issue?"

"A small bomb is attached to the door handles," whispered Security.

"Stand back and let me deal with it. I need wire cutters," Curtis urged.

"I am in charge here. I cannot allow anyone else to handle this."

"Please let me fix this. I'm a soldier. I know what to do," Curtis pleaded. "Please. Take the women down the escalator and sound the fire alarm to evacuate the building."

"No. I cannot allow that. I must take responsibility. It's my job to deal with all security issues in the shopping complex."

As Security was making his case, Curtis had looked past him at the doors and saw what is commonly called a baseball grenade.

"Please, please allow me the chance to deal with the hand grenade," he urged. "I can see the safety pin is wired to the handles of both doors. If somebody opened a door the pin would be extracted, releasing the spring-loaded lever and kaboom!"

"How do you know the bomb is a hand grenade? How can I trust you? For all I know, you may have planted this thing. I've never seen you here before." Security was becoming anxious.

Pointing at the device and in a convincing tone Curtis said, "I can see what that is from here. It's a M67 fragmentation grenade. It packs quite a punch and will kill anyone within about five metres. It will seriously injure anyone within a further twenty or so metres, so you need to get these women away from here. You need to trust me on this."

"Okay, okay," said Security anxiously. "But I cannot leave here. This is my responsibility. You take the women out of the building. Attached to a pillar at the bottom of the escalator there is a glass cabinet containing a fire extinguisher and an alarm button. Break the glass and push the button. Get the women out and come straight back. I'll wait for you before we decide what to do. Go now before I call the police."

Curtis was left with no choice. He didn't want to create a scene or cause panic. Before moving off he turned to Security and asked, "Might there be someone inside the hall? Is there another entrance? If there is, you should immediately secure that door."

"Nobody inside," replied Security.

Walking briskly to the far side of the room, Curtis asked the gathering of women to leave the premises. A security matter needed to be addressed without endangering anyone.

At the bottom of the escalator he found the box to which Security referred, broke the glass and slammed his fist onto the alarm button. A fire alarm immediately sounded. Five seconds of shrill noise and then a recorded message, "This is not a drill. Please leave the building. Do not run. Move to the muster point across the road." The message stopped and the alarm sounded again for another five seconds. The cycle continued.

When Curtis hit the alarm button it also triggered an alarm on the computerised system at the central fire station a few blocks away. Shortly after, fire appliance sirens could be heard.

Curtis hastily directed the group to the escalator on the first level. That's when it happened. An explosion. Panic set in amongst the group, and most immediately started to run.

"Don't panic. Exit the building. Don't run. The explosion was localised," Curtis yelled. It made no difference, fear and momentum kept them moving down the escalators and outside the building without slowing.

At the front of the complex Curtis dialled 999, stated his name and number, his location and the nature of the emergency. "Get the bomb squad here. There has been an explosion. It was probably a hand grenade but it sounded louder with the reverberation. We don't know if there is another device inside."

The fire service arrived first. Curtis reassured the captain the alarm was activated only for the purpose of evacuating the building. "But stand by," he instructed.

The police arrived, accompanied by two officers wearing full body blast suits. Curtis quickly told them what he had seen on the fourth floor. Dressed in advanced bomb suits with the appearance of space suits, without waiting for instructions the officers lumbered up the escalators. One carried a metal case containing equipment used for rendering safe an explosive device. His colleague carried equipment used in circumstances of a high order detonation, intended to contain an explosion.

Ten minutes passed. The police officer in charge, a station inspector, spoke into his hand-held radio and then immediately ordered a group of nearby officers to enter the building and assist the bomb squad in searching for any unexploded devices.

In the meantime, Curtis had turned to the gathering of women, calmly telling them the involvement of bomb detectors was precautionary. He was intent on reassuring the group that had now expanded to include other conference attendees, and shop assistants who had arrived for work.

The station inspector looked quizzically at Curtis.

This big man is a leader. Seems to know what he is doing.

He approached the big man. "Who are you? What are you doing here?"

Moving away from the group, Curtis quietly informed the officer he had been engaged as security for the convention centre conference. The inspector seemed satisfied, although he gazed at Curtis until distracted by the crackle of his radio.

Concluding his radio communication, the station inspector again turned to Curtis and said grimly, "Tell the conference organisers the Stamford Room will be closed. You will have to move to the Atrium ballroom, which I understand is free today, or cancel the conference altogether. Your call."

"I understand," Curtis replied. "How serious is it?" Curtis knew there was almost certainly a fatality. He surmised that Security had messed with the grenade.

"Two dead."

"Two! There was only one other security person on the floor. He told me there was no-one inside the conference room."

"Unfortunately, there was. Two of the conference organisers were in the hall making some last-minute preparations. One of them opened the door. In so doing, she pulled the grenade pin, releasing the lever. Two persons are deceased. I'm sorry, your colleague, the other security officer, and the woman who opened the door from inside."

Curtis suddenly realised he hadn't seen Jolanta. "Do we know the names?" he asked anxiously.

"Until we contact next of kin please keep this information quiet. Sadly, the woman was one of our people. The blast threw her back inside the room. She had no chance. The security officer was also killed instantly. It's a mess up there."

"Who was she? A name."

The inspector hesitated. "Our police force counsellor."

"Jolanta?"

"Yes, unfortunately. Jolanta Chan."

Chapter 45

Curtis made a secure call to Frenchy to brief him on the tragedy.

"I am aware of the act of terrorism, as the media are describing it," Frenchy said. "It was on the midday news."

With more than a hint of sarcasm in his voice Curtis asked, "Is it just a coincidence that Nelson has been here and left in the last twenty-four hours?"

Frenchy ignored the question, instead asking for more detail on the tragedy. "The media said there was an explosion and two people have been killed. You were there. How did it play out? Where was the device placed and what type of bomb was it? Has anyone claimed responsibility?"

Curtis gave a detailed, almost minute-by-minute precise description of the tragic event. He told Frenchy of the type of hand grenade and, just in case the latter had forgotten, having not been in operations for some time, he described the impact of an M67 detonation. He described how Security had insisted he take the women from the building. In return he had insisted that Security wait for his return before taking any further action. Security hadn't triggered the grenade.

His voice quivered slightly when he said, "A woman opened the door from inside the conference room. The pin had been wired to the door handle. Opening the door extracted the pin and you know what happened next."

Frenchy was silent for a few moments. "You knew her, didn't you, Curtis?"

Yes, and I should never have allowed it to happen. I could have prevented this tragedy if I had followed my instincts and not the insistence of Security.

"Yes… I knew her."

"Does this make it more difficult for you, Curtis? Should we give this task to someone else?"

A huge sigh was released by Curtis before formally and firmly responding, "No, sir! We shouldn't. This is my job. I have a plan and I shall follow it through."

"Care to share your plan with me?" Frenchy asked.

"It will take too long to elaborate on right now, although if that is an order... Besides, I am not getting a clear signal here, sir."

"It's clear at this end. Okay... I won't push the point but I remain concerned. Tell me what transpired after the explosion. Bell will want to know. Has anyone claimed responsibility, any suspects?"

"The Singapore Police have been most cooperative. The woman who was killed had provided me with a security pass for the conference. The police recognised the status afforded me by the official pass. Together with senior police I viewed the CCTV footage from several different camera positions at the entrance to the convention centre and within the shopping precinct."

"Get to the point, Curtis. Did you learn anything? Are you able to make a connection with Nelson or Wallace?"

"No, but I will, sir. Rest assured, I will."

Chapter 46

Undeterred by the tragedy and the intimidation directed at the women participating in the conference, the organisers stood firm. A press statement issued within two hours assured the public the conference would proceed. Proceedings would commence in the afternoon in an alternative meeting room, The Atrium, providing forensic police the time and space to thoroughly complete their work.

Flanked by police officers, the convention centre chief of security viewed the CCTV high-resolution discs. Curtis watched patiently as they trolled through footage from every camera in the building. He stood behind and looked over their shoulders. He was only interested in seeing the footage within the vicinity of the main door of the Stamford Room. If that did not reveal a clear image of the perpetrator, there were two other cameras that surely would.

At 0545 a small figure came into view. He wore tight brown trousers and a brown loose-fitting jacket with a large hood pulled forward to hide his face. He carried a backpack. The man walked slowly towards the entrance to the Stamford Room.

"Slow the action," Curtis said.

Security did so. The hooded man now walked in slow motion towards the door, stopped, placed his backpack on the floor near the door and knelt to open it. He retrieved an object that wasn't visible to the camera and a strand of wire.

"Stop there," Curtis instructed. "Wind it back five frames."

Curtis leant in towards the screen. "Back another three frames, please." He could now see the diminutive figure's footwear as he knelt down.

He's wearing army boots. Combat boots used in tropical countries. Low profile. Light leather and canvas. Vented behind the ankles. I've seen that type of boot recently.

The figure stood and glanced around without lifting his head. The hood shadowed his face. Noting he was still on his own in the conference room lobby he walked quickly to the door and busied himself. Facing away from the surveillance cameras. Fixing a grenade to the door handles. Job done, he walked briskly to the escalator. Face still hidden.

"Can we look at the view from the surveillance camera on level four facing the top of the escalator please. There is a powerful spotlight situated directly above, also facing the escalator. He either won't see the camera or won't expect one there. With the extra light we might get a glimpse of his face."

The CCTV controller glanced sideways at the police officer in charge, the station inspector, who quickly nodded agreement. After examining a hard copy of a building plan to find the correct camera, he shuffled through the discs and inserted one into the player.

"We know he is a military man," Curtis said with certainty. "The question is which country?"

The police officers looked at each other sceptically.

"Play it slowly, please," Curtis urged.

The perpetrator's face was clearly visible for a few seconds whilst he descended to the floor below. It was enough for the police officers to point to his features and state with confidence that the man was most likely from Thailand.

Of course he is. The third soldier Nelson worked closely with at the NCO school.

"Definitely not a local," the inspector barked. "Get that disc to our station as quickly as possible. Our technical people will freeze the clearest frame and enhance the image. I urgently want that face widely circulated. Go!"

Turning to Curtis he said, "That was very observant of you. We would have discovered that image eventually of course. You probably just sped up the process. Thank you."

After exchanging mobile phone numbers, Curtis and the station inspector went their separate ways. The inspector had undertaken to keep Curtis informed of any developments. Curtis decided to spend the next twenty-four hours within the vicinity of the rescheduled conference. Although not expecting any other incidents, he needed to be sure.

After the conference and the funeral, I need to pay a visit to Colonel Juntarsa.

Chapter 47

"Jaruth… er, Rat, where are you? I have booked into the Grand Centara in Hua Hin and the receptionist told me you have left the hotel's employ. Please call. *Ka pun karp*. Thank you, Curtis."

The conference in Singapore had proceeded without further interruption and was deemed to be a huge success. Curtis had attended some of the sessions, lingering around the perimeter of the hall. Eyes constantly darting from door to door, person to person. Scanning the attendees.

He listened with interest to the speaker who talked about a conference in Bangkok sponsored by the Thinking and Working Politically group. This group had made gender equality a major part of the Bangkok agenda, focusing on local community practice. Dao Shinawatra was meant to deliver this speech. It was uncontroversial but Curtis sensed it would nevertheless raise the ire of Nelson and his group.

His immediate mission was to determine if Colonel Juntarsa was part of the Wallace/Nelson cadre.

If he is, I will need to adopt a new approach. Alter my plans to bring these people down.

Within minutes Jaruth Ratnamphod returned his call. "*Sawardee karp*. My friend, it is so good to hear from you. Where have you been?"

"It doesn't matter where I've been, Rat, I'm now back in Thailand. You have left the Hua Hin Centara Resort," said Curtis. "Where are you right now?"

"I'm in Bangkok. I have a new job as a security adviser."

"I know. Dao is in good hands."

"How did you know I'm working for her?"

"I'm an investigator remember," Curtis chuckled quietly. "What are her plans? Will she pursue a political career?"

Rat hesitated for a few moments before responding in a desultory tone. "Unsure. She is still assessing her level of support. Understandably too, she is concerned for her own safety but also has ambitions."

Curtis smiled at the memory of his last meeting with Dao Shinawatra.

Rat continued. "Only this morning Dao told me your comment to her is ringing in her ears. Apparently, you made quite an impression, my friend." Rat's mood seemed to change with the last comment. "You told her to pursue her dreams. You said something like, 'do not be deterred from chasing your ambition', remember?"

"Of course."

"What are your plans? Why have you returned to Thailand? Why don't you visit Bangkok?" Rat fired off the questions without waiting for an answer. Then, more softly, "I'm sure Dao would like to see you."

Curtis ignored the comment.

"Rat, do you know anything about the background of Colonel Juntarsa from the NCO training school?"

"No, nothing. I shall make enquiries."

"Call me if you learn anything about him. I think you know the type of things I would find interesting," Curtis said. "I plan to visit the colonel."

The sun was commencing its rapid descent towards the Gulf of Thailand. A large number of squid fishing boats were making their way along the western side of the Gulf. Boats from the Khao Takiap fishing village several kilometres to the south of Hua Hin. Green lights would soon flood the waters surrounding them.

From his favourite bar near the beach Curtis watched the small boats manoeuvre their way around rocky outcrops and subsurface reef. He was fascinated by the design of the vessels. A large motor and long shaft holding a propeller well clear of the stern. This was deftly swivelled and turned by the skipper to drag nets without entangling them. *Skilled operators at the helm. The squid have no chance.*

A waiter approached and he ordered a lime soda, no ice. Piped easy listening music from the seventies played quietly in the background. Curtis reclined slightly in a poolside wicker day chair and closed his eyes. Soaking up the last of the late afternoon sun. Feet moving to the rhythm of the music — *I Will Survive*, the female emancipation anthem

"Good evening, Mr Curtis."

Curtis was jolted out of a semi-slumber. The resort general manager stood next to his day chair, hand extended. Curtis stood quickly and the two shook hands.

"We are pleased to welcome you back so soon after your most recent visit," the GM said as if Curtis was a regular visitor. "If we can make your stay more enjoyable in any way, or if there are any particular needs you may have, please don't hesitate to contact me or another member of my staff."

"Thank you. I like the Grand Centara very much even though this stay is again short. I will return."

"Pleased to hear it. As I say, if we can make your stay more pleasant just ask," the general manager concluded, turned and walked away.

Curtis slowly sipped on his lime soda without further interruption. His thoughts drifted to the meeting he proposed with Colonel Juntarsa.

I need to know if you are part of the bigger picture, Colonel. Are you friend or foe? Your answer to my questions will determine how widely this disease has spread.

Curtis thought long and hard about the order of questions. Not only was it important to determine if Juntarsa was closely involved with Wallace and his cohorts, he needed to know if his own identity had been revealed to Nelson. To be forewarned is to be forearmed.

Now, time to visit Rat's friend at the Grand Night Market. Noi, the cook at the Lucky Star Restaurant.

Ambling past the market stalls, as before he hesitated briefly at the Dar Restaurant. Tempted by the aromas of genuine Thai food being enjoyed by a large group of diners.

I'm sure Noi will satisfy my taste buds too.

"*Sawardee karp*," said Noi. "*Oliang* without sugar or lime soda, no ice?"

Curtis smiled. Noi has a good memory. "The latter please."

"Latter? What does 'latter' mean?"

"The last mentioned."

"Okay," Noi acknowledged, "but why didn't you say that? Lime soda, no ice." He walked away to welcome two new diners to the restaurant with a friendly '*sawardee karp*' accompanied by a smile. Curtis noticed the change in Noi's demeanour with the arrival of new guests.

Three couples now sat at separate tables within close proximity to each other. At two of the tables casually dressed locals shared several plates of seafood, stir-fried vegetables, crispy deep-fried fish, a green curry and steamed rice. The third couple was from Europe. Curtis heard them conversing in German. They chatted with enthusiasm about their travel plans in the following days whilst sipping continuously from their beer glasses.

After ten minutes or so the Germans summoned Noi. In sharp tones and a heavy accent, they ordered more beer and requested the cook and waiter expedite their order. Noi explained that his waiter had taken ill and he was left to do three jobs — drinks waiter, food waiter and chef. His guests were totally uninterested in his excuse. Not the slightest bit sympathetic. Their mood softened when he returned quickly with more beers and complimentary nuts.

Business must be improving if Noi has employed someone.

More food arrived for the now three tables of local customers and more beer for the Europeans. They again appeared restless and Noi reassured them their food was almost ready. Their order arrived soon thereafter.

Curtis's eyes darted from table to table and watched with amusement at the eagerness with which the locals ate and the Europeans drank. His stomach rumbled a little, reminding him that he hadn't eaten since breakfast on his flight from Singapore.

Noi returned a few minutes later and set the lime soda at Curtis's side. "What do you like to eat?" he asked impatiently as Curtis turned the pages of the menu. "What do you want?"

Grumpy tonight, aren't we, Noi?

Noting the spelling hadn't been corrected on the menu, Curtis smiled at the reference to 'crap fried rice' and 'moaning glory'. He ordered the crab fried rice, morning glory, and his favourite, beef Massaman curry.

Noi repeated the order, grunted and walked away. Curtis was sensitive to the moods of those with whom he conversed. He sensed that Noi had a grievance towards him and he wanted to get to the bottom of that disquiet.

When his food was delivered, Curtis ate slowly, anticipating the other guests would eat and leave before he was finished. He wanted time alone with Captain Grumpy. Noi returned to his table with a piece of paper, which he immediately thrust in front of his customer. The bill.

"Can we chat for a few minutes, Noi? Let me buy you a drink."

Noi hesitated. Curtis pointed to the chair opposite and Noi appeared to sit reluctantly.

"Do we have a problem, you and I?" Curtis asked.

"What do you mean?"

"You seem to be somewhat grumpy tonight. Towards me anyway. That's most unusual. Not your usual demeanour. I say again, do we have a problem?"

"I'm sorry, Mr Curtis. I should not talk. You have caused me the problem."

"Curtis. No mister, just Curtis. Now, what problem?" Curtis asked anxiously. "Please explain."

Noi looked down, shuffling his feet. He was obviously reluctant to open up.

"Please, Noi. It may be important to your friend Rat."

That comment hit the right button just as Curtis had thought it might. Noi was concerned for his close friend Jaruth Ratnamphod.

"After the incident at the training school an investigation was held into how you entered the base without going through the normal procedures. The commanding officer was concerned that protocol had been ignored."

"How did that affect you?" Curtis asked.

"The sentry at the front entrance was questioned and he informed them I carried an extra passenger in my car that morning. I was taken to the lock-up and spent the night there. Not very comfortable, Curtis," he sneered as he made that remark. "They threatened to have me court martialled for deliberately ignoring the security protocol."

"But they only threatened you," Curtis said. "What happened next?"

"I was physically beaten in the lock-up."

Noi stood, removed his apron and raised his polo shirt revealing bruising on his torso.

"Why? It's not as if you committed a criminal offence. In fact, your involvement ensured a crime wasn't committed."

"They wanted to know more about you. Where you came from? Who is assisting you? If there are others involved?"

Curtis wanted the names of those involved in the interrogation. "You said 'they'. Who are 'they', Noi? And what did you tell them?"

"Please, Mr Curtis. Don't let this go any further." Noi's anxiety showed in his features.

Reassuringly Curtis said, "It won't, Noi, I promise you. I just need to know who it was that wanted to know more about me. The commanding officer already knows everything he needs to know."

Noi hesitated before responding. He looked directly into Curtis's eyes. Probably deeper.

"I told him you are European, that's all. I told him you forced me to drive you into the battalion grounds. I said I don't even know your name but you are a big man and you frightened me."

That's plausible and convincing, thought Curtis. "But, Noi, who are 'they'? Was it one man or more?"

Noi hesitated again, obviously nervous about the possible consequences of disclosing too much information, before saying, "The Regimental Sergeant Major. Only the RSM. He is responsible for the training programme, the movement or transfer of soldiers and, of course, discipline."

Curtis nodded, pensively.

Noi continued, "You told me about the Australian who was a consultant to the NCO school. The RSM is his friend."

Chapter 48

Curtis rose early from a fitful sleep. The nightmare had returned after the events in Singapore. An early morning run along the beautiful white sands of the Hua Hin beach was in order. He pushed himself hard in the loose sands. South in the direction of Khao Takiap and the direction of the army base.

Too early to drop in on you now, Colonel, but I will certainly visit you when you least expect.

Curtis sprinted harder for a few minutes, perspiration pouring from his forehead. Sprint, walk, sprint, walk. The beach attracted guests from the various adjacent hotels. As they emerged from behind brick and glass walls, most stopped to watch the large man, obviously a fitness fanatic, punish his body with insane running.

Three hundred metres from the beach entrance to the Grand Centara, Curtis slowed to a walking pace. Early morning beach-goers, most of whom obviously saved their exercise regime until their annual visit to the beach, stopped and gawked at him. Some were Thais. Most were oversized and unfit Europeans. The women gawked, the men took sneaky sideways glances, not wanting to appear too impressed. Some of the latter group puffed out their chests and flexed their somewhat scrawny muscles in a silent and probably futile effort to impress their companions.

Curtis scaled the steps from the beach, through a small foot-wash pond to remove excess sand and onto the paved area near a pavilion. The rear entrance security attendant emerged from behind the commanding structure and said, "*Sawardee karp*, Mr Curtis. Welcome back."

"*Kopun karp*, thank you," replied Curtis.

"Your friend has been waiting for you. He is sitting by the pool."

Curtis walked in the direction of the main pool and there he was. The diminutive figure of the Rat.

"What brings you here, Rat?" Curtis asked.

Rat stood, bowed his head slightly and gave the traditional Y, hands clasped in front of his chest. "*Sawardee karp*, Curtis," he said with his customary grin. "I came to see you of course. You are in my country; how could I not visit?"

Curtis reciprocated with the Y gesture and replied, "Join me for breakfast. I shall take a shower and then we can chat. See you at the restaurant."

At breakfast Curtis informed the Rat about the tragic event in Singapore and the apparent 'coincidence' of Nelson's visit there in the preceding days.

"I have a hunch you intend interrogating Colonel Juntarsa," Rat said emphatically.

Curtis laughed. "Hunch. Did you say 'hunch'? I told you yesterday I intended meeting with him. Remember? I asked if you know anything about his background."

"Yes, of course you did. There is nothing unusual about the colonel. My sources tell me Juntarsa is a well-respected officer who will be considered for promotion in the near future. He runs a tight operation here and never goes over budget. If he is to have any weakness it is that he puts a great deal of trust in some of his junior officers and NCOs, some of whom have let him down in the past."

"How? How have they let him down?" Curtis was anxious to learn of any weakness.

"I understand the most recent example was when an NCO allowed a stranger to enter the training school without authority." The Rat winked at Curtis and smiled broadly as he made the comment.

"Surely that matter wasn't reported up the chain of command, beyond the school?" Curtis asked, rhetorically. "Surely the commanding officer dealt with the matter internally."

"That is his other potential weakness."

Rat paused and slurped on his cup of tea. Curtis looked intently across the table at his little friend, waiting for him to be more forthcoming.

"He is very honest and transparent with the top brass in Bangkok. He shares too much information about what is happening at his training school. Having said that, I gather he has honoured his commitment to the Australian authorities not to disclose any information about you.

"Shall we call ahead and arrange the meeting with Colonel Juntarsa or shall we just go to the battalion and hope to see him?"

"What do you mean by 'we'? Are you expecting to attend my meeting with the colonel?" Curtis asked.

Rat looked somewhat surprised with the question. "I assumed…"

"Did you now," Curtis interrupted. "You assumed. Okay, Rat, you can attend the meeting but I will ask the questions. I'll do the talking. If I want your advice, I will ask for it."

They ate in silence. Curtis crunched on toast, American crispy bacon, three fried eggs, four hash browns and a generous scoop of baked beans washed down with a second mug of coffee delivered by the ubiquitous waiting staff. Rat ate tropical fruit followed by fried rice and steamed fish. Neither spoke.

After several minutes Rat broke the silence with an apology. "I'm sorry, Curtis, I didn't mean to gate-crash your party but I thought I could be of some help."

Realising he had been a little harsh in his tone, Curtis reached across the table and patted Rat on the arm. "I'm sure your local knowledge and better understanding of the Thai culture and body language will be valuable."

Rat nodded in acknowledgement. Suddenly his face lit up with his characteristic smile. A change of subject. "Don't be surprised if Dao is here when we return from the meeting," he said eagerly. "She might well decide to again thank you in person for saving her life. Just a thought."

As they left the garden area of the large restaurant, flanked by old and heavily flowering frangipani trees, Curtis spoke to the food and beverage manager. "Please arrange for the extra meal to be charged to my room," he instructed.

"No need, sir. You are an honoured guest and, of course, Mr Jaruth Ratnamphod is really one of ours. It is our pleasure. No charge."

"*Kopun karp*, thank you," Curtis responded with surprise.

Chapter 49

The Rat drove his hire car as close as possible to the boom gate contiguous to the sentry box at the entrance to the NCO training school. The duty private first class sauntered out of the cubicle and lowered his gaze to meet the eyes of the diminutive figure behind the steering wheel.

"*Sawardee karp*, how can I help you?" the sentry asked.

"Stand fast. Major Nelson, Australian Army," Rat barked, pointing his thumb over his left shoulder in the direction of the large man sitting in the rear of the vehicle. "To see the RSM. Lift the boom barrier."

In the shadow of the trees, the sentry could just make out a large figure seated on the left rear passenger side. He recalled that Major Nelson was a large man and a friend of the RSM. He hesitated though, unsure of his next move.

"Lift that damn barrier," a booming voice demanded from the back seat.

The guard quickly did as instructed, stood to attention and saluted. Although in civilian clothes, Rat returned the salute and drove forward past the sentry box, kicking up some dust as the tyres bit into the loose road surface.

Confidence confuses. Timing is everything. Shadows from the trees. Barking instructions. Vulnerable and uncertain sentry. Yes, timing is everything.

Rat drove the hire car directly to the battalion headquarters. Not wanting to attract attention, he resisted the urge to drive faster than permitted in the battalion grounds. He brought the vehicle to a halt directly in front of the wide stairs that swept up to a landing in front of a large sign. The pair quickly scaled the stairs, glanced at the sign that pointed them in the correct direction, and walked briskly to the commanding officer's reception.

A relatively short man sat at a desk in front of Colonel Juntarsa's elaborately carved office door. He had a swarthy complexion, a heavy brow and dark-rimmed glasses sat atop a slightly protruding nasal bone. Tinges of silver threaded through thick black hair, collecting in a triangle at the temples.

Hearing heavy footsteps approaching, he peered above his reading glasses, head stationary, just the eyes moving towards the heavy brow. Two men approached. Anticipating the footsteps stopping and the visitors giving due respect to the staff officer, he lounged back in his chair. To his surprise, they didn't. The small man stopped momentarily but not the big man.

"Excuse me, what is going on here? What do you want?"

Curtis didn't reply but took long steps and pushed open the heavy pivoted door. The Rat was right behind him, almost running.

"Hold it right there," the staff officer yelled from his desk. "The military police are on their way."

Colonel Juntarsa stood by the window of a very large room, coffee mug in hand. For the first time Curtis saw the colonel without his heavily braided visor cap. He saw a man of distinguished appearance with a full head of pitch-black hair, meticulously combed. No grey. Curtis assumed it was dyed. His hair neatly pushed back revealed an unintentional parting near his left temple. Unintentional because Curtis noticed the narrow scar was in line with a small gap at the top of Juntarsa's left ear.

A close shave. Someone took a shot at him and nearly found its mark.

Juntarsa had turned at the commotion. He carried an air of arrogance. He raised his hand in the direction of the angry staff officer who was now standing in the doorway.

"No need, Kraisee," Juntarsa reassured him. "I know this gentleman."

Curtis glared at Rat as the latter broke into laughter. "What are you laughing at?" he muttered. "The colonel calling me a gentleman?"

"No, no, not that," Rat replied without offering an explanation.

The air of arrogance transformed into words. "Sergeant Curtis. I have been expecting you. Be seated."

Colonel Juntarsa pointed to two wooden chairs. He walked briskly to a large desk with ornately carved legs and similar ornate patterns on the top perimeter. He slid into a high-backed wood framed chair with dark green leather inlay and placed his coffee mug on the table.

The office had all of the usual photographs and framed certificates one would expect in the office of a commanding officer. Photographs of the colonel shaking hands with other senior officers and politicians.

One photograph depicted the colonel in full dress uniform with head bowed standing in front of the late King of Thailand, the much-loved King Bhumibol Adulyadej. Behind the colonel's chair was a photograph of the former king's son, His Royal Highness King Maha Vajiralongkorn. To the side, near a door leading to an en-suite, stood a suit rack and hat stand. The colonel's dress uniform hung neatly in place.

Noticing the colonel looking quizzically at Rat, Curtis introduced the latter as a friend and confidante. Juntarsa's gaze remained fixed on Rat but softened a little when Curtis quickly added, "And he works closely with your National Intelligence Agency under the office of the prime minister."

Rat hid his surprise at this latest addition to his curriculum vitae.

"Colonel, you said you have been expecting me. How so?" Curtis asked.

"Coffee?"

"No, thank you. Just answer my question."

"Your people in Australia told me you will leave no stone unturned in your investigations on violations of international law or suspected crimes against humanity," Juntarsa said. "It is logical that you would return to conduct further investigations after the incident in Singapore."

"What do you know about the Singapore incident?" Curtis asked.

"The media reported a Thai national was possibly involved. That's all."

"You know more than you are revealing," Curtis said abruptly. "How did you make a connection between the Singapore 'incident', as you called it, and my return visit here?"

"If you accept that I am trying to assist you in your enquiries, I am happy to answer your questions, Sergeant… er, Agent Curtis. But I don't like your tone and I don't like your insinuation that I am withholding information."

Curtis said nothing. Rat intervened, "My friend is anxious to wrap this up before anyone else is hurt or worse still, killed. He doesn't intend any disrespect."

Wrong, Rat. My level of respect depends upon how serious Juntarsa is about helping. Is he part of the team or part of the problem?

"Why did you release the prisoner, Colonel?"

"It became a matter of law. I consulted with my superiors. After a thorough briefing in which I took senior legal counsel through every aspect of the matter, including my discussions with your superior officer in Australia, counsel conducted a lengthy telephone interview with the soldier in custody. Counsel insisted we did not have sufficient evidence to detain him in the lock-up."

With that Curtis looked stunned. "An accessory to the crime. He was present at the scene of the crime and knowingly participated."

"The soldier claimed he had no knowledge of his colleague's intention," Juntarsa continued. "As far as he was concerned, they were part of an exercise. His troop leader did not fire live rounds."

"I saw him acting as the spotter for the sniper!" Curtis again raised his voice in exasperation. "He turned his weapon on me. Does legal counsel seriously think I was merely engaging in target practice on the rooftop?"

"Counsel said there was no evidence to suggest either soldier intended to commit a crime."

"I'm not convinced of the competence of the army's legal counsel," Curtis said firmly. "So, you released him. Free to go back to his NCO training."

"Not quite. Like you, I had some concerns given that counsel had not conducted an interview in person and had not inspected the site. I had to release him from the lock-up, but he was confined to barracks pending further investigation.

"Soon after he was released and before he joined the other CBs on the parade ground, he went AWOL. My staff officer and I then searched his room."

"What did you find?" Curtis asked.

"Nothing of interest, although it is rather unusual for a soldier in the Royal Thai Army to have such a fascination with international politics."

Curtis and Rat exchanged glances before the latter asked, "Perhaps an interest in the politics of Thailand is understandable for a patriotic

Thai soldier, but where else? What other countries has the decamped soldier shown an interest in?"

Rat the MI6 agent, thought Curtis.

"Yes, good question. And how thorough was your inspection? Where did you search?" Curtis continued this line of questioning.

"Our search included his locker, his desk, under his mattress, inside his mattress and his laptop computer. A thorough search. We found information on Russian politics, the legal system and judiciary in Russia and we found information on French politics."

Is the next target in France?

"Can you be more specific about his interest in France? Where in France? Did you find any names in your search of his laptop?"

"He had downloaded information on the local and regional government of Reims and, in particular, information about the mayor of the city of Reims. Is that significant?"

"Perhaps," Curtis said. He changed direction. "Had the soldier recently served in southern Thailand?"

"Yes, but not on patrols. He was in the supply division at the munitions dump at our facility near Pattani."

"The same facility from which firearms were allegedly stolen a few months back? Is that a coincidence, Colonel?"

"How do you know about that?"

"It was reported in the Bangkok Post."

"Of course. Yes, the same facility but there isn't necessarily a connection. The RKK insurgents are very resourceful. They can also be ruthless and they repeatedly attack our facilities and... er, personnel." Juntarsa subconsciously touched his left temple.

Curtis nodded and changed direction. "Do you recall I asked you to check the prisoner for a tattoo? Did you do that?"

"The RSM did on my instructions when he returned the soldier to his barrack. Nothing."

"Was it also the RSM who investigated the rooftop shooting? Did he recover any weapons? Any rubber bullets? A weapon that hadn't been fired?"

"As I'm sure you know, Agent Curtis, the RSM is always responsible for such investigations, in conjunction with the MPs. No, there were no rubber bullets."

Curtis said nothing immediately, contemplating the recent events and those involved. He was now convinced Colonel Juntarsa was not involved in any wrongdoing, but the Regimental Sergeant Major probably was.

Juntarsa broke the silence. "What is the significance of the tattoo?"

"I'm not sure. Here's my advice, Colonel, for what it's worth. If you have concerns about any of your NCO trainees and a potential connection with the Singapore incident, or the rooftop incident here on your base, you should perhaps check to see if any other soldiers have a tattoo the same as the one you saw on the deceased soldier. Those soldiers might be the next to go AWOL. I would start with any soldiers who have served at Pattani.

"Think about whether your RSM spent time at Pattani?

"Finally, as a matter of curiosity explain this to me, Colonel. Why wasn't I arrested for shooting the sniper when I re-entered the country?"

"Why would that be, Agent Curtis? It appears there was an accidental shooting in the barracks. One of the soldiers was cleaning his weapon when it discharged. He wasn't aware there was one in the chamber. He shot his friend and because of that — his fear of a court martial — he went AWOL."

Juntarsa and Curtis looked at each other knowingly, and there was a long pause in the conversation before Curtis acknowledged, "I understand."

Before leaving the NCO school, Rat called the Lucky Star Restaurant. He spoke briefly to Noi.

"Time to mend bridges. Again," he told Curtis. "We shall have some food."

"You Thai people, love your food, don't you?" Curtis commented. "Rat, I detect a tone of annoyance and sarcasm in your voice. Perhaps I was a little harsh in my approach to Noi yesterday but I needed information and he was initially reluctant to cooperate."

"I know, Curtis, but we still need to mend bridges."

"Any excuse for a feed."

The restaurant was empty but coincidentally the food was already prepared upon their arrival a few minutes later. Four plates of deep-fried soft-shell crab, two bowls of chicken and coconut soup, a large plate of crab fried rice, and more. Rat and Curtis ate while Noi sipped on a watermelon juice.

After a convivial conversation and Curtis having paid the bill adding a healthy tip, all seemed forgiven. Noi gave Curtis a firm handshake and waved goodbye. A satiated Rat rubbed his stomach in satisfaction as they made their way back to the car.

On the drive back to the Centara, Curtis was in a pensive mood. There was much to think about. He was contemplating a course of action.

Do I intercept a possible hit in France, warn the target? Is there a target in France? Mayor of Reims? Or do I go straight to the snake's head? But where is the snake?

After several minutes of contemplation in silence, Curtis turned towards Rat and asked, "By the way, what were you laughing at back there? You were not laughing at the colonel's description of me as a 'gentleman' were you?"

Rat laughed again. "No, Curtis. I was laughing at the name of the colonel's staff officer. His name is Kraisee. That means 'as brave as a lion'."

Curtis pictured the small staff officer almost cowering in the doorway to the colonel's office, body half turned as if about to run if the giant even looked at him.

"As brave as a lion," Curtis repeated. They both laughed.

Chapter 50

Wallace was booked into the London Mayfair Apartments near the Green Park Hilton where Coolidge was staying. Coolidge had arranged a series of meetings with nomads for presentations on the public floating of Green Solutions. Wallace had other business he wanted to attend to.

The luxury Mayfair Apartments provided security and, most importantly, privacy. He could safely hold meetings and telephone conversations without the fear of being overheard.

He placed a call to Nelson's throwaway mobile phone thirty minutes after checking in. It was agreed that all telephone conversations were to be straight to the point and as far as possible in code.

"Are you free to talk without interruption?" Wallace asked.

"Yes."

"Do you have any feedback on Singapore? Did we succeed?"

"Everything went according to plan but the conference was only delayed. Unfortunately, we didn't stop it." Nelson pushed on before Wallace could interrupt. "There were unintended consequences. Two people, a security officer and one of the women involved in organising the conference. A prominent woman in the Singaporean Police Department."

Wallace pointedly, "Too bad about the security officer. As you often say, Craig, there may be collateral damage. Always a possibility. Where is our agent?"

"Probably in southern Thailand with his brothers by now. The scarlet pimpernel. Awaiting my instructions."

"Ironic you should mention the scarlet pimpernel, Nelson. As you might know, that play was set in France." Wallace continued firing questions at Nelson. "How good is his French? Is he capable of doing a job without your involvement? Can he follow our business model without you looking over his shoulder?"

"I believe he is perfectly capable of doing so. Do you have a meeting for him to attend in France?"

"Yes, with the mayor of Reims, but not until he assesses the lay of the land. He should go to Reims and make a business assessment," Wallace was still talking in his code.

"See if a takeover bid is viable. Before he proceeds with the meeting, I want you to approve of his plan. Are you absolutely certain our company representative can be relied upon? Can you guarantee that he would never divulge his connections? You understand how important that is in our line of business, of course."

"Absolutely, and yes, I am certain he would represent our interests faultlessly. He knows only part of the business plan, enough to get the job done and he doesn't know of any of my business connections."

"Proceed on that basis. Have him arrange a meeting with the mayor of Reims," Wallace instructed.

"Reims is not exactly on the world stage. You may know better than me but I have to ask the question, do you seriously believe she is a contender for higher office?"

"We have thoroughly researched her background and political power base. She is ambitious. She apparently aspires to higher office. If our man meets with her that will be a huge plus for our business in the long term."

"With respect, this woman is a lightweight, isn't she? Surely not a leader?"

Wallace was starting to become impatient with Nelson but answered, "Perhaps a lightweight as they all are but an aspirant. But know this, Reims is symbolic too. It is the city where the kings of France were crowned. The Reims Cathedral. You know Edgar and I like symbolism. Don't you wear a tattoo?"

"Of course, but I just thought our focus…"

Wallace interrupted, "We should never risk our own safety, our security. Never place our movement at risk. Go for the low-hanging fruit. Plan for the long term."

"Our agent will travel to France as soon as I can contact him. Is this part of your plan to expand the business and involve more players?"

"We have decided you should not only be involved at the coal-face but should join the executive team, Craig. A meeting is scheduled here next week with the entire group and I would like you to attend. It is a major strategy meeting."

"I am honoured to be part of the bigger picture, and I'm looking forward to meeting the others."

"Keep me informed of progress in France," Wallace concluded and terminated the call.

Chapter 51

Back in his room at the resort, Curtis had sent a message to Frenchy requesting information about the mayor of the French city of Reims. Before Frenchy had responded, Curtis received a call from Coolidge.

"Alexeev, I promised to keep you informed of the movements of Wallace and Nelson," Coolidge said after the usual cordial greetings. "Wallace is staying in the UK for at least the next two weeks and Nelson is on his way here."

"Is Nelson flying direct to London?" Curtis asked in a heavy Russian accent. He hadn't revealed his true self to Coolidge, instead preferring to maintain the subterfuge. There was no need for Coolidge to know his identity. Should Nelson or Wallace somehow learn that Coolidge had provided information about their operations without authority, it was preferable they believe him to be a Russian.

"Yes, from Melbourne."

"Are you certain of that? He is not stopping elsewhere in Europe by any chance?

"No, he is flying here. Direct. I have arranged a series of meetings for next week."

"Is it possible you don't have all of the details of his movements, Geoffrey? If the meetings are next week, he has ample time to stop over in, say, Paris?"

"Wallace told me to make the flight arrangements so I know he is flying directly to Heathrow."

"What meetings have you arranged?"

"Meetings with nomads. Wallace and Nelson are both attending those meetings."

Curtis wasn't familiar with the process of preparing a company for listing on the London Stock Exchange. "What do you mean by that?" he asked. "Nomads?"

"Nominated advisers," Coolidge responded. "If they are convinced of a company's bona fides and capability of raising public money, the nomads, as they are commonly called, will assist with the preparation of an initial public offering. They will attract investors to the company."

"Why are they still trying to attract investors? Hasn't the new Russian shareholder's investment, met their financial needs?"

"I guess it is a combination of two things," Coolidge replied. "They certainly have all the funds the company needs for some considerable time, with the promise of more from the new investor. But Wallace needs to satisfy the shareholders who contributed the early seed capital that they are proceeding towards a listing on AIM."

"Why so? And what is 'aim'?"

"The Alternative Investment Market. The AIM is an alternative option for small companies that do not necessarily meet the criteria for the London Stock Exchange. An AIM listing provides an exit strategy. The early shareholders will be looking for an exit from Green Solutions at some point. The public float provides them the opportunity to sell their shares on the market with an expected strong return on their initial investment."

Coolidge waited a moment for more questions but Curtis was satisfied with his answer. He continued, "If your theory is correct, Alexeev, the second reason for the meetings is to maintain the appearance of a genuine developing business." Coolidge emphasised 'appearance'.

Curtis ignored the reference to his 'theory'. Nor was he really interested in the process of listing the company on the stock exchange.

"You're not attending those meetings?"

"Wallace said I should return to Australia. He doesn't need me here. As usual, he is keeping me away from anything to do with Green Solutions' finances."

"When do you plan to leave?" Curtis asked anxiously.

"I haven't made arrangements yet but probably within the next few days. Certainly, before Nelson arrives. That man makes me nervous," Coolidge added.

Curtis was concerned about losing his informant. "Can you find a reason to hang around there?" he asked. "It would be handy to obtain more precise details of their movements."

"I'll see if that's possible," Coolidge said. "I don't really want to be here whilst Nelson is around, but perhaps there is something else I can do that doesn't involve me crossing his path."

"For our mutual benefit," Curtis said. "The more information I have the better. Remember what I told you in Moscow too. You have been inadvertently caught up in Wallace's illegal operation and it is in your best interest to fully cooperate with Interpol."

"I'm doing everything you have asked me, Alexeev," Coolidge sounded worried.

"Yes indeed," Curtis reassured him. "On another matter, have you met Jim Wallace's brother?"

"Brother? I didn't know he had a brother."

"Hang around in England please, Geoffrey, and keep me informed. Let me know of any other meetings Wallace and Nelson attend. Keep me up to date with their location."

As soon as the call was terminated, a message arrived from Frenchy asking Curtis to call. He immediately went to his safe and retrieved his secure satellite phone. Next, the usual routine of checking for potential eavesdroppers. He exited the room and walked a dozen paces in both directions along the corridor. Satisfied there was nobody in the vicinity he returned to his room and made the call.

"Are we secure?" Frenchy asked.

Curtis sighed. *He knows the answer, why bother asking?*

"Yes, Frenchy, of course we are secure as always. What do you have for me?"

"The mayor of Reims is sixty years old — not old for French politics — and has held the mayoral position for ten years. She is also president of the wider regional government."

Now, how about that, thought Curtis. *A woman.*

"Before becoming involved in politics, the mayor was a judge."

Another judge.

"She has also held significant positions in the government of France as a ministerial adviser or similar, and has played a major role in the European Parliament," Frenchy continued.

"In recent times she has been prominent in promoting equality of opportunity for minorities, and gender equality in particular. Additionally, she has been an influential figure in French politics and has held senior positions in her political party."

That all adds up. The type of person who might be a target for the Nelson group. Something else doesn't add up though. Coolidge said Nelson is travelling to England, not France.

"Why the interest in the mayor of Reims?"

"She might be a target, Frenchy."

"Do you have any evidence, Curtis, or is this another one of your obscure hunches?"

"Time will tell, Frenchy. Time will tell."

Chapter 52

"Où te caches-tu? Sortir! Je te trouverai, n'en doute pas. [Where are you hiding? Come on out! I will find you, I have no doubt.]

The powerful French voice could be heard above the clatter of rain on the tin roof. An angry voice, fuelled by alcohol.

The boy cowered in the corner of the room behind a sofa. Large flickering shadows danced across the wall to his side. The crackle of fire bursting small fissures in the eucalyptus wood. Sparks shooting into narrow, dark space.

"Ne jamais cacher de moi!" [Never hide from me!]

He found the courage to peek below the sofa. Suddenly there were four feet. One pair definitely his mother's. The other pair larger, wearing familiar boots. He could not see much higher than the ankles but he could hear. Not the thuds of thunder in the hills. A different sound.

The boy clasped both hands over his ears. Head close to the floor behind the sofa he suddenly saw his mother on the living room floor. She looked directly at him. Eyes pleading for him to stay hidden.

Curtis threw the bed cover back and sat upright. A lather of perspiration.

It was early morning. Rat had left late the night before and went to the family home after he and Curtis had said their goodbyes. Curtis had reserved the hotel car and planned to depart for Bangkok Airport early in the morning, much earlier than Rat could contemplate.

Is Coolidge right? Is Nelson flying to London or France?

Chapter 53

Frenchy briefed Bell on the latest news. Curtis was asking questions about the mayor of Reims but Frenchy had no concrete reason to think the mayor was in danger. Neither did Curtis, it seemed.

Bell was supportive of Curtis but had to agree with Frenchy on this occasion. There was no evidence to suggest extremists would target the mayor.

"She certainly fits the profile in terms of gender in leadership," Bell opined.

"Correct but Curtis did not offer any shred of evidence or information that might cause us concern. Perhaps he has another hunch," Frenchy offered sarcastically.

"Enough of the sarcasm, Frenchy. Curtis has a very good track record. Do you think we should give him more support on the ground? We both know his family history and I am hoping he doesn't possess inner demons that put him and those he is protecting at risk," Bell said.

"We also know Curtis is most effective when we give him enough room to conduct his own investigations without anyone looking over his shoulder," replied Frenchy. "He may be a little unconventional at times but so long as he acts within the boundaries we set, I consider he is best left alone."

"No argument from me. If an Australian commits an offence in another jurisdiction that person must face the consequences. I have complete confidence in Curtis to handle that. We should provide whatever resources he requires. If he should ask for assistance, deliver it, Frenchy," Bell instructed.

'Must face the consequences', thought Frenchy. *Bell could have said 'the full force of the law'*.

Frenchy continued the briefing. "I have again been directly contacted by the commanding officer of the NCO training school in Thailand, Colonel Juntarsa. The colonel collaborated the issues raised by

Curtis and gave me an insight into why Curtis has such an interest in the mayor of Reims.

"He was forced to release the second person involved in the attempted shooting of Dao Shinawatra. The army's legal counsel insisted there was insufficient evidence to hold him.

"As an aside, the colonel said he found Curtis to be very forthright. He speaks his mind. Apparently." Frenchy chuckled. "Curtis was not enamoured of the army's lawyer."

"Because of his family history, I suspect Curtis probably holds the same feeling about most lawyers." Bell joined in the humour.

"Curtis also raised concerns there may be soldiers at the training school who cannot be trusted. Something to do with a tattoo. The colonel was unable to shed any light on that but said Curtis was convinced there is a connection between soldiers who wear a particular tattoo and have spent time in southern Thailand, where the RKK have been active.

"As for the soldier who was released from the battalion lock-up, the colonel personally undertook a search of his room. A forensic analysis of his computer revealed an interest in the mayor of Reims. That explains why Curtis asked about the mayor."

"So, Curtis may be onto something," Bell said, emphasising 'may'.

"The other interesting discovery from the forensic computer search was the soldier in question also had an interest in Russian politics. I doubt that would be a coincidence," Frenchy added.

"And what explanation did the soldier give for the collection of such material?" Bell asked.

"That's another interesting thing. Curiously, he has gone AWOL."

Bell had the impression Frenchy was about to reveal more and didn't respond to this latest revelation.

"Curtis has aroused Colonel Juntarsa's interest in a possible connection between NCO trainees who have served in the south of Thailand and, shall we say, extra-curricular activities," Frenchy continued.

"After Curtis left, the colonel obtained a list of those who were in the south immediately prior to attending the school. There were not many but they included a soldier who was recently sent to Singapore for further training. Juntarsa has personally been in touch with the appropriate division commander in the Singapore Army. You'll never guess…"

"What?" interrupted Bell, "He has gone AWOL too?"

"There is no record of him having attended anything in Singapore."

Chapter 54

Chop the snake's head. That was his decision. On the three-hour drive to Bangkok Airport Curtis had decided it was time to confront Wallace and Nelson. Whilst he still didn't have the evidence to link either man to an attempted assassination in Thailand or the murder of two people in Singapore, he had to bring the matter to a head.

Time to end this once and for all. Tackle this head on. Perhaps they will make a mistake. Perhaps that mistake can lead to evidence of their crimes and I can have the local gendarmes make an arrest.

Curtis was working through the options on the long drive. His driver spoke very little English. The silence suited Curtis. Time to think. Time to make phone calls.

I need to confront them. I doubt they would admit to any wrongdoing. Nelson will not cave in easily. Their misguided ideological views provide the motivation for them to carry on. There may be unforeseen consequences.

He contacted Frenchy and asked him to send someone to Reims to warn the mayor of her vulnerability. A terrorist group's potential target.

"Frenchy, it will have to be someone who is convincing. The mayor appears to be a popular figure and I doubt she would ever expect to be threatened."

"Do you have someone in mind? It's your theory. Why don't you meet with her?" Frenchy asked.

"It would give me a reason to visit my ancestral region of Rouen, but I have a job to do in England. I'm following a lead. It is best I go straight to the source of the problem and not just chase those acting on instructions. If I don't do that, this problem might get out of control.

"As for someone to meet with the mayor, why don't you go to Reims, Frenchy? As a senior Australian officer, you would certainly get her attention."

"Not possible," Frenchy replied. "You do what you have to do. Reims will not be an issue."

Frenchy ended the call in typically abrupt fashion. Curtis then made other calls, one to Rat, another to set up a meeting with Sir Edward Creighton, and a third to arrange accommodation in London. The call to Creighton was for backup. A possible source of information if Coolidge was unable to assist.

"It is such a pity you have to leave, Curtis. Dao arrived this morning to meet with her support base in the Hua Hin region," Rat told him.

"I have a job to do," Curtis replied. "This is just a social call. I have to leave Thailand now but I'm sure we will meet again one day."

"We will, my *naawng* [friend], we will."

Chapter 55

Creighton agreed to meet at Haling Park. The estate in London's southern-most borough of Croydon was where Rat had spent his holidays when schooling in England.

Curtis had telephoned and told the senior MI5 public servant that he worked closely with Jaruth Ratnamphod. He needed to talk to him about some important matters he believed his son had been working on. Curtis was scheduled to arrive in London late on Friday afternoon. It was therefore most convenient to meet Creighton at his residence the following day. Hopefully after a good night's sleep.

The Creighton family home was a fully detached house backing onto Purley Way playing fields in South Croydon. The large but friendly-looking house was just as the Rat had described in one of their many conversations. A two-storey family home with a lock-up garage to the right of a front porch. Grand columns reaching up to the second level announced the entrance to the house.

Curtis pressed a small button beside the door. Loud bell chimes signalled his arrival.

Footsteps approached on a tiled floor. A tall, distinguished man opened the door soon after. He stood at six feet three, not as tall as Curtis, a mop of white hair neatly combed and parted on the left, penetrating blue moist eyes, a large nose and a square chin with a small dimple in the middle.

Curtis thrust his hand forward and introduced himself. "Rhys Curtis but my friends call me 'Curtis'. I prefer that," he said.

"My friends call me 'Ed'," Creighton said before chuckling quietly.

He took Curtis by the elbow and pointed him down a wide passageway, past a wall of family photographs, towards the rear of the house. At the end of a line of photographs Curtis noticed a number of medals mounted on the wall but decided it would be impolite and possibly too nosey to look at them, especially having not looked closely at the photos.

They entered a large, well-furnished and carpeted sunroom. Curtis imagined this is where Creighton would watch a disciplined Rat perform his exercises on the playing fields when he was younger. The smell of freshly brewed coffee lingered in the air.

"Before I tell you the purpose of my visit, Sir Edward… er, Ed… allow me to provide you some of my background," Curtis said as he was directed to a large cream-coloured sofa.

"Let's not be formal. There is no need to tell me about your background. Do you really think a person in my position would not have checked on you?"

Creighton sat across from the sofa in a high-back green fabric chair. A long oval-shaped coffee table, with ornate dark timber legs of a similar design to the high-back chair, was positioned between them. Atop the table were a silver tray, a chinaware coffee jug, a matching milk jug and two white coffee mugs.

Without asking, Creighton reached forward and poured two coffees. "Strong with just a dash of milk for you and a little more milk for me," he said and winked.

Curtis smiled in the knowledge his host had indeed checked on him.

Thoroughly checked it appears.

Both men exchanged small talk interposed by polite sips of steaming coffee.

"Our mutual friend Rat… Jaruth… told me about your son's collision with the truck. I am sorry for your loss, Ed, but I do not believe your son's death was an accident."

Creighton showed no emotion. He nodded and said, "Go on."

"Did Edward talk to you about his investigations?" Curtis asked.

"No, other than to say he would be travelling in Thailand for a week, perhaps longer."

"I have reason to believe he may have been investigating a link between the theft of military equipment, the disappearance of soldiers and the involvement of the RKK."

"RKK?"

"The most radical of the militant insurgency groups in southern Thailand, the *Runda Kumpulan Kecil*, meaning 'small patrol units'. I also have reason to believe some soldiers in the Thai Special Ops Unit may have been compromised. They have been trained by an Australian. That's why I am involved."

Creighton shifted in his seat, lent forward and, without asking, topped up Curtis's coffee mug. He picked up the milk jug and showed it to Curtis who simply shook his head.

Curtis took another sip of coffee before continuing. "The involvement of your son and the secret intelligence service suggests a concern to gather information about potential terrorist groups, or individuals that may have an impact on the UK."

"From your own investigations, Agent Curtis, is that a reasonable assumption? What would their interest be in the UK? How can a little-known insurgent group in southern Thailand, however radical, affect the peace and security of this country?"

"Perfectly reasonable questions," Curtis offered. He paused before replying. "Did you hear that noise? Somebody at the front of your house."

"That would be my wife returning home from her regular Saturday luncheon with her friends. I have encouraged her to maintain her usual lifestyle after the devastating loss of our only child."

Curtis nodded in acknowledgement.

"You have very good hearing, Curtis. I didn't hear the garage door opening."

Not just very good, thought Creighton, *outstanding. Exceptional.*

Before the discussion resumed a tall, elegant woman with flecks of blond in otherwise dark hair, entered the room. Sad eyes. Curtis stood and turned to greet her with a half-smile and an extended hand.

"Pleased to meet you, Mrs Creighton. Curtis. I have heard so much about you from Jaruth."

Comments made and questions asked about Rat's welfare and pleasantries were exchanged. Heather Creighton left the two men to resume their discussion.

"The RKK. An insurgent group that very little is known about outside of Thailand," continued Curtis.

Exceptional hearing and a good memory too, thought Creighton. *Took up precisely where we left off.*

Without interruption, Curtis spent the next twenty minutes providing detailed information about the RKK, Nelson, and the attack on Dao Shinawatra. He told Creighton about the events in St Petersburg and Singapore. He reiterated his belief the presence of Nelson, and possibly his colleague at the same time as these attacks, was no coincidence. He just could not be certain of the real purpose behind the attacks.

For the most part Creighton listened intently without any reaction but nodded, seemingly in agreement, when Curtis said, "I don't believe in coincidences."

"Tell me about your understanding of this fellow Nelson's connection with the UK," Creighton asked when it appeared Curtis was completing his discourse. "You have obviously been thorough in your investigations."

Curtis told him about the company Green Solutions and its principle shareholder and founder Jim Wallace being a Brit. He explained as much as he knew about the company's technology and attraction to potential investors, without revealing Geoffrey Coolidge as the source of much of that information. He gave limited details of the company's newest investor from Russia, Lumovski.

"I know Nelson from my military training, Ed. Not a nice man. Aggressive. A misogynist of the worst type. It was rumoured he was responsible for some atrocities in the Middle East. I know little about Wallace other than the fact he migrated to Australia from the UK about six years ago."

Curtis looked hard at Creighton and added, "You might ask about my evidence linking Nelson, Wallace and the RKK. Lumovski too."

Creighton looked up from his coffee and again nodded. His expression told Curtis that the issue of 'evidence' had been raised with him.

Frenchy!

"I assume this same matter has been discussed with you already," he told Creighton. "My belief is your son was pursuing a link between those people and possibly an organisation based here in the UK."

They sat in silence for a few moments. If Creighton knew more information about the acts of terror or any plans for intervention by MI5, he didn't reveal it.

"My understanding is you are obliged, on behalf of both ASIO and Interpol, to investigate any possible criminal activity involving an Australian outside your country's jurisdiction," Creighton eventually broke the silence. "I would encourage you to continue, even if it is only to bring peace of mind to Heather.

"We have drawn a blank with police investigations into the 'accident' in Thailand and have nobody else to turn to. As you would expect, my wife has taken the loss of our son very, very badly. We both have."

Chapter 56

"Your superior in Australia told me you believe there may be some strange connection involving a tattoo and the various perpetrators of the crimes," Creighton said. "Can you describe this tattoo?"

"I can do better than that. I have a photograph."

Curtis turned his hand phone on. He waited patiently for it to power up. It sprang to life after he entered his passcode. The 'home' page appeared. As he scrolled to find the photograph, he told Creighton how he had received it from the commanding officer of the NCO school. It had been taken by the army coroner; tattooed on the back of the soldier he had unfortunately disposed of.

The same tattoo was also on the deceased AWOL soldier in St Petersburg. The man who was partly responsible for mayhem at the front of the courthouse when he met with a car accident. He saw the tattoo.

He reached across the coffee table and passed the phone to Creighton who gazed hard at the grainy photograph. Creases were forming across his brow. He returned the phone to Curtis without comment, the photograph still open on the screen.

"Jim Wallace has a brother. After my discussion with your senior officer, I made some further enquiries," Creighton informed Curtis.

"I know he has a brother but that is all I know."

"This is where it gets interesting," Creighton said. "His brother was born Anthony Lynton Wallace but when he attained the age of majority, he changed his first given name to Edgar."

"Why would he do that?"

"Because he might be just a little bit mad," Creighton continued. "You see, he has a fixation on the first King of All England, King Edgar.

"Some English history for you, Curtis. King Edgar took the throne in 959 but surprisingly his coronation wasn't held until 973, fourteen years later. He chose Bath Abbey for his coronation.

"Edgar was most commonly known as 'Edgar the Peacemaker'," Creighton told Curtis. "But that was probably something of a misnomer. He kept the peace through iron-fisted military control.

"It is doubtful that Edgar was actually a man of peace. It appears he liked the display of power. History tells the story of his demonstration of power with the threat of military force immediately following his coronation in 973. It is said he took his army to Chester where the presence of his army, joined by his navy, threatened King Kenneth II of Scotland. The threat was extended to other leaders, earls and bishops. They were forced to pay homage to him.

"There were other examples of his use of force too. He ordered the plundering of the Kent island of Thanet in 969. It is not entirely clear why that might have occurred but some historians have suggested it had something to do with goods being imported from Europe by the locals, the women in particular.

"Unfortunately, the Anglo-Saxon Chronicles provide a rather biased view of many leaders. The degree of support expressed for royals in the Chronicles depended very much on the level of their commitment to the church. In these circumstances, the writers, being theologians would not want royalty to be depicted in a negative way."

"With respect, Ed, this is all very interesting but why are you telling me this?"

"I want you to know your activities, your line of investigation, may lead you to deal with a man who might have a screw loose," Creighton said grimly. "I know your focus appears to be on Jim Wallace, but it's possible Edgar might also be involved in whatever you think they are doing. You need to be aware, that's all.

"Just imagine if Jim Wallace is as fanatical as his brother," Creighton opined. "You would have three nutters involved. The Wallace brothers and Nelson. I don't have any intelligence on the latter, but from your description he sounds like a nasty piece of work."

Curtis nodded agreement.

"You're right. You obviously know a great deal of English history too, but do you know anything about the tattoo, Ed? I think I noticed a look of recognition on your face."

Creighton chuckled. "You're very perceptive," he told Curtis. "I recognised the tattoo. It's a portrayal of the Greek goddess Medusa. If you are familiar with Greek mythology you will know that Medusa was a monster. That's appropriate, isn't it?"

Not expecting a response to his rhetorical question, Creighton continued, "It was written in ancient Greek literature that she had two sisters. The three of them were described as Gorgons. Venomous snakes replaced their hair. Medusa was not immortal like her sisters and she was eventually killed. There is hope, isn't there?" Creighton chuckled at his last comment.

"What might be the significance of a Medusa tattoo?" Curtis asked.

"I'm not sure. In Greek mythology, the head of Medusa, a Gorgon's head, was used to ward off evil people and evil spirits. It is said that if one stared upon Medusa's head — presumably a facsimile of her head too — that person would be petrified. Turned to stone. Don't stare too hard at that photograph, Curtis, we want you to continue your good work."

This time Creighton didn't chuckle, he burst into laughter at his joke. Curtis didn't join in the laughter. Not being the superstitious type, he was still gazing at the photo on his phone.

Neither man spoke for a few minutes, seemingly deep in thought. When Curtis arrived at Haling Park a light, misty rain had greeted him. He looked out across the playing fields and noticed the rain was now quite heavy. He couldn't see far onto the playing fields. The darkened sky and thought of Medusa's head sent a small shiver along his spine.

Heather Creighton broke the verbal silence as she re-entered the room. "More coffee, gentlemen? Curtis, would you like to join us for dinner?"

Curtis declined. He thanked Heather for her kind offer but said he had plans to meet a friend. A late afternoon meeting.

"Fortuitously, my wife is a student of ancient Greek literature and mythology," Creighton announced. "Heather may be able to help us with this mystery."

Creighton didn't inform his wife about anything Curtis had told him. He repeated what he had said about Medusa, and then asked, "Is my description of the Gorgon correct? Can you imagine why anyone might take pride in keeping a picture of Medusa? Of almost worshipping her?"

Heather said her husband was correct in his description of Medusa. She explained that some archaeological sites have displayed images of the Gorgon's head. "It is likely the purpose was to protect the people who enter those buildings."

"Can you provide some examples? What buildings? Where?" asked Curtis hurriedly. He could see the story developing and providing vital information.

Heather sat down on another high-backed chair matching that occupied by her husband. She raked her hair across her forehead with her right hand as she sat back. Still looking very dignified and straight backed. But sad eyes.

"There is definitely one prominent example of a Gorgon image. There is a cathedral in France that has an image of a smiling woman, sometimes called the 'Smiling Angel' but also, probably erroneously described as a Gorgon's image. In the most common Medusa image, she appears to be smiling and that is probably why the 'Smiling Angel' is so described."

Curtis stiffened. He sat upright on the sofa and asked, "A cathedral in France, where is it? What city?"

"The cathedral in which the coronations occurred for most of the French kings. Reims Cathedral."

"But that is not the most prominent example?" Curtis asked.

"No. A stone pediment at the entrance to hot spring baths here in England has sometimes been called a depiction of the Roman water god Oceanus. Some have suggested the image is of Sol Invictus, the Roman sun god. Some say it is Sulis Minerva although it doesn't conform to other images of her in Roman Britain. Others have suggested it is an image of a smiling Medusa. In truth, nobody knows. I suspect most believe it to be the latter, Medusa."

Curtis glanced at Creighton before asking, "Where is the pediment in England?"

"At the entrance to the Roman baths in our city of Bath, Somerset."

Chapter 57

Curtis left the Creighton estate having to dash through the rain to his car. Creighton had urged him to wait for the rain to stop and cancel his appointment, but Curtis was adamant he had important matters with which to follow up.

"If you won't cancel, at least take this," Creighton said, handing Curtis a package wrapped in cloth. Without unwrapping it, Curtis knew it was a gun. "I suspect you might need it."

Curtis didn't reveal his clandestine plans to meet with Coolidge for an update on the movements of Wallace and Nelson. His plan was to eyeball Coolidge and extract as much information as possible. Meeting in person is always preferred to a telephone call.

He also needed to have Coolidge explain the meaning of his cryptic text message sent following their last telephone call. The discussion with Heather Creighton was illuminating and may have given some clarity to the message, but he needed to be certain. Coolidge had said, "W takes a bath in hot spring water at night, last Thurs of each month."

Curtis had a reservation at the Royal Lancaster in London. As usual, he chose a hotel for both convenience and the standard of equipment in the hotel's gymnasium. The refurbished hotel was perfect for his needs.

Most importantly, it was located conveniently near Hyde Park; a convenient car park at Paddington Station within half a mile; convenient access for his meeting with the Creightons; an outstanding Thai restaurant; and, most importantly for Curtis, a very good gymnasium. A gymnasium with all the essential equipment. A designated weights area, treadmills, rowing machines, cross trainers and more.

When he registered at the hotel, he had no idea he wouldn't have the opportunity to use the gymnasium.

Soon after his arrival in London, Curtis made an arrangement to meet with Coolidge in Kensington Gardens. From his window at the Lancaster he could look southwest across Bayswater Road to the Italian

Gardens with its old Italian style fountains and architecture. Only a short distance from his hotel.

He was to meet Coolidge in a clearing behind the Peter Pan statue, about half way along the quaintly named lake, The Long Water. The long lake that separated Hyde Park from Kensington Gardens.

By text message Coolidge had given clear directions: 'From your hotel cross Bayswater Road near Lancaster Gate underground station. Follow the path next to the Italian Gardens fountain directly in front. You will see the Peter Pan statue. Behind the statue there is a small rise and trees and shrubs. Walk over the rise to the clearing.'

Despite the inclement weather to the south of London, with the aid of the GPS that came with the hire car Curtis made good time in returning to the Lancaster. But he was still later than he would have liked. It meant he had no time to reconnoitre the Hyde Park area, nor Kensington Gardens, nor time to visit the gymnasium.

The rain had stopped earlier in the afternoon. After two hours of heavy cloud a mist crept across Hyde Park, seemingly thickening as it went. Along the Serpentine waterway, across the bridge, past the Princess Diana Memorial Fountain, past Queen Caroline's Temple, past a statue of a man on a horse, the Physical Energy Statue, and past the Speke Monument. A slowly rolling wall of fog. Not a real pea-souper but a heavy London type that crept in without any warning from the Met Office.

Not having had time to reconnoitre, Curtis obtained a map of Kensington Gardens and Hyde Park from the hotel's concierge. Despite his trust in Coolidge, he decided he would follow a different route to the Peter Pan statue. There was sufficient time before the gardens closed at dusk.

Curtis crossed Bayswater Road as instructed but instead of following the path recommended by Coolidge, map in hand, he passed the Two Bears Fountain and made his way along Budge's Walk to where it intersected Lancaster Walk near the Speke Monument. He paused for only a few moments to look at the red granite monument erected soon after the death of John Speke at the age of thirty-seven.

Another map inspection. He hesitated as two joggers approached along Lancaster Walk, running north towards the exit. They were appropriately attired for a run in the park, wearing close fitting compression shorts, tracksuit hoodies and black energy boost running shoes. They wore almost identical outfits, save for the colour of the shorts. Curtis tensed as they approached him. A natural reaction, but it seemed they were genuine runners as they continued up the path. He relaxed.

Soon after they ran past, he rounded the monument and walked as quietly as possible in the general direction of the rendezvous destination, taking care not to step on any twigs or other debris that might signal any movement.

By now the fog was setting for the evening. It was becoming thicker and visibility was far less than when Curtis left the hotel. A matter of metres. He weaved his way around trees and shrubs in the direction he believed his rendezvous to be, planning to enter the clearing on the opposite side of where he would be expected to arrive. Not near the Peter Pan statue.

After a few more minutes, he could just make out another path directly in front. Not the path that Coolidge expected him to take but another further to the west. He anticipated meeting it near a clump of trees, but there was a grassed area directly in front. Winding through the trees had taken him a short distance further north.

He turned onto the path in a southerly direction. He thought he could see the outline of a clump of trees about forty metres ahead. That was when it happened. The runners had crossed over a grassed area alongside Budge's Walk and moved stealthily south onto the path Curtis was now on. He hadn't heard them.

One of the runners stepped out of the trees onto his path and took a confrontational stance. Curtis glanced quickly around expecting to see others but, surprisingly, this man appeared to be alone. He wasn't sure if he was one of the same men he had seen six or seven minutes earlier. He was certainly dressed in a similar fashion. The man stood at five feet eleven, shorter than Curtis. Broad-shouldered and solid build.

Time on the weights and juiced up.

For Curtis, being on the offensive was always best in such a situation. He took a long but balanced step forward. He saw the man was holding an object in his right hand. The stranger meant business.

A knife. Easy pickings.

Curtis took another step, closing the gap between them to only two metres. As he started another smaller step forward, he feinted to his right but his left foot kicked out at lightning fast pace and collected the runner on the neck. Despite being tensed for action, the man was slow to react. He never saw it coming and it threw him off balance momentarily.

But Curtis was not waiting for him to regain his composure. He again feinted, this time to the left and his right fist hit the man squarely on the side of his head below his temple. He went to ground very heavily. His knees buckling and his body crumbling onto the grass.

Curtis moved closer and lifted the hoodie away from the unconscious man's face. He never heard the other runner behind him but he certainly felt the electronic pulse of a Taser. He jolted but kept his feet. At the end of the Taser's five-second cycle, Curtis felt as if he had been in the gym lifting excessively heavy weights, but anger took over and he was ready to lash out.

A second bout of the stun gun prevented that. This time Curtis's legs gave way with a simultaneous hit on the back of his neck. A rabbit punch. He was kicked twice. Heavy boots, not running shoes. As a boot came at him a third time, Curtis rolled to the side and attempted to grab hold of a leg but another pair of boots emerged from the bushes and one of them hit him under his chin.

As Curtis was fading into darkness, he heard a voice. It sounded distant but it wasn't. Close to Curtis's ear the voice said, "Stay out of my business, boy. You're an amateur. Go back to your country or next time will be worse."

Curtis tried to talk but couldn't. The dark consumed him.

Chapter 58

Gradually Curtis started to regain consciousness. He was lying amongst a clump of trees on damp grass. It was dark. No stars, no moon, just the glow of lights in contiguous Hyde Park. He had the sense he had been out to it for quite some time but, in reality, it was only a few minutes.

After a short time of disorientation Curtis gradually stood. He wobbled slightly. Although he ached in parts of his body, he was sure there were no broken bones. He felt the warmth of fresh blood on his top lip, certain it was his. He drew his right arm across his mouth, wiping the blood away with his sleeve.

Kensington Park closes at dusk. With some initial difficulty Curtis scaled the fence. Hunched over, he made his way along the path near Bayswater Road. Passing traffic would assume he was 'tired and emotional', a euphemism for being stone drunk. At one point he stopped walking in an attempt to regain his composure before crossing the road.

He looked ill at ease as he walked towards the hotel entrance, framed by two large marble columns. As he pushed against the revolving door he stumbled slightly.

"Are you okay, sir?" asked the doorman at the Lancaster. The doorman had earlier acknowledged Curtis when he left the hotel so, although he now had the appearance of a vagrant, the doorman didn't ask for a room number.

"Yes, yes I'm fine," Curtis replied through swollen lips.

This reply was greeted with a concerned expression and the doorman quickly added, "Do you need a doctor?"

Curtis realised he must look as if he had just completed ten rounds with Mike Tyson. He conjured a smile of sorts that looked to the doorman more of a grimace.

"No, I don't need a doctor. I can assure you I'm fine. A terrible misjudgement. I was walking through the park, tripped and fell heavily against some rocks." Curtis remembered seeing a pile of limestone rocks near a path where landscapers had been working. "The fog was heavy and I couldn't see easily. Landscapers should erect barriers when they have unfinished work."

He sounded convincing. The doorman walked to the elevator and pushed the arrow that pointed up.

"I'm concerned for you, sir. Please dial reception if you require anything. Have a good night."

Outside his room, Curtis touched the key-card against the receptor and pushed the door open. On the floor was a yellow A4 envelope. He opened it and slid the contents out. Two photographs of Coolidge on the one page. A 'before' and an 'after'. He would not have recognised Coolidge except for the 'before'. He had been badly beaten, confirming what Curtis had assumed. Somehow Nelson or his cohorts had discovered Coolidge had communicated with him.

Curtis now knew he had to visit the city of Bath. There was no choice. *What is the connection between a so-called Greek goddess Medusa, Wallace and Nelson*, he pondered? *There may be a clue in the information provided by the Creightons.*

First, he needed to brief Frenchy on the latest happenings. He also needed to sleep. And food. He needed food. Having looked at his image in the mirror above the vanity Curtis decided eating out was not an option. It had to be room service.

They did a reasonable job but they made a big mistake. I'm alive.

Whilst waiting for room service to arrive, he made the call to Frenchy. It was a short, one-sided conversation. Curtis admitted to Frenchy he had been assaulted and warned off by several assailants but didn't elaborate on how he was beaten or how badly he was beaten. He told Frenchy the meeting with Coolidge never happened. Frenchy only asked if he was jet-lagged and needed to take a break before pushing on. A firm "No!" was the reply.

Room service had taken a backwards step whilst pushing the trolley towards Curtis after he answered the door. Not a picture postcard.

Having not eaten all day he hastily ate his meal although with some discomfort with each bite. He thought of his comment to Rat in the Thai language, '*Lin jor aa kae*' [a tongue like a crocodile] referring to the speed with which he ate, and managed a smile.

Curtis showered, inspecting his bruises as he dried. He boiled the room kettle and made a decaffeinated coffee although he doubted caffeine would keep him awake. He confessed to himself that he was a little tired.

The room had a very large overstuffed lounge chair adorned by several cushions next to a small coffee table. He made himself comfortable, sipped from an oversized coffee mug and pushed back against the cushions. His mind wandered.

How could I allow myself to get ambushed like that? Perhaps I was a little jet-lagged. Is Coolidge alive? My fault, I shouldn't have insisted he stay. If he's alive, I need to find him. He will need help. I sense I'm closing in on these people. Thailand, Russia and Singapore. The work of two madmen, Wallace and Nelson? Is the mayor of Reims next? I have to stop it.

He drifted into a deep sleep. The nightmare returned.

Chapter 59

Curtis woke with a jolt and scrambled to his feet, fists clenched. He had sensed a stranger in his room.

"I'm terribly sorry, sir," the housekeeper trembled, "I rang the doorbell and called 'housekeeping' but there was no reply. I thought the room was empty."

"What are you doing in my room?" he growled.

"I clean this room every day, sir. Always between ten o'clock and midday."

Curtis rubbed his fingers though his hair, massaged his neck, interlaced his fingers, stretched and yawned. His arms extended above his head making him look even bigger and more fearsome to the housekeeper who had reversed slowly towards the door.

"What time is it?" Curtis asked in a quieter and more mellow tone.

"It's half past eleven, sir. I'm sorry to have disturbed you. I will come back later."

"No need. I didn't sleep in the bed," Curtis replied with a reassuring smile. The swelling had eased and smiling was less difficult now.

An extraordinarily long sleep, over thirteen hours. Perhaps slight concussion.

As the duty housekeeper left the room Curtis found his mobile phone and turned it on. The home screen had a calendar app that he touched, revealing it was the last Monday of the month. He reflected upon the cryptic comment from Coolidge via text.

The last Thursday of each month. Hot springs. Bath. Wallace will be there this week.

Curtis knew he had time to rest before driving to Bath. He would relax today and leave on Tuesday afternoon, giving him at least a full day in Bath to become familiar with the layout of the city. The extra day would mean recovery time from the beating. No gymnasium, just rest.

He thought about phoning Coolidge or at least sending him a text but decided against it. Coolidge was unlikely to have his phone. Instead he punched in the following message to Coolidge's number, 'I'm coming for you, Wallace and Nelson.' Before pressing 'send' he stopped.

What am I doing? No point in telling them. If they think they have warned me off I have the element of surprise. My judgement is skew-whiff. I definitely need a rest.

Curtis shaved, showered and dressed in jeans, a thermal navy-blue high collar polo shirt and his RM Williams boots. Whilst shaving he closely inspected his wounds and decided the swelling had receded enough for him to venture beyond the Lancaster without attracting too much attention.

His stomach rumbled, reminding him that he hadn't eaten. He was feeling ordinary. A walk through the park might help clear the cobwebs from his head. He would find a decent café that served good coffee and have a relaxing lunch. But first he would return to Kensington Gardens and the clearing where the failed rendezvous with Coolidge was to have occurred.

Unlikely but one never knows. There may be something from Coolidge.

He crossed Bayswater Road and retraced his steps past the Italian Garden and along Budge's Walk to its intersection with Lancaster Walk. He again stopped at the Speke Monument. This time he read the inscription that acknowledged John Speke as the first European explorer to discover Lake Victoria in Africa, and the source of the River Nile.

As he walked past the spot where he thought he had been ambushed he noticed some large footprints. They came from the direction of the clearing. Curtis walked through the shrubs and trees and emerged into the clearing. He walked around the area looking for any clues that may have been left by Coolidge but found nothing. The ground had been disturbed by heavy boots. Nothing more. He decided not to waste any more time.

Curtis meandered through the gardens and crossed Hyde Park. He exited the park at Deanery Street and walked aimlessly along Curzon Street until he found himself on Shepherd. He remembered seeing some cafés on Shepherd Street when he was last in London. He had stayed at a very neat but small hotel near Green Park Station.

The Piccolo Bar looked a likely spot for a good coffee and meal. There were several black cabs parked along Shepherd Street in front of the café. That was a good enough recommendation for Curtis.

He entered the bar and immediately ordered a large English breakfast from the all-day breakfast menu together with a large mug of strong coffee with a dash of milk. At the end of the bar he saw a sign, 'eating down stairs', and an arrow pointing to the staircase.

At the top of the stairs Curtis turned to the man who took his order and said, "Excuse me, can I cancel that order please? Instead, I'll have my coffee to go. I'd also like the baguette with a poached egg, asparagus and cheese to take away. Oh, and I'll have a chunk of that homemade apple pie too." He pointed at the plate-sized pie behind the glass.

Curtis had decided to return to Hyde Park with his lunch. A chance to soak up the sun and absorb some vitamin D. The sun could be seen less often these days and in Hyde Park he could enjoy the warmth for the short time it would be available.

The Piccolo Bar in Mayfair is not far from Mayfair Apartments. It was a favourite of Wallace. At the same time as Curtis was re-ordering his meal at the upstairs bar, two plates of apricot Danish and two cappuccinos were being delivered downstairs. One for Wallace and one for Nelson.

Chapter 60

The drive to Bath was slow. The GPS gave Curtis the option of driving on the main highway, a direct route on the M25 and M4 that would take two and a half hours or deviate to some interesting towns and parklands. With time on his hands Curtis took a leisurely drive to the northwest of London, through the university city of Oxford.

He arrived in Bath after five hours, almost four of which was driving time with the additional time to refuel both the vehicle and the man. Although not paranoid about sharing his plans, it was best to make his hotel reservation online. He did so whilst taking a coffee break in Oxford. His accommodation was perfect. About a mile from central Bath, Bath Abbey and the Roman baths. An easy walk along the banks of the Avon River.

After checking in, Curtis added a scarf and thermal jacket to his attire, left the hotel and walked into the city centre. It was early evening and the temperature had dropped substantially. Mist settled on the river making the dim lighting along the riverside path even dimmer, even ghost-like.

A brisk walk across Midland Bridge Road, through Bath's Green Park and along Stall Street took him straight to the Roman baths. Some tourists were leaving the complex but, surprisingly, there were very few people in the vicinity of the historic site. He found the main entrance and realised why. Closing time during the off-season was 1700 with a required exit time of 1800.

Curtis decided he would visit the baths at his leisure the following day. Time to eat. He walked past the complex, past Bath Abbey and crossed Cheap Street to a restaurant simply called 'Bill's'. The street name surely implied a meal at a reasonable price. He was not disappointed. He found a quiet corner where he could dine without being obvious. A quaint restaurant to hang out in. He certainly wasn't disappointed in the food either.

Whilst waiting for his meal of bangers, potato patties, chorizo, tomatoes and toast he browsed through his hotel's magazine. It contained a detailed map of central Bath. An opportunity to become familiarised with the juxtaposition of streets and buildings. To double- and triple-check street names having already walked part of the area.

Curtis washed down a large slice of pecan pie with a hot mug of strong coffee. Always conscious of the possibility Wallace or Nelson might appear, he kept his head down and occasionally glanced over the rim of his coffee mug. Wallace would not know him but Nelson obviously did. He had bruises and a lacerated lip to confirm that.

Despite having more than enough sleep in the last two days the internal heating caused Curtis to yawn. He paid the bill, lifted the scarf around his mouth and braced himself for the cold night air. He followed the same route back to the hotel.

Chapter 61

Curtis awoke to a cool but sunny day in Bath. Forecast, 15 degrees Celsius, a slight south-westerly breeze strengthening later in the day. His first visit to this picturesque city situated in the Avon Valley. An exquisite blend of modernity and antiquity. What he saw on his first night whetted his appetite to visit again when this mission was completed.

He checked his phone. No messages from Coolidge. He hadn't really expected any. He touched on the calendar app knowing it was the last Wednesday in the month but still checking. He showered and dressed in the same clothes he wore the previous night, changing socks and underwear. Curtis ventured to the hotel dining room for breakfast. It was two hours before the Roman baths were open to the public. He could take his time and enjoy a leisurely breakfast.

Concierge informed him the weather was expected to change so he might care to 'rug up'. With a scarf loose around his neck and a thermal jacket slung over his shoulders, Curtis left the hotel at 0955, following the same route as the previous evening.

Arriving at the Roman baths he noticed a small group of tourists mingling to the side of the entrance. It appeared to be an organised tour group. He requested to join the tour and was directed to the money collector.

Curtis blended in with the group, which was now more substantial in numbers. At 1045 the tour leader joined them. He was a tall man with salt and pepper hair, short back and sides, and a wispy moustache. Eyes sunk deep into their sockets but red 'road maps' were still easily discernible. His cheekbones protruded. He wore black trousers, a fawn coloured shirt and a dark brown fur-lined sleeveless jacket. Embroidered on his shirt was the word 'Tourist' and part of a second word was visible. Curtis extrapolated that to be 'Information'.

Gaunt. Looks like he has been sucking on lemons.

"Good morning and welcome to the Roman baths," the tour leader said in a gravelly voice, thick from smoking. He coughed before adding, "Stay close to me as I lead you through the rooms and around the baths. I will explain the purpose of each area as we proceed. Feel free to ask any questions. Follow me." He coughed again.

A fine specimen of health, Curtis thought sarcastically. *I'd like to see this man's boots. Does he have residue from Kensington Gardens on them?*

The tour leader led the group past the ticketing area, into a side passage and out onto an elevated terrace that surrounded the Great Bath situated on the lower level. He talked as he went, punctuated by the occasional rasping cough. Curtis tuned out, more intent on examining points of ingress and egress and, of course, any closed-circuit television cameras.

"The hypocausts can be seen through this door…" The tour leader talked on as Curtis drifted off to a different side door. Two paces through an archway there was a solid wooden door. Curious, he moved away from the tour group and pulled at the brass door handle. It didn't move. He pushed. Still nothing. It was solidly locked.

"Excuse me, sir," said Gravelvoice. "That room is locked for a reason [cough]. It is not open to the public. Please stay with the group."

Gravelvoice gave the direction with his hand raised, palm pointing towards Curtis. As he did so, his turned down cuff revealed a mark on his forearm.

The tattoo!

With ten pairs of eyes gazing at him, Curtis returned to the group. As he moved out of the shadow of the archway he peered back at the locked door. He hesitated and looked harder. Above the door the entablature caught his eye. It was shadowed but he could see enough of it. The tattoo in relief.

What did Heather Creighton say? Sol Invictus, Sulus Minerva, a smiling Medusa or some other dude. What does it mean?

The tour continued with the leader constantly talking and at the same time showing considerably more interest in what the big man at the rear of the group was looking at. For his part, Curtis tried to appear interested in what the tour leader was saying but was fully aware that if required to sit an exam at the end of the tour he would fail miserably. When another person in the group asked a question demanding the leader's attention, Curtis's eyes darted in all directions.

Eventually they entered the Temple Pediment.

"On this wall you can see the most significant and most studied of the images throughout the baths," Gravelvoice announced and emitted a loud cough. "There have been many arguments amongst historians and archaeologists about who the image represents. It could be an image of the Greek water god, Oceanus. Or it could be the goddess Sulis Minerva [cough]. Or possibly the head of the Gorgon, Medusa. Who knows?"

Gravelvoice didn't remove his eyes from Curtis whilst he made those comments. Curtis stared hard at the so-called Gorgon's head whilst Gravelvoice continued, "You are looking at the pediment that sat above the entrance to the Roman baths. It stood some fifteen metres above the entrance, [cough] supported by four very large Corinthian columns."

I don't buy it. A Gorgon is a female. This er, thing, is clearly a male. It has a beard and a thick moustache. Blind Freddy can see that.

As if reading Curtis's mind, Gravelvoice concluded with this comment. "Strange, isn't it, how historians think. The Gorgon looks more like a man to me. Whatever or whoever it is, the Gorgon's head is recognised by everyone to be a welcoming face to the Roman baths."

Gravelvoice stared intently at Curtis as he made that remark. Curtis didn't flinch. Not a move. Not the smallest hint of recognition, disagreement or concern.

Chapter 62

The group moved on but Curtis sat in the small amphitheatre gazing at the pediment.

He had heard all of the suggestions about the meaning of the centrepiece of the pediment, the so-called Gorgon's head. From her research, Heather Creighton had gleaned several options, namely Sulis Minerva, Sol Invictus, Oceanus, and Medusa. Perhaps there were others but this appeared to be pure speculation. Nobody really knows what was going through the minds of the Romans when the original temple was constructed in about 60 AD.

One thing is certain. The historians who claim the head to be a woman are clearly wrong. I have never seen a woman with a full beard and moustache like that. The head of Medusa? Not likely. Why would the head of a Greek goddess adorn the entrance to a Roman temple and bath?

Curtis continued to stare at the pediment looking for clues. The same head that was in his mobile phone photograph collection. The head on the back of the sniper who attempted to kill Dao Shinawatra. The head on the back of the driver in the St Petersburg attack.

His training at the SAS regiment was deeply ingrained. Never look at a map, a statue, a photograph or a symbol just once, he was told. Look at it many times and each time you will see something different. Walk away and take a few deep breaths. Clear your head. Return and look at it again. You will see roads, creases, coloured areas or lines you didn't see before.

After fifteen minutes Curtis decided to leave the room. He ventured into the shop where one could buy a range of items to commemorate one's visit. Some of the tour group to which he had been attached were buying items, others were mulling over potential purchases.

Another group was just completing their guided tour. Curtis approached the leader of that group when she finished her presentation and asked for her take on the centrepiece of the pediment. He didn't use the term 'Gorgon's head' because he didn't accept that description.

The second tour leader was very happy to chat but indicated her knowledge of classical history was 'somewhat limited'. She went on, "There is a room here in the baths that is now apparently used for storage. Above the entrance to that room is a smaller version of that same head. It may be a myth, but someone once said the image was designed to be a deterrent to women entering that room. It was a 'men only' room."

That is more informative than you know, young lady.

Curtis returned to the small amphitheatre in front of the partially reconstructed pediment to take a fresh look. He knew he might see something different. His SAS colleagues would say an object might reveal different patterns. A map might reveal contours one didn't see initially. A map may reveal streets or street names one didn't see initially. The street names might take on a different meaning. Are there structures on the map one didn't see before? Is there something hidden behind the façade of a statue?

Everyone claims this to be a Gorgon's head but Gorgons are women. This is most definitely a man. Some say this is meant to be a welcoming face. Revisiting it now and looking harder at the pediment I believe this is a face of aggression. Of hatred. What did the female tour leader say? The image above the door 'was designed to be a deterrent to women'.

The tattoos tell me this is the symbol of an organisation aiming to be aggressive towards women. My original hunch was correct. An organised campaign of aggression aimed at women in leadership positions or potentially in the same. It's not just Wallace and Nelson. There are others involved.

Before returning to his hotel, Curtis went to his new favourite restaurant, Bill's. He had enough information to develop a plan to finalise matters and needed time over a substantial meal and a strong coffee to strategise.

He was now certain of the outcome of his investigation; it was only a matter of devising a solid plan. He recalled Frenchy's words in the early days of his investigative work — 'Find the problem and fix it'. It was clear from a later conversation that he had Bell's support even if Frenchy was not convinced. Frenchy had given the green light to continue and Curtis had asked him, "Until when?" Frenchy had said, "Until the job is completed," or words to that effect.

Frenchy had confirmed Bell's instructions with a nod when he asked him in Singapore if he should 'deal with any situation that may cause embarrassment to the Australian Government'. As far as he was concerned that meant clean up the problem by any means.

***

The envelope under his door was addressed to Alexeev Lomot. Before opening it, he went to his bag of tricks and extracted a pair of latex gloves. He then opened it with caution. The note inside was typed.

'Alexeev Lomot. I'm sure that isn't your real name but that is the name we were given by your friend Geoffrey Coolidge. We should meet, Alexeev, isn't that what you want? My colleague gave you a message but you didn't heed his request to stay away. Since you won't stay away you might like to join the team. At least find out what we have to offer.

'Meet me at the main entrance to the Roman baths at nine o'clock on Thursday night and we can have a little chat. I would welcome that. Geoffrey might even attend. He is not feeling at all well at the moment but he would love to see you.'

The note was unsigned but the letters JW were typed at the bottom.

How did they find me? They knew I was staying at the Royal Lancaster in London. They planted a tracking device on my car.

Yes, Wallace. I shall meet you tomorrow.

Chapter 63

The package Creighton handed Curtis after their meeting included a handgun, throwing knives and ammunition. His preferred weapons. The same as he used in Thailand.

Creighton has been talking to the Rat.

Fully equipped, Curtis arrived at the Roman baths before closing time. He wore a long pale brown coat over black cotton combat trousers with fitted cuffs, a black polo shirt and a baseball cap. He would discard the coat later. It was only to avoid the attention he would receive with the rest of his attire.

He purchased a ticket and a tourist's map of the complex. He was given an information brochure with his tickets and was informed that he must exit the premises before 1800.

Curtis walked slowly around the premises, head lowered and intermittently looking at the brochure and the associated attractions. He knew precisely where every CCTV was located and at each point he more carefully examined the brochure, avoiding closer scrutiny.

Soon after the last tickets sales were issued and well before exit time, Curtis had moved within the vicinity of the 'men only' room. He was confident this locked room, that was not available to the public at large and apparently used for storage purposes, was the venue for Wallace's meeting. More than a hunch. The 'men only' concept combined with the smaller version of the pediment above the door encouraged him to this belief.

He was unsure of the number of men involved but he believed he had the element of surprise and was confident in his own ability.

Picking the lock was easy. Curtis pulled the door slightly ajar, sufficient to squeeze inside. Although the room was windowless, there was just enough light from the gap in the door for him to see a large rectangular stone table surrounded by solid wooden chairs. There were ten chairs, two of which had high backs and armrests and were contiguous to each other at one end of the table. Presumably the head.

A quick visual survey was sufficient for him to locate the best place to stay hidden. A musty smelling recess behind a stone column. Unfortunately, from that position he was unable to see what he assumed to be the foot of the table.

Surprisingly he only had to wait for about forty-five minutes before he heard a rattle of keys at the door. Within seconds, a line of men wearing black hooded knee-length capes entered the room. Three were carrying lanterns that emitted an even light — fluorescent lights with rechargeable batteries. The man in the lead carrying the keys coughed and said, "'Scuse me," and coughed again.

Gravelvoice.

Careful not to be seen, Curtis noticed one of the men, more rotund, was not dressed in a knee-length cape the same as the others. From his hiding spot in the shadows Curtis could just make out a man dressed in jeans and a pullover. Another shorter man barked orders and instructed him to remain standing.

Badly beaten, Coolidge stood hunched over at the opposite end of the room from where Curtis was secluded. He was clearly struggling to remain upright.

A scrape of chairs on the stone floor. The rest of the hooded gathering was seated. The noise masked the sound of footsteps on the opposite side of the column behind which he was shielded. He was focused on the men at the head of the table.

Suddenly there was a cough behind him and he felt the cool steel of a barrel behind his ear. Before the others took their seats Gravelvoice had coughed and made a comment about water. In the darkness Curtis hadn't seen a small water fountain behind the column. Rounding the column towards the fountain Gravelvoice saw the back of a stranger in their midst.

Curtis cursed quietly, not expecting to be exposed. He had lost the element of surprise. A right hand firmly between his shoulder blades pushed him out of the recess into the light. Curtis recalled from the tour the previous day that Gravelvoice was right-handed. That meant he had transferred the weapon to his left hand. His weaker hand.

"Look what I have found," Gravelvoice hissed. "An intruder. A skilful intruder to be in this room in advance of our meeting." His voice had an ominous, menacing tone to it as it echoed off the stone walls.

"Aah, Mr Lomot, no doubt," growled one of the caped men seated in a high-backed chair. He addressed the man to his right, "Edgar, he is early for our planned meeting at the entrance to the baths," and then laughed. A sinister laugh.

JW. Jim Wallace.

"You have disappointed me. I thought you might be interested in an offer to join our team but your presence here tells me you are obviously not."

As he spoke, Wallace lifted a handgun from under his cape and placed it on the table slightly to his right between him and Edgar who was occupying the other high-backed chair. He turned his gaze away from Curtis and addressed the others.

"Gentlemen, allow me to inform you of the agenda for this evening." Wallace ticked them off on his fingers as he listed the matters for consideration. "Firstly, we need to make a decision about the order of our targets, where and when. Secondly, we have the trial of this disloyal and untrustworthy man behind me and now," he raised his voice, "we have a second trial to conduct after we hear his pleadings. Perhaps Mr Nelson will help extract his pleadings."

Wallace laughing at his own pathetic joke.

"Firstly, gentlemen, I should warmly welcome our newest member, Craig Nelson. You will soon, very soon, come to realise what an important addition Craig is to our organisation. In many ways he has already demonstrated his value. We are winning the war against women imposters aspiring to leadership."

Light applause followed. Whilst Wallace was talking, Curtis quickly scanned the gathering. Looking for weaknesses, assessing as far as possible the size of each man, assessing whom he should attack first.

Curtis couldn't see any faces but noticed one caped man did not join in the applause. He assumed that was Nelson. Wallace confirmed that assumption with a simultaneous nod towards him when he mentioned his name.

With the applause the group's focus of attention was shifted. Gravelvoice made the mistake of lowering his firearm, presumably to show his enthusiasm and support for their newest member.

Sycophant. Dumb sycophant.

That was the second mistake. The first mistake was to wear a loosely fitting cape that could easily be grasped and entangled.

Lowering the firearm slightly was an opportunity. Curtis caught him unaware and in one action twisted his body away and to the right of Gravelvoice. One hand shot to the weapon and the other to the cape at his chest. Curtis had large, fast hands. One hand wrenched the gun away from a shocked Gravelvoice and the other clenched a fistful of cloth tightening around his body. He unwound like a golfer driving off the tee on a par five. In one action he threw Gravelvoice across the table in the direction of Wallace.

Without hesitating to look at his handiwork, Curtis immediately launched a size fourteen RM Williams boot at the side of Nelson's head. An audible crack. Out for the count with a broken jaw.

It was mayhem. As he skidded across the stone face up, yelling and almost choking on phlegm simultaneously, Gravelvoice had knocked the weapon from the table. It skidded behind Wallace and stopped at the feet of Geoffrey Coolidge.

Time almost stood still. Coolidge slowly bent and grasped the weapon in both hands. Wallace turned to find the muzzle of his Glock pointing at his chest and laughed. He reached forward, hand up beckoning Coolidge to hand over the weapon. With some difficulty Coolidge pulled the slide back to slot a round in the chamber. Wallace laughed again. This time a nervous, uncertain laugh. His last laugh. Coolidge closed on the trigger.

Chapter 64

An apparent madman had shot one of their leaders and was still waving his weapon around. Another, bigger madman, unleashed heavy blows to those nearest him, seemingly picking his mark and applying a boot here, an elbow and fist there. Some of the group cowered towards the end of the room. Two had thrown open the heavy wooden door and dashed outside.

Although there were several bodies lying at odd angles on the stone floor, Curtis was not taking any chances. His Glock and a throwing knife were at the ready but not required. The remaining caped men standing had their hands in the air in meek surrender.

Curtis bent close to Nelson's ear. In a firm, deep voice sans the Russian accent he said, "Who's the amateur now, boy? You will have a long time behind bars to think about that."

He felt Nelson's pulse, turned him face up, and searched him for a concealed weapon. Under the cape he found a semi-automatic Walther P99. He unholstered the pistol, stepped over the prone body and felt for a pulse on the bloodied body slumped against the base of the table.

Wallace lay still with one arm outstretched and the other twisted under his body. There was no pulse. Curtis placed the Walther in his open hand, closed it and wrapped his index finger around the trigger.

Through puffy eyes Coolidge watched Curtis's every move. He realised Alexeev Lomot had lost his Russian accent. Curtis noticed that Coolidge was still waving the gun from side to side but the movement was more to do with unsteadiness in his legs than any threatening gesture. He stepped around Wallace and pulled a high-backed chair to Coolidge's side, away from the body on the floor.

"Sit down, Geoffrey. Give me the gun."

Coolidge sat as instructed. He slumped forward and placed his head on the table. He was exhausted from the physical beating. His emotions were a mixture of relief and anxiety. Relief from no longer being the captive of brutal men who used him as a punching bag. Anxiety from the shooting. He had never used a pistol before and the first time he did so he had shot someone.

As if reading Coolidge's mind Curtis reassured him. "You shot him in self-defence, Geoffrey. He lunged at you, gun in hand, and you were fortunate and quick enough to retrieve and put to good use the weapon that had fallen from the table. Probably the brother's gun. I saw it happen."

Edgar Wallace!

The emotion of the occasion took its toll on Coolidge. His head rested on his forearm across the table. He sobbed quietly. Curtis put his hand on Coolidge's shoulder and gripped it firmly. Comforting and reassuring.

The wooden door was pushed wide open. Curtis immediately half crouched, assumed a shooting stance and raised his Glock.

"Police! Nobody move!" This command preceded the welcoming sound of hustling police officers as they entered the room. Four police firearms at eye level, at the ready if required.

Curtis raised his hands still holding his weapon in an open palm. Finger no longer on the trigger.

"Name?" shouted the leading officer weapon pointing at Curtis.

"Curtis."

"Okay, Curtis. Place your weapon slowly on the table and slowly, very slowly, show me your creds. One false move and I'll know you're not Agent Curtis. One false move and you're dead meat," he growled.

Agent Curtis. Who informed him?

Curtis followed instructions, slowly lifting a velcro flap to a pocket on his combat trousers and retrieving his credentials. He revealed them to the senior police officer who had barked the instructions.

The officer lowered his weapon and greeted Curtis with a handshake. He turned to his subordinates, waved his firearm in the direction of the conscious caped men and said, "Take them in for questioning."

Curtis pointed at the large body on the stone floor. He had heard Nelson emitting painful groans as he regained consciousness. "You should read the Miranda to this one," he said. "You will need to hold him pending extradition to Australia."

The senior officer barked further instructions to a colleague. "You do not have to say anything. But it may harm your defence if you do not…" He listened to his colleague for a few moments and then, satisfied, he turned his attention to Curtis.

"Good work, Agent Curtis. Are you alone responsible for this?" he asked as he surveyed the carnage.

"I had some help," Curtis replied, glancing in Coolidge's direction.

"It's over, my friend. I'm sorry to mislead you about my name. I'm even sorrier to have you stay in England and suffer at the hands of these lunatics."

Coolidge nodded having regained his composure and having watched the offenders being marched from the room.

"You can take comfort in the knowledge you have helped save lives," Curtis said. "This bunch of misfits will no longer threaten the lives of innocent and courageous women. No longer a threat to democracy."

Epilogue

Nelson spent several days under police guard in hospital. The National Crime Agency treated him as the perpetrator of very serious international crimes after consultation with Interpol and the Australian Federal Police.

Curtis was questioned by the NCA about the use of excessive force but had no difficulty in convincing the interviewing officers the force was 'reasonable in the circumstances'.

"Apart from that," Curtis had told them, "his injuries were exacerbated when he fell and hit his head on the stone floor. Poor fellow."

Frenchy arranged for an investigation into any involvement or wrongdoing by the staff at the Australian Embassy in Moscow. It revealed nothing. Senior trade commissioner Hunter was nevertheless counselled and redeployed to a desk job in Canberra.

"Do you remember I told you King Edgar chose Bath Abbey for his coronation?" Creighton asked when Curtis visited. "I didn't tell you the reason for that but now, with the recent events, I probably should have.

"By the time of the coronation, the then abbot of Bath had introduced a rule by which he expected the monks to live by. The Rule of St Benedict became the main teaching principles by which the monastery would operate. It was expected society at large would follow the Rule.

"Put simply," Creighton continued, "the Rule was an acknowledgement of fraternal power. It sought to restore the natural order of human relations. It planned for a strict interpretation of relationships. Man is superior.

"What motivated these brothers and their followers? Our information is that Edgar Wallace and his twin brother, Jim, made a conscious decision to adopt their own twisted interpretation of the Rule of St Benedict."

"Twin! Did you say Edgar is Jim Wallace's twin?" For Curtis this news was alarming, especially since one of the Wallaces had disappeared. Now he was not sure which one. The second surprise in the last few days.

"Yes, they were identical twins," replied Creighton. "Impossible to tell them apart."

Earlier, upon his return to London Curtis had debriefed Frenchy over his secure line.

"Bell is happy, Curtis. She was enormously pleased with your work in Thailand…"

"She!" Curtis interrupted with incredulity. "Did you say 'she'?"

"Yes, Curtis," he paused. "I thought you knew."

Frenchy suddenly realised the extent to which he had kept Curtis in the dark.

"I thought you knew who Bell really is."

Curtis had no idea. He had assumed IB or Bell to be a senior male officer in ASIO or the military. Making that assumption was easy because most often women were overlooked in favour of possibly even less qualified men for senior positions in government. Based on his experience it was a safe assumption to make. Or so he thought.

He grinned broadly. "You never told me about the complete chain of command. I only ever spoke to you, sir. What else is there to know about Bell? Please tell me more."

"For your ears only," Frenchy stressed. "Ina Bell is the minister for foreign affairs and defence. Formerly a colonel in the army, she has also held positions in the Australian Security and Intelligence Organisation. Purely coincidentally too, diplomatic posts in Moscow, Washington DC, Beijing, and Indonesia to name just a few. Do you get my drift?

"Bell heads up the Cabinet National Security Committee, a post usually occupied by the prime minister. Such is the regard with which she is held in government. She is very much a 'hands on' person. I take my orders directly from her. Don't be mistaken by the fact she likes to remain anonymous. She is no shrinking violet.

"Keep this information to yourself, Curtis. Nobody else needs to know. Bell has to deal diplomatically with governments around the world and it is best she stays below the radar on operational matters."

"Understood," acknowledged Curtis.

He terminated the call before Frenchy had the chance to do so. A wide grin enveloped his face and a warm glow of deep satisfaction embraced him.

THE END